CITY OF CROWS

Chris Womersley

CITY OF CROWS

Europa
editions

Europa Editions
214 West 29th Street
New York, N.Y. 10001
www.europaeditions.com
info@europaeditions.com

Library of Congress Cataloging in Publication Data is available
ISBN 978-1-60945-470-8

Womersley, Chris
City of Crows

Book design by Emanuele Ragnisco
www.mekkanografici.com

Cover photo: © Pexels /Pixabay

Prepress by Grafica Punto Print – Rome

Printed in the USA

For Minka

I have never seen a greater monster
or miracle in the world than myself
—MICHEL DE MONTAIGNE

Faith is to believe what you do not see;
the reward of this faith is to see what you believe
—SAINT AUGUSTINE

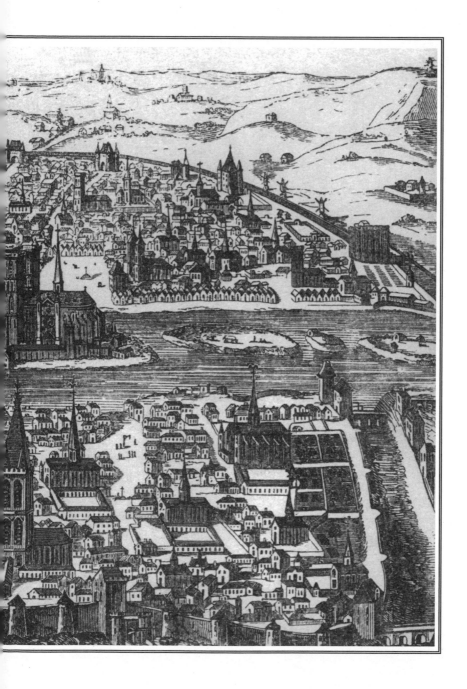

FRANCE 1673

1

S ummer stole across the country, bringing its heat and its fevers to their side of the mountain, to the cluster of cottages known locally as Saint-Gilles, and some days Charlotte Picot thought that all of them, one by one, would surely die from the plague. It had its own particular smell, said those who had encountered it up close. Slightly sour, of things turned bad, like meat gone to rot or the woollen rags found sometimes by the old bridge.

They attempted innumerable cures, as always. Scented grasses were burned in a special brass bowl, orisons were murmured, promises of one sort or another made to the stars and moon. A group of local women ventured to a nearby rock that was shaped like a crouching devil and berated the mute thing, threatened all sorts of reprisals should their families die of the sickness. *Spare our mother, our sister, oh please, you little bastard.*

One afternoon a travelling merchant named Hugo appeared in Saint-Gilles, a man no one recalled ever seeing before and, with much fanfare and brandishing of instruments, he set about cutting the lump from the armpit of Céline, the midwife, as others held her down.

"It's a method I learned in Venice," he told them. "You're lucky I happened past! All the greatest doctors in the world are performing this procedure. In Naples, in Toulouse. You people know nothing of the wider world."

And they deferred politely to him—because that was the

kind of people they were—but said outside, privately: "Certainly we know nothing of the world, but what is there, really, to know?"

The smell of her exposed gristle, they said later, was putrid, and pus bubbled from Céline's ugly wound thick and yellow, as if she had been storing soft cheese for too long beneath the folds of her skin. The operation was grotesque, a failure, and the peddler was hounded from the village with sticks, with rocks and a mighty kick up the arse. All up and down the other side of the valley he taunted them as he went, his shouts echoing against the rocks like those of a drunken soldier, all laughter and scorn and *You tribe of fucking peasants, if the fever won't get you then the bandits eventually will, peasants . . . eventually will . . . will . . .*

Poor Céline's cries and moans disturbed the sleep of everyone in the vicinity until her husband, acting from kindness, from sorrow, and on a vision that had visited him in a dream, smothered the woman with a blanket. There was no money for a coffin, certainly no time to fashion one, so she was sewn into a winding sheet, a coin placed into her clawed hand, and then buried in the cemetery further up the mountain. Happy as a corpse was the saying in their country, and never was it truer. They remarked, those who attended her burial, that Céline sighed in her sheet like a saint when the first spadeful of dirt splashed onto her face, as if she were a burning woman sensing the cool water that might ease her agonies.

When Charlotte was a girl, her father had delighted in frightening her and her brother with descriptions of the Wild Horde who roamed the countryside with the strange Hellequin at their head, leading fresh souls to the underworld. Sometimes he would tell her of having spied this unruly parade of the dead on the previous night and how he had been forced to bar the door against their entrance. And now, on some nights in the midst of this latest outbreak of fever, she heard the sinister gambolling of the Wild Horde as it passed through their country, the hem of Hellequin's cloak swishing in the dirt, fingers scratching his bristly chin as he pondered where next to make his dreaded visit. Yes, thinking, thinking, thinking.

In the morning, Charlotte's husband Michel Picot left their cottage to organise the sale of several horses in a nearby town, but Charlotte forbade her young son Nicolas to go outside unless he needed to shit. Already she had lost three children. Two daughters in the same year to fever and a son who couldn't survive his infancy. She would not lose another. No. No. No. The thick curtain lapped at the window frame. They crouched in near darkness, a single candle burning, silent, their hands wedged beneath their thighs as if already entombed. Nicolas was afraid and sullen and he spoke even less than usual. He had always been easily frightened and now he sat on the edge of the bed rocking back and forth, occasionally murmuring prayers, his head overflowing with crickets.

The other villagers also remained indoors if they could. Occasionally they called out encouragements to each other. *Still alive over there, are you, my dear? Have courage. It will be over soon enough.* There were more prayers offered to Saint Roque and his faithful dog. Prayers they had all offered before, with limited success.

From the centre of their low ceiling, in a hard shaft of sunlight, a spider dangled on her silken thread. The sight of the creature chilled Charlotte because, as everyone knew, it was bad luck to see a spider in the morning. Charlotte watched the creature for a long time, thinking how like an abyss must this room be for one so tiny. Did she feel fear, this spider, spinning around on her thread? What did she see with her tiny eyes? Did she wonder at the largeness and strangeness of this world? The tiny black creature hung there for a long time, revolving slowly as if admiring the room and its meagre fittings, before clambering, leg over leg, back up her thread.

At that time of the year, the days were hot and long, but Charlotte was nothing if not patient. She and Nicolas and Michel would outlast this fever. Yes. She and Nicolas and Michel would outlast this fever. In this way, time passed.

But when it came, oh, it came. Just as she feared it would.

2

Three days later, the villagers filed into the cottage and said their prayers over Michel Picot's body before they arranged themselves on the low bench along the wall to mutter and pray. It was late afternoon. At times the dark cottage overflowed with the earnest sounds of devotion, and this comforted Charlotte somewhat. When the cottage became too crowded, the village men gathered outside in the warm breeze, smoking their pipes and talking in low tones. The women stayed indoors, moving around unhurriedly like murmuring ghosts.

Charlotte listened vaguely to their condolences, to their assurances as to Michel's entry into heaven, of the friends and relatives he would surely encounter there. His children, his parents, God himself on his great throne. Think, also, of the suffering he would no longer have to endure. No hunger or sorrow. The curé, Monsieur Larouche, who had not been able to come over from the church in time to hear his last confession, sprinkled holy water over Michel and prayed loudly. He felt certain, he said, that Michel's soul had been in good order before he died. Charlotte sensed this to be true; although the parish church was some leagues away, she and Michel and Nicolas had attended Mass there almost every Sunday.

Late in the day, the villagers left her and Nicolas alone to finalise preparations for Michel's burial. As was the custom in their country, Charlotte leaned close to her husband's face and said his name three times to offer him a final opportunity to prove he was alive.

"Michel," she said. "Michel. Michel."

No response, of course. No flicker of eyelid, no warmth of breath, no pulse of blood. A thick and empty body. Dry teeth. Michel's mortal suffering had ended, but never again would he press his face to a horse's mane or bite into an apple. He would not pause a moment in the day to watch his son wrestling with friends or playing a game with the other boys of the village, never gaze upon her as she undressed for him. A drop of holy water glistened on his temple, like a dead man's tear. Sorrow, then, was the price of this life. With a finger she wiped away the drop of water and put it on her tongue.

How difficult it was to believe there was no one behind that waxen mask. Where had he gone? They all said to heaven, and yet it was tempting to imagine her husband somewhere deep inside his own body, as if in a labyrinth of vast caverns, becoming ever smaller and fainter as he journeyed away. Charlotte pictured this miniature version of Michel hearing her voice calling his name and pausing momentarily to ponder its echo before continuing onwards, downwards, until he was finally out of earshot. For a long time she observed his face for any sign of such fanciful interior activity, then placed her palm to the cool, dry skin of his forehead. No. He was gone. The dead, at least, cannot die again; this was some consolation.

As she had done for each of her children when they had died, she took up a knife and gently cut off a curl of her husband's dark hair. Michel's hair was coarser, naturally, and as she rolled the lock between her fingers, she was overcome. Her own tears dripped from her eyes and bloomed momentarily dark on the white linen of the winding sheet before they dried. Her husband had been quiet, dependable, kind. Yes, she had loved him in her way.

When she had composed herself, she tied this lock of hair with a short length of twine and deposited it in an envelope of paper with the others. She took out her needle and twine and began to sew the winding sheet closed. The tiny pock and draw of the thread was the only sound in the cottage; Nicolas was quiet, even the stove burned silent. She concentrated, took her time. This final act of tenderness she performed most diligently, pinching the sheet well clear of her husband's chest, his throat, his chin. Skin slack, his plum-coloured mouth, silver bristles. Nicolas shifted impatiently on the bench behind her.

Earlier today she and her son had washed Michel's body with a damp cloth and dressed him for burial in his wedding clothes, softly and superstitiously explaining their movements to him as they worked, so that he might find no reason to object to their ministrations were he able to hear them. *There, your arm in the shirt like so, Father. Your best shoes. Your hands are cold, my dear. Remember when we were married, the storm that night so loud?*

Into his nostrils they had stuffed plugs of cloth. She could see the blood already pooling under the skin at his shoulders, along his thighs. His body lolling as they moved him, arm flopping at an awkward angle, eyes stubbornly open but unseeing. The only purpose of a corpse was to display the boundaries of life.

And now her husband, the only man she had ever known, was gradually being sealed away, as if inside another skin.

Nicolas broke the silence. "What do you think it's like?"

Charlotte paused, one hand in the air holding the needle. She cleared her throat. "What is what like?"

"For my father."

"What can you mean, Nicolas?"

"What does he—I don't know—what can he see?"

Charlotte considered the sheet in which they had wrapped her husband. His milky eyes and the blackened mouth that had been locked open so hard they had been unable to force it shut, try as they might. Beneath his earlobe was a tiny speck of dried blood they had missed. She restrained herself from wiping it away.

"Louis once told me that he saw a woman having her head cut off and after it was done, her eyes were still wide open in her head. While it was on the ground. And that the woman looked at him and *spoke*."

Charlotte had heard this kind of fantastic story before—and many others like it. It seemed they were living in an age of terrible wonders. She had heard of nuns who spat nails from their mouths, of men who could fly through the air on greased sticks, of the woman with cat's paws instead of hands hidden beneath the sleeves of her gown. These tales she didn't quite believe, but nor did she discount them altogether.

She turned to her son. "And what did this headless woman say?"

As if to ensure they were not overheard, Nicolas glanced around before speaking. It was clear this was something he had long wanted to tell her but had been too fearful to—until now.

"She said: 'It's getting late, my child. I see dark halls and so many vast underground chambers. It is surely time for you to go home for the night.' This was while her body was still tied to the chair. Then she blinked because there was blood in her eyes, blood all over the ground. Her own blood. Then she died."

Nicolas watched Charlotte intently to gauge her reaction to his anecdote. Firelight played over his ruddy cheeks. She remembered vividly the night he was born nine or so winters ago—the forest wolves howling at the scent of her fresh blood, snow banking up around the cottage—and felt a surge of love for the boy, her only child still living; the only son, now, that she would ever produce. The love for one's child, she thought, was forever braided with an intense fear of his loss. It was an inescapable fact that the birth of a child meant disquiet for the mother.

Charlotte coughed into her hand. "Well. I don't know if we should trust the stories of young shepherd boys like Louis. I'm sure your father is by now in heaven. You have been listening to the curé, I hope?"

"And what's it like in heaven?"

This son of hers, always full of questions, convinced there might actually be an ultimate answer to everything. The first word he uttered—*why*—would doubtless be his last.

"I try not to think about it," she said eventually. Which was a lie, of course; it was impossible, in these fevered days, not to think of death and what might be beyond. Brood on it she did, and often. But, in order to forestall further interrogation, she added: "You have heard what the curé has told you, have you not? He knows what it is like there. He knows all there is to know about such things."

Nicolas shrugged.

"It's beautiful in heaven," she continued. "It's sunny and there is always enough to eat. All the people you have ever loved will be there. Which is why you must always try to be good, so you can meet them again."

"My sisters? My brother?"

Charlotte took a moment to answer. "Yes," she murmured at last. "And there are angels playing beautiful music. Green fields, sunlight. Lovely sweet wine."

"My father would enjoy that, at least."

She was uncertain if this was intended as a joke, for Nicolas was not renowned among his fellows for his sense of humour. She smiled for the first time in days and felt ashamed for doing so. "Indeed he would."

A sudden gust of wind skittered down the chimney and nudged a glowing coal from the grate. The coal landed on the dirt floor, where it throbbed several times with orange light before expiring.

But, of course, the boy's interrogation was not yet complete. "What did you say to my father? Before, you leaned over him and spoke with him. I saw you."

Charlotte was sad and weary and this conversation was only making her more so. "I wished him well on his journey and said that I would see him again in heaven one day. That's all I said."

Nicolas sniffled. "Should you not have said a prayer for him?"

"I did, Nicolas. And I prayed for us, too. God has a lot to do in these times, I think, and we need his help. Your father's time had come. He has left us. He has gone from this earth."

Nicolas sniffed, wiped his eyes. "He won't come back?"

"No."

"We must have done something terrible to be visited by such things," Nicolas said. "My father dead. My brother, my sisters."

Charlotte shook her head, eager to finish this conversation. "Your father died of the fever, there's nothing more to it than that. Like my own mother. And your sisters . . . " She swallowed a sob, tried to dispel the image of the corpses of those she had loved piled in a corner of her mind. Her girls and her infant boy, forever young, their bleak smiles, stony eyes in their sockets. Gone. Barely formed before they were taken from her.

"Death visits everyone," she said.

"Not the way it comes to us."

"Yes, Nicolas. Exactly like it comes to us. There is no order to it. Remember Ann Waites's people? The Blois family? They are all gone. The dead are many. They surely outnumber us by now."

"Mother?"

She put down her needle and twine. "What now?" she asked, trying, unsuccessfully, to keep exasperation from her voice.

"What is hell like, then?"

Her son waited, staring up at her, one of his fingers tracing a complex pattern of his own design on his knee. Like a drunk surprised by his reproachful wife, the candle beside him on the bench buckled at the waist, weaved, then managed to halt its collapse. She glanced around the cottage—at the torn curtain hanging across the window, at the rickety table, the shelf warped and corroded by years of use. As always, the place smelled of tallow, of smoke, and of ash.

Charlotte turned again to regard her husband's unmoving face, the only part of him yet to be sealed away. She ran a finger along the seam she had already made in the winding sheet. She had done a good job; it would hold for a long time. Much longer than his skin would hold his bones. Sorrow flared in her throat, and was gone.

Probably like this, she thought, although she said nothing. Hell is probably like this. She took up her needle and bent wordlessly to her wifely duty.

Soon afterwards, three men of the village came and lifted Michel's body away in his sheet for burial. By this time it was almost dark. Charlotte took up a lantern and she and Nicolas walked behind them. The other villagers followed silently. Footsteps, the crack of twig, some low murmurs. The grave had already been dug and Michel was laid gently in it, the clumsy farmer Samuel Garance stumbling and swearing at the edge of the hole as they did so. The curé offered some final words. "*Pater noster, qui es in caelis . . .* "

When the men started to shovel the dirt back in, the sound of soil hitting the taut linen winding sheet had nothing of the living about it. It was unbearable to Charlotte's ears and she turned away weeping. Nicolas clung to her dress, for her unspoken anxiety as to what would happen to them now had communicated itself to him. When at last she opened her eyes, all she saw in front of her was the dense and complicated forest darkness. The villagers had trickled back to their own hearths. Doubtless they had muttered consolations to her and patted her shoulder as they passed, but of these actions she had been unaware.

Night fell. Charlotte sensed a lurch in the atmosphere, the wind changing direction, as she stood with one hand pressed to her lower back, the other resting on a spade's rough wooden handle. It was a clear night and the rising June moon was as full and low as a monk's belly. She paused to listen to the last gossiping sounds of robins and the hiss of the wind through the oak trees, their slow-creaking limbs, the rattle of ivy that clung to their trunks. It was only the forest muttering its difficult speech. It was a language she had heard her entire life, but it never failed to imbue her with fear and melancholy, as if it were reminding her, perpetually, of some malevolence close at hand, of sprites and other unknown vermin scuttling about in the dark. There were stories, after all, of an odd man in the forest who became a wolf at night and tore people's bodies to pieces. Other things, too. Ghosts, demons, spirits.

Charlotte's chin was crumbed with dirt. Her cheeks and neck were pitted here and there with half-a-dozen scars from her childhood pox, as if she had long ago been splashed with hot oil. There were other less visible scars scattered across her body. Fifteen of them; Michel had insisted on counting them every so often. *To make sure none have escaped*, he would chortle as he crouched over her stomach, her thighs. They used to call her Fever Girl in the village, on account of these scars— although there were plenty of others nearby similarly afflicted; such blemishes were hardly rare. Of course, most who contracted any one of the many fevers—her daughters, now her husband—died of it. This fact of her survival she hoarded like a mysterious talisman to take out and ponder in private, fondling its indentations in the hope its meaning would eventually reveal itself. It calmed her somehow, this intimation of destiny.

Nicolas tugged at her dress. Absent-mindedly, Charlotte ran her hand through his hair and pulled him against her hip. She scanned the other side of the valley for signs of smoke or soldiers, but saw nothing out of the ordinary. She swept aside her hair and crouched to smooth over the ground as best she could with the flat of her spade. Once this had been done to her satisfaction, she took up the cross Nicolas had fashioned from two sticks tied together with twine and jammed it into the earth. Like those for her daughters and her infant son who were all under the ground, there were no words on the marker, no flowers for the grave. Death was the final word. What was there to add? More family under the ground than walking on it, she thought as she got to her feet. She made the sign of the cross across her chest and muttered a prayer. "*In nomine Patris, et Filii, et Spiritus Sancti.* Amen. Goodbye, my husband."

"Come on, Mother. We should go indoors. It's getting dark."

She stared at the rough ground, breathing hard, suddenly afraid. A worm that had been sliced in half by someone's spade writhed about on the freshly turned earth like the pink, waggling finger of a miniature creature otherwise hidden beneath the soil. The sight of it disgusted her; it took vast effort not to mash the vile thing utterly with her spade. Eventually, she took the whimpering Nicolas by the hand, and together they picked their way back across the uneven ground to their cottage.

The village goats complained as they were shoved indoors for the night. There came the hoot of a bird. Coughing, soft words, latches falling into place in the houses around them, then silence.

3

By daybreak the following morning, Charlotte and Nicolas had tidied away their few pots and plates and cups, nailed the cottage door shut and were on their way. She had told none of the villagers of her plans, for she knew some of them viewed such departures as a kind of betrayal. They trusted in prayers and isolation, but Charlotte had placed her faith in these things before and been disappointed. Someone would see or hear them leave, of course, and it would take no time for reports of their departure to spread, but by then they would be gone. She was resolved to flee and there was nothing anyone might say to change her mind.

They took turns tugging the skittering goat along behind them on a length of rope. The animal regarded them with anger and contempt, an old creature forced against its will. Charlotte carried a cane basket with two chickens, and over her shoulder was a sack containing a few turnips and beets, a blanket, some dried fruit, bread, sausage and a flask of water drawn from the well.

It was not long before they left the village environs and entered the forest. The whistles of orioles and the skirring of finches filled the air around them, and the light from the early-morning sun spattered upon the flowers. Charlotte had never before seen a body of water as large as the ocean, let alone swum in its depths, yet she imagined this was how it was beneath its surface; it would not surprise her unduly to spy a mermaid or leviathan floating through the treetops overhead.

Beneath their shoes, leaves crackled and crunched with a sound like that of damp insect shells. Lizards scurried across the rocky path. Ancient oak trees furred with green lichen, drone of huge wasps, the incessant chatter of birds. Despite the outbreak of fever, it had been a favourable start to summer and they were able to collect plenty of mulberries and plums as they walked. They ate what they could and filled their pockets with the surplus. Charlotte urged Nicolas on, eager to leave the valley. Her son was nimble on his feet but easily distracted and often had to be coaxed onwards after becoming entranced by a bee clinging awkwardly to a head of purple thistle or some martens in the undergrowth.

The only signs of human life they encountered that morning were the ancient stone crosses slumped along the path at irregular intervals, most of them worn almost to the bone by weather and time, by thousands of penitent caresses. The fields and lanes of their country were dotted with such powerful shrines: for fertility, for good crops, for protection from disease. Charlotte knew that Madame Solange from the village sometimes put the scrapings of one of these crosses in her husband's dinner to assist him in the bedroom.

After a time, she heard voices and presently a small group of people approached from the opposite direction. None of them she recognised. The party—two women and a young man dragging behind him a stretcher or bier—waited a moment on the narrow track as silent and cautious as deer. They were dressed as pilgrims, with numerous amulets and icons slung around their necks and crosses at their belts. Charlotte clutched her husband's knife beneath her shawl.

The woman at the head of the little procession stared at her and Nicolas until, evidently deciding they were not to be feared, she indicated for her companions to continue. She was old and walnut-faced, her grey hair wispy and only partly covered with a scarf. When they had approached to within hailing distance, the woman halted again and nodded in greeting to Charlotte.

"Good morning, madame."

"Good morning."

"Where are you going?"

Charlotte paused. "To Lyon. We are escaping an outbreak of the plague in Saint-Gilles. And you, madame?"

The woman sighed and indicated the path ahead of her with her staff. "To the shrine of the Virgin to pray for this boy."

Although she had never visited it, Charlotte knew of this shrine, which was on a hill some leagues from here. It had grown up at the site where, many years ago, the Virgin had appeared to a shepherd girl and given her a wooden cross. Céline, the village midwife, had journeyed there long ago to pray for the health of her own sick daughter and, on her return, had excitedly described to Charlotte how the tree near the shrine was so garlanded with flowers and icons and votive candles that it fairly trembled, even at night.

"The plague is in this poor child," the old woman went on, and gestured to a boy lying on the bier attached with ropes to the young man, as if he were an ox in the field and the sick boy his plough. Charlotte and Nicolas craned to see this afflicted boy, who was bundled in a blanket with only his face, thin as a hatchet blade, visible over the coverlet. He was turned aside. His lips were dry and chalky. Charlotte shrank back, for he reminded her of Michel bound in his winding sheet.

"The shrine is two days' walk from here," Charlotte said. "The boy will not last long enough, I fear."

The woman shrugged and made a face, as if agreeing with her but reluctant to speak aloud her thoughts on the matter. She crossed herself. "We must do what we can. He is the only boy left in his family. We have been bleeding him and he is much better for it. And we will pray, of course, casting his fate into the hands of the Lord. He may yet help us."

The woman's companions nodded and smiled vigorously at this and fondled their crosses and icons. Each of them had sprigs of lavender tied around their necks to ward off disease. Charlotte smiled, greatly touched by their devotion. Each soul contained an entire world, after all. At that moment, the boy on the bier opened his eyes and turned to look at Charlotte. His face showed alarm. Agitated, breathing heavily, he strained to say something. The old woman leaned over him and put her ear close by his mouth. She nodded and stood.

"He says you must be an angel, madame," she said to Charlotte. "Because you are so beautiful. Are you an angel? Will you help us?"

Taken aback, Charlotte shook her head. "No, madame. It is the fever talking. They sometimes see odd things when it has hold of them."

The old woman took a step closer to Charlotte. White whiskers sprouted from her cheeks, lending her the appearance of a strange and leathery cat. Her mouth worked away as she scrutinised Charlotte for a long time with her pale blue eyes until, finally, she turned back to the sick boy, leaned down once more and consoled him with a few words.

Charlotte tugged Nicolas back by his sleeve and the two of them stood aside on the path to allow the pilgrims to continue on their way. "God be with you," she said as they shuffled onwards.

She and Nicolas stared after the group. She crossed herself. "They will all die of it, I think," she murmured to her son.

Their last sight of the strangers was of the sick boy on the bier, of his milky face fading, becoming ever smaller as they drew away. A wood dove cooed nearby and fluttered up from the undergrowth, startling them. By the time Charlotte looked back, there was no sign of the pilgrims, prompting her to wonder if they had encountered anyone at all.

4

They worked their way up along the wooded side of the mountain until, in the middle of the day, they emerged into a bright landscape of rolling fields that stretched as far as they could see. Wheat shimmered in the breeze. Here and there an orchard or a stand of trees. The spire of a distant church, its grey roof and, closer at hand, an ancient shepherd's hut built a thousand summers ago. The world had never seemed so vast and immeasurable to Charlotte and she experienced an unfamiliar swooning thrill as she gazed around. The air was fresher up here, but the sun was blazing and it stunned her and Nicolas like the blow of a mallet. She retied the scarf on her head, wiped sweat from her face. For a moment she was uncertain which direction to take, but then she saw the landmark she sought beneath a chestnut tree several fields away. With the sun hot upon their heads and the sharp smell of the countryside filling their nostrils, they paused to drink from their flask before hurrying on, two people with their burdens toiling across the enormous face of the earth. Stalks of wheat swayed about their waists, and butterflies erupted from the crop and fluttered in their faces as they crunched through the fields.

The so-called Giant's Table consisted of three huge slabs of lichen-scabbed rock arranged to form a rough shelter. Charlotte had heard of similar structures in the surrounding area, but this was the only one she knew of personally. Some people called it a *cromlech*, but she did not know the true name for such a thing. An unfamiliar four-pointed cross was carved into the surface of one of the massive slabs, along with various other symbols she didn't understand, scratches perhaps made by Druids or their ilk a long time ago. Cathars or Saracens. The villagers said, variously, that this place had been used by such heretics as a gateway to other worlds, or that it was a burial chamber or church of some sort. Consideration of odd tribes crouching here, perhaps eating and drinking, speaking in their strange tongues, made her most uneasy.

Charlotte placed the basket containing the fretting chickens on the ground while Nicolas tied the goat to the chestnut tree. Avoiding the *cromlech*, they crouched in the shade of the tree to eat some apples and bread. The shaggy tops of the trees in the forest below moved slowly from side to side, as if they were being shaken by men at their trunks.

"Was this place really made by giants?" Nicolas asked her.

Charlotte drank some tepid water from their flask and removed her headscarf. "Yes, I think so. But don't worry, they are long gone. They died in the great floods years ago. No one has seen them for many years. Not while I have been alive. Not even when my own mother and father were alive."

Nicolas pointed across the shallow valley. "And what is that country over there?"

Charlotte shrugged. She had no idea. Their country ended at the edge of the valley and it had always been enough to know that. Or it had been enough until now.

"Perhaps the giants live there these days?"

"No. They are long gone. I told you." She indicated the forest below them to the west. "We are going through there, anyway."

She could see that the prospect of going through an unfamiliar forest made Nicolas nervous, as it did her.

"There is a path," she continued before the boy could voice further objections, "that leads to the old chapel overlooking the river. We can sleep there tonight, and tomorrow we'll take the other path through to Lyon. It's quite simple. Your father explained it all to me before he died. He said it should take us two days."

She choked on the memory of Michel grasping weakly at her in the night and exhorting her, over and over, to leave Saint-Gilles and go to Lyon, where he thought it would be safe. *Save yourself*, he had murmured. *Save our boy*.

Charlotte placed a hand across her mouth, as if allowing the grief to escape her body would make it worse. He was gone, she was on her own, she needed to be strong.

Nicolas thought on this for a moment. "What is it like in Lyon?"

She had never in her life travelled further than one or two days from Saint-Gilles and the thought of such a journey filled her with dread, as if silt were accumulating thickly around her heart. She had been born and grown up in the village, as had her parents. Only a few times in her life had she even crossed the river to the other side of the valley, and that was with her husband or father. She had never needed to until now.

"It will be bigger, with more people. They have an enormous cathedral there, your father told me. Larger than anything you have ever seen, he said."

"Will it be safe?"

The question surprised her. Surely even a nine-year-old village boy such as Nicolas knew nowhere was absolutely safe these days. There were constant rumours of banditry, of outbreaks of unrest and damaging weather. A travelling merchant last summer told her he'd seen a five-legged dog.

She nodded nonetheless. "Safer. They have special doctors there. Plague doctors. And places for the sick. Pest houses. The plague is coming from the north-east, they say. Soldiers are bringing it with them from the wars in the Low Countries. We shall head west, where the air is much better. Don't worry."

The goat twitched an ear and altered her position on the ground. She fussed loudly, then rested her whiskery chin in the cool dirt, observing them with her twitchy, slipshod eyes. Charlotte reached into her pocket and pulled out a handful of mulberries. She nibbled the sour fruit from their stems until her lips were bruised with dark juice. Nicolas did the same. Together they watched a lone hawk lofting soundlessly on the breeze, going higher, drifting in ever wider circles until, finally, it arched its wings, veered away and dissolved against the brown and green patterns of the earth. It was, somehow, a sorrowful sight and Charlotte feared that the tide of dread she had managed to contain within her would soon split her skin.

"Perhaps all the mice died of fever, too?" Nicolas ventured.

Despite herself, Charlotte laughed. "Yes. Perhaps."

Presently, they heard the distant tinkling of a bell, followed by the bark of a dog. Nicolas stood and looked around.

"It's Anton," he said, delighted, and stepped from the shelter to wave him down.

Eventually, the grubby peddler noticed the boy waving and hooting to him and changed direction, leaving the track and bearing straight through the field. His voice became clearer as he approached, goading his dog onwards with a combination of endearments and furious curses. "Come on, you lazy bastard, my beautiful boy, my evil whore, that's the way . . . "

Soon he loomed through the wheat, the large black dog ahead of him pulling a trunk which had been adapted, ingeniously, with wooden wheels and a canine leather bridle. A brass bell dangled at the poor hound's throat.

On his own back, Anton lugged a massive woven basket which was itself packed with numberless other canisters and packages, each of which was, in turn, stuffed with pins and needles and bobbins and tools and knives and who knew what else—probably Anton didn't even remember everything he carried anymore. He sold household items, sharpened knives, dispensed worldly advice and attempted to seduce all the prettiest women.

They exchanged greetings as the peddler and his hound moved into the shade of the chestnut tree. Anton uncoupled the dog's trunk of goods and the poor animal flopped, panting, to the ground, pink tongue lolling. Then, with much grunting and sighing, Anton steadied his walking staff—which was fashioned with a curved seat at its top—against his ample arse and leaned back until it supported him against the earth. A contented smile seeped from his lips and spread across his face.

Anton was a big man, always sweaty, roughly bearded. His nose was missing its tip after a corsair hacked at him with his cutlass in Saint-Malo, or so he had always claimed, and this aspect of his face gave him a decidedly sinister appearance. His white shirt was poorly patched, as were his breeches. He had come every summer for as long as Charlotte could remember, beetling across the countryside, stopping here and there, accumulating gossip and sweethearts, ridding himself of his wares, drinking most happily the wine of strangers.

Charlotte observed him suspiciously, this fellow who claimed to have sailed at sea, to have killed a bear in the Spanish mountains. There were those who adored him and welcomed his seasonal arrival, while others maintained he was no more than a sly villain whose principal skill lay in divining and exploiting the weakness particular to each person's heart. It was whispered that, in addition to household goods, he stocked more unsavoury items—the teeth of hanged men, dried rabbit hearts, the finger bones of saints. Who knew, really, what to believe about such a man? As usual, he smelled of rotten onions, of things overripe and old.

"And what are you doing up here, so far from home, my little ones?" he asked in his creamy northern accent, untying the thin blue scarf from his neck to wipe sweat from his face and brow. He breathed like the bellows at a blacksmith's forge.

"The plague has come," Nicolas said.

Anton spat on the ground. "Ah. Here as well?" He scrutinised Charlotte, then Nicolas, eyes slitted with mistrust. "And you have it too, I believe."

"We don't," said Nicolas.

"Yes. I think so. Both of you." He tapped his dirty fingers to his lips. "Here. Do you not taste blood on your mouths?"

Charlotte touched her lips, heart thrumming. No. Surely not. It couldn't be true. She put a hand to her throat, felt the sweat on her face. It was from the heat of the day, surely, and the arduous walk? She spat into her own palm and was dismayed to see her saliva was thin and discoloured with dollops of red. She stared at it, disbelieving.

Anton made a face at once sympathetic to their plight and triumphant at being the first to diagnose it. Nicolas had grown pale and he ran his hands over his body, under his arms, feeling for swelling or heat.

"It can't be," Charlotte muttered, panic swelling in her throat. Then she understood. From her dress pocket she produced the remaining mulberries, which glistened in her palm like freshly hacked clots of blood. She held up her hands, displaying as proof the resemblance between the two globs. "It's only mulberry pulp. Not blood at all."

Anton chuckled, hands on his belly, then wiped his face again with his kerchief.

"But my father died of it," Nicolas added. "And Mother says we will too if we don't get away."

Anton stopped laughing. None of them spoke for some time. Charlotte wiped the mulberry spittle on the tree trunk.

"That's a shame," Anton said eventually. "Michel was a good fellow." He paused. "Did he have a good death, at least?"

Charlotte considered the question. It was one that people asked and yet she was never entirely sure what they meant by it. Was the death fast, or slow? Painful? Her husband had developed the sickness in the morning and died the following day. During the night he had suffered greatly and cried out and wept with the agony of it. Blood leaked from his nose. His skin was as slick as that of a fish. The air in their cottage grew soupy and close as she and Nicolas had prayed over Michel and attempted to bathe him in lavender water. They wrapped him in blankets until he cast them off with screams and groans. It was a terrible sight, to see such a strong man reduced to shivers and sweats. Nicolas went to fetch the curé, but he was nowhere to be found. And the moment of his death? The moment of his death? Merely a gasp, as if he were preparing to dive under water, or had seen something incredible, and then he was gone.

Charlotte cleared her dusty throat. "Before he died, Michel said, 'Help me, help me.' He was not calm, as some others are. He feared for us, for Nicolas and me. Feared what would become of us, I mean."

She was unsure if she had answered his question, but Anton absorbed this information with a grave expression on his face.

"Did you not think to take him to the Forest Queen?" he asked.

Charlotte, now weeping softly, shook her head. She had heard of the Forest Queen, who lived in a low house in the forest; an old woman who could speak with animals and knew all sorts of powerful magic. Some even claimed to have seen her floating high above the ground. "I would not do business with a witch, monsieur."

Anton shrugged. "The woman knows all manner of things about the world, Madame Picot. She can heal many ailments, you know. She has a particular book . . . "

"Have you seen her?" Nicolas asked Anton.

"Indeed I have. Most years we cross paths at least once. I have seen her in the forest gathering herbs and barks for her medicines. On her head she wore a crown of yellow flowers, like a rickety old bride. A strange sight it was. Most strange. They say she has taken the form of different women over the years. Sometimes she is young, sometimes old. Tall, short. And many others? Did the fever take many others yet?"

"The midwife is dead," Charlotte said. "As are the wood-cutter's daughters."

"The woodcutter's daughters? Shame. Most unfortunate. They were pretty. I had hoped to fuck them both one day. Well, I shall bypass Saint-Gilles this summer, I think. It's a bad season for it. And these crops will go to waste if there is no man to harvest them." Anton considered their possessions. "And you are—what?—going away, are you?"

Nicolas nodded. "Yes. To Lyon, to escape the fever. My father said we should go there."

Anton shook his shaggy head. "No, no, no. It's not safe there. I was in Lyon—let me see—only two days ago. The pest house is full. Besides, the town gates are closed. They'll not let anyone in for anything. There are far too many people wandering the countryside seeking refuge these days, what with one thing and another. I've heard that even Paris might soon close its gates. You should return to your village."

To Charlotte it seemed as if the earth were momentarily jolted, and she experienced the unnerving sensation of losing her balance even while squatting on the ground. "No. We cannot go back to Saint-Gilles. The plague is rife. Everyone is dying."

Anton scratched his hairy throat and retrieved a wineskin from some sack or other hanging about his person. He removed the stopper with his teeth, gulped loudly from it, then wiped his mouth on his sleeve. He was a disgusting man, a peddler of bad tidings, and Charlotte wished they had not encountered him at all.

"What were you intending to do in Lyon?" he asked. "Do you have some family there?"

"No. I have some money. I can sew, run a house, make cheese. I could be taken on as a servant, perhaps?"

"You have a brother, though. I remember."

She shook her head. "I don't know where he is. I have not heard from him in many years."

"You are not so old, madame. And, of course, you are quite a beauty. You might be married again. Have some more children to replace those you have lost. You'll need a man to care for you now. Why not be my wife?"

Charlotte's anger overcame her instinct to ignore such impertinence. "I do not think you are a suitable man for me, monsieur. Besides, I am in mourning. My husband is only one day in his grave."

"I am not as bad as some. I could take care of you and the boy. I have a good business. Not as wealthy as some men, but certainly you would never starve with me."

"You have enough wives scattered across the country, I think."

Anton laughed and patted his capacious belly, as if she were referring not to women he'd had but to meals consumed. "A man can never have enough wives. This you will understand one day. There is no point being faithful to a dead man."

The sneaky old peddler let this last statement hang in the air, then passed his wineskin to her. Charlotte took a draught of the warm, sour liquid before passing it to Nicolas, who also drank.

"That's lousy wine," Nicolas exclaimed, wiping his mouth. "Tastes like piss."

"I suppose you would know, my piss-drinking young fool," Anton said. "But it's better than no wine at all, believe me. It's good for keeping the fever at bay. I've never had it in all these years and I have seen some dreadful plagues. Bodies piled like giant, hairless rats. You know, sometimes they bury you alive to save time. Might as well, because you won't last long anyway.

It's true! Outside Marseille many seasons ago I saw people trying to crawl out of the pits, grown men weeping like infants,
pleading'—here he made his voice like that of a girl's—"*Please,
please, please, lift me out of here.*

"And I remember your own fever, madame," he said to
Charlotte. "All those years ago. You were probably the age
your son is now. Covered in spots—not like the one this year.
Your father was already dead of it when I arrived. A terrible
thing. Your mother begged me to help her. She was very afraid.
Your father was a decent fellow, and she prayed for three days
on her knees to save him. On her knees. And when you fell
sick, too . . . You were fortunate to survive, madame. Once it
has you in its grip . . . " Anton shook his head, overcome.

Charlotte's memories of that time were akin to glimpses of
a stranger's vision. A woman weeping, a boy crying out, the
shape of the Wild Horde skulking beyond the fire's flickering
light. She took the flask of wine from her son and drank deeply
from it. It did indeed taste sour but she was glad of it nonetheless. And perhaps the peddler was correct when he said it pro-
tected one against the plague?

They sat in silence for a while until Nicolas said in his small
voice: "What will we do now, Mother?"

In lieu of an answer, Charlotte picked up an ancient shard of
pottery and thumbed a scab of dirt from its surface to reveal a
clumsy image of a dragon or winged lizard. She silently considered the flying creature. How beautiful it would be to escape
into the sky, she thought, to escape the bounds of this earth.

Anton belched. "You could go to the abbey at Saint
Bridget. They are taking people in, especially if you have a goat
and chickens to offer. It is only two or three days' walk."

"Are you sure about Lyon?"

"Oh yes. I'm sure." He held up a clenched fist. "Sealed tighter
than a chestnut."

Charlotte pondered this. "How do we get to this abbey?"

Anton shook his head, as if he already regretted telling her of it. "I don't think you should go alone. It's not safe. Plenty of bandits about these days. If you wait for one day while I do some business nearby, then I can accompany you there. I will take you there myself."

"No. Thank you. We need to get away from here. We will be careful. God will provide a safe passage for us."

Anton paused, shrugged. "So be it. But you need to be wary. The roads can be dangerous. Sleep in the forest, but do not light a large fire, only something to keep the wolves at bay. Avoid groups of men, soldiers especially. There are people who would kill you for the goat. Kill you for their pleasure. Worse things, if you know what I mean. Give them what they want if you have to."

Charlotte did indeed know what he meant. She showed him her knife.

"That's not a very big knife," Anton said.

"But knife enough to slice a man's throat."

"Then, by all means, go for their throats," he said admiringly.

Then Anton took her by the shoulder and led her into the field where the sun was hot on their heads. He explained how to get to Saint Bridget—back down the valley and up the other side, across the hill shaped like a mole's back and in the direction of a distant stand of birch trees that huddled as pale and thin as skeletons waiting for their graves to be readied.

"Cross the old Roman bridge and follow the path up the mountain. From the top you will see the ruins of the old castle—you know the one I mean. Spend the night there, but be careful of snakes. Head north-west along the ridge until you come to a fork. Let me see. Oh, yes. The next day bear to the right, heading more directly west. A day's walk. You might see the camp of the troubadours if they are still there. They'll not trouble you. The path leads downwards and you'll come to the abbey by the river. Ask for Sister Junius. Tell her your husband is dead."

"The truth."

"Yes. They'll put you to work washing clothes or in the garden. The boy can help, too. They'll pray for you, at least. And you will be safe, or as safe as anywhere, until the fever passes. Who knows? You might even take the veil."

"I do not wish to be a nun."

Anton found this highly amusing and glanced over to where Nicolas squatted in the shade to involve him in the joke. "Ha ha. Does your mother think she's the queen or something?" he called out to him. Then, to Charlotte: "You might as well become a nun if you're not intending to put that cunt of yours to its proper use."

Charlotte ignored him and stared out over the countryside, going over his directions to the abbey in her mind, memorising the route. Anton ambled back to the shade of the chestnut tree. He tousled Nicolas's hair and set about hitching his dog to its tiny wagon, a procedure the creature accepted with gloomy resignation, looking sidelong at Charlotte as if she might intervene to spare him this indignity.

When it was done, Anton pissed against the tree, sighing loudly with satisfaction. Then he wished them well, urged his hound on and strode away.

Charlotte watched him go, then joined Nicolas in the shade of the tree. The peddler's wine, combined with the awful heat, had made her sleepy. The sun was high overhead; there was still plenty of daylight remaining. She lay down and closed her eyes. A short rest, she thought, before we continue on our way.

She grew aware, gradually, of all her children huddled close and hot and sweating around her, even her infant son Philippe. Michel was there, too, his grumbling laughter, tallying numbers in his ledger. The dusky scent of their hair, their kisses. Oh, their milky kisses! They had returned to her. She drank them in. Skin as soft as flour, eyes like gems. Their limbs, their knees, their grasping hands. Something loomed over her. Glimpse of ring, a whisper and grunt. She was conscious, dimly, of a rustling. The chickens clucked frantically. Her children called out. One child. Such a strange darkness. *Mother! Mother!* Nicolas's voice. It was Nicolas, his voice high-pitched and strangely distant. But her body was unwieldy and her legs oddly encumbered. She saw a flicker of light behind her eyelids, felt her tongue dry and sluggish in her mouth. Sweated brow, body tangled in the lark-net of sleep.

She woke at last to find herself in the dirt. The hot afternoon, drool on her mouth. The wine. The damn peddler's wine had put her to sleep. She gazed around. The Giant's Table, the chestnut tree. But where was the goat, the basket with the chickens? A dream. Of course, of course. Still she heard Nicolas's distant cry. She got up woozily and staggered into the hard, gleaming daylight. Red and purple shapes danced across her vision. When her eyes finally adjusted she saw that further down the hill, at the edge of the forest, were some people. Men on horseback and a wagon. Another cry. But where was Nicolas? Where was her son? She looked around, panicked.

There. Her son was down there with them, his arms flailing, mouth opening and closing, his cry reaching her a moment later. *Mother! Mother!* Something was happening, but what was it? Charlotte grasped the trunk of the chestnut tree for balance. She felt sick. A glint in the air but she barely had time to wonder what it might be before something punched her mightily in the shoulder.

A blast of pain and she stumbled. A cheer, followed by ragged laughter, the rocky ground under her knees, stones digging into the palms of her hands, blood soaking into her clothes like wine into bread. Her life; all of her poor life. An arrow, she realised. The thing she'd glimpsed was an arrow. And she plunged headlong into darkness.

5

Charlotte found herself lying on her back on hard, ice-cold stones. Her shoulder and left arm ached dully. A grey darkness. Moan of wind, a chill breeze across her face, the distant wails of men and women. She was unable to move. Each breath was an effort. She recalled, but only dimly, someone leaning over her and muttering. Nicolas. Where was her son? She croaked his name, then felt around her in the surrounding darkness. Nothing. She crossed herself. *"Pater Noster, qui es in caelis, sanctificetur nomen tuum . . . "*

Slowly, she moved one part of her body, then another. Feet, legs, her head. Blood heavy all over her clothes. How long had she been lying here? It felt, strangely, like days or seasons, forever. Time seemed to have broken free of itself. She raised herself stage by stage, onto one hip, then to her knees. She had no sense of the size of the space she found herself in until, gradually, her eyes adjusted to the gloom. Perhaps a tunnel of sorts, a chamber, the intimation of flickering light in the distance. Lamenting voices again echoed up from somewhere. Distant laughter, and not genial, crumbling as if into dust.

Feeling carefully around her as she did so, Charlotte got to her feet. She felt both weightless and heavy. At her shoulder, a wall slimy with moss, the space between the stones filled with a gritty mortar. With her hands held out in front of her, she began walking towards the pale light until she found herself in a large underground chamber lit by several flaming torches, one of which she managed to prise from the wall. The room was vast, its dimensions untroubled by her torch's light. Her shuffling footsteps echoed in the space. Rats and mice skittered here and there across the floor in front of her. There was a blundering movement high overhead, of bats or moths. Chipped columns wider than any oak tree she'd ever seen rose up and up and out of sight into the darkness.

Finally, as she stared in wonder, she made out something far above her. It was a mechanical contraption of some sort, with dangling ropes and chains. A huge metal wheel, perhaps. She stared upwards for a long time, craning her neck. Suddenly, the machine whirred and moved, lowering a wooden drawbridge, across which hurried a number of—what? People in rags? Or were they merely the undulating shadows cast by the torches? Wraiths? There, the shuffle of feet, a voice. She called out—timidly at first, and then, when there was no response, louder still.

No answer, only the echo of her own voice. *Hello . . . hello . . . hello*, grinding of gears, the creak of wood against wood, *there . . . there . . . there*. The people far above—if, in fact, they were people—had vanished and the two sides of the drawbridge lifted apart. One of these sides swung around ponderously and was eventually lowered at a different location, where it was joined by another bridge similar to the first. Again several figures crossing, the sense of hurrying movement high overhead, grim laughter.

Charlotte clasped her shawl tight about her and held out her torch, trying to see anything in the gloom that might identify this monstrous palace. Cobbles and bricks, rotten timber beams, old bolts and joints. There were rusted steel grilles in the walls and floors. With her toe she nudged a rock into one of these grilles and waited, in vain, for the sound of its landing. Nothing. In various places along the walls, iron rings were fixed with broken lengths of chain attached to them. Scattered here and there over the floor were piles of animal pelts, hanks of hair, bones large and small, hundreds of teeth, pieces of rotten clothing, ancient weapons and large splotches of wax. A deep fear settled in her bones, and Charlotte shrank back against one of the vast pillars. Where was she? Where was her son?

She walked on and, after some time, heard what sounded like a fete. Voices, music, laughter. With her torch held out in front of her, uncertain whether she wanted to meet the inhabitants of this ghastly place or not, she shuffled across the vast expanse of the chamber. The sound grew louder. She ventured along another passage until she found herself in yet another massive room. The scene inside was horrifying and compelling, a bleak carnival, like nothing she had even dreamed before. The room was lit by several torches sprouting from the stone walls and jammed into the floor, and the air was filled with a thick and putrid miasma. A stench of pipe smoke and death.

She had never before seen such a large assembly in a single place. Dozens of people of all ages and stations jostled for space. No one paid her the slightest attention, so absorbed were they in their various diversions. Babies played among the bones and rags on the floor, demure ladies fanned themselves. There were crippled beggars on crutches, riders on horseback. Nobles and peasants, lepers with their warning clappers. Some men crouched on the floor nearby playing cards and passing a jug of wine or beer between them. Hooting and weeping. Merchants with baskets strapped to their backs, old men, courtiers. A group of women divided an orange among themselves as they chatted serenely, three or four boys wrestled among the rubble, lovers wandered arm in arm beside the walls. And the air all around rang with a fearful din.

A cough at her back and Charlotte wheeled around to find an inordinately tall gentleman standing beside her. He was thin-faced, with a black cape draped across his shoulders.

With a bony hand he swept a wing of long, grey hair back off his high forehead. This gentleman obviously occupied a position of some authority among the assembly. Large rings glinted on his fingers and he nodded indulgently at passers-by when they paused to smile, doff their caps or be otherwise acknowledged by him. He wore an expression of forbearance, much like a schoolmaster overlooking his unruly flock and barely keeping any disciplinary blows in check. Every so often one of the revellers bumped into him, whereupon he would shove the offender away forcefully into the crowd, prompting further angry exclamations or drunken laughter.

"What is this place?" Charlotte murmured, probably not even loud enough for anyone to hear her.

But hear her the tall man did. He looked down at her, but paused before answering, as if uncertain of the true meaning of her question. "Merely a pause on our long journey, madame."

"Is my son here? Have you seen my son?"

The fellow shrugged and gestured vaguely at the heaving crowd. The question appeared to interest him not at all.

Charlotte persisted. "But where are you going, monsieur? Who are all these people?"

The man sighed. His cool breath smelled of bones and soil, as if he carried a graveyard within. He cast his eyes over the crowd. "There. See that woman, the one with the scarf about her neck? She was set upon the other night in Rue de la Poterie in Paris. Six men bent her to their will, one after another. She begged them to spare her, as if they would care. Put a knife right up inside her when they were done. The bloodstains are probably still on the road if you wish to look. Then they tossed her baby into the river."

Charlotte followed his gaze and spied the woman in question, who winced as she wandered through the crowd with a hand pressed to her belly. The lower part of her dress was stained with blood and she carried a bundle in the crook of her arm. Even in the dim, flickering torchlight, it was plain to see that her cheeks were wet with tears.

"Did she survive this attack, then?"

The gentleman paid no heed to her question. He was too busy pointing out others in the gathering and enumerating the gruesome fates that had befallen them. Fever, rape, murder, execution, madness. The man who fell from a window, a child trampled by a horse. There a girl whose leg rotted right off her body, there a man poisoned by his wife.

Charlotte looked again at the crowd and this time she saw their injuries: the swollen necks, the blood glistening on faces and hands. A man tugged at a knife embedded in his chest, a woman fiddled impatiently with dirty bandages wrapped around her head. Some appeared to be unhurt and yet their faces were pallid, their lips blue. Some wept or picked at scabs in disbelief, other beat their chests and tugged handfuls of hair from their heads. Anger and resignation. Fear, despair, hysteria and, for others, exultation. Such a fearsome reverie.

She closed her eyes and crossed herself. "*Ave Maria, gratia plena, Dominus tecum . . .*"

But when she opened her eyes again, the infernal scene was unchanged. The tall gentleman had by this time stopped talking and was instead watching with desultory interest as three men nearby squabbled over a purse. Among the crowd was a familiar face: that of the boy who had been on the bier in the forest earlier that day.

"Ah!" the gentleman exclaimed with arch delight. "Are we not so aptly named?"

Charlotte felt sick and her surrounds began to liquefy and whirl. She reached out to steady herself but could gain purchase only on the strange man's clothing, which she grasped as tightly as she could. So many. Of course there were so many. The Wild Horde. Of course.

At that moment, Michel—his face as grey and greasy as the

afternoon on which he died—emerged from the throng and it seemed to Charlotte that he glimpsed her only momentarily before melting back into the crush. She called his name, reached out, then lost sight of him.

"My husband," she whimpered.

The tall man took her hand to steady her before lowering himself onto one knee so that his great face was level with her own. He was kindly, concerned, so very sympathetic. "Your husband?"

She nodded. It was only then she realised she was sobbing and, judging by the tears already on her cheeks, had been for some time. It happened, this weeping, for often she woke salt-lipped from dreams in which all her children still lived.

The man smiled. "There is always something to say, isn't there? Apologies, tokens of this or that, last words, reminders, confessions. Ghosts, apparitions, dreams. The call of the end-less dead. For they certainly are many."

"And my poor children? Are they here?"

The man glanced around, then returned his gaze to her. Charlotte composed herself. "My daughters Aliénor and Béatrice died of scarlet fever in the same summer. Their older brother Philippe died in his infancy. The midwife told me it was for lack of milk. Such a tiny thing he was, like a kitten."

"Why don't you join us, then?" the man asked. "Come with us and you can spend time with them again, and see your hus-band. Did you tell him you loved him in time? Did you tell your children?"

"But what of Nicolas?"

A deep and melancholy shrug. "One boy."

"And are you . . . Who are you, monsieur? Are you the Devil?"

An indulgent smile and a shake of his head. "Oh, no. I am merely the sexton, gathering my dead."

"Then why would you tempt me so?"

"It is no struggle, surely, when the offer is as sweet as this? I seek to help you, madame. Can you not see for yourself how joyous they look?"

Charlotte cast her eye over the assembled mob and, yes, she was compelled to acknowledge they appeared happier than many living people she had seen, as if they had been released. "But where are you taking them? What is it like there?"

"Oh, madame. You have listened to the curé, I am sure. How to describe it? A grand palace fit for kings and queens. There are numberless rooms, huge lush gardens and sunshine. You would finally know what it is to be liberated from earthly concerns, free of disease and further death. No mourning, no weeping, for it is where all former things have passed away. Beautiful wine, meat, nectar."

It sounded beguiling. Charlotte's shoulder pained her and her heart tolled heavy in her chest. She gazed around. "Is it somewhere nearby?"

"No. All those things are much further along. First one must pass through here with me, madame."

"But my children? Are they . . . ?"

The man arched an eyebrow and waited for her to finish her question. He glanced around, evidently wearying of her and her womanly hesitations. Then, when she faltered once more under the burden of her sobs: "Are they what, woman? Happy? Warm enough on cold nights? Staying clear of those terrible wolves and bears? Is there sunlight and sweetmeats? Angels? Do they grow old or remain exactly as they were when they died? Do they think of you? Long for you? Do they know how often you think of them, how much you pray for their poor, childish souls?"

Foolish questions, all of them, but yes, that was exactly what she wanted to know.

At that moment she heard a woman's voice at her ear, felt a hand pulling at her sleeve. "Come with me, chicken. Come. I need you." Then, directed to the strange man: "Leave her alone. I need this one."

There followed an urgent conversation between the fellow and the newly arrived woman but Charlotte was unable to determine the nature of their business. When finally they reached their agreement, the man turned his attention to the crowd as it congregated around a man and woman—husband and wife, perhaps—engaged in a shrill quarrel. The woman struck the man on the chest, much to the crowd's delight, before she turned her anger on them with her fists balled, calling them sluts and purse-cutters, among other things in languages Charlotte didn't understand.

"Be on your way, then, Madame Picot," the cloaked man muttered as he lumbered to his feet. "I am certain we will meet again one day. The time has come to gather my flock."

He is Hellequin, Charlotte thought, and she was overcome with wonder and fear. The strange fellow raised one of his hands and, although he did not speak, the clamour subsided and the assembly turned their gleaming faces towards him. Their attention thus commanded, he nodded a curt farewell to her and mounted a large horse that had materialised from the gloom.

And, with that, the assembly moved off, his horse snorting, bridle clanking, cloak fluttering in the wind. Horns sounded and weapons and implements clattered as the crowd—still grumbling, still laughing and cursing and jeering and weeping and praying—trailed behind him across the chamber in a shuffling, chaotic procession until they disappeared from sight.

Charlotte remained where she was, a woman's murmuring voice still at her side, a tugging still at her clothes. These things sensed rather than seen, like seasons or weather, the tides of blood. An old woman with a crown of yellow flowers took her hand and led her in the opposite direction. The riotous clamour of the Wild Horde faded away behind her.

Soon the floor began to slope slightly upwards. Charlotte felt a fresher breeze upon her cheek. She glimpsed a thread of light near the floor, of sunlight this time, and she pulled ahead of the old woman. She came to a wooden door, its construction and purpose determined easily by feel alone. Charlotte ran her palms all over this door's splintered surface, searching for its latch. There. She fumbled with it. With effort, for the mechanism was stiff and unyielding, she lifted it and put her shoulder against the door's considerable weight. But it would not move. The old woman joined her and together they heaved, this time with all their strength. The door opened, at last.

6

In the winter months the prisoner yearned to be on the water, and when on the sea chained to his bench, rowing for hours and hours every day, he wished to be back here in the port prison, in the turbid dark, among the dead and almost dead, far from the overseer and his terrible lash.

He heard the slopping of water in the distance, and the cries of the Mediterranean seagulls, their sound so different to the gulls of his own infinitely more civilised country. Even after all these years, the noise of the birds startled him; on his first few mornings here, when he was woken by the cries of the atrocious creatures, he was horrified in his mistaken belief they were, in fact, the hellish shrieks of unwanted babies being disposed of by the angel makers, dozens of them all at once, so many that the docks below must surely be greasy with their infant blood. But that was many years ago, at another port to the west—what was its name? What *was* its name? Or was it here, after all? He thought on this for a long time, most pleased to have something to ponder, for it filled the long days. What *was* that place? Famous, he knew, and yet its name pranced mischievously in the outermost shadows of his memory, enjoying its diversion, darting away, reappearing to leer at him before vanishing again. Bah! He shook his head and cast off the thought. Let memory play its foolish games.

He crouched on his stone ledge in the darkness with his heels drawn up under his arse for warmth. The prison provided a threadbare straw mattress to sleep on, but little else—a paltry blanket, a thin cloak, whatever meagre comfort or sustenance one might buy after the poor-box donations had been distributed among his fellow convicts. There were deals to be done, of course, but any trade with these men was akin to dealing with actual devils. Turks and murderers. No, he thought. Better to make one's own way.

The stone of the wall beside him was cold and slick with moss. The chain bolted to his ankle clanked whenever he changed position. The vast room reeked of sweat and shit, of unwashed men, of their scabrous bodies and drooling sores. There was the incessant chitter and squeak of rats.

He removed his cap of red cloth and ran a hand over his bristly scalp, over the notches and the scars, the fresh wound over his right ear. It was still tender, this most recent one, and encrusted with just-dried blood. He busied himself picking at it, his mouth puckered with pain and concentration. Finally, he tore away the scab. In the meagre light afforded him by the barred window set high into the wall, he inspected it lying in his grubby palm. He sensed the line of blood that trickled down his shorn scalp. Some warmth. At least my blood is still warm. He was most fortunate; the surgeon at the hospital had told him this many times as he bandaged him and treated his wounds with camphored brandy. Several others on his bench were killed in the skirmish. Bourdin didn't survive, nor the fellow next to him, Sevignon, whose whole arm was severed by grapeshot. The water all around them was soupy with bobbing bodies, lengths of timber, clothes and barrels, pieces of burnt sailcloth. And, oh, the hideous screaming, the wailing of dying men. Was it good fortune to survive such an assault, or bad? Never mind, he thought. Never mind. Never mind. Never mind. The name of the place would come to him eventually. Patience. At least one learned patience in the dungeon. It came with other, much less savoury lessons, naturally, but he steered his mind away from those for now. He pressed a hand to his left cheek to stay its twitching.

From a pocket in his breeches he produced a shabby silk purse no larger than the palm of his hand. He loosened the string that secured it and took from it a folded square of paper. It was a map of a part of Paris. This map had been given to him by a blacksmith named Bertrand who'd died three years ago. The prisoner held it in his closed fist. He had pored over the map's trembling lines and instructions so often that he no longer needed to look for it to calm him. The former town-house in Rue Saint-Antoine. Through the courtyard, down the stone stairs, find the rock with its eight-pointed star. But beware. A true witch must banish Baicher, the Guardian of Lost Treasure, with a crow that is stolen, never bought.

As had become his custom, the prisoner held the little square of paper between middle and index finger, pressed it against his lips and murmured those words he knew to be magical: "*Sator Arepo Tenet Opera Rotas*'. This invocation—which might also be uttered in reverse—had been taught to him by a Jew in Toledo many years earlier. This was ancient wisdom, old magic, handed down through the centuries and transcribed and deciphered by the scholar Trithemius from manuscripts written by Simon Magus himself. Yes. Not a great deal of such magic remained, the Jew had assured him. It was now as rare as myrrh. And now the prisoner waited, eyes closed, lashes vibrating. His heart beat more rapidly. A prayer. Yes, yes, it was a coded prayer, he supposed—to whom exactly he didn't know. Whoever might be listening to a man as wretched as he. God, the King, the Devil himself, for all he cared.

There. The frail dandelion of his imagination floated up through the rusty grille set high in the stone wall and right over this filthy harbour—across green fields and magnificent chateaux, to cities suffused with soft northern light. He glimpsed church steeples, boys on horseback, a cartload of red apples, gaggles of young women with their clothing falling away just so. The world beyond. So close! So maddeningly close! *There*, beyond these thick walls. And, ah, breathing deeply now, the far more agreeable smells of fresh bread and loamy soil.

A man nearby coughed and spat. This was followed by a loud, wet fart. The spell, such as it was, was broken.

The prisoner returned the treasure map to his purse, retied it and cupped the purse for a moment in his hand, thinking, dreaming, wishing. Then he put the purse back in his pocket. Under his breath he sang a childhood song that also never failed to comfort him. "*Mes amis, que reste-t-il? À ce Dauphin si gentil? Orléans, Beaugency, Notre-Dame de Cléry . . .*"

Around him in the gloom other men slowly stirred and sipped water from their cups. Most of the convicts were unfamiliar to him, having arrived on the chain from Paris a few days earlier. There arose a general murmuring, yawns, more coughing, the clank of chains and, now and then, the steady burr of old and tired cocks pissing into wooden buckets already brimming with human waste. And weeping. There was always someone weeping—sometimes the same man, at other times a different fellow—so much sorrow that they distributed the weight of it among themselves, passing it from slave to slave until it came around again.

From the other side of the dungeon there came the sound of a key opening a lock. The heavy door swung open and the turnkey Laurent stood in the doorway, silhouetted against the flickering yellow lamplight from the damp passageway. Jangling his iron ring of keys as usual, thoroughly enjoying his brief moment of authority. One of his guards stood behind him.

The turnkey scratched his bearded throat and stepped among the waking men like a farmer among a crop of giant mushrooms. A grumble, quickly swallowed, as he kicked some poor fellow in the head. Rats skittered out of his way. Shuffle and exclamation, someone crying out with a complaint, a request to see the surgeon.

Laurent approached the prisoner, peered at him. "Double one five double four?"

The prisoner showed him the small tin plate that was stamped with his number and sewn to the front of his red jacket. "Yes."

The turnkey sorted through his massive ring of keys and crouched to unlock the prisoner's chain from its bolt. He stood back. "Governor wishes to see you. Bring your bag."

"Why? What have I done?"

"How would I know?" Laurent laughed heartily and glanced around, seeking allies to share in and bolster his mirth. "You're the fortune teller, aren't you? Aren't you? You should know, not me. Ha ha. Isn't that right? Isn't it? Look into your magic cards, my friend. Look to the fucking moon."

The prisoner clasped his knees and forced a smile. Oh yes, how they loved to tease him. Laurent mocked his tarot cards—as did many of the other guards and prisoners—but visited him occasionally, in secret, to enquire about his future. *Will I marry? Will my wife survive her illness? Will I have a son?* The prisoner bore the jeering in good humour because his cards—and his skill in interpreting them—had secured his survival. After all, one needed brutality or wisdom to survive the galleys.

And so he held his tongue. His shoulders ached, his heart shivered in his chest. He gazed around at his fellow prisoners. A few desultory stares in his direction, grinning mouths. They would laugh at anything the turnkey said in order to ingratiate themselves and possibly be spared a beating in the future. Yes. Hilarious. Shaven heads and pairs of eyes glinting and unglinting like old coins pressed into the sockets of the dead. Most of them barely cared. After all, what was he to them? Another mouth to feed, another slave chained to his bench, one more worthless rogue destined to die in the dungeon or at his oar. Such scum. Oh, but how little they knew. How little.

Laurent jabbed him in the ribs with the wooden club he always carried. "Anyway," he growled, "that's enough fun for now. Come along, convict. I don't have all fucking day. Gather your things."

The prisoner picked up his battered satchel and followed the turnkey from the dungeon.

The Governor's office was in the east tower. Progress was slow. The prisoner's ankles were shackled together with a short length of chain. The dreary warren of passageways was so dank and dripping with moisture that it seemed he was not being taken to see the Governor at all but, rather, King Neptune in his network of caverns beneath the sea. They shuffled past similarly chained prisoners who were on their way to work at the arsenal or for tradesmen in the port, and they were admitted through numerous rusty iron gates that slammed shut and were locked behind them.

Perhaps he was to be given a position in the port, off the actual galleys? Yes. He'd heard of it happening. His old friend—what was his name, Jean?—who had rowed on the same bench as he some years ago, he was given, for no apparent reason, an administrative post in the treasury or some such. Good with numbers, they said. So, it was not out of the question. No. After all, he could read and write, speak several languages, perform sums. He had skills. Chances came along in this life, didn't they? It was merely a matter of determining their design. And of being in the right place. And, of course, *recognising* them when they appeared. Yes, that was a huge part of it. The pattern of things could be deciphered if one had the necessary skills. There was design, he knew, but this might be nudged in certain directions, might even be yoked to one's own desires if one knew how.

When at last they arrived at his humid office, the Governor was seated behind his desk shuffling through a sheaf of papers.

Round-shouldered, with his sallow, unshaven face close to the papers and records. The guard announced the prisoner, but the Governor merely went on reading. He didn't even look up. Most boorish, really. The prisoner removed his red cap and cast his eyes about the room. A window looked out over the harbour. High, thin clouds, a strip of cornflower-blue sky. One, two, three seagulls wheeled about before vanishing, as if hauled from sight on a length of string. On one wall hung a plan of the prison, on another a map of the port. He inspected this port map, attempting to orient himself. Streets, churches, a chunk of the Mediterranean—that body of tepid water he had come to loathe.

A well-fed orange cat luxuriated in a slab of pale morning light that fell upon the stone floor. Momentarily startled at the noise of their entrance, the cat had glanced up at the prisoner and the guard before relaxing again, half closing its green eyes and licking a grubby paw. The cat, he knew, was named Athénaïs. The shadow queen, the one who really ruled the prison. A local joke. If only they knew—as he did—what Madame de Montespan was really capable of. The prisoner shuddered at memories of what she'd been involved in—at what he had been required to do. The infant, the chalice, the knife, the blood.

The cat, perhaps sensible to these morbid thoughts, stopped bathing and eyed the prisoner as if committing his face to memory for future reference, or trying to place where they might have met before. Either way, it was most unnerving. The prisoner glanced away.

Then the Governor, who was rumoured to be a decent enough fellow, screwed up his face and nodded to himself with—what? Satisfaction? Surprise? Bafflement? He looked up and inspected the tin plate affixed to the prisoner's jacket. "Ah. Double one five double four."

"Yes, monsieur."

The Governor glanced again through the papers in front of him. "Let me see. You have been here since . . . September '68? Five years. Quite a long time. A survivor, eh? Monsieur Adam du Coeuret . . . "

The prisoner flinched at hearing his name spoken so plainly. *Adam du Coeuret.* Yes, that was his name but it had been so long since he had been addressed in such a manner that he had almost ceased to think of himself as a man. After all, was it not the purpose of the galleys to transform men into compliant beasts, to take a man's name from him and expose him? The guards called him by his number—by other, worse names—or referred to him sarcastically as the Magician. They flogged the convicts, denied them food, forced them to perform all manner of unnatural acts. Oh, the things he'd seen. Most of the time the prisoner—this Adam du Coeuret—managed to act as if these terrible things were happening to other men but, suddenly, he could deceive himself no longer. And now what? Were they preparing to execute him? Was he guilty of some new crime? It was all too much. He began to weep softly.

"I see that you are from Caen in Normandy," the Governor went on blithely. "I went to Caen once. Very nice. I had a cousin there. But you were sentenced for . . . for impieties and sacrileges, it says here. Uttering incantations. Spells. Found in possession of a black book. *Frogs.* Worked with an Abbé Mariette. François Mariette." A sort of *harrumph*—of disdain, of disbelief, who knew. "And what happened to this Mariette fellow? He was not here with you, was he?"

The prisoner composed himself. "Oh. No. I believe he was, ah, he was banished, monsieur. But it was nothing, really. Harmless tricks, nothing more than that. Really. Nothing. As if I would—as if I even *could*—do anything of the sort of which I was accused. Well. I don't know. Mysterious, quite unfathomable. François Mariette is a most devout man. Or he was. As am I. It's true I was involved in the production of certain creams that might whiten a lady's complexion, but that's all. Frogs are well known for this, of course. I am a wool merchant, sir, that is my profession. Of a quite favourable repute, might I add . . . "

The Governor waved a hand for him to shut up, then scrutinised him anew, as if unable to reconcile the criminal charges with the ruined man standing before him. Probably he wondered at the twitch in the prisoner's cheek, although certainly he had seen much worse in his years here. The confinement. The confinement and the months of rowing. The uncertainty, the rats (oh, the rats!), the mosquitoes, the whippings, the damp, the salt, the blisters, the endless diet of beans, the perpetual fear of the bastinado, of drowning. It all did terrible things to a man. All those nightmares wriggling away like maggots in his brain. Ugh. He, the prisoner, had himself seen men reduced to no more than rubble and rags. Men trembling, unable to speak in actual words or, worse, speaking in languages intelligible only to themselves. In madness and despair they scooped out their own eyes with spoons, hacked off their fingers, killed themselves in all manner of ways. Why, more than once he had seen a fellow bequeath to another all he owned in return for a knife pounded into his heart with a mallet. Promises. Promises and threats, all of it made immeasurably worse because he understood it so intimately. Life reduced to its bones, wherein you could see how it all truly worked, like a man rotting away in a gibbet. And, yes, it was certainly an ugly business.

The Governor glanced down once more at his papers. "But on June the twelfth you were injured at Genoa. In the assault."

"Yes, monsieur. Yes, yes. Some shot in my head. Quite close, they were, the bastards. Came right up alongside." The prisoner angled his head to display his injury.

Again the Governor waved his hand, not eager to see such a wound. Doubtless he had seen plenty of the sort.

"Well," he continued, "it would seem that you acquitted yourself quite admirably on that day. The Secretary of State of the Navy has sent word through Monsieur Arnoul that fifteen men who served on that vessel are to be freed. And, as it happens, Monsieur du Coeuret, you are to be one of those men."

The prisoner remained still. Stunned. Everything slowed down. The gulls outside fell silent. The cat halted its ablutions to watch him. Blinked. Blinked again. Somewhere outside a woman cried out, in what at first sounded like anger, then amusement, "*Oh, you sly old devil!*"

This moment. This was the precise moment he had dreamed about for so many years. Although, to be sure, it had never been exactly like this. Usually an escape, flight across the water or, better still, belated recognition of their egregious mistake in jailing him in the first place. There would be grovelling excuses; perhaps a royal pardon; invitations to the court; the attentions of young ladies who vied with each other to minister to his wounds, to his poor heart, to other—equally tender, equally mistreated, equally neglected—organs.

"Sorry," the Governor said, "did you say something?"

The prisoner shook his head. "Pardon? No, monsieur. I don't think so."

A confused lull.

"Congratulations," the Governor added, although it seemed clear from his tone of voice that he felt no such praise was necessary. Then, when there was still no response: "Did you understand what I said?"

Another pause. *Did* he understand? "Yes, monsieur," he said at last in a whisper. "I understand. Thank you. Thank you."

The Governor smiled. "You did not foresee this in your cards, then?"

The prisoner hesitated, said nothing.

"It must be quite a shock."

"Indeed."

"But a pleasant one."

"Oh, yes, yes. Of course, monsieur. Thank you."

"Not many get out of the galleys. We've had some here for ten years, twelve—longer. Old lags, no good to anyone, really. But Monsieur Colbert is quite determined to build up the fleet and, as we have already seen in this part of the world, defiance does not pay. Still. The punishment for impieties is usually death by burning. You are lucky twice over, monsieur. I assume you have been praying?"

"Every day."

"And it seems your prayers have been answered."

"I know it, monsieur."

"A bonfire, eh? They might easily have turned you into ashes. Spread you all over the garden beds of Paris." And here the Governor gestured, as if casting his powdered remains to the wind.

"Yes."

Silence. The Governor appeared puzzled, and glanced again at the papers on his desk before returning his attention to the prisoner with his chin perched on his fist. His face shone with sweat. "Do you have somewhere to go?"

The prisoner considered. Swallowed. He felt dreamy, as if his head were filling with wine. Again tears pricked his eyes. "I do have a wife, monsieur. Claudette. If she is still alive, that is. If she'll have me. She still lives in Normandy, I assume. It has been a long time since I had word from her. We are a long way from Normandy."

"Yes. Well, a wife is a good start. Some children, I presume?"

Adam du Coeuret was taken aback. He had indeed fathered two sons who survived, but he'd heard no word of them for many years. Doubtless the long-suffering Claudette had remarried, for no reasonable person expected a man to survive the galleys, let alone ever be released. His sons André and Étienne

would be in their twenties, if they were still living. He recalled
the two of them as children, standing in a green field when he
returned from some journey or other, watching his approach as
if uncertain of who he was.

"Yes, I have two sons," he said, when he realised the Governor was still waiting for his response. "They would be men
by now."

"And have you given much thought as to what you might
do upon your release?"

*Had he given much thought to what he might do upon his
release?* Was the man a complete idiot? What else was there to
do in prison aside from dreaming of such things? There was
survival, avoiding the salacious attentions of sodomites,
scrounging for favours. That all took time, naturally (and more
than one might think), but there was plenty left over. Like an
oafish and ungainly squirrel in its nest he had hoarded plans
and ideas, returning to them over and over—discarding some,
embroidering others, stitching and filing and whittling and
crafting—until they were so magnificent that it seemed a pity
not to share them. But what could he tell this man of these
plans? That he was intending to go back to Paris as quickly as
possible and that, there, he would find a sorceress powerful
enough to banish several terrible demons so he might take possession of treasure hidden in a cellar? And then—what?—live
a life of luxury and indolence? Probably. Why not? After all he
had endured.

But if there was one thing prison had taught him, it was
when to keep silent. Yes, indeed. Adam du Coeuret giggled,
then cleared his throat. "I think I shall return to Normandy,
monsieur, and take up my profession again. I am forty-five
years of age. It is the serene life for me from now on."

The Governor smiled ruefully, as if he envied the prisoner
his good fortune in departing this wretched port. Then he
stood and handed several sheets of paper to the guard. "These

are the official documents for Monsieur du Coeuret's release. Take him through to the guardhouse and tell them to sign him out."

The prisoner flinched. He dabbed at his tears with the frayed cuffs of his blouse. "*Today?* I am to leave today, monsieur? Right now?"

"Yes. Why not? Unless you wish to spend another night with us? Because I feel sure that can be arranged."

"Well. No. No. Of course not." He glanced around. An unfamiliar taste in his throat. Bilious, salty, as if his heart were attempting to shoulder its way into his mouth.

"The guardhouse will give you new clothes and some money to see you on your way. Is there anything else from the dungeon you need to take?"

A stupid question. What could he want? Adam du Coeuret shook his head. "No, monsieur. Nothing. Thank you." He held up his satchel. "I have all I need."

7

The portcullis clanged closed behind him and Adam du Coeuret found himself outside, unshackled, free. It was all so sudden. Was it some sort of horrible trick? His feet were constricted in the tight shoes they had given him. Indeed, it felt decidedly odd to be attired in clothes other than rags. Dressed almost like a real man. The clothes were old, certainly, but not so terrible, taken from some fellow a day or so earlier, they said. Cream-coloured breeches, a blue doublet. It was humid—the morning was bright and monstrous, a too-large beast. He groaned and covered his eyes with his sleeve. In his other hand was the purse of coins they had presented him with. A few écus. Some consolation, at least. It would be enough to get him away from this stinking southern city, but probably not much further. What was the price of things these days? Bread, a portion of soup, a cup of wine? He would almost certainly need some more money, and quickly. He thought of Paris and patted the pocket containing his purse with the map. Soon, he thought. A few days, a week at most.

Thick smells of brine and bilge filled the air. The hark and endless damned hark of gulls, clatter of carts, a crate of chickens cluck-clucking somewhere nearby. Stink and din—that was nothing new. The gentle lap of sea water. Fishbones strewn over the cobbles, handcarts at rest, barrels and baskets stacked high wherever he looked.

He felt fearful, as if the world had grown so much larger

and louder in his absence. Or, more likely, he had shrunk. Almost without knowing it, he found himself with his back pressed against the prison's stone wall, like a child seeking comfort within the folds of his mother's skirts. There he loitered, in the shadows of the prison, his heart quivering in his chest—still trying to escape—his fingers plucking at his sleeves, leather satchel pressed to his chest.

He stood there for quite some time, thinking. Or not thinking, exactly. *Wondering*, really, at the machinations of the earth and the heavens. This was a fiendish miracle, almost unheard of. Certainly he had not seen it in any of the readings he had performed for himself. He waved a hand in front of his face, half expecting the buildings, the sky, the weathered sails of feluccas and galleys to vanish, like a vision roughly dreamed. But they all remained stubbornly real. Canvas fluttered in the breeze. He inspected his hand, made a fist, opened it once more. Skin, a few scars, hardened blisters, many years of grime. Fingers, nails. But there was no doubt it was a real thing, this hand, *his* hand, solid and so useful.

The working day on the docks was already underway. Washerwomen, maids on errands, sailors and children scurried back and forth with bundles of possessions, wooden carts of tools or nets. Italians and southerners and other wicked sorts laughed and cursed in their ugly, rough-hewn dialects. Arabs wearing turbans. A huge Ethiopian fellow arranged piles of crates. It was frightening, that's what it was. Disconcerting. All these people—having woken at dawn and gnawed at some week-old bread—going about their business, running here and there. Life's daily struggle. A bell clanged somewhere in the port, clatter of rigging in the breeze. He hefted his purse of coins. A satisfyingly soft, upholstered chink. Really quite reassuring. He repeated the action. This was something, at least.

Adam du Coeuret noticed he was being observed by a

scrawny barefooted boy, perhaps ten years old, who was lounging against a pile of nets some distance away. The boy had
paused in his whittling of a length of wood with a knife.

After some hesitation Adam du Coeuret motioned for the
boy to approach, which he did, spitting stickily as he sauntered
over.

"You off the galleys?" the boy asked when he was near. He
stood at a slight distance, squinting, out of Adam du Coeuret's
reach.

The question took him by surprise; perhaps his clothes
were not disguise enough after all? Although his first instinct
was, always, to lie, he nodded. "But I am free now. As free as
you are." He held out his unshackled hands and with them
indicated his legs, also unchained. "As you can plainly see."

Rather than being afraid or derisive, the boy seemed gratified by the response. "My uncle uses convicts from the prison
in his workshop. How long were you inside there?"

Adam du Coeuret glanced over at the closed gate. Shapes
moved about in the shadows. Guards, prisoners, their forms as
slender and indistinguishable as phantoms. "Oh, quite a long
time. It felt like forever."

"Did you kill someone?"

He swung his gaze around to the boy. "No, no, no, no.
Nothing like that."

"Then what did you do?"

"Oh, I don't think that matters now, does it? They have
pardoned me anyway. Our King himself has pardoned me.
Apologised, in fact. Yes, most gracious they were. I have been
summoned to court to see the King. You wouldn't hold a man's
past against him, would you? You wouldn't appreciate it, I'm
sure, if I mocked you for some foolishness you did as a child.
Some petty thing. Pulling your sister's hair, for instance, calling
her terrible names or something."

"I don't have a sister."

It was all he could do not to clip the insolent fool over the head. "Well. You know what I mean."

The idiot seemed to consider this deeply as he leaned down to scratch his calf with the tip of his knife before jamming the knife into his belt. "I suppose not. Not many get out of there alive, you know."

"Oh, I know."

"You must know someone in authority."

"I wish."

"Or you must have prayed very hard."

"Oh, I did that."

"And God listened to your prayers."

"Ha. Well. Someone certainly listened to my prayers. Tell me. What's your name, boy?"

"Armand."

"Well, Armand, I need your help with something. I require some supplies. I need'—he indicated his notched, bristly scalp—"a hat of some sort, first of all. One cannot visit the King bare-headed. And I need some other things. And do you know of an apothecary shop in Marseille, by chance? I require a few . . . personal articles. Some wax and saltpetre, among others. An apothecary would carry such things. Could you show me where in the town I might find such a place?"

"What will you give me if I do?"

He had anticipated this and held up his hand in a gesture calculated to demonstrate the degree of thought he had given the matter and how bounteous he intended to be. "Ah. Good question. I can give you, Armand, one whole livre. A fair exchange, I think."

The boy looked around. "Very well." But, frustratingly, he gave no indication of movement other than to hold out his hand for payment.

Adam du Coeuret smiled and wagged a finger. "No. After we arrive. How do I know you won't run away with the coin?"

"How do I know you won't refuse to pay me when we get there?"

The little prick. Adam du Coeuret squeezed out a smile. "Quite. Yes. Good thinking." He fished a coin from his purse and dropped it into the boy's grubby, outstretched palm.

"What's your name, monsieur?" Armand asked.

Adam du Coeuret was taken by surprise. "My name?" It was a question he hadn't been asked in some time, although he had been certainly preparing an answer. Oh yes. Over and again he had considered a new name, for a man's name contained so much, didn't it? A fresh start was what he needed, a whole new beginning. The options had been numerous and, of course, he'd had many years in which to refine this name, as if it were a small but perfect sculpture. His new name, he felt sure, would impress people of quality and grant him access to the finest houses. It was a summation of all he'd learned, a reflection of his personality. So, on the one hand, he was pleased to be asked his name at this juncture, and yet, to be brutally honest, he was also *slightly* disappointed that the first person to hear it was to be a boy standing among the fish scales and seagull shit on a greasy Mediterranean dock. Never mind. That was the way it was. It was probably a good thing to be able to test his new name on a mere boy.

"My name is . . . Lesage," he whispered in the manner he had rehearsed over the years, the word drawn out and complemented with a little revolving wave of his right hand in front of his stomach, as if it were itself a minor spell.

Armand turned and started walking away. "I know a place. This way, monsieur."

Lesage hesitated for a few moments before pushing off the wall, out of its shade, and scurrying after Armand. He followed the boy as they left the dock area and turned down narrower, ever darker streets. Armand skipped across the cobbles, hopping over piles of food scraps and grimy puddles. He was agile, and doubtless he was a fast runner. They turned down another alleyway, this one narrower than the previous one. More piles of filth, a cat darting across their path.

Lesage glanced around to make sure there was no one about before he gave a yelp, as of pain, and crouched down. "My ankle. Something has bitten me. Ouch! My foot."

Armand, several steps ahead of him, turned around as Lesage groaned once more and made a great fuss of unbuckling his shoe. The boy sauntered back.

"What's the matter?" he asked.

"Something has attacked me."

Armand squatted beside him on the dirty ground and peered at Lesage's ankle. Before he had found his balance, however, Lesage shoved the boy as hard as he could and sent him sprawling onto his arse. Then he grabbed Armand's bare foot and twisted until the boy cried out and was compelled to flip onto his stomach to avoid wrenching his own ankle. Before the boy could fight back, Lesage pulled the boy's knife from his belt, easy as you like. One does not endure years in the galleys without learning a trick or two.

"Ha! There. Now. Give me back my coin."

"Don't kill me. Help!"

With his knee firmly in the boy's back, Lesage pressed the knife to his neck. "Hush, boy. Don't say another word or I'll cut your throat. Just the money. Give it to me and I won't kill you."

Armand released the coin from his hand and Lesage snatched it up off the ground.

"Now," Lesage said, "don't move." He pocketed the coin and looked around. Still there was no one in sight. He heard people laughing in a nearby street, again the ringing bell, a merchant's hoarse cry.

8

Charlotte woke on her back with a start. Clotted breath and a dry hack in her throat. A comforting scent of wood smoke filled her nostrils. With much effort, she turned her head and gazed around. Firelight flickering on a stone ceiling, several candles, bundles of herbs, a shelf crowded with bottles, and there, in the shadows, a human-shaped form slumped in a corner. She attempted to hoist herself onto her elbows, but the weight of her body—combined with the heavy bedding arranged over her—prompted such pain through her left shoulder that she cried out and immediately fell back.

After some shuffling out of her line of sight, an old woman's face appeared over her. The face was thin, deeply lined, the head covered with a tattered bonnet. A severe mouth, stony blue eyes and a gathering of white bristles at her flabby throat. The woman raised a wooden candlestick, in which a candle fizzled, to peer down at her. Charlotte was too terrified to speak.

"Ah," the woman said, "you have returned."

Charlotte nodded. It was all the movement she was capable of. In the woman's eyes she saw her own reflection—a pale-faced woman with dark hair adrift in a blue pool. Thin and frightened. Her throat was so dry, as if it were lined with cloth. She raised one hand to the bandages at her shoulder. "What about Nicolas? Where is my son?"

"Your son? No. There was no one else. I found only you, madame. On the ground up by the chestnut tree. So much blood there will surely grow a hanging tree on that hill. You're lucky I happened past, for I do not go that way often. I heard the commotion."

"Please, madame. Where am I?"

The old woman exhaled. Then, in a whimsical, rasping voice: "Where are you indeed. And where did you come from, woman? A long way, I think. Probably as far as one can go from here without being lost altogether."

"Some men took my son. What would they want with him?"

The woman pursed her lips and shook her head, but it was unclear whether she was communicating a lack of information on the matter or reluctance to reveal what she knew.

Charlotte closed her eyes. Her son, dear God. Again she attempted to sit up, again she sank back onto the bed. "We fell asleep in the hot afternoon and when I woke, some men were taking him away and he was screaming. I must find them. He's only a boy."

And she began, inevitably, to weep.

The old woman grunted. "I've heard that men like that take young children to Paris, where they sell them as servants."

"All the way to Paris?"

The stranger mopped Charlotte's forehead with a damp cloth, rinsed it in a wooden bowl, then wiped her face again. "But they will be far from here. Do your weeping now, woman, and be done with it. Your heart is disordered. What else did they do with you? Anything?"

She knew what the woman meant, but could detect no further signs of injury or misuse along the length of her body. She shook her head. "How long have I been here?"

"I found you yesterday. You're lucky—the injury is not as bad as it looks. You should not die of it, that's for certain. You are Madeleine Beaufort's daughter, are you not?"

"Yes." Charlotte stared at the ceiling overhead, which

appeared to be hewn roughly from rock. Firelight played comfortingly on its irregular surface and this reminded her briefly of the curious stories her mother used to tell her, and which she, in turn, had related over the years to her own children: of the monkey and the cat; of the north wind and the sun. Foolish things to pass the time, to encourage sleep or to reassure them that everything was right with the world. Lies, one might say.

"But where are we now, madame? A cave?"

"Yes."

"How did I get here?"

"I am stronger than I look, madame. One learns to manage. I have carried heavier loads than you."

Charlotte crossed herself. "*Pater noster.* Save me from this place." She struggled to a sitting position, wincing with the pain and effort of it. "I have to go and find my son. There is no time to waste."

The old woman clucked her tongue. "But they might have gone anywhere, woman. Do you have some army I do not know about? A horse hidden away nearby, perhaps?"

Charlotte shook her head. "No. Of course not."

"I did not think so. No. How will you catch up to them? They will be many leagues away already."

"Then the sooner I leave this place, the better. Let me go, madame."

"Why are you afraid of me?"

"I'm not afraid."

"Oh, you should be."

Charlotte cowered. "Are you planning to harm me, madame?"

"Me? Of course not. I'm probably the only person who can help you."

She stared at the old woman, who stared back at her in return. The woman's cheeks were sunken, her skin as brown as hide. Her hands, too, were knobbly and gnarled, blackened by dirt and burned by the sun. She had long, thick fingernails but her mouth possessed so few teeth that when she spoke, her tongue resembled a pink and fleshy eel squirming in its dark, glistening den. She wore a dress—dark blue but much worn and faded—and wooden *sabots*, also in very ill repair.

"Who are you, madame?" Charlotte asked.

The old woman considered her. "My name is Marie Rolland," she said at last.

"You live here alone?"

"Yes."

Charlotte ran a hand over her bandaged chest gingerly, as if testing a portion of the earth suspected of harbouring dangerous hollows and swamps. She lifted aside her filthy, bloodstained undershirt and peered down at herself. There, in the flickering light, above the fleshy swell of her left breast, was her wound. It had been crudely stitched with twine and was blackly and thickly scabbed. She ran her fingertips along its raised and roughly puckered length. It looked horrible. The skin around the wound was hot, tender to the touch, and slightly brown, smeared with some sort of sticky paste.

"The ashes of arrows are the only cure for an arrow wound," said the old woman, proud of her handiwork.

"I am amazed to be alive, so near to my heart went the arrow. I remember collapsing onto the earth. Voices. An enormous underground palace in which I walked for what seemed like days. A dream."

"Ah. What else do you remember of that place?"

Charlotte tried to recall. The details were indistinct, as if glimpsed through water or fog. Flickering torchlight, faces, mouths. She covered the vile wound with her bloodstained clothes and marshalled her strength from the distant outposts of her body.

"I remember bones, instruments, machinery. Odd things. I called out. People on high gantries. People weeping. I remember men crying out and laughing as if they were drunk on wine. Hellequin." She turned to the woman. "And I remember you, madame. You were there, I think."

"I have been waiting a long time for someone like you."

"Was I dead, madame?"

"No. But very close."

"But I saw Michel, my husband who is dead. And the boy the pilgrims were taking to the shrine."

The woman appeared frustrated. "Yes, yes. You were well on your way."

"But you saved me? You went . . . down there?"

"One might sometimes strike a bargain with Hellequin."

"What sort of bargain, madame?"

"I know how to do many things. Alone, here, one learns to do a lot. You do not believe me?"

"I'm not sure what to believe, madame."

"That's as well. Certainty is an ignorance of sorts." She shuffled away and clattered about nearby before returning with a bowl brimming with a sweet-smelling broth in which leaves and twigs bobbed. "Here. Drink this."

"What is it?"

The woman shook her head in annoyance. "It's not poison, madame, don't worry. Some herbs, leaves. All good things. Drink it. It will help you heal."

Charlotte was afraid, but sipped at the broth. Its flavour was raw and woody, but not unpleasant. The effort exhausted her.

Madame Rolland observed her keenly. "But tell me, Madame Picot," she said, "to what lengths would you go to find your son?"

"I would do anything. He is my last living child. I would walk through fire."

The old woman's face contorted strangely with what might have been pleasure. "And you might get a chance to do that."

Charlotte handed back the bowl and soon fell into a dark and irresistible slumber.

Charlotte drifted in and out of wakefulness and it seemed, on occasion, that she was journeying again down into the network of underground caverns and halls from which Madame Rolland had escorted her. Her body was leaden and in her nostrils were smells of damp walls, old fires, rust. She was afraid, consoled, weary. Her shoulder ached. When she woke, she saw Madame Rolland muttering to the fire and her pan of broth, conducting idle conversations with herself as she swept the floor or wrenched the skin from a hare.

It was on one of these occasions that Madame Rolland lurched over, grasped Charlotte's forearm and shook her as if she were a mischievous child. "So. What do you think will become of you now, Madame Picot?"

Charlotte shrank back, then looked away, ashamed. It was not a matter she wished to consider. "Please. I must find Nicolas . . . "

"You could go back to your village, I suppose. But who knows how they would receive you? Your husband dead, no man to look after you. You could move to a larger town, become a seamstress or maid. A washerwoman, perhaps? A nun? Be married again—if they allow you. A pretty woman like you would have no trouble finding a new husband, whether you want him or not. He might be a scoundrel. Some fellow who treats you worse than he treats his donkey. Or maybe a good man, who knows? I've heard there are some. You can work in the fields all day long, fetch water, then cook your family's dinner. Have more babies, suckle them. Maybe one or two will even survive. No. But suppose you had someone to help you find your son?"

The conversation was making Charlotte most uneasy. She wiped away her tears. "I cannot pay a mercenary or soldier. I have no family left. I don't know where my brother is. I heard he was in Italy or Spain. Perhaps I should tell the magistrate?"

The old woman scoffed and gripped her arm tighter. "No, no, no. Nobody like that. Official men are no good to you. The magistrate cannot be trusted. You are on your own now, madame. No. I meant another sort of person entirely."

"But what sort of person? You said it yourself—I have no army, no one to help me. I don't even know exactly where they might have taken him. Is it you, madame? Would you help me?"

Madame Rolland released her arm and laughed, revealing the few teeth like blackened tree stumps in her old, wet mouth. "No. I am only an old woman. Worse, even, than a young woman. I mean someone else. I know of a particular sort of man who will come if we ask correctly."

Madame Rolland attended to her bonnet, which had become loose on her head. Her hair, now uncovered, was grey and stringy, but something else caught Charlotte's attention: on the left side of the old woman's head, where an ear should be, there was instead merely a fleshy lump around the earhole.

"What happened to your ear, madame?" Charlotte asked.

Madame Rolland paused to fondle the gristly protuberance between her thumb and forefinger. She considered Charlotte closely for a long time.

"Let me tell you a story," she said eventually. "It's an old story, but it's almost always the same one. I was born on an island a long way from here. When I was a girl they hanged my mother for being a witch and then they burned her body on a pyre. The curé there said she had conspired with the Devil to curdle the milk in a neighbour's house, but she didn't do any such thing. I watched it all. The whole island watched her hang. At least she was dead when they burned her. That was some fortune. Others were not so lucky. The screams of burning women are truly terrible to hear. I was accused of nothing, but the executioner sawed off my ear with his knife and threw it to the dogs. Then they banished me forever from the island—as if I would wish to return after what they had done to my family.

"They bound my hands tightly, put me in a boat, and a fisherman called Dugret and three other men sailed me to the shores of Brittany. My father didn't even see me off, he was so afraid. It was summer, but very cold on the water. I shivered and cried all through the crossing. My head was bleeding. I had dried blood crackling all over my cheeks, on my neck. Blood as thick as honey in my hair. The gulls circled. The men laughed and said they'd throw me into the water for their entertainment if I didn't shut my weeping. On the shore they took all my money for their trouble, then they bent me to their will, all of them, and sailed away laughing. They threw my bonnet into the water when they were done. I had some bread and sausage in a basket, but that was all. My cloak was rags, everything was torn."

"You're fortunate they didn't murder you."

The old woman smiled. "I am not so easily murdered. I started walking east when I was able to, following the sun where it rose and then the stars at night. The moon was kindly. I stole food along the way, begged for money. And I did other things, of course. I slept in haylofts and fields. Some people were helpful, others not so welcoming. It was summer. Highwaymen roamed the forests and robbed people. Mercenaries were leaving the wars in the north. I came across bizarre tribes—people who bleed from their navels once each year. They were the Saracens; I don't know if you have heard of such a people. I stayed with a family of Cagots who had webbed feet. In one forest I saw a naked man who could leap as high as a deer, and I also travelled for a time with an army of boys walking to work in the fields. The winter swallows. There are many incredible things in the world. More things than you could ever truly know.

"I kept walking and, in time, I entered this forest. Here I met a woman whose name was Vivianne. She took me in and gave me shelter. I told her what had happened to me—how some men had killed my mother for being a witch, even though she was no such thing. How they had sliced off my ear, the blood, what those sailors had done to me. She lived right here in this cave."

Here Madame Rolland paused, nodding to herself at the memory, chewing on a seed, the husk of which she soon spat out. She sighed, rearranged her grey cloak about her shoulders and prodded the fire.

"Vivianne was very old. She was tiny, almost like a child, and was unable to walk without the aid of a stick she carried at all times. She had seen many, many things: hundreds of soldiers, all sorts of wars, truly unspeakable things. And she was tired. She asked me what I would wish to do to the men who had hanged my mother and cut off my ear, and I told her I wanted to kill them. When I said this she laughed so loudly and said: *I've been waiting for you.* She said she could arrange for some help to do what I wanted. She said she had something especially for me."

"She had a gift?"

"Oh, much better than any gift." Madame Rolland paused again. "And worse, too. But it is true. I wanted very much to kill the men who hanged my mother, but I was only a young woman. What could I do? I didn't have the courage. I had no means to do such a thing. Like you, I had no army of my own. No family to speak of. Vivianne said she might be able to find a certain type of man to assist me. She made me a curious offer, but it was on the condition that, if I accepted it, then I must, in turn, make the same offer to another young woman." She paused. "To a woman, perhaps, like you."

Charlotte rubbed her forearm where Madame Rolland had gripped her, and which still bore the dark, ghostly imprint of the old woman's fingers. "You are the witch, aren't you? The Forest Queen."

"I was not a witch, but they made me one."

"Is it true what they say about you?"

"Which things exactly? That I have kissed the Devil's arse? I have touched his cold, leathery skin? Felt him deep inside me? Yes. I have supped with him on many occasions. I have slaughtered children, too, and drained their blood to make a paste. I have met with hundreds of witches in the forest and we have lit fires and danced naked in the light of the flames. We have sung terrible songs and told terrible tales, and we have smeared ourselves with grease and risen into the air as if we were made of feathers."

Charlotte shrank back.

Madame Rolland shook her head and laughed with grim satisfaction. "Ha. No, Madame Picot. They are stories only. My tricks are not quite so varied or exotic. It's only simple magic. Old knowledge. I have never myself spied the Devil, although I have certainly spoken with some of his nasty servants. It's only charms and baubles. Some healing, a few prayers. That's all. You should be thankful for my skills—if anyone else had found you, you would be dead by now, that is for certain. Mostly it is harmless things. Recipes, love charms, spells for protection from bullets and fire, remedies for barrenness and ague. There is some darker magic too, of course—for there is never one without the other—but one need not seek out those particular spells. What foolish people call magic is nothing more than a way of seeing the world; of being alive to its design, understanding it for what it really is. There is some power in that. Probably the only power a woman like you or I will ever possess. They do not want a woman to take her fate into her own hands."

"No, madame."

"I have watched you longer than you know, Madame Picot,

and you are strong enough. You are the same Charlotte Picot who was bitten by a wild dog and returned home to sear the wound with a poker turned orange in the fire. You are the Charlotte Picot who fought off that merchant who tried to force you to his will when your husband was away—even with the children in the house. You are the Charlotte Picot who buried her mother and father, who has tended crops and birthed lambs. Who has kept a family alive. Yes? You are stronger than you think."

"How would you know all these things?" Charlotte looked around at the walls of the cave, at the low fire, and was moved to think how much this woman knew of her life. Her hand moved to her thigh where, indeed, a dog had bitten her many years ago. "What was the offer, Madame Rolland?" she asked.

The old woman considered her. "Do you really wish to know?"

Charlotte hesitated. Her heart was beating rapidly. "Yes."

"Because it changes everything, woman. It is a gift—that's true—but it is also a great responsibility. Most dangerous and powerful. And it can never be returned, only passed along to another woman. Never a man; they have enough power. Already they are popes and kings and prophets and gods. This is ours alone. We need to keep something special for ourselves, do we not? The only danger, Madame Picot, is that it must be passed along to another woman before you die. If it is still in your possession when you die, then your soul will be lost. This is the bargain that was struck to gain the knowledge. You must be careful."

"Please. Tell me. What was it?"

"It was a book."

The silence between them thickened. Charlotte turned aside, afraid again. "I think it is a black book. I'll not have dealings with the Devil, madame."

Madame Rolland shook her head. "Perhaps you do not

understand me. I did not spare you from old Hellequin because of the goodness of my heart. I am old; my time is almost done. Soon I will be joining the Wild Horde myself. The power of the book needs to be passed along or it will be lost altogether. As will my own poor soul. You need to take the book from me—for my good as much as your own."

"No. The curé warned me about such books. He said they are corrosive and that—"

"Monsieur Larouche? He is no saint. I can tell you many things about him. The same man who collects the tithes? The man who fucks every boy he can get his hands on? No. The book itself is not evil, woman. The choice is yours."

"No. You will not trick me, madame. A person's heart is good or bad, that is all."

"You do not know a great deal of the world, do you?"

"I know enough. I know not to handle these books."

"Imagine you are the queen of a great land, Madame Picot. The crown is yours. The sceptre. I know it is something you have thought of. You have imagined it when you were young and your brother slapped your face in anger. Imagined it after the terrible crops a few years ago when your family had to survive on milk and grass. Yes. You are queen and ruler. People look to you for guidance, to keep them safe and to protect them. It's not the power, madame—it's how that power is used. I am holding out the crown and sceptre to you. All you need do is take them."

Madame Rolland adjusted her bonnet again. "Think of your son. Alone, frightened. Are you going to allow those men to take him as easily as they have? No. You told me you would walk through fire to save your boy. They seek to limit us, but a heart contains all things, madame—especially a woman's heart. She creates life, gives suck to her baby; her heart is tender and loving. But it has other elements, as well. It contains fire and intrigue and mighty storms. Shipwrecks and all that has ever happened in the world. Murder, if need be, and dragons and quakes. This book can help you bring back your son. The boy they took is not the only child you've had, is he?"

"No, madame. There were three others. Two girls that died of fever some years ago. A boy who died in his infancy."

"God took them all?"

Charlotte hesitated. "Yes."

Madame Rolland nodded. "And did you pray to this God of yours to save the lives of your daughters and your son when they were failing from the sickness?"

"Of course I did! I prayed all night and day. And we did everything we could. We bled them, as others had done, but it was too fast. A few days. The fever was like a wind that sprang from nowhere . . . "

"And did God assist you? Were your prayers answered?"

Charlotte did not answer immediately. Their bodies laid out as cold and stiff as boards. Candlelight, prayers, dark bloom of death on their faces and necks. "I just want my son back."

"And your husband? Did you do the same for him when he was dying? Prayers and the like?"

Charlotte paused.

"Did you?"

"Yes. All the prayers I knew."

Madame Rolland clucked her tongue. "All that begging. All that asking. For nothing. Well. I think perhaps it is time for the spirits to do *our* bidding, madame."

9

L a Corne resembled any other tavern dotted at intervals along a country road. Low ceilings, the smells of smoke and wine, knots of men eating and drinking at various tables. The patrons were mostly farmers, judging by their appearance, and perhaps one or two travelling merchants. An elderly woman sat in front of the fire, roughly dunking a chicken before plucking its feathers. A goat was curled up asleep on the floor nearby. In one corner a spinning wheel stood idle.

Lesage paused in the doorway. He had been travelling for several days, mostly on the back of farmers' carts, and had managed to put some distance between himself and Marseille. This made him feel better—but also slightly anxious. He had become used to his day being tightly regulated, and he was aware that he had lost some of his expertise in dealing with people. Only this afternoon, a farmer's wife had chastised him for his ungracious manners after they had given him a ride. Yes, he needed to remember that he was a free man and that those he met on the road were also free.

There were no unoccupied tables, so he lowered himself nervously, willing himself inconspicuous, onto a low wooden bench at which a bearded, large-shouldered fellow was already seated. The other man was huddled over a ledger in which were scrawled columns of numbers. When a woman approached him to ask what he wished to eat, Lesage felt, quite suddenly, as if he were in another country altogether, its customs unknown to him; a land in which his desires might actually be heeded. He was startled, but managed—after consulting his purse to check on his money—to order a bowl of turnip soup and a cup of wine.

Unaccustomed to wearing it, Lesage adjusted the hat he had purchased in Marseille. The boy Armand's dagger was wedged snugly beneath his doublet. A lovely knife it was, too, and the boy had not been nearly as tough as he thought he was—although he put up a fair struggle. No match for a man who'd spent several years in the galleys, however. No. Not that he had harmed the boy in any serious fashion—such violence was not really in his nature. A twisted ankle and a few threats were more than enough for him to get what he needed. He tugged at his collar. Mustn't fidget, he told himself. Mustn't fidget. It marked one out as suspicious. But the truth was that he felt most conspicuous indeed, as if his years in prison were written upon his skin—which, in a way, they were. His weathered face identified him as, if not a convict, then at least a sailor. Not to mention the galley brand on his arm, which he took great pains to cover with his sleeve. Instinctively, Lesage pressed a hand to his left forearm, where the brand had been seared into his skin, and he shuddered to recall the sickening stink of coals, and of sweat and sizzling flesh. *GAL.* There was the sheer dread of the red-hot iron, of course, but also—and this was perhaps the most terrible detail—the gradual realisation that this initiation would merely be the first of countless terrors he would need to endure; in the galleys, there was always worse to come. The rough sleeve scratched his skin. This certainly didn't help matters. Again he straightened his jacket, again he reproached himself for doing so.

"What's that?" his table companion asked. A red-faced fellow he was, gruff of voice, with a felt cap pulled low over his forehead.

"Pardon, monsieur?" Lesage asked in return.

"I thought I heard you say something."

"No. I don't think so. Perhaps it was someone else. That fellow over there?"

The man looked at him and shrugged. "No matter."

Lesage's soup and wine was delivered by the woman who rested her hand (but, oh, so briefly) on his shoulder. She smelled of peeled vegetables, of tepid water and vinegar. The soup was tasty, certainly better than any fare he'd been forced to eat in recent years. And it was steaming hot! The woman waddled, had a slight limp, but was a woman nonetheless—not terribly old and, presumably, with the requisite soft and fragrant parts tucked beneath her skirts. What wouldn't he give to put his cock inside her for a while. Any hole would do, really. He was amazed to be alive. He watched her saunter into the kitchen, dip a finger into a pot and suck gravy from it. Glorious, terrifying.

"Indeed she is," said Lesage's companion.

"What?"

"She is a terrifying woman. This I know for a fact. For that woman'—he pointed with a stubby finger—"is my wife."

Lesage laughed uneasily. Was the fellow mocking him? He put a hand to where his dagger was hidden, but the man had returned to consideration of his ledger. It was a joke. Merely a joke.

"I see," said Lesage. "Yes. I see. Still, the soup she makes is excellent."

The man raised his tumbler and tossed the last of his drink into his mouth. "And the wine is good, too. My name is Pierre Scarron. I am the tavern keeper. And you, monsieur?"

Lesage made his little bow—awkwardly, on account of being seated—and introduced himself. In this fashion, they meandered into conversation. Monsieur Scarron was a former soldier who now ran the tavern with his wife—the woman in question. He puffed at a clay pipe, unleashing pungent clouds of smoke that settled over his shoulders as fog might about a mountain. His hands were wide and scarred.

It grew late. The two men traded tales and grievances, talked of women and money. They shared a jug of wine. The tavern was not a successful business, Scarron lamented, gesturing at the accounts on the table in front of him, and his wife was something of a scold. And what's more, he said, although she was satisfyingly bosomy, she had not allowed him anywhere near her (here he nudged Lesage conspiratorially in the ribs) in *months*.

"It is fortunate there is another woman nearby who sometimes grants me access to her secret parts," the tavern keeper boasted, "or my cock might explode, you know what I mean?" He became contemplative. "Her breasts are not as big, but she is younger—and quite a good deal richer."

Lesage wondered what, exactly, Scarron was telling him. The man was drunk, that was certain. And drunks almost never lied; they lost the facility.

"Then perhaps you should marry *her*," Lesage suggested with a grin, "and solve the problems of both your ledger *and* your cock."

The tavern keeper laughed. "Did you see my wife, monsieur? She is as healthy as a monk and twice as tough. No. She will live forever, I fear."

Lesage paused. "Nobody lives forever," he ventured. "I've heard there is plague about. Any number of ruffians must pass through here, monsieur. People have accidents. I've heard of women who fall and bang their heads and die. A common thing. Yes. Terrible. They go to the privy and fall down the stairs in the night."

There followed an odd silence. Scarron stared at the glowing coals in the grate and Lesage feared he had misjudged him; perhaps his ability to read the characters of men had eroded while he had been imprisoned? Had people changed so much

in the years he had been in jail? Had he? He had begun to formulate excuses in his mind, to make light of it, when the tavern keeper, with his face still averted, asked quietly: "And what
do you do, monsieur?"

Relieved to move on to other subjects, Lesage told the tavern keeper he was a wool merchant and that he had been journeying in foreign lands for some years, but was now heading
home to his own dear wife Claudette in Normandy. He scrabbled through his memory for tales he had heard during his
time in prison, and regaled the tavern keeper with some of the
more lurid examples that presented themselves. He told his
companion of the strange habits of the Moors, of encounters
with bandits and whores, a brutal shipwreck off the Italian
coast. He told him of other things, too. True stories of his former life as a wool trader—of the man he'd met in Madrid with
six fingers on each hand, of the splendours of the French
court. The food, the women . . .

"I have been all over," Lesage said, gesturing expansively,
then adding—because he could never resist, also because he
was slightly drunk—"almost to the ends of the known world. I
came through Marseille only a few days ago. Across the oceans.
My God, what a world. *Africa.* In Africa, you know, they eat
the little finger of their firstborn child because they believe it
brings them luck. Yes, yes. They do. Off the coast there I also
saw monkeys riding on the backs of dolphins, many dozens of
them at once. This is true. And laughing, too. Most incredible.
I saw also the Monster of Ravenna. Oh, hideous it was . . . I can
hardly bear to tell you of it. The size of a child. Wings on its
back, an eye on its knee, one single horn in the middle of its
head . . . "

Scarron was wide-eyed, appalled. "You actually saw this
creature?"

"Of course. Well, no. I saw illustrations. Very fine they
were, too. Done by a fellow who had seen her. I think the vile

monster was a girl. No matter; they starved it to death on orders of the Pope, thankfully. No place on God's earth for such things, is there?"

Lesage paused to sip his wine. He was pleased. Yes, he could manage again among free men, could talk and act as they did. His mood had begun to lift and he realised he was enjoying himself immensely. The unexpected camaraderie of a new friend, embers glowing in the grate, the pleasing smells of wine and tobacco smoke. How he had missed this! He felt like Lazarus raised unexpectedly from the dead. The other patrons had departed into the night long before, the tavern keeper's wife was not in sight. The old woman dozed in her seat, chicken feathers at her feet like drifts of bloodied snow. Still. Here he was. *Free.* Yes, free. He gazed down at his two feet, moved them apart. No chain. How had this happened? Remarkable, a miracle of some description. He belched and wiped his mouth.

"Well," Scarron announced, "no such marvels in this part of the world, monsieur, although they say there is a witch nearby who can fly. Some people have seen her floating above the forest, although I've not seen it myself. Once she cursed a farmer's cow and it died, and she—"

"There is a witch near here?"

"Oh yes." Scarron lowered his voice. "The Forest Queen, they call her. Quite famous in these parts. Hundreds of years old. A shapeshifter. Her appearance changes now and again. But she has a very powerful black book, one of the most powerful there is, or so I've heard. A special knife, too."

"What else can she do, this witch?"

The tavern keeper paused. "I think she does various things with herbs and leaves. Prayers, talismans. She can perform all sorts of magic, locate treasure. Even summon demons."

Unnerved and intrigued in equal measure, Lesage glanced around the tavern. "Treasure, you say? Truly?" He hesitated for a few seconds (so crucial when attempting to distance one-self from a question, to make any interest sound as casual as possible). "And have you met this—what is she called?—this Forest Queen yourself? Or does she have another name, by chance?"

Pierre Scarron shook his head so determinedly that he had to grasp the table to steady himself. "Me? Seen her? No, no, no, no."

Like so many skilled liars, Lesage was expert at detecting even the slightest deception in the words of others. He paused to sip his wine. "So you don't know where the woman lives?"

By now clearly quite drunk, the tavern owner gazed around, still shaking his head. He ran his hands over his greying beard, licked his lips. He regarded Lesage with his glistening, well-dark eyes before looking away with a shrug. "I think my wife has been to see her, maybe once or twice, nothing more. For medicinal purposes, you understand. Illness . . . "

"Ah."

Scarron gestured vaguely towards his lap. "Womanly con-cerns, if you know what I mean."

"Yes. Babies and the like?"

A tipsy pause, a belch, warm waft of wine in the air between them. "Babies and the like, yes. Why do you think my wife won't let me near her anymore at night? This tavern is not profitable enough to feed more mouths. She says she's had enough of children. But nothing further. No . . . you know, *magic*."

"I see," said Lesage. "Well. There is no real harm in that."

"Of course there isn't!"

They lapsed into contemplation of the dying fire. Lesage was excited and slipped a hand inside his jacket to pat his purse containing the treasure map pocketed there. Still there, safe. A witch was exactly the kind of person he needed to help him retrieve his treasure. But how to proceed? It was dangerous—after all, he had been imprisoned for dealing with such people. But there was the not inconsiderable problem of his declining funds. He had enough money, perhaps, to get to Paris, but not much further. Once there, he could unearth the treasure and never have to work again. Yes. He needed time to think. He needed also to piss. He stood and took up a candle.

"The privy, Monsieur Scarron? Will I find it out the back?" Scarron nodded and gestured towards the rear door.

Lesage wove his way outside. In the tavern's rear yard was a rickety barn with a straw roof, under which a mournful donkey stood. The candle in his hand flickered and spat, its light revealed now to be feeble in the greater darkness of the night. He located the privy—a shitty, reeking shack; abrupt movement of rats—and placed the candle saucer on a shelf in order to relieve himself. Ah. There. Much better. He pondered what the tavern keeper had told him of the witch. It was most intriguing. There was no harm, surely, in finding the woman, this Forest Queen, was there? He knew many witches in Paris, of course, some of them really quite powerful, but, if truth be told, their magic was occasionally wayward and unpredictable. There was that time, for instance, when Catherine Monvoison had placed a curse on a man's mistress who had become too demanding, and instead the wife had fallen into a fever and almost died. None of them, that he knew of, had ever had success with treasure and its attendant demons—not even Catherine. Much better, surely, if Lesage could find a woman who was more reliably proficient. And better, also, if he had someone with him who was unknown to the authorities—and to the other witches. Why, there was a chance he could simply arrive in the city, claim the treasure and leave with his fortune before anyone knew he'd even been there. Yes. It was dangerous, certainly, but what reward was won without risk?

Then a presence at his shoulder. It was Scarron himself,

breathing like a hog, probably come to beat him—or worse—for Lesage's ill-considered suggestion about his wife. Lesage's breeches were still undone. He fumbled and moved to draw his dagger, staggered in the gloom and almost fell. Scarron's grip upon his shoulder steadied him.

"Whoa there," the tavern keeper boomed. "Be careful, monsieur. Trust me, you do not want to fall over in here."

Lesage righted himself. "Yes, thank you. Of course not. Thank you, Monsieur Scarron." Fearing he had splashed himself with his own piss, he retreated.

The tavern keeper unleashed his own lengthy stream. Once he had finished and reordered his breeches, he shuffled outside and stared up at the sky. Lesage, who had waited for him, followed his gaze. The night was beautiful and clear. The moon a glowing shard, the stars spattered like quicksilver. As they watched, a bright, thin streak fell across the darkness and was gone. Both men gasped with the wonder of it. A sign from the heavens, Lesage thought. He took heart, for surely such a rare and glowing phenomenon was a good omen.

"What does such a thing mean?" Scarron asked, and he spat clumsily on the ground, leaving a gleaming thread of spittle swinging from his chin. Truly, the man was a pig. "They say the stars reveal our futures," he went on ruminatively, "and who wouldn't wish to know something of their future? How long one will live. How the summer will be. How long to wait for one's wife to die! Eh? Eh?"

The tavern owner doubled over in a fit of chortling, making a joke of his comments, but in the man's voice Lesage recognised a tone he knew well—an effort to express a heartfelt wish while, simultaneously, mocking such desires as outlandish lest he find himself tied to a stake for soliciting magic.

Lesage hesitated before speaking. "Well. It is only natural to wish to know of such things, isn't it? To know something of our fates? Yes. But I suspect that making our desires known only to men is not always the most reliable way to bring them about."

"Of course, monsieur. That is why I say my prayers night and day."

"Indeed. I could tell right away that you are a most pious man. But . . . has that been effective, Monsieur Scarron? Do you have all you wished for?"

Pierre Scarron snorted again and grasped one of the poles supporting the shelter. He appeared, for a moment, to be preparing to vomit, but managed, thankfully, to suppress the impulse.

Lesage realised the tavern owner was much drunker than he had first thought. Perfect. He glanced up at the heavens. The stars had been right. The moment was indeed ripe and the fellow ready to be plucked. He clapped a hand on the tavern keeper's shoulder, partly to steady him, partly to draw him closer to prevent anyone from overhearing what he was about to say.

"The world is truly a wondrous place," he said. "Full of such riches! Have you visited Paris, monsieur?"

An exclamation of disgust. "Paris. Of course not."

"Oh, Monsieur Scarron. The things I have seen. You know, there are men in that city who seem to have *everything*. Such women, fine clothes, carriages, silks and grand houses. Incredible. And most of them, I am sure, have not prayed for such things, nor have they worked hard for them. As we all know, wealth and happiness have not been evenly distributed. There is much greed and trickery and deceit. There is a pattern to things, of course, but it is a pattern from which good, hard-working, honest people like me and'—here a jab in Scarron's chest with his finger—"*you* have been excluded. Rich families, with all the luck in the world . . . "

Lesage eyed Scarron closely. In the buffoon's eyes he could discern an intimation of movement comparable with that of a

curtain ruffling prior to the opening of a theatrical performance. Doubtless the tavern keeper was assembling backstage
the very characters Lesage was describing: the beautiful, scorn-
ful women; men in their feathers and finery; their warm
houses; their sleek horses. The resentment was clearing its
throat, too, and—most importantly—the envy.

"I'm sure they have stopped by your tavern on occasion,
have they not? Perhaps on the way to their vast estates . . . ?"

Scarron nodded. "Oh yes. They have, monsieur."

"Ordered you around, ogled your wife as if she were a
maid, expected a man of your standing to water and tether
their horses? Did they care you had fought for your country
while they sat around drunk in their grand houses? No. Did
they recommend you for honours? No. Appreciate your hard
work? No." Lesage paused and shook his head sadly, as if overcome by his own little speech. "But *you*'—another judicious
prod—"you deserve so much more. So much better. Why,
Monsieur Scarron, I can tell this by looking at you. There is
God's plan, monsieur, but that plan resembles a river or
stream. It has its natural course, but sometimes this might be
altered in order to help another man's crop. Another man who
might deserve it even more . . . "

Before pressing on, Lesage paused to allow all he had said
to ferment within the tavern keeper's gut. It was, he thought
with sudden insight, a form of alchemy in itself; add a drop of
this, a pinch of that, then bring to a low but determined sim-
mer.

He glanced around before again drawing the tavern keeper
to him. "Look, monsieur, this is not an offer I make to many
people, but I feel it is my duty to help you obtain what you so
clearly deserve. Now, don't misunderstand me, there is nothing wrong with your tavern out here, but . . . "

"And how would you achieve this?"

Lesage hesitated. He was wading into dangerous territory.

"Well. Not *me*, actually. Let me rephrase that. Let's say there are others I can call upon to help you achieve your ambitions. One might send a message to powers far greater than those here on earth—if you understand my meaning?"

"But that is why I pray, monsieur. And go to church every week."

"Of course you do. *Of course*. But you and I are both men of vast experience, monsieur. Let's not pretend. Wars, plague, death. We both know who has the power on this earth."

"You are playing a dangerous game, Monsieur Lesage. There are plenty who would not take kindly to this sort of talk."

Lesage felt the man's hand heavy on his shoulder. He swallowed and glanced around. "The more dangerous the game, the greater the reward. A man of the world such as yourself knows this to be true, I am sure. Think of the freedom, think of your woman friend."

Scarron was silent for a long while. Then, almost under his breath, he murmured, "I have very little money as it is, monsieur. As I have already told you. How would I pay you? I am sure these services do not come free."

It was all Lesage could do to contain a squeak of excitement. How well had his snare been set and how perfectly had he lured this fool into it! Clearly, his skill at breaking into the hearts of men had not waned at all during his years of imprisonment; a simple appeal to lust and avarice was still the key.

"I see," Lesage said after a short pause. "Well. I understand completely, Monsieur Scarron. But let me think. There is usually a way. Perhaps there is some other manner in which I might be compensated for my services."

"Such as?"

Finger on chin, brow furrowed, Lesage made a great pantomime of consideration. "I know! How about you give me some information?"

"What sort of information?"

"Oh, I don't know. How about you tell me, for example, where I might find this so-called Forest Queen. I have a very interesting proposition for her. You *have* seen her, haven't you?"

Scarron shrugged like a schoolboy caught out in an obvious lie. "Yes. I have."

"Well, perhaps in the course of our business together you might let slip accidentally, almost in passing, where one might find this fabulous creature."

The tavern owner exhaled and some animal or other shifted in the barn behind them. Dull clock of hoof on wood. There followed a lengthy silence between the two men, and Lesage became aware of a soft mewling sound somewhere nearby. He tried to ignore it, but the noise was insistent. Was there perhaps an injured cat in the barn? No. It was something else. Could it be—no—a child? A child weeping horribly? He glanced around but there was not much to see. An intimation of pale road, buttery glow of lamplight through the tavern window, the glossy shimmer of leaves.

"What is that sound?" he asked Scarron.

The tavern keeper creased his brow and listened, then said, "Ah. That. It's nothing, monsieur."

"But there is something, Monsieur Scarron . . . "

Lesage made his way unsteadily towards the barn. The sound grew louder. Holding the candle aloft, he peered into the gloom, but could discern very little. Hay bales and dim shapes. There was an earthy, pissy smell of wet straw. Eventually, a shape consolidated into something more or less recognisable. A pale cheek, a nose, black scribble of hair. It was a boy with a torn blanket drawn to his chin. There were several children, in fact, boys and girls, most of them asleep with arms and legs so wild and askew they might have been one somnolent, many-limbed creature. Again the terrible sob.

He crept towards the fretting child and was overcome with a pang of tenderness, the like of which he had not experienced in many years. His heart sighed. Slowly, almost unwillingly, he lowered himself onto one knee. The poor boy's cheek was bruised and he had an ugly cut on his forehead. He might have been any man's son lying in the straw like a beast.

Lesage reassured the boy. "I won't hurt you, my child," he whispered. He saw now that the children were all chained together, as he had been when taken to the galleys. He reached out towards the boy—for what? to wipe the dirt from his nose? to otherwise comfort him?—before pulling back.

The whimpering boy shrank away. "Please, monsieur. Help us."

Panting with the effort, Pierre Scarron came up behind Lesage and joined him in consideration of the children.

"Who are these children?" Lesage asked him.

"They are orphans, the poor things. Lot about with the fever taking off their parents and families. They sell them in Paris. Put them to work. They make good servants or apprentices. Other things, if the price is right. Sodomites enjoy using them, I've heard. Priests, of course. Do you need an assistant, monsieur? Monsieur Horst will be here all tomorrow morning, he told me. He has some business to conclude before he travels onwards. He is their guardian."

"But they are in chains. And one of them is crying . . . "

The tavern keeper appeared ashamed at Lesage's discovery. He glanced around and scratched his throat. "Please, monsieur. Come away. Please. You must not worry about them. Monsieur Horst pays me to lodge them here on his way to Paris. I cannot refuse the money." He paused, and into his voice crept a threatening edge. "It seems that you are not the only one to do business with undesirable creatures, monsieur. But I promise not to tell anyone of your proposal if you pledge not to tell anyone about these children being kept here."

Lesage felt Pierre Scarron's meaty hand on his shoulder and turned to face him. The man's face was large, impassive. Lesage nodded.

"Come then," the tavern keeper said. "Leave them be for now. It's late. Let's go inside and send a request to your friend the Devil, since you claim to be able to do such a thing."

10

K neeling on the hard floor, Charlotte trembled as she held out her hand, palm up, as she had been instructed. Madame Rolland grabbed it and Charlotte had to fight the urge to pull away and flee the cave. But the old woman, doubtless sensing her reluctance, gripped her ever tighter. Madame Rolland pursed her lips. She brushed Charlotte's hand free of dirt, then took up a cloth from a bowl of water, wrung it out and washed Charlotte's hand.

The reflection from the water in the bowl skittered on the cave ceiling, vanishing, reappearing. They said a witch might manufacture a storm in this manner, could bend the elements to her will; that her exhalations might cause great oaks to bend and snap. Charlotte turned her attention back to Madame Rolland, who was absorbed in her task, and she felt an inexplicable urge to weep. The old woman's laboured breathing, her priestly devotion. Such tenderness. Long, long ago she'd had a mother who had cared for her in this manner. She wondered about Nicolas. Her poor son, terrified, trembling, crying out. It was an unbearable thought. The world was so cruel.

"Now," Madame Rolland said, "pay close attention, for you will need to do this for another woman one day or the knowledge will be lost forever. It's most important. You must swear to give this book—and the knife—to another woman when the time comes. It's like a fire that must never be allowed to go out. The spell for this procedure is at the back. Here? Do you see it? It's how the knowledge is absorbed. There is no other way.

Even if someone else tries to use the book, it will not be of use to them. The book can be given only in this way. And remember—if you die with the book in your possession, then your soul will be lost. Now. Do you promise, Madame Picot?"

Charlotte peered at the scrawl on the page Madame Rolland displayed for her. It was tiny and seemed to be in a language unknown to her. "But I cannot read that."

"No matter, woman. You don't need to read it. It will come to you. Did you learn your country's language from reading it? No. Of course you didn't. It came in your mother's milk. This is the same. Soon it will be like your own tongue. You'll understand it soon enough. Mostly, they are things you know already, but are unaware of. Everything I have learned, and what Vivianne learned—and the woman before her, and the woman before her—you will now know. What they call a witch is merely a woman with power. Now. Do you swear?"

Charlotte paused. "Yes. But I am afraid."

Madame Rolland paused to look up at her. Her face softened slightly and she nodded. "As you should be. You will have something other people might want. This is not common for women like us, eh? Imagine it. But you no longer have to be afraid, madame. Instead, others will have cause to fear you. After I pass along the knowledge, you will sense the world as never before. See things, smell things, hear things you have never known. I am glad to be giving it to you."

"Is there not some other magic we might use? A spell to get my son back somehow?"

"There is a limit to this magic, woman. If you live to be old, you might learn how to do all manner of things."

"But the spirit we wish to summon—is it not unruly? Dangerous?"

"Oh yes," the old woman conceded. She picked up the book in one gnarled hand. "But it can also be controlled. It must be controlled."

"Where does it come from?"

Madame Rolland paused. "From places beyond. But when he arrives, you will be his only mistress. Don't worry, I will help you to summon him."

The old woman put the book aside. Then, from within the folds of her clothing, she produced a short knife with a bone handle. "This knife offers protection. It has been blessed by an angel. Guard it well. It can make a circle that cannot be penetrated by anything except God himself."

Then, in a single movement, she drew the blade across Charlotte's palm. Charlotte gasped with pain and surprise and tried to wrest her hand back, to no avail. Madame Rolland held her fast until the worst of the pain subsided. Blood bubbled on her palm and dripped to the cave's dusty floor. Madame Rolland released Charlotte and made a similar incision in her own palm. Then she took Charlotte's bleeding hand once more and pressed their two hands together, wound to wound, in a sort of handshake, like men did. Their blood mingled. Madame Rolland closed her eyes and muttered a few words under her breath.

Finally, when it was done, Madame Rolland got to her feet in stages, like an ancient horse.

Still kneeling, Charlotte gradually came back to herself. It felt as if much had happened. She feared she might swoon. Her hand was sticky. There was blood on her dress, drops of dark blood on the floor. She gazed around at the cave walls, at the candle sagging on its saucer, a broken axe in a dim corner. Her hand was sore, and her shoulder, where the arrow had lodged, also ached. She felt heartsick and weary.

"I don't feel any different," she murmured.

"Oh, you will. You will. Here." Madame Rolland held the book out to her. "Take this, woman. Take it if you want to see your son again."

Charlotte did as she was told. The book was small, like some

books of hours she had seen, and fitted snugly in her hand.
The black leather cover was rough, its corners battered and
torn. It gave no indication of what it might contain.
Awkwardly, for she was loath to smear it with her blood, she
opened it on her lap. The cover was almost as stiff and weighty
as a church door. She sensed Madame Rolland observing her
keenly. The sight of the book's innards sent a chill through her.
There were crosses, circles, pentagrams, a drawing of a nun,
and many others of herbs and flowers. Sunflowers, ginger,
lavender. Some of the drawings had been made with coloured
inks—mainly green and red and brown—while others were
only in black. Some entries appeared more recent than others,
many more were difficult to discern in the low light. She
turned the thin pages. There was a naked woman frolicking in
a cane basket, a red flower, a mortar, two lions intertwined,
smiling suns and moons, diagrams, arrows, various other heav-
enly bodies. Words, too, although she was faintly relieved to
see that many of them were illegible, almost impossible for her
to decipher, while other pages were in scripts utterly unknown
to her. Lines of minuscule words, like those made by an insect
having crawled through a dollop of ink. She thumbed further
through the book and discovered several pages in the middle
that were sealed with a small, metal clasp.

"What are these?" she asked, although she already suspected the answer.

"That's the magic you did not want to know, Madame
Picot. The part of your heart you wished to keep hidden."

"Dark magic?"

"Yes."

"Did you ever open these pages, madame?"

Madame Rolland paused, made a face. "They are hard to
resist."

"I will resist."

"Of course. Now, turn to the last page."

On the final page of the book were dozens of whorled fingerprints that resembled roughly severed heads gazing out mutely from the past.

"They are the thumb prints of each of the women who have owned this book before you. Heloise, Jeanne, the Maid, Vivianne, myself. Now, dip your thumb in your blood and make a print alongside them."

"Are you sure, madame, that my soul will be unstained by this?"

"Everything can be forgiven."

"Everything?"

"Did God not make everything?"

"Yes, madame."

"Then whatever is, is God."

Aware of Madame Rolland's stern gaze on her, Charlotte pressed her bloodied thumb to the paper and joined the serried ranks.

Madame Rolland handed her the knife. "The book and the knife belong to you now. The knife for protection, the book for its magic." Then, wheezing with effort and satisfaction, she began to move away. "But it's time to go. Let's find someone who might help you to rescue your son. Come now, chicken. Before it grows too late."

Charlotte didn't move. When she was a girl, there was a blind man in Saint-Gilles called Thomas who ran his hands over objects to identify them—faces, fruit, leaves, furniture—and many said his understanding of the world was greater than those people with eyes that functioned. She ran her fingers over the writing as Thomas might have done.

She felt the little indentations. The smell of the vellum, its dimpled texture. Her fingertips, rough as they were, grew sensitive to the myriad scratches and curls. And, gradually, she heard whispers, muttering, incantations—the individual words initially as difficult to comprehend as those of immured women—but, eventually, the clamour splintered into distinct voices, both old and young. *The feather of a week-old sparrow,* one of them said. *A winter chestnut, summer moon. This one is for protection from sweating fevers and pox. Here are love charms, a cure for insomnia.* There were directions for summoning spirits, for sending them back, as well as countless other things: for finding treasure; the health of a child; to keep a man hard in the night. *Avaunt, avaunt, avaunt. Take mandrake, yarrow, a lock of hair. Belladonna, coriander, chicory. The Devil is as old as the world, you know. Female demons came first. Hellebore for madness, thistle for love. Birds live four times longer than a man, a deer four times longer than a bird and a crow five times longer than a deer. In Spain, healers are born with a mark on their bodies in the shape of half a wheel.* The spells and charms and recipes were familiar somehow to Charlotte, as if she were being reminded of them rather than learning them for the first time. *Mandragore, the noonday demon, appears as a small, dark man without a beard. The moon governs the brain but the kidney is governed by Venus. Astaroth, In Subito, Eloim. The teeth of a hanged man have great power. The blood of a freshly executed person is the only cure for epileptics. Petrica, Agora, Valentia.*

And, beneath all these words, weighty as ballast, she detected the dull knock of her own heartbeat, itself like an ancient chant she had never before deciphered. *Your blood, your blood, your blood.*

LE BATELEUR

11

Charlotte was relieved to leave the cave at last, although it was unclear how long she had spent there, and Madame Rolland seemed unable to advise her. It had been some days and nights, at least. The late afternoon was warm, quite cloudless. Her injured shoulder made movement of her upper body awkward and painful. Madame Rolland followed, urging her on, muttering angrily upon encountering any tree roots, rocks or uneven ground that hampered their progress. She chattered as they walked, telling stories of her life in the forest, explaining the magic. How to make vinegar, a prayer for warding off foxes. The summer a noblewoman came to consult her for her warts. Starlings were not to be trusted. Circles and signs and incantations. There was an order to the world, she said, to the movement of the stars and the life of plants and animals—but one might, with the proper tools, alter its course.

"Our gift is to be able to interpret it," she wheezed. "The magic is imperfect, of course. It's like throwing a line into a river or stream—you can never be sure exactly what kind of fish you'll get until you see it on the bank. You can try, of course, and I've seen people use all sorts of special tricks to catch the fish they want, but it doesn't always work. Don't fret, woman. It will become clear. There is hope and trust. Command the elements and they can be yours."

Their progress was slow, but, eventually, they cleared the forest and arrived at a barren crossroad. Madame Rolland called out for her to stop. Charlotte was sweating, breathing heavily. The bandage on her hand was moist with blood. The sun was sinking slowly into the west and the pale dirt of each of the four roads faded into the distance, their surfaces rutted from the carts that had travelled this way. There was no wind in this part of the forest, only silence, like that of an abandoned world. Soon it would be night and Charlotte felt uneasy. She worried about wild animals, about mercenaries and ghosts.

Madame Rolland, now at her side, surveyed the site and nodded approvingly. She squatted, produced a tinderbox and, after several attempts, managed to light a lantern.

"Now," she said, "take your knife and draw a circle the way I told you. Come, woman. Quickly. While the time is right."

Charlotte pulled the knife Madame Rolland had given her from her dress pocket, crouched down and, ensuring she remained in its centre, she carefully scratched a wide circle around her in the gravel road. The sound of the blade across the pebbles was loud and even, like a little animal's spitty hiss. Then, prompted once more by Madame Rolland, she drew a triangle within the circle, dividing it into three more or less equal parts. This, the old woman had told her, was part of the sacred formula.

"Now. Write the letters *J*, *H* and *S* along the bottom length of the triangle. Make it precise. And draw a cross at the beginning and end of those letters. There. Yes. Like so. Good."

Charlotte hesitated. She felt sick with fear. Madame Rolland, perhaps sensing her anxiety, shuffled over to her.

"Remember what I have been telling you. Treat him as you would a disobedient cur. Firmly, and with authority. It is sometimes difficult, for men do not take kindly to a woman telling them what to do. They think they are something better than they are, always unwilling to know what they truly deserve. They are like dogs; you must never let them sense your fear.

And—most important of all—be very careful of any deals he might try to strike with you, for such creatures can never be trusted."

"And I can send him back whenever I wish?"

"Of course. He is yours, madame. You will summon him and you are able to banish him. Like any old servant." She clicked her fingers. "A single word said three times and he will be returned, as it is written in your book. Sending him on his way is easier than calling him up."

She paused again. The lantern on the ground had attracted a frantic maelstrom of insects that eddied in its light. Around they went. Closer, further away, now closer. Gone again. The night beyond the lantern's meagre glow was black and vast and filled with a multitude of unknown things. She thought of Nicolas, her poor son. *I would walk through fire.*

"Come, Madame Picot. It's time. Take up the book. Close your eyes. Say the words. We are between the dog and the wolf. When all great and wondrous things happen."

Dusk, the old woman meant; when the moon rose to replace the sun in the sky. Charlotte hesitated. She looked around, as if farewelling the world she had known. She held her book in one hand and the knife in her other. Finally, she closed her eyes and listened to the voices. They swirled in the air around her, close to her face, like smoke, like moths, they whispered to her and to her alone. And she repeated what they said.

"In the name of Adonay, Eloim, Ariel, Jehovah and Tagla. I beseech you to release a spirit from his domain to come and speak with me in a decent voice without undue noise or stench. To do as I command. *Venite, venite.* In the name of God and our Father. Come now, without delay. *Venite, venite. In subito. Ainsi soit-il.*"

A wind through the forest's many trees. Charlotte opened her eyes. She waited. Nothing. She was relieved, disappointed, exhilarated. Time passed. She turned to Madame Rolland.

"But there is no one coming."

"Don't move," the old woman hissed. "These things take time."

"How long?"

"As long as it takes. But you must wait inside the circle. It's your only protection. You cannot leave now. But I must go. Goodbye, Madame Picot. May God be with you."

"No, madame. Don't leave me here alone!"

But Madame Rolland had turned away. "Don't fret. You'll not be alone for long."

"Please. What if some other man comes to do me harm? Thieves? How will I know?"

"Oh, you'll know."

And with that the old woman shuffled away until she disappeared from sight, as if borne on the evening's warm tide.

Charlotte glanced around at the forest, up at the darkening sky, at the road stretching out until it dissolved from sight. She considered the circle in which she stood, and she felt even more afraid.

The night passed. The lantern's light grew faint and eventually it sputtered out. Such awful solitude. She prayed under her breath. "*Ave Maria, gratia plena, Dominus tecum. Benedicta tu in mulieribus . . .*"

Overhead the immense apparatus of God wheeled ceaselessly around the earth. She kneeled on the hard road and licked salty sweat from her lips. A nightingale sang out— tremulous, urgent, quite beautiful. Crickets, the insistent musical abrasion of their tiny legs. A petal tumbled from its stalk to the forest floor. She heard the scrabble of animals over fallen logs—foxes, perhaps, or martens—their paws on rotting wood, pausing to scratch behind an ear, blinking. The smell of soil filled her nostrils, decaying bugs, the stink of a dead hare several leagues away.

Then finally, towards dawn, she detected a human noise.

Petrified, exhilarated, she stayed her breathing and cocked her head to listen. Dear God, what had she done? There, footsteps on the road, a long way away but drawing closer, a man murmuring a children's rhyme to himself.

And, by this time almost familiar, her heart singing its own strange song. *Your blood, your blood, your blood.*

She stood and tucked her knife beneath her shawl.

12

Lesage strolled with a new-found jauntiness until the tavern and the cluster of cottages fell away behind him and he found himself on a dark and empty road. How strange and luxurious it felt to be in the fresh night air, all alone, inhaling deeply of the cool forest scents. He had heard of men who had been unable to bear a life so unconstrained after prison, who were content to be caught and sentenced again, but he himself felt no such anxiety. After all, who could not wish for this? His boots crunched on the gravel as he sang under his breath. *"Mes amis, que reste-t-il? À ce Dauphin si gentil? Orléans, Beaugency, Notre-Dame de Cléry . . . "*

While in prison his concerns had been so immediate. There was survival from one day to the next and, sometimes, from moment to moment. Aside from the physical rigour of rowing for endless days in the summer heat under virtually no shade, there were worries over food, the countless rats, money for bribes, avoiding the attentions of the many villains. The constant, shifting loyalties of convicts were a great, infernal contraption of pulleys and wheels and gears that would crush a man if he made the slightest misstep. Friends slaughtered friends over perceived slights or made enemies of those who might otherwise be sympathetic to them. He recalled a convict who took it into his mind that another prisoner, who until then had been his bosom friend, was conspiring to steal his food and wine—and brutally stabbed him while he slept. All this limited a fellow, made his world not only physically unnatural, but philosophically stunted as well. The brain cowered in the skull, as did the convict at his bench, and, despite one's best efforts, the outside world felt as distant as the upper reaches of heaven.

But now, as if in sympathy with his unexpected freedom, Lesage's thoughts roused themselves, stood up, stretched and looked around. Experimentally at first, and then with increasing confidence, they wandered far and wide. As he walked, Lesage assembled Paris in his mind. The green gurgling river with its flotsam and boats, men bathing in its shallows. The Pont Neuf, Rue Beauregard, its sly beggars. He wondered also what had become of his former accomplice, Abbé Mariette, about La Voisin and her idiotic husband Antoine.

Overhead the sky was growing pale; daybreak was, thankfully, not far away. Lesage heard a frightful high-pitched yelp from somewhere in the forest. He froze and held his breath to listen. Silence. He shuddered and stepped off the road. He flapped at a mosquito whining past his face. He had always hated forests. Dark, sinister places full of animals and vermin, boars and wolves. One never knew where one was, which direction was east or west. Trees covered in ivy, bracken, spiders. Ugh. He muttered a prayer under his breath and fondled the knife he'd taken from the boy in Marseille. "*Sic ergo vos orabitis Pater noster . . .* " The sound came again. He listened, then relaxed. A fox. It was merely a fox calling to its mate. Still. He was unnerved, he had to admit it, and he hesitated before setting off again.

Scarron, the tavern keeper, had warned him about travelling alone at night (bandits, bears), but Lesage was most eager to find this so-called Forest Queen. In addition, he felt curiously invulnerable. After all, he had survived five years in the galleys—five whole years!—and thought it improbable he would be murdered on a lonely road by mercenaries. His fortunes had changed. After so many years on the decks of the galleys, his hide was as tough as an old boot and he felt as reckless as an acrobat. The galleys. God, what hell. Men dying all around him from disease, murder, floggings, all manner of barbarism. But he was sure he had been rescued for a purpose. As with most things—the stars, the whims of men, the weave of cloth, the very elements of the world—there was surely a pattern of reasoning for his survival. If only he could decipher it. Then, and only then, might he be able to alter the course of his life to his best advantage.

He had, of course, studied these matters widely, and so much else besides (the cards, alchemy, the lines of the hand), but his knowledge was still somewhat shallow. He knew a little about many things; this was a painful truth to admit. Unfortunately, so much of the scholarship on these matters was completely fraudulent. Ancient books, false talismans, indecipherable marginalia. He had applied himself most diligently to his tarot cards in particular, but felt that—although close to doing so—he had never quite unlocked their great and mysterious secrets. This was most frustrating. He had no doubt that true magic existed in the world—he had seen it with his own eyes—but his own expertise was, sadly, more akin to sleight of hand. Still, his favourite trick was enough to impress the likes of the tavern keeper Pierre Scarron, who was a drunken old goat, certainly, but not a complete fool. The note on which the tavern keeper had scrawled his murderous wish was still in Lesage's pocket. *Please make my wife die of natural causes without pain and also give me some money.* Pathetic, really.

People had not really changed in the years he had been in prison, he mused, and although the methods were ever shifting, the results people yearned for were inevitably similar the world over: men desired wealth and other women to fuck, while women sought wealth and men to marry; there was almost always someone wished dead or otherwise disposed of.

He could almost write the notes himself and save his customers the trouble. Their wishes were, of course, never for anything admirable; never a plea for happiness or peace, for the health of the King or an ailing neighbour. No. Hardly a surprise, he supposed, considering who they thought they were writing to; to God they revealed who they aspired to be, but to the Devil they revealed their true selves.

He was preoccupied with such thoughts when, after walking several leagues further, he glanced up and saw, in the distance, a startling apparition. There, in the middle of the road, probably a hundred feet away, stood a solitary figure. He stopped to squint. It was a woman by the look of it, standing all by herself, and although her features were smudged by distance and dim light, he sensed her staring at him. He glanced around. He had heard before of this kind of trap; of robbers using an injured person or pretty maid as bait, prompting a good Samaritan to stop, whereupon he would be robbed and beaten. He licked his lips and clutched his satchel to his chest. He felt the bulge of his knife beneath his doublet. He waited, looked around. After a few moments of uncertainty, he slowly approached but halted again when within hailing distance.

The woman observed his every move. He bade her good morning, for indeed it was almost morning, night having finally begun its retreat to the more heavily wooded parts of the forest. She looked startled, as if incredulous at the sound of his voice, and didn't respond.

Trying again, he raised a hand. "Good morning, madame."

This time the woman nodded, but said nothing. And so he advanced. The neckline of her dress was dark with what might have been blood. On the ground beside her was a sack tied with string. Perhaps she was some sort of imbecile, abandoned in the woods by her family? But her gaze, he saw as he drew closer, was keen and inquisitive—not at all like that of an idiot.

She wore a scarf on her head and a green dress which was muddy and ragged at its hem.

Lesage glanced around. There was only the forest, the roads, birds flitting through the air.

"Is there somebody else here?" he called out. "Are you injured, madame?"

The woman shook her head. Would she not say anything?

"Then what are you doing here all alone in this place?"

"I might ask the same of you, monsieur."

A fair response. He hesitated. Why not tell her? After all, she might be able to help him. Again he glanced around, but saw no sign of anyone else. "I'm looking for a woman who I'm told lives near here."

The woman flinched, as if he had said something wholly unexpected, before she recomposed herself. "Who is she? What does she look like, this woman?"

"I'm not sure. It changes, they say."

"It changes?"

"Yes. Sometimes she is one woman, then another. Sometimes old, sometimes younger. I don't know for certain."

"You are seeking the sorceress," she whispered.

It was his turn to be surprised. "Yes. But how did you know?" he asked cautiously.

"What is your business with her?"

Lesage examined the woman's pale features, her green eyes and her sharp little nose. Really quite a lovely peasant woman judging from her attire, although the skin of her face was as pocked as the moon and her lips were dry and cracked.

"I have a . . . proposition for her," he said eventually. "There is something she might assist me with. Do you know where she lives?"

The woman merely stared at him, expressionless, and he was horribly conscious of her gaze as it trickled like tepid water down the length of his body—from his face and his hat to his shoulders, then down to his breeches and dirty, broken shoes. He felt suddenly ashamed; there was nothing like an attractive woman to make a man feel grubby and inadequate. He tugged at his sleeves and straightened his posture as best he could.

Then the strangest thing. In one hand she held up a book, like a Bible or a book of hours, while, haltingly, with eyes closed, she spoke aloud several sentences in a strange tongue. Greek, perhaps. The meaning of the words meant nothing to Lesage and yet a chill coursed through his blood, for he knew intimately that one did not need to understand the words of a charm to be subject to the dark undertow of its power.

"What . . . what are you doing, madame?"

She didn't answer, but when she had finished speaking, she swung her gaze again to him. Her bottom lip, he saw, was trembling.

"You are afraid?" he said.

"I have never seen a . . . man like you before."

"I'm sure you have."

"Oh no. I can assure you. Or not to my knowledge." She winced as she drew breath. "And what is your name, monsieur? What shall I call you?"

He performed his bow, accompanied by the subtle flourish of his hand. "My name is Lesage. At your service, madame."

Despite her apparent nervousness (who knew; perhaps because of it?) her gaze was clear-eyed and bold. Was it—could it be possible?—that she was flirting with him? The thought stirred him. Women had been an endlessly popular topic of conversation among his fellow convicts on the galleys, of course, and the collective memories of those they had loved and admired glowed like coals in their bellies. It had been so long, and now—look at this!—here was a fine specimen, a little coquette, out all by herself in the forest. Perhaps he should drag her behind a tree and bend her to his will? Who could blame him for some harmless fun after all these years?

"And is it true what people say about you?" the woman asked. "About . . . men like you, I mean? That you can talk with the Devil?"

Lesage was taken aback. "You have heard of me?"

The woman appeared amused at this. She dropped her book into the pocket of her dress. "A woman like me hears many things."

"And what kind of woman would that be, madame?"

She paused to fiddle with her scarf and he saw that her left hand was bandaged. "I brought you to me," she went on, "and if you don't do as I command, then I will send you back."

"Oh? Really? Send me back, will you?"

The woman snapped her fingers in the cool dawn air. "Yes. Like that. A few words from me is all it takes."

Her assured manner and the bony click of her fingers disturbed him. He cleared his throat. "And what would you know . . . of that particular place, madame?"

She faltered, but only momentarily. "Only what I have heard of it. Enough to know it is a place to which anyone would rather not go. A stinking place of agony and suffering, where men are treated worse than beasts."

This much was true. Lesage nodded distractedly and wiped sweat from his throat. He felt faint. A glass of brandy would be lovely right now. He ran his fingertips across his bristly cheek to reassure himself that, indeed, he was all here and that, no, he was not dreaming. He swivelled on his heel and looked around—at the forest, at the roads stretching away into the distance. Sunlight was rising like a tide between the pine trees and insects were passing through its cloudy beams, lighting up then vanishing, lighting up again. He felt distinctly uneasy and wished that someone—a coach or travelling merchant—might appear to interrupt this strange encounter. But there was no one in sight.

"It was you who brought me here?" he said at last, turning back to the woman.

"Yes. Of course. I have been waiting for you."

It was only then that Lesage noticed she was standing inside a large circle scratched into the dirt of the road. There were other patterns as well, signs and words he couldn't decipher. A circle, symbols. A circle and a book.

"*You* are the sorceress?" he whispered, his voice faint with amazement. She was the woman he had been seeking? This was most strange and most fortuitous.

The woman watched him, as if waiting for him to perform a trick. "Yes, monsieur. It is most fortuitous."

"But what would you want with a . . . with a low man like me, madame?"

The woman set her jaw and gazed along the length of the road by which he had arrived. "I need the help of a man such as yourself to find my son. He was taken away by some men. You must help me find him and bring him back to me. Do you have a weapon of some sort?"

Lesage touched a hand to the knife he'd taken from the boy, which was hidden beneath his clothes. "Yes," he murmured at last, although he was not really paying attention to what he was saying. "I have a knife." He cast about for a stump or rock on which he might sit and rest for a moment. Nothing. "Well. Yes. Of course. Of course."

She looked at him with disappointment, as if he were something purchased and found to be faulty or rotten. Despite himself, Lesage felt insulted, and he attempted to draw himself up once more. "But tell me, madame: why did they take your son away?"

"There are men roaming the countryside who steal children and take them to Paris to sell. There is such a trade. But what is it? Why do you look at me like that?"

Lesage cowered as the odd woman reached out and grabbed his forearm, although he dared not strike out for fear of further antagonising her.

She shook him as one might a child. Her eyes were wide and wild. "Tell me. What is it you know? Have you seen my son?"

He glanced down at the hand that gripped him so tightly, tendons flexed against the freckled skin of her knuckles, nub of bone at her slender wrist. Finally, he nodded. "Yes, perhaps. Last night I saw some children at the back of a tavern. But the tavern keeper assured me they were orphans." Only then did he remember he had promised the tavern keeper he wouldn't tell anyone of the children, and silently he cursed himself.

"Where is this place?" the woman asked.

"It's called La Corne, several leagues back that way."

The woman stared at him for a while longer before releasing him. "Come. Quickly, monsieur. Take me there. You can carry my bag, for it is hard on my shoulder."

The day promised to be hot; already sweat was forming on Lesage's forehead and seeping like oil into his eyes. He was exhausted and felt quite unwell after the wine and carousing of the previous evening with Scarron. He blinked, blinked again. "But I should get to Paris," he said, and was horrified at the plaintive note of misery in his voice.

The mysterious woman laughed scornfully. "We have no time to waste."

"I'm not going back there, madame. Besides, I have been walking all through the night."

"Come, Monsieur Lesage. You sought me out, and now you have found me."

Unsure how else to respond, he spat on the ground.

The woman glared at him. A moment passed. "You must do as I tell you, monsieur. I called you out from where you were with a charm so that you might walk the earth like a man. Enjoy its pleasures, eat its foods."

"Then it was indeed magic that freed me?"

"Of course. What else? And, as I explained, you are bound to me until I release you. You are now my servant, monsieur."

Servant? Lesage attempted to smile and make light of the woman's madness, but there was something in her tone and in the set of her mouth that forestalled such mockery. The sow was talking to him as if he were no better than an animal or child. The entire encounter was most peculiar. "But what if I refuse?"

"Then I shall cast you back. And I wouldn't even think of harming me—for if I die, you will also be sent back immediately. You are here by my grace alone, monsieur."

Forest birds called out. Dawn was breaking. Lesage glanced around. "Cast me back?" he whispered.

"Yes."

He considered her warily for a moment longer before shaking his head in disgust. Taking orders from a woman! How shameful. He recalled a bear he had seen once in a sordid village in the Pyrenees, tethered to its scruffy handler by a ring through its snout. Was he no better than a wild beast? A familiar? Perhaps it was preferable to return to the galleys? No, no, no. That was ridiculous. Anything was better than that. And, besides, this was the very woman he sought. Was it not better to attempt to take advantage of the situation in order to further his own cause? But, as she brushed dirt from her dress, she appeared to him so . . . ordinary. Her clothes were dirty and patched, her boots as cracked as his own. A peasant woman.

"You are truly the Forest Queen?"

"I am."

"But I have told you where to find your son, madame. La Corne is not so far . . . "

She straightened her hair and adjusted her scarf. "It's not enough. They are dangerous men. They already attacked me once before." She indicated the bloodied neckline of her dress.

"What did they do to you?"

"It is an arrow wound. I am fortunate to be alive, I think."

"I see. And what is your name, madame? What shall I call you?"

"My name is Madame Picot."

"And would you really send me back?"

The pock-faced witch nodded. "Indeed I would, monsieur. Now come. There's no time to waste. Take my sack, please."

"What is in it, madame?"

"A few things. Bread and sausage, some wine." Then the woman, this Madame Picot, began to walk away. Frustrated and angry and unsure what else to do, Lesage wiped his forehead on his sleeve and picked up the sack. He caught up with her and they walked on in silence.

They encountered no one on the forest road and they barely spoke, which afforded Lesage ample time to ponder his strange new predicament from as many angles as possible. It was, he had to admit, one of his great skills: an ability to assess a situation and determine immediately where any advantages might lie. When to parry, when to thrust and when to do nothing at all. It was how he had survived—not only recently in the galleys and dungeons of Marseille, but in the filthy squares and alleyways of Paris, where he had lived on the balls of his feet. Confidence was a large part of it. Confidence and wit. Yes, yes. And he smiled at the thought of La Voisin shaking her head in wonderment as he recounted the latest trick he had perpetrated against some gullible duchess or duke. *Ah*, she'd say as she caressed his cheek with the back of her soft, pudgy hand. *You could fool the Devil himself.*

"And what else can you do?" Madame Picot asked after some time. "What other arts?"

He hesitated. She appeared to be guileless—but perhaps this itself was a ruse? He perceived, deep in his bones (this intuition another of his many talents), that it was wise to make himself valuable to her, and a sense of his own importance—

itself chained and cowering for so long in the dungeon of his heart—stirred in his breast. He cleared his throat.

"Well, I can, ah, combine ingredients—metals and the like—in favourable combinations. Some alchemy, if you will. If called upon I am most experienced in making good marriages, so if you should need any assistance in that area—unlikely for a woman as beautiful as yourself—then I would be delighted to oblige. I have some knowledge of the stars and their movements and, as such, I can read a person's destiny. Make a map of their life yet to come. Such a thing takes time, of course. Paper. Charts and so forth."

Madame Picot seemed impressed. "You can see the future? And are you good at this?"

He affected a grimace of embarrassed humility. "Sometimes. Yes. Many, many noble people used to visit me in Paris when I was working there."

"And did you predict your own fate, then?"

He could not suppress a sour laugh. The little bitch. This was the very taunt they had employed when he was arrested all those years ago with Abbé Mariette. *If you are so accomplished*, they mocked, *then why are you in the Conciergerie with the rest of us?*

"It is much harder to read one's own destiny, Madame Picot. Besides, it is a fickle business at the best of times. Not perfect. There are many things to consider and it is complicated, too much to even begin to explain to someone such as yourself. If I did not see my own fate clearly enough, it was not through lack of study or expertise but, rather, because of unexplained variations in the order of the universe. The cards, however. Now. They are much more accurate."

As he walked, Lesage rummaged through his satchel for his tarot cards, which were bundled in an old red scarf. He slowly unwound the scarf and displayed the deck facedown in the palm of his hand. Madame Picot glanced at them but, although clearly intrigued, turned away as if he were displaying a dead rat.

"And what exactly can these . . . cards do, monsieur? Are they themselves magic?"

"No. It's not really like that. It's all in the interpretation, if you understand what I mean." He gestured helplessly, as if attempting to conjure an explanation from the surrounding forest. "Like a song!" he offered with sudden and unexpected perception. "A song might well be pleasing and melodious, but if the singer himself is terrible, then it will not be so enjoyable."

"Then you are a good singer?"

Lesage leaned in and assumed a more intimate tone, as if revealing a mystery to her alone; women loved that kind of thing. "This is the tarot, madame. The future, the past. Everything you need to know is contained in this deck. These cards were given to me a long, long time ago in Toledo by a very old and wise Arabic scholar who entrusted me with the great learning needed to use them."

This was not strictly true, but a good story never did any harm. In fact, the cards were given to Lesage years ago by a slutty Parisian fish merchant called Alexandra in exchange for facilitating an introduction to a woman who might help her daughter with an inconvenient pregnancy. Stolen, most likely. The cards were more than beautiful. He had studied them in great detail over the years and come to love them more than anything he had ever possessed: the intricate batons; the red and gold cups; the King of Coins with his broad hat; the poor Hanged Man dangling upside down in his sling. How many days had he spent poring over the battered cards, marvelling at their colours and designs, unravelling their symbols and codes—those snakes, wolves, towers, queens, moons and lobsters? The permutations were fascinating and endless and they comforted him somehow.

"And where did you learn such things, monsieur?"

Lesage looked at her as he walked. He was wary. How far did her skills extend? Could she see directly into a man's heart? "Even when I was a child I was fascinated by the world beneath. The hidden world, if you like. The darkest part of the forest, the deepest bend in the river. I don't know why. I loved it when the peddlers and merchants passed through our village with their stories of distant places. Venice, London, Jerusalem. I became a wool trader and travelled to some of these places and met all sorts of people along the roads. Conjurers and magicians who claimed to have access to the secret parts of the world, to its hidden design. Like a . . . like the mechanism beneath everything, if you understand my meaning, madame. The bones beneath the skin. Then, in Paris, I met people who knew all sorts of magic and had all manner of powerful books and I was able to refine my skills. I hoped they might be able to help me with something in particular. Learning, that's what it is. Learning. It's science, madame, as much as a magic. One needs to learn the rules and systems. Such knowledge doesn't come from nowhere. Oh no. Study and diligence. How I pored over those great books written by Arab scholars. And I am still learning, even after all these years. My skills in some areas are still quite rudimentary, I'm afraid."

It felt oddly satisfying to tell the truth for a change—to be relieved of his characteristic bravado—but he was overcome by a blush of embarrassment, as if she had somehow hoodwinked him into revealing too much. How had she drawn such an admission from him? He gestured towards the stack of tarot cards still resting on the scarf in his hand.

"Perhaps I could do a reading for you now?"

She paused walking to stare at the cards for a long while, but eventually shook her head and continued on. Lesage was amazed and disappointed that anyone could resist their dark allure.

"Are you quite sure, madame? It might give us some indication of your son's whereabouts?"

This seemed to have the desired effect. Again she hesitated

for some time, apparently deep in thought, before waving for
him to take them from her sight. "No. Put them away, monsieur. I fear enough for my soul as it is."

Reluctantly, Lesage rewrapped the cards in the scarf and
slipped them back into his satchel before scurrying after her.
He heard a rattle of planks. A donkey cart approached them
from behind. The cart was being driven by an elderly man with
a long, straggly beard. Madame Picot hailed this ancient creature and asked if he might take them to the tavern called La
Corne, a request to which the man acquiesced with no dis-
cernible enthusiasm.

Madame Picot climbed aboard the low cart. "Come, Monsieur Lesage," she said.

He looked around helplessly. No one in sight, of course.
Only trees, rocks, sky. The terrible forest. The thought of running away into the woods crossed his mind, but this Madame
Picot—as if reading his thoughts—shook her head at him. A
sort of futile anger coursed through his bones. How could this
be? Had he merely exchanged one form of slavery for another?
It was worse than cruel. He felt like weeping as he eased himself onto the back of the cart. So, he thought with a chilly stab
of despair, this is the pattern of the world revealing itself.

13

M adame Rolland had been right; Charlotte knew as soon as she spied him on the road that he was the one she had summoned. He was awkward and slump-shouldered, ruddy of cheek and almost as ugly as she had imagined such a creature might be. He was like a man, but ill-made, as if he had once been pulled apart and reassembled in haste. He smelled powerfully of stale wine and old sweat, and his cheek twitched as if at the behest of a puppeteer's invisible thread. When he had materialised, she had felt very afraid—despite Madame Rolland's assurances about the consecrated safety of the circle she had scratched in the road—and had to resist a powerful urge to flee into the forest at his approach.

The old woman had been right, too, about his surly and querulous demeanour. The fellow—who called himself Lesage—was stubborn and uncooperative. He complained that he was too tired—too tired!—to walk back to the tavern where he had seen Nicolas, and she'd been forced to threaten him with return whence he came to make him do as she asked.

The two of them sat in the back of the ambling cart. Lesage sighed loudly at regular intervals and muttered intermittently to himself, rather like a perplexed hog grumbling in its stall. The wound in Charlotte's shoulder still troubled her greatly, especially if she twisted her torso, and at times it was painful merely to draw breath. She feared her skin would tear apart if she weren't careful and open her heart afresh to the elements.

From her sack, Charlotte withdrew a lump of bread and some sausage that Madame Rolland had supplied her with. She held it out to Lesage. "Do . . . men such as yourself eat, monsieur?"

He looked at her with something like disgust, although it was hard to tell, for it might have been the natural cast of his unlovely features. "Of course I do."

She tore off a portion of each and handed them to him.

"I'm still not sure what you expect me to do," he muttered in a low voice, his mouth stuffed with food.

Charlotte glanced at the old cart driver, who displayed no interest in their conversation and most likely could not even hear them above the clatter of his cart and clop of his donkey. "Take me to where my son is. Help me to free him."

"But the boy is chained up. I told you this. What do you think I can do for him?"

"Do you not have some special talents in that area? Some way to free him?"

The fellow wiped breadcrumbs from his greasy lips. "And are you not a sorceress, madame? Can *you* not do something?"

She hushed the rude fellow with a wave of her hand and looked away. After some time, the cart driver called to his donkey and the cart halted with a jerk. The driver turned around on his seat to face them, then pointed further along the road. In the distance she saw a squat building with a thatched roof. Smoke trickled from its chimney and a few chickens strutted about in the yard. She could smell the hot iron and cold sparks of a blacksmith's forge somewhere nearby. The old driver said he was leaving the road to get to his own farm, but that they might easily walk the rest of the way to the tavern, if it were all the same with them. She thanked him and lowered herself gingerly to the ground, indicating for Lesage to follow—which he did, though only after a small but pointed display of reluctance.

Charlotte brushed straw and dust from her dress and

watched the cart disappear into the forest along a narrow track. She turned to Lesage. "This is the place?"

With a throw of his chin, Lesage indicated the building she had seen. "There. He's at the back of that tavern."

She looked around. On one side were fields of barley and, further on, a dense copse of elm and oak trees, probably clustered along a river or creek. On the other side of the road the forest loomed. The breeze that drifted from between its trunks was cool and thick with the scent of night-damp foliage.

"So," Lesage said, squaring his shoulders and stretching as if they had come to an agreement after protracted negotiation, "now that you know where your son is, I think I'll wait here while you make your way. I assured the tavern keeper I wouldn't reveal anything about the children . . . "

Charlotte looked back at the tavern, thinking and worrying as Lesage made his various weak excuses. It was some time before she gathered the courage to speak. "But you have to do what I tell you or you're of no use to me, monsieur. Come. Now. We should hurry. I think perhaps we should go around the back, through this field."

The man scowled and licked his glistening lips, then peered about as if hoping to spy someone coming to rescue him before he nodded and muttered agreement.

The barley was waist high and insects sprang in front of them with tiny squeaks and twitters as they waded through its nodding, dew-heavy stalks. The tavern was one of three buildings located at the bend in the road. There also appeared to be a forge, as she had smelled, and another cottage set some distance away from the others. Thankfully, there appeared to be no one about as they neared the low-roofed barn at the rear of the tavern.

"There," Lesage whispered. "He's in there."

"Where is your weapon?"

Lesage produced a knife from beneath his clothes. It was

not long past dawn; the sun was rising in the east. Charlotte had a sudden sense of the largeness and strangeness of the world, and felt uncertain and alone. She thought of Saint-Gilles, of her cottage, of her stove.

She considered the rickety barn. Her poor son. She tucked a strand of loose hair beneath her scarf, picked up her sack of supplies, and they pressed on. Her mouth was dry and her heart beat hard. They emerged from the field of barley and crossed a low wooden fence into the rear yard of the tavern. The privy reeked. With her strange new companion at her side, Charlotte approached the barn. A goat tethered to a nearby tree gazed at them with its slotted eyes and, for a moment, she glimpsed herself and Lesage as the goat doubtless saw them— a woman with a sack in one hand, and an older fellow carrying a knife and trailing after her muttering and tugging at the sleeves of his ill-fitting coat. Like a pair of grubby thieves or murderers creeping through the watery morning light. And she saw, also, with a sickening jolt of recognition, the fear glittering in her own green eyes as she gripped one of the struts of the shelter and peered into the gloom.

A grey donkey gazed back at her from beneath its long, courtly lashes. Bundles of straw, pieces of equipment, a disordered stack of cane baskets. Nothing else.

She turned to Lesage. "But there's no one here. Nothing."

Lesage shuffled up alongside her. His cheek twitched and he scratched the bristles on his chin with stubby fingers. He shrugged and looked around as if confident that Nicolas had perhaps merely been misplaced nearby. "He was here last night. Several children, chained up right here."

"You're sure this was the place?"

"Of course, madame. Yes. Definitely."

Charlotte glanced at the rear of the tavern. One of the shutters hung awkwardly from its upstairs window, lending the place the appearance of a man cradling his broken shoulder. A rake and hoe leaned against a dirty white wall. A pile of broken bricks and a dungheap.

"Perhaps they are inside the tavern?" she ventured, although she thought it unlikely.

At that moment, as if summoned by her query, the tavern's back door opened and the shadow of a man appeared in the doorway. Fearing it was one of the men who had attacked her, Charlotte stepped back. The man regarded her and Lesage as he sauntered in their direction, pushing his undershirt into his breeches and weaving from side to side as he did so.

"Who is that?" she whispered.

Lesage jammed his knife into his belt. "That is the tavern keeper, Monsieur Scarron."

Indeed, Charlotte could smell wine and tobacco on the man's breath as he drew near. She relaxed, but only slightly.

This Scarron called out as he approached. "You again, monsieur? Lesage! You are back. I did not think to see you so soon. You were in such a great hurry to leave last night . . . "

The two men shook hands. It was clear to Charlotte that this tavern owner was quite drunk; even when standing still he wobbled about like a newborn foal and his face was so sweaty that his cheeks resembled a pair of soft, dewy plums.

"Where is my son?" she asked him.

Scarron stared at her, as if bewildered she should speak at all. "Pardon, madame?" Then, to Lesage: "What is she –?"

"My son, monsieur. The children. Monsieur Lesage told me there were children here last night. Chained up. But where are they now? Please."

Scarron turned to Lesage. "And who is this lovely lady?"

"This is . . . Madame Picot," Lesage said.

"Well, I'm charmed, Madame Picot." Scarron gestured so expansively towards his establishment that he almost toppled over. "Welcome to my tavern. It's always a pleasure to see a beautiful woman in—"

"Please, monsieur. My son. Where are the children?"

The fellow's expression darkened. "There are no children here, madame. I'm not sure what you—"

"My son was taken from me by some men several days ago." She gestured to Lesage. "This man said he saw them here last night, monsieur."

The tavern keeper glanced at Lesage. "That's impossible, madame."

"Please, monsieur. My son."

The fellow sighed and his features contorted with what might have been anguish or guilt. "Your son, madame?"

"Yes."

"But he told me they were orphans, madame. Honestly, I had no idea. I have children myself. I would never allow such goings-on at my establishment . . . "

"Where are they now?"

Monsieur Scarron waved in the direction of the forest. "They have gone, madame. To Paris. Monsieur Horst took them away at first light. Long way to go, he told me."

"Was my Nicolas among them, monsieur? Please. He is nine years old. He has black hair, he is slight. Nicolas Picot?"

The tavern keeper put a hand to his chin and furrowed his brow. "Yes, madame. I think there was such a child."

Charlotte reeled. She closed her eyes and covered her ears, as if she might make of her body a stoppered vessel to keep out the world. Perhaps this was all part of a terrible vision brought on by fever? It happened frequently. Oh yes. On the night before his death, Michel had imagined himself to be on a ship at sea, and she had heard also that the seamstress Agnes Popin had in her delirium believed herself to be floating about near the ceiling of her cottage. Am I still at home under heavy blankets, by the fire, being cared for by my family? Charlotte wondered. Would that it were so.

But when she opened her eyes and returned to herself, she

was still in the yard of a tavern a long way from home as men talked on around her with a conspiratorial air.

"So," the tavern keeper was saying, "did you find the woman you were seeking, monsieur?"

Lesage looked oddly at Charlotte, as if she might be expected to volunteer an answer herself. "It seems so," he said after an odd pause.

"Now," the tavern keeper said, "Lesage, tell me: how long will it take?"

Lesage seemed distinctly uneasy in the tavern keeper's company. "Pardon?" he murmured.

"My wife is hale and hearty this morning. How long does it take for the, you know, the *message* to make its way—"

Lesage stopped the fellow with a wave of his hand and glanced at Charlotte. "I think perhaps it's best not to discuss this right now, Monsieur Scarron."

The tavern keeper slapped a hand across his mouth. "Oh. Of course."

Charlotte began to walk away. "Come," she said to Lesage. "We must keep going."

She crossed the road and approached the path into the forest. Almost hidden in the long grass was a knee-high statue of the Virgin with her head bowed and both hands raised to the sky. The statue's nose was worn almost entirely away and around her neck were garlands of dried daisies and rosary beads. At her feet were a pile of burned-down candles, dead flowers and pieces of paper with messages scrawled on them in script so tiny they might have been the work of fairies. Charlotte had nothing to offer, but kneeled momentarily and crossed herself.

"*Ave Maria, gratia plena, Dominus tecum. Benedicta tu in mulieribus, et benedictus fructus ventris tui, Iesus. Sancta Maria, Mater Dei, ora pro nobis peccatoribus, nunc, et in hora mortis nostrae. Amen.*"

Then she caressed the woman's rough head, hefted her sack and plunged into the forest.

"Wait!"

She turned around. Lesage approached, breathing heavily. "Where are we going?"

"To Paris, of course."

He looked angry and determined as he wiped sweat from his forehead. "Madame, it is many days away. Can you not do some magic to get us there? Fly, if you are truly a sorceress?" He paused. "Who are you, really?"

Charlotte's heart turned in her chest. "I told you my name. Madame Picot. Charlotte Picot."

He shook his head. "I was searching for the Forest Queen. A true witch. And that fellow Scarron'—he gestured behind him towards the tavern—"didn't recognise you, although he knows exactly who she is." He peered at her sceptically. "You're just the boy's mother, aren't you? You're no one."

Charlotte displayed for him her left hand, with its grubby, bloody bandage covering the wound Madame Rolland had scored into her palm. In her other hand she held up the black book. "The old woman passed her powers along to me. *I* summoned you, and if you don't do as I tell you, then I shall cast you back into hell, where you will suffer torment and pain."

Never before had Charlotte threatened anyone in such a manner and her entire body was suffused with an unfamiliar but thrilling warmth. A draught of damp morning air blew in from the forest. She heard the murmurs of an animal. She sensed also, becoming heavier and heavier, the beating of her own heart. A wind sprang up and dry leaves rolled across the ground like a congregation fleeing before a storm.

Lesage spat on the ground and smirked. From him emanated the violent contempt the men of her country harboured in their hearts for women. "But how do I know you're not . . . "

"That I am not what?"

"Well, in the dungeons there was a fellow who thought he could fly like a bird if he flapped his arms. Another man thought he was Moses himself. It was the confinement, the heat, the terror. He went mad in that place. And they were not the only ones, oh, no . . . "

"The old woman warned me about you. Now come." Charlotte turned around and kept walking, but when he failed to follow, she faced him again. "Come, monsieur," she said, and was amazed that her voice betrayed none of the terror and fury she felt humming beneath her skin. Talking to a man in this fashion felt as if she were going against the natural order.

The hideous fellow shook his head. "You threaten to send me back, but I don't believe you can do any such thing. You're no witch. You're merely an ignorant peasant woman, and I don't have to do what you tell me."

From the book drifted the urgent voices of women. *Taking orders from one was to take orders from them all. Thistle, seventy-two princes, a demon might manufacture storms. The wolf is a more scrupulous beast than man. Stand fast and do not quail. Alazan, Mercury, Sansinena.*

Charlotte held the book out in front of her in one trembling hand and repeated the words she heard.

Lesage stood fast. Charlotte sensed a shift in the atmosphere, not only because they were on the outskirts of a sprawling forest. No, it was something else entirely. The drone of insects and the twittering of birds—so insistent a moment earlier—ceased. She detected the anxious squeak of mice nearby, a frantic scurrying in the undergrowth, followed by a pooling silence. Her heart beat harder, ever thicker, flooding her body. *Your blood, your blood, your blood.*

And then the forest around them darkened as if filling with a fine dust. Instinctively, Charlotte grasped at the air in front of her face. But it was not dust at all; the morning was, instead, closing down. The sun, having risen only a short time ago, seemed unable to accomplish what it had yesterday and the day before and every other day of her life.

Lesage groaned and looked around wildly. He cursed and hunched his shoulders as if trying to make himself smaller. Charlotte heard the thump of footfalls on the path behind her but had not time enough to turn around before a large wolf appeared from the gloom and loped past her, so close she felt its bodily warmth on her thigh. She gasped in fright and the animal stopped on the path between her and Lesage. It turned to gaze upon her with its serene and glittering eyes. Charlotte had seen wolves in the distance before and she was familiar with the aftermath of their nocturnal slaughtering of livestock, but never before had she been close enough to hear its breath or smell its rich and smoky pelt. Since she was a girl, she had been warned about these roaming killers but now, eye to eye with one, she felt not alarm but, instead, a curious sympathy. She felt certain the animal would not harm her.

The wolf revolved its great body to face Lesage, who cried out and raised both hands to his face in terror. Instead of attacking him, however, as she might have expected, the creature paced out a number of tight circles with its snout upraised before sliding into the undergrowth. She heard it moving away between the trees, its hoarse breathing, its paws bounding over logs, the sound of it growing fainter and fainter until the forest was silent again.

By now it was almost as dark as night, and when Lesage wailed again and fell to his knees—his greasy face barely visible in the gloom—he might have been speaking aloud her own thoughts. "My God. What have you done, woman? Make it stop!"

Charlotte closed her eyes, as if by creating her own darkness the greater one surrounding her might terrify her less. The book was hot in her hand. All was still and she feared it was the end of the world.

They stayed like that for some time—Charlotte standing with eyes closed and her book in one outstretched hand, Lesage on his knees in the dirt with his hands over his eyes— until, at last, from behind her eyelids she sensed the sky lightening and the forest around them awakening for the second time that morning.

When she opened her eyes, she saw Lesage staggering to his feet in the dappled sunlight. The strange man wiped his sleeve across his brow and gazed around. He raised his hands again in her direction, this time in supplication or surrender. "Very well, Madame Picot. That's enough. Please. I believe you. That's enough."

Charlotte nodded and licked her dry lips. She inspected her book for a moment before dropping it into the pocket of her dress. Eventually, they recovered themselves sufficiently to continue. Lesage smelled meaty, of sweat, and as they travelled deeper into the forest he muttered almost constantly to himself with one hand pressed to his face, apparently to stay the twitching of his cheek.

14

L esage had seen some bizarre things in his life, but as he trudged sullenly behind Madame Picot, he found it impossible to rid himself of the memory of that morning's events—the woman's great grey wolf emerging from the suddenly falling darkness, the way the creature glared at him, its rippling shoulders, the terrible silence after it had vanished. Even she had appeared stunned by what had occurred. He shuddered and shook his head.

At first glance she didn't look much—merely another thin peasant—but in her eyes there burned a strange certainty. Before his sentence on the galleys, he had spent a good portion of the past years with people who claimed to be able to perform supernatural feats: talk with the dead, conjure spirits, descry a man or woman's future in a glass ball or a bowl of water. Some of them truly had great powers, but many were no more than charlatans—fortune tellers, palm readers, abortionists, poisoners, greedy priests—preying on their rich and foolish clientele. But this Madame Picot? She was of a different order altogether. The woman was very powerful indeed, a realisation that filled him with wonderment and terror.

In the middle of the day Lesage and Madame Picot stopped by a creek in the shade, where they knelt on the bank and scooped cool water into their mouths. He was sweating heavily. It was hot and the thick forest air was oppressive. They rested beneath a tree on a cushion of moss, beside a cluster of mushrooms that resembled a miniature village perched in a bright green field. A black beetle stepped about daintily among the stalks, then up and over the milky caps of the mushrooms. A centipede ebbed through the stalks of grass. Was this, he wondered, how God viewed the world from his perch in the heavens; everything laid out, its myriad chaotic patterns so manifest? Instinctively he glanced up between the trees as if expecting to catch a glimpse of this God, as, at that moment, the beetle seemed to register Lesage's presence and waved its antennae in his direction. He lowered a hand towards the insect—who continued to wave feebly, as if brandishing tiny fists—and flicked it away. The crack of its shell against his fingernail. Gone. And then, for good measure, he plucked one of the mushrooms from its loamy soil (the sound and feel of it so like the tearing of a fairy's limb) and flung the plant—tiny roots and all—into the creek. He, too, could be capricious.

The woman produced more sausage and bread from her sack and offered him a portion. The bread was hard and the sausage tough, but it was tasty and he ate gratefully.

"And what was it you did for that tavern keeper?" Madame Picot asked after a while.

Not eager to answer, he stalled by reaching into his mouth to dislodge some gristle from between his teeth. Eventually, he turned to face her. "Pardon, madame?"

"The tavern keeper we met this morning—Monsieur Scarron. He mentioned something about a message. Did you perform an errand for him before we met on the road?"

"Ah. Yes, yes, yes. *That*. Well, I . . . " Lesage looked around and lowered his voice. "He wished me to deliver a message to . . . in order to help him with a problem he was having with his wife."

"But who was the message for?"

Normally, at this juncture in a conversation as delicate as this, Lesage might place one hand on a woman's forearm to further enhance the intimacy these exchanges required, and he prepared to do so before thinking better of it. Instead, he raised an admonitory forefinger, glanced around again, and adopted a conspiratorial expression—mouth pursed, eyes downcast, brief shake of his head—as if fearful to gossip about someone who could be in earshot. "I think you know who I mean, Madame Picot," he whispered.

She was clearly shocked. "So it's true? You can speak with the Devil himself?"

"Shhhh, madame."

Madame Picot crossed herself and muttered under her breath—a prayer presumably. "But what was the message?" she asked.

Another display of reluctance. "Monsieur Scarron is seeking a new wife. He's had enough of the woman he married and she is not—how shall I put this?—being very *wifely*."

Madame Picot tore off a chunk of bread and put it in her mouth as she considered this. "But a man cannot have two wives, monsieur. It's against the law."

"Indeed it is, Madame Picot." Then, seeing that the woman was still failing to comprehend what he was telling her: "He wished his first wife to have an accident of some sort . . . "

"My God, what a terrible business," she murmured after a shocked silence. "What a terrible man."

"It's not me," he protested. "I don't, you know, *hurt* anyone. That's not in my nature. I merely pass along the request. Besides, if the whore won't fulfil her wifely duties, then surely the poor man is entitled to find a woman who will?"

She glanced at him as if he were a vile creature, before looking away, and while her attention was on the creek, Lesage took the opportunity to inspect the woman, this witch to whom he owed his so-called freedom. Madame Picot had removed the scarf from her head. Strands of her dark and tangled hair were pasted with sweat across her forehead and had arranged themselves into hieroglyphs: a large, sloping *S* swirled over one temple, along with other, less determinate symbols—

a *T*, perhaps, and the outline of a child's surprised face high on one of her pale cheeks. The slope of her breast was visible beneath her clothes. He shifted his position and was reminded of the dagger jammed in his belt. A dull anger surged through him. Oh, how he longed to press it to her throat.

"Do women such as yourself have husbands, madame?" he asked.

She looked askance at him. "He died of fever a few days ago."

"A good man, was he?"

There was a long silence. "Yes' she said at last. "A good man. He was a horse trader. Most years he helped with the harvest. We were married for a long time."

"And are there other children?"

"Two daughters and a son. The girls died of fever and the boy didn't survive his infancy."

"Ah. No other family?"

"Why would a man such as yourself wish to know these things?"

"Curiosity, madame. Just being sociable."

She looked perplexed. "I have a brother somewhere—if he is still alive. That is all I have left."

"I see. And if we find this Monsieur Horst, what do you propose we do? Is he not armed?"

"That is why I have summoned you here, monsieur."

Lesage forced a laugh. "And you expect me to—what?— *fight* with these men?"

Madame Picot stared at him. "Of course. What else?"

"But I am no mercenary, madame. I was never a soldier. I think perhaps you have misjudged my abilities."

"Then shall I send you back where you came from?"

"No, no, no, no. That is not what I meant. Not at all. I shall, of course, be glad to assist you. But tell me: what will be my reward? If we find your son, will you release me from further . . . duties?"

Madame Picot shook her head, not only in response to this most reasonable of queries but also, it seemed, in sheer incredulity that he should ask such a thing.

"Well, if that's the case," he went on, "then why should I help you at all?"

The sorceress got to her feet, wincing as she did so. "It is the only reason you are here, monsieur. You have to assist me, as I have already told you."

"So if I help, you will send me back—and if I don't help you, you will also send me back?"

At this she appeared vexed. "I cannot leave you to wander the countryside at your leisure, monsieur."

Despite himself, Lesage laughed. "I fail to see what might be so wrong with that."

Madame Picot did not share his joke. He decided on a fresh approach and got to his feet also. "Madame! Wait, wait. I have something. I know of something you will be most interested in. It is the reason, in fact, I sought you in the first place."

"You did not seek me out, monsieur. I summoned you."

"Well, that might be a matter of perspective. In any event, I was wondering what you intend to do once you have—once *we* have—found your son safe and well?"

"There is an abbey taking people in to escape the plague. My son and I will go there."

"But how will you survive? With what money? You have no family, no man to support you. Are you able to manufacture money in some fashion with your skills?"

Madame Picot shook her head.

"Because I—and only I—know where there is a vast amount of money hidden in Paris. *Thousands* of livres. More money than you will ever see in your entire life. It could be *ours*. We can share it. Is it not true that you have the ability to cast aside spirits?"

Madame Picot laughed derisively. "Yes. As I have already

warned you. A spell to conjure spirits and one to cast them back."

"Indeed. Well. The money is locked away in a cellar beneath the city." He fumbled through his pockets until he located the purse containing the much-folded map with the instructions written on it. He drew it out. "I have a map here showing the exact location. No one else knows where it is. The treasure is guarded by several ferocious demons, but *you*, with your particular abilities . . . The instructions are right here. You see here, it says—"

"Who does the money belong to?"

"No one. It was buried by a wealthy aristocrat during the Fronde."

"And what is the Fronde?"

"A war. It was a war."

"Here?"

"Yes. In Paris, mainly. A battle for power between the King and the nobles."

"There was a war in Paris?"

"Oh yes. But it was some years ago. You don't know much about the world, do you?" Lesage said, unable to keep a note of wonder and satisfaction from his voice.

"So I have been told."

He tapped the map with a finger to draw her attention back to his proposal. "It requires a sorceress such as yourself to cast aside the demons guarding the treasure. You can mark a magic circle on the ground, as you did when we met. We could release this money and be very rich, madame."

The witch sighed as she leaned down and picked up her sack. Then she looked at him but said nothing. It was unnerving, this silence of hers. Why would she not answer him?

"Why do I not answer you?" she asked in a voice thick with scorn.

Lesage flinched. "Yes. Why not?"

"Because my son has been taken. I am tired. My heart is most painful."

Madame Picot did indeed look most unwell. She was probably a bony thing at the best of times but now, with hair stuck to her face with sweat and the neckline of her green dress dark with blood, she resembled a woman recently emerged from the earth. She had removed the bandage from her left hand and he saw that her palm was also filthy with encrusted blood. Despite himself, Lesage felt a twinge of pity for her. Most likely her son had already been sold to some farmer or sorcerer for God knew what hideous purpose and was at this moment being subjected to all sort of appalling treatment. The woman had no true idea of the wickedness of the world. Lucky, perhaps, for her.

"But do you not have some sort of magic with which you might free your son—aside from darkening the sun and summoning wolves from the forest, that is? A spell or charm of some sort? Or a curse, perhaps? Could you not . . . *kill* these fellows who took him?"

Madame Picot shook her head. "I don't know such things. My magic is only simple. Charms and healing, spells for protection."

"But can you not at least conjure some assistance for our journey to Paris? It is such a long way."

Madame Picot looked at him thoughtfully for what seemed a long time before she nodded, produced her black book and muttered something under her breath. She was making a spell, presumably, but nothing happened—even after she had returned it to her pocket.

"Well?" he said after a few moments. "Did you request something? What happens now?"

"These things can take time, monsieur."

"But your wolf didn't take long at all. That was very sudden."

Madame Picot hoisted her sack and began to walk away.

"Your fate does not come to you, monsieur. You must meet it halfway."

Lesage groaned. "What about the treasure? I think you should at least consider my offer . . . "

"No, monsieur," she said over her shoulder. "I have no need of such riches. Besides, I was warned not to strike bargains with creatures like you."

15

L esage trailed along the narrow forest tracks behind Madame Picot, fretting still about how they might get to Paris. It was, after all, much too far to walk—especially with the woman injured—and they had no money for transport. Had she made a proper spell? What kind of witch was she, really? Perhaps not a very accomplished one, after all. This thought consoled him slightly—perhaps he would be able to find someone in Paris to unwitch him? Surely La Voisin would know some sort of conjuration or could locate something in one of her many books? Then he remembered the wolf Madame Picot had summoned and his confidence ebbed.

He comforted himself with thoughts of Paris. *Paris.* The city trembled on the far horizon of his imagination. The smell of bread, its bustling women, the hoarse cries of boatmen drifting up from the muddy old Seine. Truly a city of dreams. Sometimes, while rowing in the galleys under the ferocious Mediterranean sun, he had glimpsed cities floating on the water, magical palaces with towers and churches, shimmering with life. He'd heard of convicts who, convinced of their own imminent deliverance, leaped into the water at the sight of such palaces and paddled into the distance. Always a mirage, of course; as they drew closer, the buildings would reveal themselves to be no more than a heat haze upon the water, some broken wood, three fishing vessels flinging out their nets. Paris, however, was no illusion, and he would arrive eventually and somehow escape the spell of this wretched woman.

"You're fortunate I am your guide," he called out to Madame Picot as he scurried after her. "Paris is a most dangerous city, oh yes. *Filthy*, my God. Full of rats and other vermin. Bodies lying dead in the streets. Horrible carrion birds everywhere, living off the refuse. You know, I've heard some people refer to it as the City of Crows. And a man I know told me that many of these crows are inhabited by the souls of dead witches. Yes."

Lesage paused to catch his breath. "And the Parigots themselves are a very coarse people," he continued. "It's where the worst in all of France come together. Violent, rough. Speaking all sorts of hideous tongues and dialects, several of which I speak myself, of course. Oh yes. You are lucky, madame, to have a man of the world such as myself at your disposal."

Alas, it was indeed true what he told her of the city; despite its pleasures, Paris *was* a dirty, stinking place of muddy streets and dim houses. One saw all types of people and heard all sorts of garbled languages in the street. There were men and women, it seemed, from every corner of the globe. Thanks to his years travelling as a wool merchant, however (and his time in the galleys with all manner of despicable foreigners), Lesage could understand and make himself understood in a wide variety of tongues. After all, one could not do business without at least a few words of the dialects they used in the more backward parts of the country—not to mention those merchants in other cities and ports. He understood most villagers in the Pyrenees quite well, for example, with their language like that of bears; a little of what they spoke in the Low Countries; Italian and Spanish, of course; plus an assortment of other tongues, some Latin. Versatility was what a man needed in this day and age. Versatility, oh yes. Besides, the woman might be a witch but it was clear she knew almost nothing of the wider world. What was the harm in some embellishment?

But Madame Picot stopped and raised a hand for him to be silent. Dear God, what now?

She scowled at him. *Scowled!* As if he were a child.

"Be quiet," she whispered. "Do you hear that?"

He strained, but heard nothing other than the endless bird-song of the forest and the rustle of leaves in the trees. They were probably leagues from anywhere.

Madame Picot revolved slowly on the path, features fixed, listening. Lesage was afraid she might again darken the sun or—he dreaded to think—something worse.

Then, without another word, she stepped off the track and disappeared into the undergrowth. He glanced around, then followed. Soon enough, he heard what Madame Picot had doubtless been referring to. A melody picked out on a flute—high-pitched and tremulous, like that of a lone forest angel. Soon they came to a glade in which a number of people were gathered in the dappled sunlight. A crow launched itself from a tree branch and disappeared into the arboreal murk, leaving one of its black feathers to flutter to the ground.

There was a wagon with a canopy of brightly coloured patchwork fabric affixed to its side. Another, larger tent was set up nearby. Smoke from a fire rose in a single grey thread. Clothes were spread out to dry on bushes. There was a hand-cart piled with household possessions. A donkey was tethered to a tree, a lute rested against the wheel of the wagon. It was, quite obviously, a family of troubadours.

Lesage had seen such performers, usually Italians, on numerous occasions at the fair at Saint-Germain or on the Pont Neuf—juggling, dancing, telling stories of courage and singing their bawdy songs. This one was a motley group indeed; several adults, plus a number of children scattered about. A girl with one frosted eye gazed at him and Madame Picot with her head aslant. A boy was tossing several balls up and down in the air and a tall, dark-haired woman cradled her baby in one arm as she bit into a red apple.

Madame Picot grasped his sleeve. "What is that creature?"

Lesage followed her gaze and noticed—could it really be? Yes!—a *monkey* on a chain squatting by the wagon. Good Lord.

A fellow around Lesage's age was the first of the adults to notice them hovering at the edge of the clearing, and he stood from his card game. The flute player halted his song. One by one, all the members of the group stopped what they were doing and stared at them. The forest fell silent.

"Good morning," the man called out eventually.

He was dark-skinned, narrow-shouldered and wore a beard trimmed in the Spanish style. Strands of black hair trailed from beneath his cloth cap and an uncertain smile twitched along his lips.

After an awkward pause—in which Lesage waited for the witch to speak, for it was she who had led them here—he introduced himself and Madame Picot to the troubadours.

The strangers declined to offer their names, merely nodded. A most suspicious gathering.

"You are entertainers?" Madame Picot asked.

"Yes," the bearded man answered.

"Are you performing for the birds in the trees?" she asked with a wave of her hand.

The man grinned, perhaps as surprised and impressed by her spirit as Lesage was. A gold ring glinted in his ear as he glanced around at his companions. "We would perform for them if they would pay us in anything other than song," he said.

"You are going to Paris, then?" Madame Picot asked.

"Yes, madame."

"We are searching for some men who have my son. Perhaps you have seen them?"

The fellow shrugged. "We see many people on our travels, Madame Picot. What do your friends look like?"

"These men are no friends of ours, monsieur. One of them is called Monsieur Horst. My boy is named Nicolas Picot."

Some of the troubadours exchanged glances; it was clear they had indeed seen this Monsieur Horst.

Madame Picot stepped forward. "You saw them, didn't you? When did you see them? Where?"

"They made camp not far from us here in the forest, but they left before dawn."

"Were they going to Paris?"

"I suppose so. They took the road to the north. They had several children in their covered cart. They were orphans, one of the men told me."

Madame Picot turned to Lesage. Her face, previously so wan, was flushed with colour as she smiled.

"Why do you seek them, madame?" asked the woman with the apple and the baby, who was by this time standing with one hand resting on the shoulder of her older daughter. She nibbled her apple, wiped the back of her wrist along her mouth and flung away the core. The baby emitted a little croak and was comforted by the woman.

Lesage cleared his throat. "They have stolen the boy," he said. "We think they intend to sell him in Paris."

The gaze of each of the troubadours swung across to him, like that of a many-headed creature. Even the monkey paused in its chittering to stare at him with its big brown eyes.

"These types of villain are well known hereabouts," Lesage went on. "You're lucky they didn't take any of your own beautiful children, madame. They would fetch a fair price. As servants, I mean. And other, worse things. The baby . . . There is quite a trade in this sort of thing, as I am sure you have heard. Sorceresses sometimes make use of them . . . "

The woman nodded. "I have indeed heard. And who might you be, monsieur?"

Lesage hesitated. There, in his chest, fluttered the joyful thrill of invention. He placed a hand on Madame Picot's shoulder, as the woman had done with her own daughter. "I am . . .

a friend of Madame Picot's family. An old friend of her father's. And her son's, of course. Nicolas, that is. The child's father died of fevers. The child's brothers and sisters are . . . all dead. Her brother was killed tragically in the wars. Nicolas is the only true family she has left and she will not survive very well without someone to help her. We have been seeking these terrible men for days so we might rescue the boy and alert the authorities to their trade. I can assist her for a time, but I must return to my own family in Normandy. But a woman, all alone in the world . . . "

When lying, Lesage knew, it was advisable to cleave as closely as possible to the truth. The tale he told was a convincing one and, fortunately, Madame Picot did not contradict him.

There was no need to elaborate; everyone knew that women who found themselves in the world without family were fated to become servants, whores or thieves—probably all three. If such women were fortunate, they might be taken on as a maid somewhere and not beaten or taken advantage of in a more despicable manner. Whatever happened, a miserable existence beckoned.

There was another lengthy silence as the troubadours ruminated on the paucity of Madame Picot's prospects. At last the tall woman spoke again.

"I am sorry to hear that, madame. I myself have lost children and a sister to smallpox," she said.

Lesage grimaced in an effort to convey his sympathies. "And . . . how far is Paris from here?"

It was the bearded man who answered. "Hopefully only two or three days, depending on the weather and the road. We are in a hurry. We are told they are threatening to close the city gates against plague and we need to arrive in time for the summer season."

This was pleasing information indeed. "May we travel there

with you? Monsieur Horst and his associate attacked Madame Picot when they took her son. She was badly wounded in the shoulder by an arrow and it's most painful for her to walk far. She could perhaps travel in your wagon? Show them, Madame Picot. Show them."

She drew back her shawl to reveal the blood-encrusted neckline of her dress. It was indeed a grim sight, and gasps and general grumbles of disapproval emanated from the gathering.

"I am sorry for your strife," said the man, "but we are not in the habit of taking on travellers. We have trouble enough feeding our own families."

"But we can help your performance," Madame Picot announced.

Chuckles from the troubadours. A few of them exchanged words in a dialect Lesage didn't recognise.

"Is that a fact?" one of them asked eventually, barely concealing his mirth. "Can you tell stories, madame? Sing or dance?"

"No, but my friend here is a great fortune teller. He is most accomplished at reading a person's future in his deck of tarot cards. He was taught by a great Arab scholar."

This bold declaration caught their attention and there followed a round of murmurs. The troubadours exchanged impressed glances. Lesage, however, was unsure of the wisdom of uttering such claims; travelling entertainers, after all, were themselves a deceitful and wily tribe and it was dangerous to attempt to fool them.

Madame Picot had by this time, however, grasped Lesage's hand in her own. He attempted to squirm free as discreetly as possible, but to no avail. Injured or not, the woman was strong. Stronger—and, perhaps, more cunning—than he first thought. The troubadours looked at him with renewed interest and there appeared no elegant way to escape the situation.

He loosened his collar with his free hand and smoothed his weathered coat. "Yes. My name is Lesage. At your service."

The man with the cap introduced himself as Vincent Leroux, and the woman as his wife. Then, the troubadours debated among themselves in their dialect.

"What are they saying?" Madame Picot whispered to him.

Lesage hadn't the slightest idea, but before he was compelled to confess this fact, the tall woman with the baby approached him with a faintly mocking smile.

"Is it true what Madame Picot says about your skill with these cards?" she asked.

"Of course, madame."

"Then come, Monsieur Nostradamus. I am most curious, for I have never seen this done before. Tell me what these cards say about my future."

Lesage sensed Madame Leroux appraising him sceptically as he settled himself beneath the coloured canopy on a stool facing her. As usual, a woman's scorn aroused in him a complicated amalgam of resentment, self-pity and reassurance; there was no doubt that his unlovely physiognomy—in these matters, at least—comforted his customers, for no one fully trusted a handsome man. Still, he wondered how a mere travelling entertainer had acquired such hauteur. If honest, he would be compelled to admit the woman intimidated him.

He glanced around to ensure they were sheltered from prying eyes, as he had requested. Over the years, he had found that a sense of intimacy—not always possible—generally aided the experience, especially with married or widowed women; they invariably delighted in someone giving them their full attention, even if the man doing so was as unattractive as he.

Lesage heard people talking outside, the clucking of tongues, as the troubadours dismantled their camp. He took his tarot cards from his satchel, but Madame Leroux spoke before he could begin, and her voice was laced with suspicion.

"Do you not sense, monsieur, that we have met before?"

He hesitated. Did he recognise her? Leroux, Leroux, Leroux. Did he? No, but who could tell? How many thousands of cards had he interpreted over the years, how many charts had he drawn up?

At last he shook his head. "No. I don't believe so, madame. I would certainly have remembered a woman as lovely as yourself."

Clearly unimpressed by this cheap flattery, she continued to inspect him, brow furrowed, before shrugging off the matter. "Come then, monsieur."

Lesage unwrapped the cards from the threadbare scarf. He muttered a few Latin words under his breath, in prayer or supplication, before taking up the deck and shuffling them with a show of great concentration. Then he held out the cards to her. "Now, Madame Leroux. I want you to place one hand on these and close your eyes."

She did as he asked, thus affording Lesage the opportunity to scrutinise her face and any other uncovered parts of her body, such as her weathered forearms and neck. There was much to be deduced about someone from the clothes they wore, the way they sat and the pendants or trophies they hung about themselves. Like many of her ilk, Madame Leroux wore battered silver rings on several of her brown fingers—some of them bearing astrological markings—but there were no remarkable scars or bruises on her body. She was thin-lipped and strong-jawed, a woman who had seen many places. Her black hair was greying around the temples. Her headscarf was green and blue, probably foreign, her dress made of brown fabric. Around her neck a rough wooden cross hung on its length of string. She was an attractive woman, no doubt, simultaneously sturdy and soft. Strong nose, dark lashes and brow. A luxurious, piquant warmth rose from her throat. The back of her hand covering the deck of cards had a few minor scars, but her nails were in quite good order. No missing fingers, no fever blemishes in evidence. In short, there was nothing from which he might hang a bold prognostication. He would do a simple spread, then. Five cards.

The baby, he noticed with a slight start, was staring at him with its watery black eyes, which resembled a pair of plums marinating in oil. The child looked sweaty, unwell. A fly landed on its cheek and walked around in erratic circles before buzzing away again. The child didn't even appear to notice, let alone object. Most unsettling.

"You may open your eyes now, Madame Leroux. Thank you."

On his scarf Lesage laid out five cards in a loose cross, making cryptic noises of surprise and deliberation as he did so. Madame Leroux watched him attentively.

With fingers interlaced beneath his chin, Lesage stared for a long time at the cards. Three of Batons, the Chariot, Knight of Cups, Page of Coins and, lastly, the Star. He nodded thoughtfully and waggled his head from side to side as if in mute discussion with himself. What he had understood instinctively upon encountering this magical world all those years ago was that people were really paying for the performance of magic as much as for the magic itself. It was like seeing a theatre show of Molière's. A black mass, some mumbled words in Latin, the *tap-tap* on the bedhead with a wand made of hazel. Smoke and mirrors. Why, his own particular monkey trick—which had been so successful for him, and of which he was inordinately proud—involved little more than a ball of wax, some saltpetre and a fireplace. Poof! Your message has been delivered to the Devil. They paid for warnings, yes, but also—and perhaps more importantly—for reassurance, for hope and some version of faith. On one hand they desired mystery, but on the other hand they wished it explained.

"Well?" Madame Leroux urged with some impatience. "What does it all mean?"

"Yes, madame. Here we have the past in these two cards, so

things which may have happened to you already. The things that perhaps influence your future, of course. Three of Batons. A lot of responsibility, a heavy load. It indicates that you are a most caring woman. This, in symmetry with the Chariot—do you notice the beautiful, yellow-haired lady borne by the two white horses?—indicates devotion and fertility, both of which are most important in a woman, of course. It suggests to me that you are also most devout. Important also in these godless times, what with the heretics of the reformed church everywhere. Don't touch the cards, please. Thank you, Madame Leroux. Only I may handle the cards while a reading is in progress. But it really is an excellent spread. Here, the Knight of Cups, also on horseback. But I *can* see some sadness in your life, something damaged right *here*—do you notice the cracked vessel? A broken heart when you were a young woman, perhaps? Was there another man who might have gone away? And has there been pox somewhere in the immediate family?"

"My sister. And two children. As I told you."

"Ah yes, of course. How sad."

"Common, too."

He ignored the scorn in her voice; best, perhaps, to concentrate on her future. "Yes. It is the times we are in, I am afraid. But here, this is more pleasing. There seems to be no suggestion of shameful death for you, madame. No indication of melancholy, I am happy to say . . . Your health is robust, Madame Leroux. That is clear. There is some wealth, but not a great deal. The times will sometimes be hard for you. But wait. Oh . . . "

Madame Leroux fixed him with her blue eyes. "Yes? What is it?"

Lesage nodded, as if an idea were being communicated to him from a voice audible to him alone. "I see more death in your family."

Surprisingly, the woman laughed. "You will need to do better than that, Monsieur Lesage. Predicting death in these days is a simple matter. We are all fated to die, are we not? And most of us before our allotted time. What can you see that I myself could never foretell?"

"Well, I—"

"Who will die, and of what?"

"I am reluctant to predict with precision, madame."

"You should try to if you wish to travel with us. A peasant audience can be a dangerous beast if you do not give them what they have paid for. I have seen them throw men into a pond if they suspect anyone of cheating them out of their money."

Lesage exhaled and attempted to smile. The woman was right, of course. People were unpredictable.

"Water," he said at last.

"Water? What of it?"

"You should take great care around water, madame. See this here? The woman of the Star card with her vessel beside the river?" He shrugged, as if to convey that he had seen this all along but had been reluctant to speak it for fear of upsetting her. "I see death by water."

"My own death?"

"Well, these are *your* cards, madame."

"Rivers? Ponds? Buckets?"

"River, I would say."

"At what age? Soon?"

He looked again at the cards. "Not for some time," he said after further thought. After all, it was wise not to be too explicit.

"And these cards of yours . . . ?"

"The tarot."

"This is the future, then?"

Lesage repeated for her the analogy he had given Monsieur Scarron—of God's plan resembling a river and how its natural course might be altered if one is forewarned. Madame Leroux gazed down at the cards for a long time, stroking her cheek with a beringed thumb, apparently ruminating on all he'd told her. Then, abruptly, she indicated the baby wedged in her arms. "Read my baby's cards. Tell me what the future holds for my boy, Jean."

Lesage was reluctant. "I'm not sure there is much to be read for such a baby."

"But surely there is everything? An entire life?"

"How old is he?"

"He was born not long after Easter."

Less than a season old. Lesage took up the cards and shuffled them. "Very well," he said. "Three cards will be enough for the baby, I think. *Ab aeterno . . .*" He touched the deck to the child's forehead, then put out three cards.

They were not good cards at all. Lesage recoiled. Never before had he seen such a combination. The House of God, the Devil, and the Nameless Arcanum with his bloodied scythe. They suggested bloodshed, chaos, violent death. The child would be lucky to survive the year. Despite this, Lesage reassured Madame Leroux and made one or two vague predictions—Jean could become a good blacksmith, he should be alert around strange women, the boy needed to be wary of the plague, for it would surely seek him out if she weren't careful.

When he had finished, Madame Leroux nodded and rose from her stool. She seemed impressed. "Thank you for the warnings, monsieur. I will keep my son as safe as I can from the disease. I myself will take great care around water, for it is true that I cannot swim."

Lesage got to his feet. "Do we have an arrangement, then, Madame Leroux? Will you take us to Paris?"

Madame Leroux looked perplexed. "Of course, monsieur. The woman's child is missing. We must assist her as best we can."

Lesage's warning over baby Jean's possible encounter with plague added more urgency to the troubadours' journey and they made swift progress. Despite his odd circumstances, Lesage was pleased; Paris was all he wanted to see and now they would get there soon enough.

Including Lesage and Madame Picot, there were nine of them in the troupe. Vincent and Agnes Leroux and their three children: Marguerite, Antoine and the baby boy, Jean. The other man was Guillaume Boucher, Agnes's young brother-in-law, a widower travelling with his only surviving son, Charles.

On account of her injury, Madame Picot was persuaded to ride in the donkey-drawn cart, along with Marguerite and Charles. She sat staring straight ahead, chin tilted upwards, as if expecting to detect the presence of her son or Monsieur Horst by smell, rather than any other sense. Whenever they encountered a merchant or trader on the road, she asked if they had seen some men with several children in a carriage. A Monsieur Horst? Nicolas Picot? Some shrugged, others nodded, a vague pointing finger indicating further along the road. *That way*, they said, or, *This morning we saw some people very much like that, it might have been them, who knows, we didn't ask who they were.* There were further rumours of plague, warnings of bandits, stories of the King's victory at a siege in the Low Countries.

The other members of the troupe took turns pushing the handcart, which was piled with cooking utensils, clothing and the various costumes and other items they needed for their performances. They stopped at a market town, where Madame Leroux told several lively stories to the children and adults gathered in the square by the church. She was a wonderful storyteller and regaled them with the tale of "The Ant and the Grasshopper," of "The Milkmaid and her Bucket." Next, Monsieur Leroux sang the famous *"Ballade des dames du temps jadis,"* accompanied by his daughter Marguerite on her recorder. Lesage knew the song, of course—who in the world had not heard it?—but was touched afresh by its lament for Heloise, and by its persistent refrain: *Mais où sont les neiges d'antan?* So beautiful that the audience was struck quiet.

Meanwhile, the hideous monkey, Roland, wearing a red hat on its head and a bell around its neck, cavorted and was a great asset to the show, frightening and delighting the crowd with its antics. The boys juggled and Lesage read the tarot cards for several villagers using a simple wooden box as a makeshift table. Madame Picot assisted him in this, moving through the crowds to ask if anyone wanted their futures told by the one and only Lesage, and then escorting them to where he sat. Those she brought to his table were simple folk, farmers and merchants, a sad-eyed former soldier with only one arm. And what did Lesage see in his cards; what did the Wise One foretell? Death, of course, the infidelity of woman or man, perhaps an accident with a plough. *Take great care around Italians, my dear; be wary of women with green eyes; never ride a grey horse; don't take in a three-legged dog.* The usual things.

Afterwards, Lesage watched Madame Picot as she moved among the crowd collecting coins and asking if anyone had seen her son or this Monsieur Horst. None had, or none who admitted to it. Then the troubadours tallied the money they had made, packed up all their things and set off.

16

They established camp that evening in a thinly wooded area beside a field, not far from the road. The site appeared well used. The ground was flat and a stream of clear water flowed nearby. Charlotte sat on a low stool and leaned against the wheel of the wagon. It was almost dark. She was weary after the day's travel and had been growing increasingly anxious as they approached Paris. She thought if she concentrated enough, she might detect something of Nicolas's whereabouts, so she sat by the wagon and slowed her breathing.

Nothing. Only the troubadours murmuring over their soup, forest sounds, the munching of the donkey nearby.

She heard footsteps, and the girl Marguerite appeared with a bundle of blue fabric clutched to her chest. She smiled uncertainly. One of her eyes was clouded over and she was unable to see from it very well. She tended to tilt her face away, as if looking to the side of things, and because of this flaw she couldn't take part in any of her family's complicated acrobatic feats. Charlotte liked the girl and was pleased to see her.

She handed Charlotte the fabric. It was a dress. "My mother told me to bring you this," she said. "It belonged to my uncle's wife before she died. She says you should not travel with us in such torn rags."

Charlotte thanked Marguerite for the rare kindness and accepted the dress. The girl looked to be about thirteen years old, the age her own daughter Aliénor would have been had she survived her fever. This, then, was how she might have looked and acted. Her height, her abrupt manner of movement, the way she leaned over to scratch her calf. It was a strange thought, almost unbearable. It rendered Charlotte speechless. She thought of Michel so recently in his grave, of his ears and mouth filling with dirt. What would he say of this journey of hers? He was a kind man, but given to unpredictable judgements. Tears filled Charlotte's eyes. Grief was surely the hardiest of emotions, a splinter forever lodged beneath the skin of one's heart.

She cleared her throat. "I had a daughter once. Two daughters. Aliénor and Béatrice. They died of scarlet fever in the same week. That was three summers ago."

The girl winced. "How old were they?"

"Béatrice was five, Aliénor was ten. Had Aliénor survived, I think she would be about as old as you are."

"I saw some children with scarlet fever last year."

Their swollen tongues, their burning skin, their tears.

"It is not a good death," Charlotte said after a pause, and it surprised her to hear herself say it so plainly.

The girl opened her mouth as if to speak, but she hesitated and instead fiddled with a loose thread on her pale orange dress. "I think I saw your boy," she said at last.

"What?"

"Your son. In a cart. I saw him."

Charlotte wiped her tears and sat up. "Nicolas? Where? And he was alive?"

"Yes, he was alive. They had beaten him, I think. I went across to them in the evening where they were camped nearby in the forest and looked into the wagon where the children were. One of the men caught me and he threatened me. He said . . . "

"What? He said what?"

"He said he would take me with them if I wasn't more careful. Said he'd cut my tongue out, that he'd steal me away from my family."

"When was this?"

"A few days ago. The night before you came to us."

They sat for a moment in silence.

Then the girl coughed. "I heard Monsieur Lesage telling my uncle there is, in Paris, a secret trade in children for use in black masses and such ceremonies. All sorts of people, even nobles and priests. They use them to request things of the Devil. He said your son is probably already dead."

Charlotte didn't answer. Just as speaking one's desires could make them true, a person could conjure what she feared simply by uttering the words. This, after all, was the essence of magic and prayer. But what kind of person would kill a child for their own ends? Her mouth was dry. She felt sick. Her last child. Her son. Nicolas.

Marguerite watched her, nibbling her lip. "Why do you not help us in our show, Madame Picot?"

"I am a village woman. My husband was a horse trader. I can make cheese, sew. I can bind a broken arm, help birth a child. But I have never learned the kind of tricks your family knows. I am no acrobat, in case you couldn't tell by looking at me."

The girl nodded, but seemed unconvinced. She glanced around before speaking. "But are you not a sorceress, madame?"

What had the girl seen? Charlotte flinched and considered carefully before responding. "No," she said. "Why would you say such a thing?"

"Because you have this," Marguerite said, and she produced something from behind her back.

Charlotte was appalled to see in the girl's hand the book Madame Rolland had given her. Her black book. Foolishly, she patted the pocket of her dress where she usually kept it, but it was empty. Panicked, she reached out towards Marguerite. "Give that back to me." The sudden movement caused pain to flare anew in Charlotte's chest and shoulder.

The girl stepped backwards, smirking, as the horrible monkey clambered from beneath the wagon and onto her shoulder, where it bared its yellow teeth and made its chattering sounds. Marguerite fed the creature a morsel of food directly into its brown, leather-lipped mouth.

Charlotte cowered on her stool, disgusted and afraid. The animal brought to mind a tiny man from a children's tale, hairy and loud and unpredictable; a stealer of babies.

"You are a thief," Charlotte hissed.

Marguerite scratched her animal's head. "I am no thief, Madame Picot. Roland stole your black book, not me."

"But is not the animal under your power?"

The girl shrugged and turned the book's pages with her fingertips, as if fearful they might be poisoned. "Yes, but sometimes he has his own mind. Where did you find a book such as this, madame?"

"That's not your affair."

"It is now."

"An old woman gave it to me," Charlotte said.

Marguerite turned the book over in her hands, inspecting it from all sides. "You should be careful, Madame Picot. They'll burn you alive if they find you with such a book."

"As they will burn you if they find you with it."

"Can you read all the strange words and symbols written here?"

"One does not need to read it in order to understand it. The book . . . speaks to me."

"Speaks to you?"

How strange it was to hear it said out loud. "Yes. It tells me what I need to know."

"Could you not do something to help find your son? Make a curse against those men who took him?"

Charlotte swooned with a sort of fury. "I would if I could," she whispered.

Marguerite closed the book with a snap. "What *can* you do, then? What sort of magic?"

Charlotte paused. Sometimes, when no one was looking, she opened the book and listened to its voices, inhaled them so deeply that she felt her blood becoming steeped in its ancient perfumes—of spices, desert winds and grass; of ink, blood, vellum; of smoke and the aftertaste of sparks.

"There are prayers for protection from bullets or fevers," she said. "But there are other things, too. I know the simpler things only. Spells to help people find things they have lost, the names of the herbs needed to rid a woman of her pregnancy. There are some love charms."

The girl nodded thoughtfully. "Love charms? How do they work?"

"You need a lock of the man's hair or a piece of his fingernail and some of the woman's monthly blood. A pigeon's heart, too. There are special orisons, some prayers to be said aloud."

Marguerite pondered this for a while, before asking: "Can you see into the future, like Monsieur Lesage?"

"No, and I am not sure I would wish to."

"And what are these pages? The ones that are locked?"

"Don't open them. Please. That's dark magic I do not wish to know. Harmful spells. Deals with the Devil, raising the dead. Curses and murder. They are spells that cannot be unknown once they are known."

Marguerite considered the book in her hand with trepidation, as if it might harm her.

"I used to be able to juggle better than any of my brothers," she said. "Perform all sorts of acrobatic tricks. Before my eye was damaged, I mean. I could pick the pocket of almost any man in a crowd. Now Roland does it for me. A Spaniard helped me to train him."

"What happened to your eye?"

"An accident. I fell from a great height onto my head. For three days I was asleep and when I woke up my eye was broken."

Charlotte indicated her book. "You cannot steal such a book, you know. It has to be a gift. None of the conjurations will work if the book is obtained by theft. Besides, you cannot read it. Give it back to me now, mademoiselle. It's of no use to you."

"Could you fix my eye with a spell?"

"Maybe. I can see if the book contains anything for such an ailment. There might be a lotion."

"We will be staying in Paris for the summer, near the fair at Saint-Germain."

Finally, Marguerite handed back the book. It was still warm from her sweaty palm.

"This book is many hundreds of years old. Many others have owned it before me. I have to protect it carefully or its magic will be lost."

A corner of the heavy canopy covering the wagon flapped in the breeze, like a slow handclap. The sound of a flute trickled in from elsewhere, accompanied by the voices of Lesage and the troubadours laughing and swapping stories. She had observed the odd fellow closely over the past two days—reading palms, chatting with strangers, flirting with women—and been amazed at how animated he'd become. How *alive*.

She came back to herself. "How far is Paris from here?"

The city occupied the dim space in her imagination reserved for things she had never seen but which terrified her nonetheless: oceans, ghosts, dragons.

"We will be there tomorrow night, I think."

"Is it truly an island?"

Marguerite laughed. "No, although there are some islands in its river. But it is very large. How will you find your son?"

Charlotte had no idea. Instead of answering the girl, she glanced around to ensure none of the men could see her, then eased off her muddy, bloodstained dress. Although it was healing, her shoulder injury was still inflamed, encrusted with dried blood and the remnants of the poultice Madame Rolland had applied. It pained her a great deal to lift her arm. She gasped and flinched as her linen shift—also bloodied and torn—slipped from her shoulder.

Marguerite was observing her intently. She extended a trembling finger towards her. "Is that where the arrow pierced you?"

Charlotte stopped what she was doing, leaving the dress puddled about her waist and thighs. The girl made her uneasy but, equally, she longed for her touch—as if it might, in some fashion, connect her with one of her own lost daughters. She resisted the urge to shy away as Marguerite brushed a fingertip lightly along the scab beneath her collarbone. She nodded.

The girl drew back her hand. "My mother told me the Maid was pierced by an arrow in her shoulder. Like you. The fellow who caught me at the wagon with the children said he had shot a woman with an arrow and that they had left her lying near the edge of a great forest. He said the wolves and foxes would eat her and that soon enough she would be nothing more than shit and bones scattered everywhere."

The girl appeared to take grim pleasure in this augury, and Charlotte recoiled at the disgusting thought.

"Are you an angel, madame?"

"The injury is not as bad as it appears," she said. "I am no angel, Marguerite. An old woman found me and nursed me back to health."

"Was that the woman who gave you the book? The witch?"

The word chilled Charlotte, as if it were alone a curse. *Witch.* She considered her hand, revolved it in the dim light. Fingers, veins, bones hidden beneath the skin. I am a woman of power, she thought, and I will find my son. She finished dressing.

"She was a kindly woman, that's all. A rare thing in these times, perhaps. If it weren't for her I would have died. Have you told anyone about this book? Your mother?"

"No."

"Please don't. The book can help me save Nicolas. He is the only child I have left. The only family. I love him dearly."

The girl hesitated, perhaps torn between her fear of Charlotte and relishing her own rare moment of authority.

"Great harm will come to you and your family if you breathe a word about it," Charlotte whispered.

Her warning had the desired effect. The girl looked afraid. "What sort of harm?"

"The worst you can imagine."

"You said you only knew simple things. Not dark magic."

"It is not me you need to fear. It is my companion, Lesage. He is wicked, and he is under my control as surely as that monkey is under yours." She paused. "But he is more dangerous than a mere thief. He seems a man, but he is really a demon and he will murder you if I command him to do so."

Marguerite looked around nervously. It was clear she longed to flee Charlotte's presence, but was equally compelled not to betray her fear. She was a resolute girl.

"He is certainly a strange man," she admitted, "with his face all twitching the way it does. And the symbols scratched into his arm."

"What symbols?"

Marguerite indicated her own forearm. "Have you not seen them? Yesterday, when he was bathing, he rolled up his sleeve and I saw something here on his arm. Devilish symbols, like nothing I had ever seen before. Was it true what he saw in my mother's future? That she would one day drown in a river? And he said that my brother Jean could die of the plague."

"How do you know what he told her?"

The girl blushed. "I was hiding nearby."

"Well. Our fate can be what we make it. Your mother needs to be careful, that's all. As do all of us." Charlotte heard a woman's voice calling out. "There. Do you hear that? She is looking for you now."

The girl backed away, then turned and ran.

17

That night, when everyone was asleep, Charlotte could bear it no longer. She slipped from beneath her thin blanket and sat up for a moment to orient herself in the gloom. She patted her pocket where she kept her black book and its weight against her hip reassured her. The fire over which they had cooked soup was now merely smouldering embers. Around her the dim shapes of travellers huddled under their blankets. Marguerite and Madame Leroux were in the cart with the baby, while the men slept on the ground wrapped in blankets. The donkey stood beside the wagon with its head bowed, dozing. Overhead, through the leaves, the night sky was black, dotted here and there with pinpricks of light. Stars. The moon was low, a few days past full. No one moved. A fox cried out, an animal crept through the undergrowth. The forest went about its business.

Charlotte picked her way over to where Lesage was asleep under his own bedding. She shook him until he woke, startled and wild-eyed, flailing clumsily at her.

"What? What's happening? What is it, woman?"

"Is it true what you told Monsieur Boucher?"

He looked around blearily. "What did I tell him?"

"That my son is probably dead? That there are sorcerers in Paris who might use him for their own purposes? Murder him? Tell me. What do they do with them?"

Lesage wiped a hand across his greasy face. His breath stank of wine. "How do you know what I told him?"

Charlotte shook him again. "Tell me," she hissed.

"I only told him that to frighten them. A story, that's all. I told him that to give our situation more *urgency*, you see. So these damned troubadours would move faster. No, no, no, Madame Picot. You misunderstand. They won't hurt him. They might . . . might make the children work as servants or maids, that's all. They hire them out as mourners at funerals and the like. Nothing more than that. I'm sure no harm will come to your boy. We'll find him soon enough."

"Are you telling me the truth?"

"Of course."

She hesitated. "I want you to read my cards for me."

"Now, madame? But it's so late . . . "

She pulled his blanket off him. "Yes. Immediately."

Finally, cursing to himself, Lesage got to his feet, scrabbled through his satchel and produced his deck of tarot cards. Squatting on the ground with his blanket draped like a cloak across his shoulders, he unwrapped the cards from their filthy scarf and held them out to her. They shone dully in the moonlight. Charlotte was fearful. She shivered in her shawl.

"Now," Lesage said, "close your eyes and place your hand on the deck for a moment. There. Like that. Thank you."

When, at his instruction, she opened her eyes again, he arranged five cards in the shape of a cross, mumbling several incantations or curses under his breath as he did so. He had removed his hat to sleep and Charlotte could see where his hair had grown on his scalp, but patchily, like a blighted crop. His own hands were rough. His fingers were calloused and the backs of his hands were as scarred and leathered as those of a field worker. With each card he laid down, he muttered with surprise and rumination. Charlotte drew breath, as if scorched. Indeed, the cards were as beautiful and terrifying as fire.

"Very interesting," he said at last, and tapped the cards one by one, as if she were unable to read their names for herself.

"Here is the Empress, the Magician, the Queen of Coins, the Hanged Man and, there, this last one is Judgement."

"Do they say if my son is still alive?"

"Not exactly. Alone, the cards have varied and inconclusive meanings, but together we might draw forth some predictions about your future." Here Lesage made a scooping gesture with his hands, as if gathering these disparate meanings together. "I think you have had a troubled life, madame, but perhaps no more so than any woman. I can tell you are a very caring woman. Most fertile, which is important, of course, and you have been a valuable wife. You are also devout, madame. That's excellent, and so important in these godless times. You should live to a good age, I think. No madness that I can see. A content enough childhood, I think?"

She shrugged and tucked a strand of hair behind her ear. Her own contentment was not something she'd had occasion to consider. But yes, she supposed so. More content than some, less so than others. She was moved to think it might be so visible on these cards. "But what of Nicolas?"

"Patience, madame. Let me see. I can also see death and sorrow. Children lost . . . to plague, I think?"

"Yes. Two of them to scarlet fever. Another of something else. We never knew what. He lasted only one year. Less."

"A terrible thing."

She nodded but was unable to speak. Yes, a terrible thing. A most terrible thing. The candles, their skin slackening as it fell away from the bones that supported it, the suffocating sense of inevitability when they first fell ill. Oh, oh, oh. This is how it is, how it had been, how it will always be. Prayers and a coin in their hands before they were rolled gently into their graves. *A grave.* No more than a hole with a dignified name. She wondered often about her son and her daughters all these years later and was glad, at least, they each had the company of their siblings.

"This card. The Empress is there in your past. She is a messenger from God, with her wings. Do you see the distaff in her left hand? This is usually women's business. And the shield with the eagle as its crest? This card is a woman because she is the only means by which one might be brought across from one world to another . . . "

Madame Rolland, the Empress. Her crown and robes, her face looking off to one side.

Lesage talked on. "How one might be born, as it were. She is the giver of life. She might summon an angel, for example—"

"Or a demon?"

Lesage laughed. "Or a demon, yes. The Empress offers great power and knowledge. And here'—he tapped the second card he had laid out—"is the Magician. In a physical sense it refers to the liver, trouble with bodily fluids and various humours. Do you have trouble with these things? No. It might also mean an element of trickery or sleight of hand. Someone to be wary of . . . "

Like you, she thought.

" . . . but in this position in the spread it might also mean things moving out of sight, hidden from plain view, like the great creatures of the sea. That vast region of things we don't understand. Have you ever attended the theatre, madame? No? Of course not. Well, sometimes they move items behind the curtain. There are unseen elements that play a role at a later moment in the show; things to appear on the stage much later in the performance, if you understand what I mean?"

Charlotte was unsure if she did understand. She leaned over to look at the card, which bore the illustration of a man in a wide-brimmed hat standing behind a table with coins and cups upon it—the sort of fellow one saw gulling people out of their money at markets and fairs. "And what is this third card? The woman holding the round object in her hand?"

"This card represents the near future. That is the Queen of

Coins, madame. The round shape in her hand is a coin. A coin. This is interesting. You know, this is one card I have rarely put out for anyone in all my years of doing this." Lesage licked his lips. He seemed greatly excited to see this particular card. "This indicates . . . great prosperity, madame. Money in your future. How far distant I could not say. But perhaps not very far."

Lesage paused and nodded, as if in dialogue with himself. He grunted ruminatively. "And this card here is the Hanged Man."

The card bore a colourful illustration of a man hanging upside down in a sling with his legs crossed at the knee. His breeches were blue, his shoes red and his hair a flaming yellow. She drew breath, for surely such a card was a bad omen, but Lesage sought to reassure her.

"It's true that this card *appears* rather forbidding, but it is, in fact, very good," he said. "It signifies change, that's all. Not necessarily death or anything of the sort. No. The Hanged Man. It's the twelfth card, as you can see. For the twelfth apostle. Some think it represents Judas, but remember the cards do not have definitive meanings. And remember, it was Judas who set the events in motion that led to our salvation. Think about that. Maybe he was actually the most loyal of all the disciples? See his face? Quite calm. Personally, I think the fact the fellow's legs are crossed in that way is most important. It's a crossing of sorts to another side. Perhaps the transformation is of a more personal nature. You might get leave to remarry, for instance. Or it's time to return to your village, perhaps. After all, you are not so old . . . "

Charlotte stared at the card. The man's face did not look so calm to her. She shook her head, weary of Lesage's tiresome riddles. "Say it plainly, monsieur. Please."

He ignored her. "But here. Do you see this card here? This represents your future. This last card is Judgement. And it's an interesting place for this to fall, madame."

She inspected the card. It showed God, or one of his angels, reaching out from red and yellow clouds with his trumpet. A naked, prayerful man and woman were standing below with their eyes cast to the heavens above. The illustration was compelling and Charlotte had to stop herself from reaching out to touch the card, as if by clasping it to her breast she might be relieved, magically, of the pain that had settled there. Oh, my son, she thought. My son, my son, my son. Tears welled in her eyes. Was it better to think of Nicolas constantly, or not at all? For years she had brooded on her dead daughters and her other son, fretted over where they might be, but had her thoughts assisted them or did they merely pain them—and her—even more? Could they hear her weeping all through the night? What could it be like to listen to the longings of those who have loved you, and whom you have loved, drifting across from another realm, one impossible to visit, one barely possible to even imagine? The curé had told her—as he told all the women who lost family to plague or accident—that her children would always be in her heart ("*There*," he would say, pressing a finger to his own breastbone so hard that his fingertip would redden), but this was not enough for Charlotte. She wanted her children in her arms, although she never said this aloud for fear of appearing ungrateful, or deficient in her faith.

"Please, monsieur," she said. "Will I see my son again? Does it tell you that? Please."

"I'm sure your son is still alive, madame."

"But do you see it in the cards?"

Lesage glanced at her—a little pityingly, perhaps—before looking down once more at his tarot cards. Finally, he tapped the last card, Judgement. "Yes. This one here is all about resurrection. Life eternal. God sacrificing his child to save us. You can see the Lord blowing his great horn and the dead rising from their graves to be borne aloft to heaven. All will be well, madame. This is what the card says to me. Do not worry." He patted her arm.

Charlotte wiped tears from her eyes. She felt overwhelmed and it was all she could do not to clasp Lesage's hand in her own to communicate her appreciation to him. "And peace? Will we find some peace?"

Lesage seemed perplexed by the question and gazed around at the dark forest beyond the clearing, as if the answer might be found among the trunks and vines growing there in such riotous profusion. He hesitated, and when at last he spoke his voice was thin and dry. "I think few people have complete peace in this life, madame."

"What does that mean?"

He regarded her as if he considered the answer to her question obvious. "It means that there is always a cost, madame."

The following day the countryside became flatter and greener. There were many more people on the roads, and in the fields loomed giant haystacks and windmills larger than any Charlotte had seen before. There were boats on canals and flocks of birds drifting like dirty thumbprints across the cloudless sky. Villages, taverns, carts, cottages, herds of cattle, great houses shining in the distance. Women humpbacked in the fields stood upright—one hand cupped across a sweaty brow—to watch them pass. Groups of labourers squatted beside the road playing piquet on upturned barrels, a procession of monks. There were elegant ladies in carriages, travellers, merchants, beggars, lepers hovering in the shade with their clappers and bowls for coins. And corpses, sometimes, of children and old women and men, at first glimpse a skinny grey foot poking from a bundle of rags, then something body-shaped, purple-lipped, reeking.

Then, late in the day, Paris appeared. At first merely a grey smudge on the otherwise green horizon, but gradually the city resolved into buildings and spires, drifts of brown smoke and the glint of glass in the afternoon light. Black spots drifted in the grey sky over the city. Crows, Charlotte realised as they drew closer, and she slipped a hand into her dress pocket to touch her book.

She soon heard the human throb of the city, smelled mud drying in the streets after a summer storm. The road became more congested. There were plenty of other carts, people on foot, shepherd boys beating their flocks to market, nobles and priests and pilgrims and thieves. They joined the procession— the saved and the damned—and passed through its gates.

REYNE·DEDENIERS

LE BATELEUR

18

To be imprisoned is to spend all of one's time longing for the life one can no longer experience. In the dungeons, convicts spoke of the countless things they missed from their lives as free men; memories that, like coals, needed to be banked diligently to ensure their continued warmth. Women were always a favoured topic, of course—those they had been with and those they would never again see. Whores, wives, food, children, the dark thrill of particular forests. The smell and flavour of a lemon found on the ground beneath a tree. A river near a man's farm where he could catch magnificent eels, a famous night of debauchery, a much-loved hound. But, for Lesage, it had always been Paris. Over the years he had worked hard at keeping the city alive in his mind; even in his worst moments he could recall almost every road, every building and bridge of the great metropolis. At night, deep in his dreams, he had strolled past the grand townhouses of the Place Royale, across the river to the fair at Saint-Germain, then back beneath the benevolent, lurid sculptures that adorned Notre-Dame before crossing the Pont Neuf with its gaggle of boats and barges floating on the river beneath like geese awaiting scraps of food.

The city had grown larger and busier in his absence. The previous evening, as soon as they entered through the Port Saint-Jacques, he noticed more signs of industry, many more houses, greater numbers of carts and barrels, larger piles of rubbish and ordure in the streets. When it came time to part ways with the troubadours, Monsieur Leroux had recommended the house of the widow Madame Simon in Rue Françoise, where Lesage was indeed able to find dingy rooms for Madame Picot and himself. It was clear that Madame Picot was terrified; as they hurried through the dimming city, she had gazed apprehensively upon the buildings and the crowds of people, at the runnels of muck in the streets. And this morning, when he suggested she remain indoors until he returned with intelligence about her son, she nodded with evident relief. She was a strange creature, as if she were uncertain, exactly, of how to use her own abilities.

He ruminated on the Queen of Coins he had turned up for her. It indicated the treasure, of that there was no doubt. But should he mention this to Catherine Monvoisin? Or wait? Something told him to wait. Prudence was generally the best course of action, he thought. Patience. Yes. He hurried across Rue Montorgueil with his chin tucked to his breastbone, unsure if he wished to be recognised or not. While imprisoned he had, of course, envisioned his return to Paris (men and women stopping him in the street to shake his hand, general outpouring of emotion), but now that he was here he thought it wise to keep a low profile. Besides, he felt ashamed of his threadbare clothes, of his wigless scalp. He certainly did not look his best.

Gravel crunched beneath his boots as he headed into the outskirts of the city. It was still sparsely inhabited, but there seemed to be more villas in Villeneuve than he recalled. Even here, he thought. The city has spread even to here. Although it was still early morning, there were quite a lot of people in the streets. Ladies, maids, merchants and beggars. Grey pigeons waddled here and there like little tutting nuns, their fat necks bobbing with disapproval. A cobbler was repairing shoes with his hammer. A scrawny peddler woman with a cane basket at her hip and two infants clawing at her skirts sang out her wares. *"Peau d'agneau, conil, peau de veau . . ."*

Three bearded gentlemen stood talking by the road. Smartly dressed, they were, with fine leather boots, luxurious-looking wigs, bright cloaks and ostrich feathers jammed into their hats. One of these men observed Lesage as he passed them, and the man's idle, wholly uninterested gaze again made him aware, suddenly, of his own appearance and attire. Once he had commanded a degree of notoriety in this part of the city. *There goes Adam du Coeuret*, people would whisper. *The magician who works with La Voisin. The great fortune teller.* But no longer. Thus far he had managed to keep at bay his concerns that the world had irreversibly moved on and left him sinking as if into a swamp, but now this fear returned with renewed vigour.

He paused glumly at a street corner and considered how terrible it was to have once had prestige, to have been someone whom ladies and gentlemen sought for advice. Not only had he been able to imagine the future, but he could—with La Voisin's assistance—even fashion it on occasion. Fate was certainly cruel.

A carriage rattled behind him. He adjusted his sleeves, then lifted his hat momentarily to arrange the little hair that had finally grown back upon his head. The hat, purchased in Marseille, was ill-fitting; it had been a hasty purchase. And the clothes they had given him at the port prison! Dirty, torn. He pondered the probable fate of the man whose clothes he now wore, however, and this cheered him up somewhat. In addition, the injury to his scalp was, at least, adequately covered. That was something. Yes, something.

But how strange it was to be back in Paris again after all these years—and at the street of his lover, no less. It was a moment he had fantasised about so fervently while imprisoned in the dungeons that, here at last, he feared it might reveal itself to be merely another cruel dream. A dream within a vision. He wondered about Catherine's husband, the feeble Antoine. Was he still living or had she managed at last to kill him off? Many years earlier—when their love and desire was fresher and more impatient—they had cursed the poor fellow and buried a sheep's heart in the garden, only for Lesage to lose his resolve and urge her to disinter the fetid thing when Antoine fell gravely ill. After all, to cuckold a man was one thing, to murder him quite another. Was anyone he knew still alive, for that matter? La Bosse? François Mariette? Abbé Guibourg? Lesage prayed that Catherine would still be living at Rue Beauregard, near the city's northern walls, for she was his best hope of escaping the clutches of Madame Picot.

The high, ivy-covered wall bordering Catherine's house was as he remembered. Lesage paused to catch his breath, then glanced around before opening the heavy door and entering the garden.

Catherine's consulting pavilion was at the rear of the property. Lesage crept along the side of the main house, lifted the latch on a low wooden gate and, once inside, peered around the corner of the villa. The past assailed him like a great hound loosed from its chain, and he pressed a hand to his throat as if to prevent it from mauling him. Those walls, the gravel path, the windows glinting in the morning sun.

He had met Catherine when he first came to Paris in the spring of '67, and had fallen under her spell almost immediately—as, it seemed, she had fallen under his. They were introduced by the Norman, Pierre Galet, whom Lesage knew from his youth. Ostensibly a shepherd, Galet had a profitable sideline supplying herbs, flowers and other useful and hard-to-obtain substances to numerous Parisian midwives, witches and apothecaries. Foxglove, powdered diamond, mandrake, unicorn horn, Spanish fly. With her curious mixture of piety and ruthlessness, Catherine Monvoisin was unlike any woman Lesage had ever met. Indeed, she often swore her powers were

God-given, and that she had been using them since she was a girl—in which case, how on earth could they be wrong?

There followed a profitable partnership. Lesage and La Voisin had become famous among the city's witches and fortune tellers and they rapidly established a loyal clientele and helped a great many people—for a suitable price, of course. People from all over the city consulted La Voisin: tanners, ladies, fishwives, sailors, soldiers, tallow chandlers, priests, seamstresses, butchers, laundresses, nobles. Each of them with their heart swollen with secrets and desires—which rarely differed from person to person. *Please, madame, my husband beats me. My daughter is pregnant. My wife is standing in the way of my inheritance, if you understand what I mean . . .* The appetite among aristocrats and commoners alike for a little illicit ritual was insatiable. Often it was no more than enhancement of a lady's breasts or a cosmetic paste to improve the complexion, but Lesage and La Voisin also arranged marriages, drew up astrological charts and conducted ceremonies to secure loyalty or desire. There were the occasional concoctions to dispatch family members, of course, and Catherine specialised in taking care of prospective unmarried mothers, while Abbé Mariette could perform the necessary priestly devotions that gave charms their necessary power. Strictly speaking it was illegal, but no one bothered them. Besides, it was well known that half the priests in the city were engaged in some mischief or other; those that weren't living with whores were drinking and brawling in taverns. La Voisin heard more about the goings-on in the city than almost any other person; if anyone knew or had heard of Nicolas's whereabouts, it would be her. There was even a good chance she was involved in his sale.

And then, suddenly, there she was, Catherine Monvoisin, looking more regal than ever, if that were possible. She had grown plump, slightly rounder in the face and body, although this in no way detracted from her beauty. Her fine mouth, her compassionate blue eyes, her pale throat. She stepped from the shadows on the far side of the garden but did not notice him, so absorbed was she in securing a red velvet robe at her throat with a gold clasp. The cloak was thick, most handsomely decorated with gold trim and lined with dark fur; sibylline, as if she had finally ascended the throne she had coveted for so long. She was, truly, the queen of the Parisian underworld. Lesage stepped back and covered his mouth to stifle a gasp of admiration and alarm.

Catherine was muttering to herself, doubtless any number of the curses or prayers usually ready on her tongue, but upon hearing his footfall, she glanced up angrily. She narrowed her eyes. "You there. Who are you? Do you have an appointment?"

Lesage stepped out of the shadows.

"What do you want?" Catherine bellowed. "I am not ready. I'll call my servant . . . "

"Catherine, it's me—Adam."

She looked again, this time more closely. Her eyes widened. She whimpered and pressed a hand to her bosom. "My God, Adam. Is that really you?"

He took another step. "It is."

She drew away, crossing herself and muttering more entreaties. "*Ave Maria . . . *" She did not look afraid, for La Voisin seldom displayed fear but, rather, merely scorn for those things she did not yet fully understand. The woman was momentarily speechless, however, and glanced around, as if for assistance. The unfastened cloak dropped to the ground.

"No, Catherine. Please. Don't cry out."

"Is it a miracle?"

"No."

"Have you come to torment me? But . . . I have confessed all my sins. Ask Abbé Davot. I have done nothing wrong."

Lesage smiled. Still the same Catherine, whose motto might be: *Always be bolder than the next woman.* "That I doubt," he said, then added the phrase which Catherine herself employed to console those who were wary of requesting some occult task of her: "But we are all sinners in our way. It is how God made us, is it not? Imperfect."

"Please, monsieur. What I do is ordained by God himself. You can ask anyone. Helping people is all I do. Helping women. Men, too. Some charms, cosmetics, a little enhancing of the bust or other features. Women sometimes need help, that's all. I baptise the babies if they show signs of life. They are buried in consecrated ground, if possible. I *save* their poor souls. As for the women, if they are whores, it is no fault of mine."

Lesage knew that some of this, at least, was untrue, but he smiled nonetheless and walked across the garden towards her. "Let me help you with your cloak."

She shrank away slightly, then stood her ground. "Is it really you, Adam?"

Lesage stopped and held out his hand. "Come, Catherine. I told you I would return. Do you remember when you visited me in Châtelet when I was arrested? And you promised to welcome me home, however long it took? Do you remember that?"

She laughed almost girlishly, obviously relieved. "I thought you were a spirit come to torment me. But you're not, are you?"

"Of course not. It's me, Catherine."

After a moment's hesitation, she reached out and grasped his hand. She released him quickly, however, nodding approvingly, but seemed unconvinced. "You are much changed, Adam."

Lesage began to weep. He was ashamed but unable to stop, as if some sorrowful tide had burst its banks. Finally, he managed to contain himself. "Oh, Catherine. I have spent years chained to a bench, rowing like a Turk. The things I have seen. Things no man should see. Disease, murder, violence, the vilest sodomy. No one could remain unchanged by such things. They made monsters of us."

"But is your sentence finished already, Adam? It has not been nine years."

He shook his head. "No, no."

"Did you escape the galleys, then?"

"Oh, it is far more bizarre than that."

"Then it must be bizarre indeed."

He nodded, gathering his thoughts, still overwhelmed.

"I saw you on the chain when you left Paris," she said.

Although it was five years ago, and much had happened in those intervening years, Lesage remembered that terrifying day only too well; the heavy chain at his waist and neck, the crowds along the route as the column of desperate thieves and killers shuffled along the muddy streets from the prison of Bicêtre in their convict attire of red cap, jacket and pants. It was not long after the feast day for the Nativity of Mary, but there was already a chill in the air. He had searched for her face in the crowd, looked for anyone he might recognise, but did not see a soul he knew. Certainly not Catherine. Boys jeered and threw fruit at the convicts. The Parisian summer had already been grim—river trade had been suspended due to an outbreak of plague and anyone with means had fled the city—but on leaving Paris that day, Lesage felt as if he were being herded into hell itself.

Catherine smiled and appeared to soften. "I promise I was there."

He did not quite believe her but, as ever, a mysterious and painful tenderness towards her swelled in his chest. It was a sensation no other woman—not even his poor, long-suffering wife Claudette—had ever aroused in him. It was love, he supposed, or its nearest relative.

"We walked all the way to Toulon chained together like that," he said when at last he could speak. He bent down to retrieve her heavy cloak and patted it free of dirt. "Please, Catherine. Let me help you with this."

She considered him, then turned around so that he might secure the clasp at her throat. "I need your help," he said when it was done.

Catherine spun around. "What have you done, Adam?"

"No. Nothing. I have done nothing." Suddenly exhausted, he lowered his voice and shook his head. "I can barely bring myself to say the words out loud."

"What is it, man? I hope you are not bringing trouble to my door."

"May I sit down?"

She hesitated. "Of course."

Lesage eased himself onto one of the chairs beneath the tree and rubbed a hand across his face. "I have been thoroughly *bewitched*. A young woman . . . "

Catherine narrowed her eyes, then held up one hand for him to pause in the telling of his tale. She turned aside. "Marie!" she yelled in the direction of the main section of the villa. "Get out here now."

There was a sound of running feet and, presently, a fretful-looking girl with a coal smudge on her chin peered out through the doorway. Lesage recognised Catherine's daughter, who was no longer the child she'd been when Lesage had last seen her, but was probably now thirteen or fourteen years old. Almost a grown woman, good enough to eat.

Marie started at seeing Lesage, but greeted him courteously, then cowered in the doorway. And no wonder—God alone knew what tasks the poor girl's mother had her do around the villa. Helping at her ghastly ceremonies and holding the hands of ladies while Catherine poked about inside them with her giant syringe, burning blood-heavy cloth and the curdled clots of vestigial babies. He shuddered at the thought of the oven in the nearby consulting pavilion and those who'd been devoured in its fiery mouth. No. Catherine Monvoisin's business was certainly not suitable for such a sensitive girl—or any girl, for that matter.

"Is there anyone here to see me?" Catherine asked Marie.

"One lady has arrived in her carriage, madame. She asked me—"

"Tell her she will have to come back later. And leave us alone for a little longer."

The girl hesitated, perhaps considering whose wrath it might be preferable to incur, but Catherine shot her an impatient glance, effectively deciding her daughter's mind for her. Marie curtsied and vanished. "Yes, madame."

A wise decision, Lesage thought; he suspected there were few ladies in the capital who could be as fearsome as Catherine Monvoisin. She indicated for him to continue.

Lesage herded his unruly thoughts. Where to begin? So many years of suffering since he left Paris in chains. Already it was hard to believe he had survived. Men falling dead by the road, the lashings and hunger, nights knee-deep in snow, murder and rape. Eventually, he told Catherine a little of his time in prison, of the battle with the Genoese galley, of his miraculous release from the dungeons and of meeting Madame Picot—the Forest Queen—on the road at dawn. He told her of the woman's black book and her knife, of the enormous wolf she had conjured from the forest, of travelling with the family of troubadours. Of the darkness she had invoked and of her apparent—what was the word?—unworldliness, despite her powers.

"She seems to know very little," he said, "but at the same time she knows so much. I think perhaps she has never even left her village before."

His voice trembled as he told his tale. Catherine did not

interrupt him, merely listened with hands clasped in her lap, nodding every so often, exclaiming with interest or surprise. When he finished, she said nothing for some time. This only increased his anxiety.

"Power does not always come with the experience to use it wisely," she said at last.

This wasn't a useful observation, but Lesage nodded nonetheless.

"And this woman freed you from the dungeons to help find her son?"

"Yes, although I am not sure what she expects me to accomplish."

"You have many skills, Adam."

"That is true, but they do not extend that far. I cannot see through walls. I am no mercenary. No soldier."

"Nor are you a saint."

"Indeed. But she seems to believe that I am some sort of, I don't know, *spirit*."

"Perhaps you are?"

"Catherine, please. That's not funny."

"But she will free you if you find her son?"

"No. That is the worst of it. She says not. She says I am not fit to be left to my own devices. Besides, who knows where the boy is? He might be anywhere."

"What's the name of the man who took the boy?"

"Horst. Monsieur Horst. Do you know anything of him?"

"Horst, you say? No."

"Are you sure?"

She scratched at her ear. "Yes."

"Who knows what these ruffians might do with him. One of them shot Madame Picot with an arrow and left her to die. The boy is probably already dead by now."

He said this hoping that Catherine would contradict him. But no.

"Yes," she muttered, "quite possibly."

"Then I will surely be sent back to the dungeons. It is even more imperative you help me. Please. Is there some way you might be able to free me from her? A charm or spell? I spent years in the galleys and not once did I mention your name to anyone—not even when they threatened to put me to the question." This was not quite true—he had never been threatened with torture—but Lesage felt the need to press his case. "I was loyal, Catherine. *Loyal.* Remember what we always pledged? *Corvus oculum corvi non eruit.*"

Catherine seemed annoyed to be reminded of this. From the cleft of her ample bosom she fished out the gold cross she wore on a chain around her neck and lodged it between her crooked front teeth. Thinking, thinking. Lesage waited, perched on the edge of his chair. He felt sick with worry.

"The woman has only one child?" Catherine asked.

"Only one still alive."

"Why not simply . . . get rid of her?"

He groaned. "I wish it were that simple. I must, in fact, look after her. If she dies, then I will be returned immediately to the galleys. I am like her . . . her *shadow.* Without her I cannot exist in this world."

"I see. Well, that is quite an impressive charm. Often with this kind of enchantment it is only the conjurer himself who might dispel it. She has a book, you say?"

"Yes."

"I suppose the first thing is to ensure this woman does not suspect her son is dead. As long as she believes there is hope for him, then you remain useful to her. I'll ask some people if they have heard of him. This is a terrible situation. And I'll look at my books today to see if there is some way to unwitch you."

"Sometimes she can hear what I am *thinking.*"

"Truly?"

"I told you. She has great powers, Catherine. But what if she doesn't believe me?"

Catherine dropped her cross beneath her blouse, as if into a grave. "Dear God, man. Did you lose all your sense in the galleys? You can convince her that her son is still alive. I suspect you will not have lost your gifts of persuasion. *Lie* to the bitch. I know you're capable of that. If she really is as provincial as you claim, then she'll believe you. Besides, a mother will wait a lifetime to be contradicted over the death of her child. Trust me. Some sorts of love make fools of us all."

Despite his despair, Lesage allowed himself a wry chuckle. "Except you, Catherine."

She blushed at this—a little pleased, a little irritated—and shifted in her chair. "Oh, no. Even me. Tell Madame Picot you have heard no word of this Horst fellow. Reassure her. Bide your time while we find a solution to your troubles."

Lesage was flooded with relief. Any previous misunderstandings between he and Catherine—and there had been several over the years—seemed to have been forgotten during their time apart. They spoke further, of different things. She told him that his former accomplice, Abbé Mariette, was back in Paris. This was no surprise; although Mariette had been arrested and put on trial in '68 with Lesage for their various impieties, the priest—whose cousin was a magistrate—had merely been banished from Paris and had, Catherine said, reappeared in the capital after only a few months.

"He is living now in Rue de la Tannerie with his latest whore. You should go and see him. I'm sure he would be happy to see you. Go over there this morning. Mariette will almost certainly be in. Priests like to fuck in the morning, you know, so they have plenty of time to confess before the day is out." At this witticism—doubtless well-used—she laughed uproariously. "And your wife? Does she know you have been freed?"

Freed, he thought bitterly. Hardly. "No. I am sure she thinks of me as long dead."

Of this Catherine approved. "Is there anything else, Adam? Your cheek is twitching. Why does it do that?"

He began to prepare an explanation but, really, there was none. He was sometimes aware of this tic, which had begun in the earliest days of his imprisonment, but was powerless to control it. He shook his head, embarrassed. "I don't know. Something happened. So much has happened to me in the past few years."

"You poor man. My poor Adam."

They sat in silence for a time.

"I have changed my name," he said at last.

"Oh yes? Why is that?"

"I felt it would reflect a new beginning, my new life as a free man. I am now . . . Lesage."

She smiled and leaned forward on her chair. "Very good. Very suitable, too. Come now. Give me your hand. Let me see what lies in store for you from now on, *Lesage*. Let's see about your future."

There was no point resisting. He placed his right hand in hers and for a moment she caressed his fingers. The touch of a woman. Dear God. Hot tears welled in his eyes again. Displays of tenderness were agony for a man who had not experienced such a thing in so many years. Lovely. Many of the things Parisians said about Catherine Monvoisin were indeed true. That she was ferocious; that she had dealings with agents of the Devil; that she drank far too much wine. Yes, but what of her feminine softness, her willingness to help people in need, her vast store of kindness and wisdom? Her nature was more varied than most people knew, and it was almost certain that her great powers had been granted to her by God himself. She was not always charming, not always sweet—who could claim to be?—but she meant well.

"You know, that bastard La Reynie is still making life hard for us," she said.

Lesage groaned at mention of the man's name. Nicolas de La Reynie, that inveterate quibbler, had been appointed to the new position of lieutenant general of the Parisian police shortly before Lesage was sentenced to the galleys. Although Lesage had never actually met the fellow, he had glimpsed him during his time at Châtelet prison. He was renowned as a fierce man, so scrupulous—always casting his imperious eye over crowds, seeking felons among them as a weaver sought frayed thread in his cloth.

"He has the ear of Louvois and the King," Catherine went on. "One can barely do a thing these days. You know, they even have lanterns on some street corners that are kept lit all through the night! Imagine that. Absurd. As if we cannot handle a little darkness. Lucky we are so far away up here. Did you hear that La Brinvilliers was almost arrested for murder, but she managed to escape to England? Scandalous. They got her lover's valet instead. Hamelin. Tortured and broke him on the wheel only a few months ago. Quite the gruesome performance, it was. The executioner certainly took his time with *that* one."

Catherine enjoyed executions and always attended them if she could. It was the spectacle, the sense that justice had been served, the opportunity to pray ostentatiously for a damned soul. She was well acquainted with the executioner—some said that they were lovers—and he passed along items stripped from the dead that were useful for her conjurations: hair, fingers, teeth.

"He confessed to everything, of course, poor fellow. Poison. La Brinvilliers had been providing this Hamelin fellow with arsenic to kill all sorts of people. Her father, her two brothers. She herself had been visiting patients at the Hôtel Dieu for years in order to perfect her potions. Killed *dozens* of

people before turning on her own family. It has been the talk
of the whole town."

"And did you . . . ?

She shook her head. "No, no, no, no. It was nothing to do
with me. Her lover cooked up the mixtures. A cavalry captain
called Sainte-Croix. He poisoned himself accidentally, the fool."

Catherine gripped Lesage's hand more firmly and lowered
her voice to a growl. "Let me ask you again, Adam: you have
not brought any trouble to my door?"

"Pardon? No. Of course not. Do you think I am a spy of
some sort? Catherine!"

Catherine didn't answer. Instead, she scrutinised him for a
moment longer before closing her eyes and arranging her features into her most genial expression. Summoning the muse,
she called this. Then she opened her eyes and inspected his
palm. "Your lines have grown prominent, Adam."

"Lesage."

"Oh yes—Lesage."

"Great suffering, that is easy to see. Your years on those
boats must have been difficult. Hardship. Yes. But here, *this* is
interesting. The line of wealth has grown much stronger. How
could that be?"

Lesage peered at his palm. She was right. His money line
had grown much clearer.

She pressed him in creamy tones. "Is there anything you're
not telling me? Did you become rich?"

Such probing disturbed Lesage. La Voisin had always been
able to see the truth behind what people said. This, after all,
was part of her gift. He thought of the treasure map folded in
the purse in his pocket. Already that morning he had sauntered
past the site in Rue Saint-Antoine where the money was hidden. He had, in fact, intended all along to share the fortune
with her, but his circumstances had changed in the past few
days and he thought it wiser to keep this particular secret for a

while longer. It was a skill, wasn't it? Knowing when to divulge certain things. Speak too soon and the advantage was often lost. For one thing, there was Madame Picot, who—despite her apparent naivety—seemed more powerful than Catherine. He sensed, also, that Madame Picot could be more easily swindled once she had helped him retrieve the money. Besides, he was as yet unsure if he wished Catherine Monvoisin to share in his good fortune. So he shook his head and hoped neither his manner nor his tone of voice would betray him, for if La Voisin was a formidable ally, she was a deadlier foe.

"No," he said as lightly as he could, "of course there is nothing I'm not telling you. One cannot make money in the galleys, Catherine."

Still with his hand in hers, she leaned closer until their foreheads almost touched and he was enveloped in her fragrant female humidity. A storm of memory sprang up; she had always generated her own weather. So many happy afternoons had he spent with Catherine at the wooden table here beneath the linden tree—drinking wine, flirting, spinning their vast and intricate web. Her ambition, Lesage often thought, was to gather a compromising scrap of information about every man and woman in the capital to use as leverage for her own success. The department of births, deaths and marriages, they called themselves, to roars of laughter.

"I have missed you," she murmured. "Paris has not been the same without you."

His throat was so thickened with desire he was unable to speak for a moment. He coughed. "And I have missed you, Catherine. But what of your husband? Is he . . . ?"

"Antoine is still alive," she said ruefully, "but knows enough to stay out of my way. I barely see the man. But I thought of you often. Said so many prayers for you, lit candles at Bonne Nouvelle. Yes, perhaps it was *my* magic that freed you?"

"I only wish it were so," he said. And regretted it instantly.

She cast aside his hand and fell back into her chair. "You think this woman of yours is more powerful than me, is that it? This *Madame Picot*? This fucking peasant?"

"No, no. It's not that, Catherine. I only meant that it would, of course, be preferable to be under *your* spell. I would—willingly, of course—fall under your power. I'm sorry. My God. I didn't mean anything by it. Please . . . "

He reached for her hand, which she surrendered—but only after a display of reluctance. Her mouth creased into a shy smile.

"I'm sorry, Adam—"

"It's Lesage now, remember."

"Oh, yes. Lesage. I'm sorry. But pay me no heed. I am a foolish woman, sometimes. Jealous. It's only because I have missed you so much. I'll find a way to release you from this woman." She smiled, this time coquettishly. "And where are you staying?"

"We have rooms in Rue Françoise, with Madame Simon. A widow."

"I see." She paused. "And this peasant? Has she beguiled you in other ways?"

"No. No. It's nothing like that. To be honest—and I know this sounds absurd—I am afraid of her."

Catherine brushed his cheek with her finger. "But you are afraid of me, and that has not stopped you from enjoying *my* company on many occasions."

Lesage opened his mouth to speak then hesitated, unsure if he could articulate a denial with adequate conviction. "Well," he said at last, "love makes fools of us all, Catherine. Is that not so?"

She smirked, appreciative of his wit, then rummaged in her robes to produce a purse that chinked when hefted in her palm. "Here. I told you your money line had grown prominent and, of course, I was right. Here's a start." She held out the bag of coins by its tied-off neck, but mockingly, as one might dangle a parcel of sweetmeats before an ungrateful beggar. A fresh smile formed on her lips. Or, rather, not quite a smile but, at the same time, so much more. "And meanwhile, I will seek a solution to your dilemma, Adam. I'm sure we can think of something. Come and see me again tomorrow. And why don't you bring Madame Picot? I would very much like to meet Paris's latest witch."

He paused. How best to phrase this? "I'm not sure, Catherine. At the moment, she knows no one in Paris. She doesn't know the city at all. She's afraid and I think that the fewer people she knows, the better it is for me—for us. Wouldn't you agree?" He cupped his hands, as if cradling a bird. "Then I can keep her contained, at least."

Catherine appeared dissatisfied with his answer but nodded nonetheless. "Very well. Off you go, then. I have clients waiting already. But please—buy some new clothes before you come back here. You look like a bear handler."

Lesage accepted the pouch. He loved money, of course—its very sound and smell—and yet this particular bag of coins did not make him feel as cheerful as it ordinarily would, for it seemed he was now indebted to not one witch, but two.

19

C harlotte's room contained a lumpy straw mattress in one corner, a low stool, a candle holder with a glob of old tallow and a chamber-pot. It was late afternoon and her odd companion, Lesage, had been out all day seeking word on Nicolas's whereabouts. A wedge of sunlight slunk across the dusty floor. Perched on the stool, she watched the portion of the street the window afforded her.

Her stomach groaned with hunger. Although she had watched bread and cheese sellers passing in the street below, she had been too afraid to leave her room. Carriages, people, beggars, cats. It was a peculiar feeling to be in such proximity to so many strangers, these people whose names or relations or professions were utterly mysterious to her. Who were their brothers or fathers or wives? How on earth might she situate them in her imagination? Hundreds of them going about their business, gossiping with acquaintances, speaking in their foreign languages, laughing and cursing. And all of them at home in this place. To her it was sheer chaos. She ran her thumb idly along a groove in the wooden window ledge. Back and forth, back and forth, back and forth, expecting—half hoping for— a splinter to lodge beneath her nail at any moment.

Household sounds drifted up from the courtyard down-stairs. Madame Simon with her voice like that of an old door— chastising tenants, arguing with merchants. People came and went. Foreigners. Mysterious tongues, murmurs, the clatter of tools. Charlotte smelled the neighbourhood's muddy, shitty drains and heard the thick slap of washerwomen beating wet clothes in the courtyard. Soot from the city's greasy fires stained the skin of her cheek, dust gathered in her hair, and through the floor she sensed vibrations from passing carriages. A brandy seller had set up his cup and flagon in the street. A man called out something to his animal or wife before his laughter shattered like glass into ever smaller pieces and trailed away. In the courtyard a chicken clucked. Somewhere a woman wept. It seemed there was always a woman weeping. Always a child crying, always a peddler singing out: *"Qui veut de l'eau? Qui veut de l'eau?"* *"Fromage d'Hollande . . ."*

Her husband Michel had been to Paris when he was young and had described the city to her many times. He was excited, as if he had encountered a wondrous beast, and his voice took on a note of wary admiration as he told her of its buildings and streets, of the people loitering in doorways, its water sellers and thieves. "They have as many people living in one street as we have in the entire village," he'd claimed. But for Charlotte, Paris resembled a dark and horrible labyrinth of blind alleys and grime. Lesage had been right; it was a frightening place indeed. *Where the worst in all of France come together.* She had not been able to sleep the previous night, and had instead lain awake wondering at the voices of strangers out in the darkness, listening for her son. Now she was exhausted.

Where in this terrible warren of a city could Nicolas be? It seemed hopeless. Unwillingly, Charlotte thought of her other children. She closed her eyes. She heard their whispers around her shoulders, smelled their little sour exhalations, almost sensed their trusting hands in her palm; that tender weight. Oh, how she had prayed for them, over and over, shuffling the words as if they might accidentally transform into a secret cure; the terrible sense, when no such cure materialised, that the failure was her own. The gaze of a child preparing to die—so fearful, so forlorn—was surely the cruellest sight imaginable. They would remain children forever, people said, as if that might offer some consolation. *We must have done something terrible to be visited by such things.* Perhaps Nicolas had been right?

She shook her head to free herself of the cobweb of memories, then stood and paced about the dim room. Idleness was no friend to sorrow.

There were voices on the landing, a soft knock at the door. It opened and a woman's smiling face peered in. "Ah. You are Madame Picot?" the stranger asked.

Charlotte stood. Instinctively her hand moved to the book in the pocket of her dress. "Yes. Who are you, madame? I do not know you, do I?"

The woman eased inside, shutting the door behind her. She was short and plump, kindly-looking. She wore a deep green dress with lace cuffs and a grey bonnet on her head. She looked around the room. "I understand you are looking for your son, Madame Picot?"

"Yes! Have you seen him? Do you know anything, madame?"

The woman shook her head sadly. She hesitated before crossing to where Charlotte stood by the window and taking her hands. "I am afraid not. But such a frightening thing to happen. I heard that someone took him? You poor woman. I am a mother myself, of course." She shook her head and squeezed Charlotte's hands with an intense maternal affection. She appeared to be on the verge of tears herself. "I can't even *imagine* such events. How old is your boy?"

"He is nine."

"*Nine?*" The woman clucked her tongue sympathetically and released Charlotte's hands to steer her over to the stool. "Here, Madame Picot. Sit, sit, sit. Please, madame. You must be terribly worried."

Grateful to have someone—even a stranger—take her well-being in hand, Charlotte sat on the stool. "I have someone helping me. He is out looking right now. Finding out what he can."

"A man is helping you?"

Charlotte didn't answer for a moment. How to describe Lesage? "Yes. A man of sorts," she said eventually. "But, madame, please tell me: how did you know about us? About Nicolas?"

The woman glanced out the window, then hoisted her dress and squatted beside Charlotte, so close that she could sense the warmth of the woman's shoulder. She smelled earthy, of spices, of lemons and washed linen. "Oh, there is not much that happens in Paris I do not know about, Madame Picot. The comings and goings. Who does what with whom. I'm like a . . . a mother to the city." She tapped Charlotte conspiratorially on the arm. "You know there's a baker in Rue du Lour—not so far from here, actually—Monsieur Balon. He has three mistresses. *Three!* His wife has no clue. I know many other things. Even secrets from those at court. Some people are amazing. Yes. Many sorts of people come to me with their problems. This city is overflowing with rogues. A very dangerous place."

And at that moment—as if summoned by this woman to underscore what she was saying—there came from the street outside the voices of men brawling. "*Scoundrel, you fucking thief, I'll kill you . . .*"

The voices died away. From her voluminous clothing, the woman drew forth a shiny cross attached to a chain around her neck. This she placed in her mouth. Wet clink of gold against teeth. "I cannot help everyone, but I might be able to help you. I shall pray for your son. Light some candles at my church. Yes. As if he were my own child. I will do this for you, madame. And who knows? Perhaps the Lord will listen to our entreaties?"

Charlotte was overcome with emotion. Warm tears ran

down her cheeks. "Thank you, madame," she said when at last she could speak.

The woman leaned in closer still. "But tell me, madame," she whispered. "I understand you have particular skills?"

Charlotte wiped her eyes. "What do you mean? How would you know such a thing about me?"

The woman chuckled. "As I told you: there is not much that happens in Paris without my knowing of it. Don't worry, Madame Picot. I have quite some expertise in that area myself. Some spells and things. Remedies of one sort and another. Simple charms." She dropped her voice. "But you must be very careful in Paris with that particular knowledge, madame. You know, they are hanging some people any day now. Justine Gallant and her lover Monsieur Olivier, who attempted to contact the Devil. A nasty business. If the authorities found out about your abilities, you might find yourself in grave trouble . . . "

Charlotte was unsure if this was intended as a warning, but before she could formulate a response, the stranger continued, "But I'm sure it won't come to that, will it?" Then, after a moment, she said, "Tell me: where did you learn your craft, Madame Picot?"

"It was passed along to me by an old woman in my country."

"Ah. An old woman? Charms? Healing? Women's special business?"

Charlotte nodded.

"Anything else? Darker magic?"

"No, madame. Nothing like that."

"I see. And do you have a particular book that helps with these things?"

"Yes, madame."

"Does the book have a name?"

"A name? No."

"Is the book with you now? Perhaps you might show it to me?"

The woman's manner was making Charlotte most uneasy. She was aware of the book in the pocket of her dress but made no move to draw it out. "The book is only useful if it has been freely given, madame. It cannot even be bought or sold—"

The woman removed the cross from her mouth and tucked a stray curl of hair beneath her bonnet. "Yes. But it surely wouldn't hurt to show it to me, would it? I'm most curious. I—" She stopped speaking and peered towards the door. "Who are you?"

Charlotte followed the woman's startled gaze to the doorway, where someone hovered. It was Marguerite, the troubadour girl. Charlotte was suffused with tenderness for her; she would not have considered herself lonely until the sight of a single familiar face. She stood, as did the stranger—who seemed disgruntled to have been interrupted.

"This girl's family helped bring us to Paris," Charlotte explained.

The woman appeared unimpressed. "I see. And what do you want, girl?"

Marguerite blinked, said nothing. There followed an odd silence, broken only when the stranger muttered some excuses and slipped from the room, forcing Marguerite against the doorframe to allow her past.

Charlotte strode to the passageway and called out after her. "Madame? Madame?" But the woman was gone.

"Who was that?" Marguerite asked.

"I don't know," Charlotte said, looking out to the dim landing. "She knew about what happened to Nicolas. She said she would pray for us . . . "

"You have been crying, madame?"

"Yes."

"There is no word of your son, then?"

"Lesage is searching for him. I would not know where to begin. This city frightens me."

Marguerite edged more fully into the room and Charlotte saw that in one hand she carried a small wooden cage in which a shape cooed and bobbled about. It was a dark-feathered pigeon with eyes like glittering black seeds. The girl held up the cage. "I want you to make me a charm, Madame Picot."

"What sort of charm?"

The girl told Charlotte that she had met a handsome fellow the previous summer when she was working in Paris with her family. It seemed that romantic words had been exchanged. "He said he loved me," the girl said, "and wanted to marry me. He does not even mind about my eye."

"Then you are most fortunate. What is his name?"

"His name is Francis Bernard. He is one of the King's musketeers. He is very witty."

Charlotte nodded. She sat again on the low stool while the girl squatted on the straw mattress with the birdcage beside her on the floor.

Marguerite fumbled through her pockets and held up a dark vial, similar to what an apothecary might use to store his unguents. In it was a dark liquid, faintly red against the afternoon light. "I have some of my blood," she said. "Woman's blood. The malady started for me recently. And here is a lock of hair he gave me last summer. These—and the pigeon—are what you said you need to make a love charm. That's what you told me. Do you remember, madame? Only a few days ago."

"But if this man said he loved you, why do you need a charm?"

"To make sure, madame. I do not wish him to find another woman to marry, do I?" Marguerite frowned, apparently puzzled by Charlotte's lack of enthusiasm. She withdrew a purse from her dress pocket. "And, of course, I can pay you, madame."

Charlotte stared at the purse. "It's getting late," she said finally. "I am hungry. Step outside and buy a candle and some bread for me. I'll need a scrap of paper, too."

By the time the girl returned, Charlotte had removed the pigeon from its cage, twisted its neck and sliced out its warm heart, which was about the size of a cherry stone. After worrying all day about Nicolas, she was grateful to have something practical to do. Her fingers were greasy with the bird's blood and grey feathers jostled on the floor at her feet. She wiped her hands on her dress and devoured some of the bread Marguerite had bought.

Finally, with the girl watching on anxiously, she picked up her book and held it unopened in her hand for a long time. The cover was rough and marked, its corners torn in places. She hefted it in her palm. The book was warm and solid and she was reassured by its weight. *Like any human heart.* Its voices were becoming more and more familiar.

"Can you write?" she asked the girl after a time.

"No, madame."

Charlotte wrote the man's name for her on the scrap of paper. *francis bernard.* Then she dripped some of Marguerite's blood from the vial over the pigeon's heart and wrapped this in the paper. This she bound as tightly as she could with the lock of Monsieur Bernard's hair. She hesitated, suddenly unsure if she should perform such magic, but reasoned that everyone did such things. At the gates of Saint-Gilles women cast dust gathered from the church floor to ward off dark spirits, they scrawled secret formulae on strips of paper that were sewn into their clothes. Her own mother had been in the habit of kissing a protective charm worn around her neck when she glimpsed lightning. There was no real harm in it.

"Now," Charlotte said. "Repeat after me: My Lady Saint Martha, worthy you are and saintly."

"My Lady Saint Martha, worthy you are and saintly."

"By My Lord Jesus Christ you were cherished and loved. By My Lady the Virgin Mary you were hosted and welcomed. Just as this is so, bring to me Francis Bernard, who is the person I desire. Calm, peaceful, bound of hand and foot and heart . . . "

As obedient as a lamb, the girl followed her example. The prayer was lengthy and by the time they finished, it was almost dark. With flint and tinder, Charlotte lit the candle. Her heart tolled heavily in her chest. *Your blood, your blood, your blood.*

"Wear this next to your heart for three days, then bury it somewhere this Monsieur Bernard will pass by."

Marguerite took the thumb-sized package. "And this will work?"

"It should. Now go. You might as well take this pigeon for your family. It will make a good pie."

Marguerite bundled the gutted pigeon in the folds of her dress. When she had finished, she looked up at Charlotte. "I was thinking, madame. When you find your son, you should order Lesage to strike down the men who took him. My mother says he is a very dangerous man."

"Your mother knows Lesage?"

"Yes. She says she met him here in Paris but couldn't recall who he was at first. He worked at the fair a lot, she says, and his name used to be Adam du Coeuret, but she had not seen him for some years."

"Adam du Coeuret?"

"Yes. He used to work with La Voisin."

"And who is that?"

The girl shook her head in wonderment. "I am surprised that someone like . . . yourself does not know her. Catherine Monvoisin is a terrible witch. She helps women who are with child. She murders the babies and burns them in her oven. Other things—worse things, if you can believe it. She has an Enchiridion, the blackest of all the black books, full of dark magic. How to raise the dead, turn people into dogs and crows. She sells inheritance powders for men to kill their wives and for wives to kill their husbands. My mother says La Voisin has met with the Devil himself. Lesage used to be her assistant."

Charlotte crossed herself, closed her eyes. "*Pater Noster, qui es in caelis, sanctificetur nomen tuum . . .*" Afterwards, her spirit felt becalmed. "Are there many such witches in Paris?" she asked.

The girl pushed her dirty hair back from her eyes. "Yes, madame. The city is full of such people. They are everywhere, even if you don't see them. They are doing the Devil's work for him here on earth, my father says. The one called Françoise Filastre has made a pact with the Devil himself. She's a fat, ugly crone. And they say La Bosse has killed dozens of people with curses and charms. They mostly live up in Villeneuve, on the outskirts of the city. You should find them and ask them if they know about your son. They deal in such matters. They might know something."

Charlotte considered what the girl had told her. Her blood trembled to think of all the people in this city crawling over each other like rats in a cellar. A man sang in the street below. "Go home now, girl," she said, "before it grows too late."

The girl seemed relieved to have been dismissed. Without another word, she stood, took her empty cage and slipped from the room into the dark passage.

20

The late afternoon was much too sunny, the merchants were barking too loudly and Rue Saint-Denis stank more pungently of rubbish and shit than Lesage recalled—and yet how wonderful it felt to be back in Paris, inhaling its unlovely urban stench. His head ached dully after the rowdy evening he had spent with François Mariette in a tavern somewhere near the river. It had been a long time since he had been able to indulge in such an exuberant manner and he was unaccustomed to such carousing. His head ached and his eyes seemed not to be working properly yet. Under his breath he sang his nursery rhyme: *"Les ennemis ont tout pris, ne lui laissant par mépris, Qu'Orléans, Beaugency . . . "*

His fears that the odd events of the past few days were merely a lovely—but, ultimately, cruel—dream were evaporating with every step. In his mind's eye he reconsidered everything as a jewel merchant might repeatedly examine a rare stone to ensure he had not, in his excitement, mistaken mere glass for a ruby: there was his visiting Catherine Monvoisin yesterday; travelling with the troubadours before that; encountering the witch Madame Picot on the road; and, where it all began, his unexpected release from the dungeons. Yes. Quite the adventure.

He glanced down at the new clothes he had purchased with the money Catherine had given him. A wonderful grey cloak, boots in the latest style, a new hat and a red wig. The wig was of horsehair only, unfortunately, but he felt it conferred on him a slight but alluring air of mystery—and a hint of eccentricity. Yes, here was the dirt under his feet, and in his ears echoed the cry of a fishmonger; here was the usual congregation of women and children clustered around the Fontaine des Innocents like flies on a fresh wound. Undoubtedly, it was all true and real.

His thoughts were interrupted by someone shouting. A bearded man was gesticulating on a street corner. He was shoeless, with ragged clothes and a large wooden cross strung around his neck. A monk, judging by his appearance, fulminating about the apocalypse and damnation and so on. Angels and trumpets and disease and the dead rising from their graves; the usual things. Lesage had heard this sort of talk on countless occasions—in the squares of Paris and Naples, in the galleys, from dozens of Christ-haunted men wandering along the roads—and never paid it much heed. A Spanish hermit named Raphael had lived in a cave near Caen, where Lesage grew up, and was notorious for accosting passers-by with his tales of hellfire and retribution from his perch upon a log in a forest clearing. The end of the world was always near, Lesage thought to himself, and such doomsayers had become even more common in the years after the London fire.

A small, sceptical crowd had assembled to watch this monk. A man cursed, some boys giggled, someone tossed a half-eaten apple at him. Lesage navigated gingerly around a cart that had halted in the road so that its driver, a man of beefy proportions, might remonstrate with a washerwoman walking in front of him.

Ah, Paris! Laughter, scorn and an appreciation of the lusty theatre of the street. Lesage inhaled the spirit of the place and ambled onwards with his head lowered, taking care not to muddy his new boots. He hailed a passing brandy seller and gulped a cupful of the scalding liquid to clear his head. Terrible, beautiful stuff.

He had been gone an entire night and half a day, but later,

when Lesage entered the tiny room at Madame Simon's, it seemed Madame Picot had barely moved since yesterday morning; her wan face and dark hair, the restless fingers of one hand worrying at her fraying shawl like a pale, fat-legged spider dancing upon her knee. In her other hand she clutched a book.

She leaped to her feet at his entrance. "Did you find my son?"

Lesage shook his head. "I'm sorry. Not yet, madame. Not yet, but I'm sure we will."

She seemed disappointed, naturally. "Where have you been?"

He wiped his sweaty brow to demonstrate his effort. "Here and there, madame. All over Paris. I have been asking some people I know. Searching for anyone who might be acquainted with Monsieur Horst or—"

"And buying new clothes?" She was regarding him with contempt.

"Ah. Yes. A few items."

"With what money?"

Dear God, would she not shut up? "Are you my wife, madame? No. I don't think so. I had a small amount of money. This is Paris. One cannot go about looking like a vagabond . . . "

"Who did you visit?"

"Oh, acquaintances. Some people. It's a large city. I'm not sure which of my old friends might even still be alive. I am working as hard as I can to locate your boy, Madame Picot."

She appeared unhappy with his answer but quizzed him no further, thankfully. Lesage's attention was drawn to several feathers ebbing about on the floor. "Why are these inside the room, madame? Did a bird fly in through the window?"

But the woman waved away his query. "I know Nicolas is still alive," she murmured after a short silence. "He is somewhere in this city."

"Oh, of *course*, madame."

"It was in the cards, wasn't it?"

"Yes, yes. You saw this for yourself. Most clearly. Alive as you or I." He indicated the book in her hand. "You have been praying, madame. A wise course of action, I think. It might settle your troubled imagination."

With a sour smile, she displayed her book. "This is no Bible, monsieur."

He saw it was, in fact, her magic book, and he recoiled.

"Your name was Adam du Coeuret before?"

He was too startled to speak. Dear God, what else did she know?

"I know that you were a great magician. And that you worked with a famous witch called La Voisin, who lives in Paris, in a place called Villeneuve."

Lesage pressed a hand to his cheek to stay its twitching. His thoughts. The woman knew his thoughts. He nodded.

"What sort of magic could you perform?" she asked.

"Oh, we helped people to achieve their desires. We told their fortunes, made predictions. Often a prayer for help with a marriage or birth. Catherine is most adept at making various concoctions for love and that sort of thing. To help women attract a rich husband. She could enhance their looks with creams. Cosmetics. Nothing serious . . . "

"And poison?"

"No," he said cautiously. "If the truth be told, most of what we did was harmless. Fooling people out of their money."

"Is it true that she murders unborn babies?"

He hesitated. "I have heard rumours of such acts, madame."

"But not seen them yourself?"

"That is women's business. I'm not privy to these things, naturally."

"Who would do such a thing?"

"People have their reasons. One can never truly know another person's heart."

"That is why you ended up where you did."

He nodded, embarrassed.

She looked him up and down. "Do you not tire of doing evil deeds?"

Aggrieved, Lesage stepped forward. Who did this fucking bitch think she was—Queen Marie-Thérèse? He was tempted to slap her face. Any other man would surely have done so—or worse—by now. "Is it not the case, Madame Picot," he hissed, "that certain unsavoury qualities of mine are precisely the reason you summoned me to your side? I think it was not for my handsome looks or my gentle manner. Nor my educated way with words. You know, I am the kind of man who might normally press you against the wall and slit your throat on a dark night. But isn't that what you desired of me? Isn't it, madame? Tell me: you didn't want a cowardly merchant, did you? A baker? A decent fellow? No. I thought not. You wanted a cutthroat, madame, and that is what you got." This was untrue, of course. He had never really physically assaulted anyone, much less carried out any threats of murder. Even that boy Armand on the docks in Marseille he left unharmed—apart from a bruised ankle, perhaps.

Madame Picot shrank back, but held his gaze. "Don't threaten me, monsieur. Take me to see this La Voisin. Perhaps she knows something about my son or Monsieur Horst?"

"No, no, no. I already visited her. Yesterday. Unfortunately, she has never heard of this Horst or of your son. But she will ask her colleagues."

"I see. Do you know of a woman called Françoise Filastre, who also lives in Paris?"

Lesage gestured vaguely. Again he was unnerved; it was impossible to determine what the woman did and didn't know. Lesage did indeed recall La Filastre, who was young, quite well-bred, lovely in appearance, married to a coachman. But he hesitated before answering. "Yes, madame. I might have heard of someone of that name, but—"

"Perhaps she would know something?"

"But how do you know of this person, madame? It seems you are more familiar with Paris than you told me."

"No, monsieur. I have never been here before in my life. But I am eager to find my son and get away from here." She crossed to the door. "Come. Take me to see this woman."

"Do you not think it would be much safer to stay indoors, madame? It's quite late. I am not certain where La Filastre lives and it might take some time to find out. I can go see her and I'll come back immediately. Yes, and—"

She flourished her black book with a trembling hand. "You have not been very useful so far, monsieur. Perhaps I should send you back to the Devil immediately? All it takes is one word, said three times, and you are banished once more."

Her threat was a hard, thin blade nosing about his ribs, and his anger drained from him immediately. Why could he not keep his mouth shut?

"Please don't send me back, madame. I beg you. These things take time. Paris is a huge place, as you can appreciate. Many thousands of people. I am doing my best. It won't take long to find your son. Please, madame. No."

He had not intended to plead in such a degrading manner and he was embarrassed and appalled to find himself on his knees with his hands clasped in supplication, as if his limbs had arranged themselves without direction.

Madame Picot lowered her black book, apparently appeased. But she shook her head authoritatively. "No. I will go with you. Come. I'm told she lives in Villeneuve, along with the other witches of Paris."

"But how would you know such a thing, Madame Picot?"

The woman gestured to the feathers on the floor. "A bird told me, monsieur."

And with that, she slung her shawl across her shoulders and disappeared down the stairs, leaving Lesage to trail after her, cursing under his breath.

21

Charlotte strode across the courtyard, trying not to reveal the fear she felt in her chest. She paused at the high gate until Lesage came up behind her and together they stepped into the street. It was late, almost dark. Several children were fighting with swords fashioned from sticks, shrieking with terror and glee as they parried and lunged. A cart rumbled past, rats snickered in the darkness.

Lesage paused, obviously pondering which direction to take, before saying, "This way, madame."

He led her north, past houses and dungheaps and piles of rubbish, past merchants and knots of people gossiping in doorways and courtyards. Lanterns were being lit in windows and servants were running out for provisions. No one paid them the least attention. They passed a crowd gathered to watch as a woman lit a lantern attached to a chain and then, by means of an ingenious pulley system, hoisted it until it hung out of reach above their heads. Lesage stopped here and there to ask something of a stranger in hushed tones, then pressed onwards. Despite his grumbling and unwillingness to share with her anything he discovered, it was clear the night suited him. There was a lightness to his step and he navigated the busy roads and drains and various other hindrances with ease. Following the advice of a sinister-looking fellow he encountered on a street corner, he disappeared into a tavern and came out shortly afterwards with new purpose.

They continued north until the jumble and noise of the city

fell away. Gardens and fields stretched out on each side of the road and there were fewer people to be seen. Moonlight glistening on leaves, the pungent waft of soil, here and there the bobbing lantern of a labourer making his way home. Behind them, Paris squatted on the horizon.

Finally, they came to a wide street of houses. Humming to himself, Lesage approached a large door with a circular knocker dangling from the mouth of a brass lion. With Charlotte at his shoulder, Lesage rapped several times.

Eventually, a sulky young maid holding a candelabrum set with three candles opened the door a crack. In the hallway behind were other candles, the glint of a mirror. "Yes? What? It's late, monsieur."

"We are hoping to see Madame Filastre on some urgent business, mademoiselle," said Lesage.

The maid scoffed and stepped back to close the door. "Madame does not see people this late, monsieur. You can come back tomorrow."

Charlotte jammed one foot against the door. "No, mademoiselle. We need to see your mistress tonight. Now."

In the hall over the maid's shoulder, there was movement as a woman—perhaps the witch herself, this vile woman who had made a pact with the Devil—loomed up from the hallway gloom. Rather than the ugly and frightening sorceress Charlotte had anticipated, however, the woman resembled a kindly wife. Wisps of dark hair at her temple, a glittering necklace at her throat, rich swish of her green silken garments along the floor.

"Who is here so late, Madeleine?" she asked.

The maid merely scowled and wiped her nose with her free hand.

The woman approached. "Well, well," she said, clearly amazed. "Look at that. It's Monsieur du Coeuret, is it? Back from the dead after all this time. Now that's a surprise."

Lesage made his little bow. "Good evening, Madame Filastre. How pleasant to see you, too. I'm flattered you should even remember me after all these years. I know it is late but we have some urgent business. May I introduce Madame Picot?" His voice dropped to a whisper. "She has a problem she wishes to ask you about."

Unsure how to acknowledge such a person, Charlotte dipped her head in greeting.

"It's very late, Monsieur du Coeuret," the sorceress muttered.

Lesage gestured vaguely towards Charlotte. "Yes. I'm sorry, madame, but . . ."

With a tight-lipped smile, Madame Filastre considered Charlotte before she stood back from the door. "Very well. Let them in, Madeleine. No good talking on the street in this fashion, is there? Come inside, Madame Picot. Come."

Charlotte hesitated and looked around. Night had settled over the city while they had been seeking this woman's house. It was dark. In the distance a man held out a candle to peer at something. A donkey clopped along the street. Crack of whip, the laughter of merchant. A cool breeze ruffled her hair. She crossed herself and muttered a prayer. "*Ave Maria, gratia plena, Dominus tecum . . .*"

Madame Filastre led them into a room appointed with mirrors and paintings on the walls and rich, red carpets covering the floor. Charlotte was seized with the urge to flee but Madame Filastre, perhaps sensing this, took Charlotte's hand in her own and guided her to a low sofa. The hand that gripped hers was not icy—as she might have imagined of one in league with the Devil—but, rather, it was soft and warm, like any other person's.

"Come, Madame Picot," Madame Filastre said. "Sit. Please. You are so cold! Madeleine, bring us a jug of wine and something to eat."

Charlotte had never before even imagined a house so luxurious. There were shelves of books, portraits of men and women hanging on the walls, and on the mantel stood a vase overflowing with wilting purple irises. Despite the mildness of the night outside, coals glowed in the hearth. The air in the room was smoky, warm, tinged with smells of perfume and burnt pine. La Filastre herself looked to be around Charlotte's age. She was pale, dark-eyed, quite beautiful, and Charlotte blushed with shame at consideration of her own dirty clothes and unkempt hair. As the women settled themselves, Lesage shuffled about uneasily, peering at books and ornaments, poking at the coals in the grate with the toe of his boot.

The grumbling maid reappeared with a jug of wine, some glasses and a platter of meats, which she set on a low table. Madame Filastre waved her away and poured wine for each of them.

"And what is the problem that brings you here so late, Madame Picot?" she asked, sipping from her glass.

"Some men took my son, madame."

"Oh, how terrible! Took him how?"

Charlotte touched the place on her shoulder where the arrow had pierced her. "They attacked me several days ago and kidnapped him as we were on our way to Lyon to escape an outbreak of fever in my village. I was injured myself. My husband is already dead from fever."

The woman considered all this. "But how might I assist you? You wish me to . . . ?"

Charlotte could barely bring herself to say it aloud. She spoke in a whisper. "I know there is a trade in these things. That there are people in Paris who . . . purchase children for their secret ceremonies. For their own purposes."

Madame Filastre tilted her head back to scratch her elegant throat. Her gaze slid over to Lesage, then back to Charlotte. "But what sort of people would buy children, madame?"

Charlotte shifted uncomfortably on the sofa. Was this woman mocking her? "Witches, madame. *Witches.*"

Lesage, who had been warming his calves in front of the hearth, stepped forward. "What Madame Picot is saying, madame, is that she is hoping you might have heard something through your various acquaintances. A man called Monsieur Horst is understood to be responsible for the kidnapping."

"And what is your role in this, Adam?" asked Madame Filastre.

"I am . . . accompanying Madame Picot."

"*Helping* her?"

"Well, her husband is dead, as she told you. She is unfamiliar with Paris—"

"Is she paying you, then?"

"No, madame."

"Then you're helping because of—what?—the kindness in your *heart*?"

Lesage laughed nervously. "Yes. Something like that."

"Were you not sentenced to several years in the galleys, Adam?"

"I was."

"But your time is now finished? Already?"

Charlotte could not bear such banal banter any longer. "Madame! Please. Do you know anything about my son?"

Apparently amused by the situation, Madame Filastre shook her head and drank her wine. "No. I have not heard of such a man, nor have I heard of these things happening in Paris. My circle of acquaintances is not large, madame. I entertain occasionally. My husband is often away on his business. I really don't know how you expect me to help you . . . "

Charlotte drank her own wine and felt it seep warmly into her blood and bones. Her legs were trembling slightly and she pressed her feet against the carpet to steady them. She felt queasy in the presence of this serene and forbidding woman.

She glanced around once more at the furnishings. In the house of a witch. How had it come to this? "But are *you* not a sorceress, madame?"

No longer quite so merry-eyed, Madame Filastre settled her feline gaze upon Charlotte. She drank her wine and wiped her mouth with a single finger. "It's true I have some expertise with remedies and so on. Charms. Particular novenas. But I cannot conjure your child from where he might be, madame."

Charlotte cleared her throat. "But have you not made a pact with the Devil, madame?"

There followed a brief silence. "And who told you that, Madame Picot?"

"A woman like me hears things."

"Oh, but I'm most intrigued. What kind of woman would that be? A milkmaid? No. A seamstress?"

Charlotte attempted to hold the woman's eye, but faltered, glancing instead at Lesage who, mercifully, stepped forward.

"Come now, Françoise," he said. "Madame Picot is most upset at what has happened, as I'm sure you can imagine. She means nothing by it. We are sorry to disturb you so late. We thought you might have heard something or could help in some way. That's all. But if you have not heard anything, then we shall try elsewhere. Come, Madame Picot. I shall escort you back to your lodgings. Just allow me to . . . "

Lesage bent over to carve himself a hunk of ham from the joint on the platter. Abashed and relieved to have a focus aside from her own discomfort, Charlotte watched him tear away the greasy flap of meat and slide it into his mouth.

Madame Filastre leaned forward and refilled her wine glass. "*I* know," she said, after a lull in which the only sound was that of Lesage wetly chewing his meat, "why don't you send one of your special messages, Adam? Perhaps the Devil himself knows where the boy is?"

Charlotte was dismayed at such an idea, but Lesage, evidently energised at the prospect of communicating with his master, began muttering and nodding and pacing around the parlour.

"Yes," he was saying. "Yes! Why did I not consider it myself? An excellent idea, Madame Filastre. Yes, yes." He appealed to Charlotte. "What do you think, madame?"

Charlotte turned to their hostess. "Are you sure, Madame Filastre, that you have not heard anything of this man or of such a trade in Paris?"

"Not a word, I'm afraid."

"But will asking a question . . . injure me in any way, or put my soul in jeopardy? Is it not dangerous, monsieur?"

Lesage shook his head. "No, no, no. Merely asking a question won't hurt you. Nor does it imperil your soul, madame. Not at all. Honestly. If it is dangerous for anyone, then it is dangerous for me. I am here to serve you, am I not? It would not be in my own interests to cause *you* any harm, would it?"

Charlotte supposed this was true enough. She imagined the city of Paris out there beyond the thick walls of this house. Its alleys and buildings and cats, its grim doorways and stinking, straw-covered courtyards. Nicolas could be anywhere, nowhere, and a fresh dread filled her heart at consideration of his possible fate. Desperation bested her fear. After a moment, she nodded her agreement. What choice was there?

Lesage clapped his hands. "Excellent. Now. Can you write, madame?"

Again she nodded. "Yes. A little."

Charlotte's odd companion was most excited as he produced from his satchel a scrap of paper, a quill and a pot of black ink. This he uncorked. Then, with great care, Lesage smoothed the grubby square of paper on his knee, jabbed his quill several times into the ink and offered it to her with a solemn dip of his head.

On the tip of the quill bulged a drop of blood-dark ink. Reflected upside down in it was the room and its occupants:

glowing coals in the fireplace; Lesage's ruddy cheeks; Charlotte's looming, outstretched hand; the attentive but disdainful gaze of Madame Filastre. An entire world, shrunken and pulled out of shape. She hesitated. Again Lesage pressed the quill upon her.

Eventually, she took it and wrote her question awkwardly, but with great care. She was not an experienced scribe. The effort was considerable and it took some time. She spelled out her question in clumsy letters: *please where is my son nicolas please.*

"Now," Lesage said, "fold the paper into as small a piece as you can. No need to show me what you have written. The message is not intended for me, of course. That's very good. Well done. Hand it here. Thank you, Madame Picot."

Lesage rummaged again in his satchel, finally producing from its depths a large glob of cream-coloured wax. He seemed most pleased with himself, humming away as he fashioned from this a smaller ball of wax—the second one about the size of an apricot stone. Then, without reading it, he stuffed Charlotte's folded message inside the smaller ball, taking care to embed it thoroughly and reshape the wax into a ball when he had done so. "Wax, of course, is a natural medium between our worlds, is it not, Madame Filastre?"

Madame Filastre nodded energetically. "Oh, indeed it is, monsieur."

"A substance both liquid and solid, a vessel for flame. This particular wax is from altar candles and has been blessed by a priest."

Charlotte observed him at his work and thought he looked almost like any man who had lived long enough to be acquainted with his human share of sorrow. With his free hand he touched his cheek, something he did often, as if to check on the pulse beneath his skin. "Did you have any children yourself, monsieur? Were you married?"

He seemed perplexed that she should ask him such a

question. He paused in his moulding of the wax ball and glanced up at Madame Filastre before answering. "Yes," he said in a low voice. "I have two sons. One daughter did not survive infancy. Some sort of illness. She was born near Easter and died by Whitsun of the same year. The boys would be men by now."

"How long is it, then, since you saw them?"

He looked at her. "It is some years," he said at last. "I am sure they are still in Normandy where they were born and raised. They were always fine boys."

"And your wife?"

"Why would you want to know these things, madame?"

It was a good question. Why indeed? "Just to be sociable."

He allowed a thin smile. "Claudette? A decent woman. Kind, came from a good family. Her father was a shipwright in Le Havre. Much too good for me, I'm afraid. That woman's only shame, perhaps, was in marrying a man such as myself."

"Were you truly so terrible to her?"

He gazed up at her from beneath his hooded eyes, as if he suspected her of mockery. "I was sent to the galleys for impieties," he hissed. "For the very thing I am about to do for you, in fact. I was most fortunate not to have been burned alive at the stake for my crimes. I think she would be pleased to be rid of me. Her family certainly would be."

Charlotte pressed him. "Do you not wish to know something of your sons' lives? To know whether they are prospering, still fine boys? Whether they are married?"

Lesage worked the wax expertly in his large hands, palming it over and over until it resembled grey marble. "There is no way to know such things, madame, but I feel sure they are prospering. André, the oldest one, was always good with numbers. He will do well in business and I know he will look after his brother. They were always good companions to each other. Fond of each other. André's favourite thing when he was a boy, believe it or not, was for me to ask him mathematical questions. Yes! It's true. What is five times eight. Nine and twenty-four. That sort of thing. I would write out sums on his slate to amuse him. I was away travelling a lot and it would sometimes be several weeks before I would return to assess his answers. But he was determined to make something of himself and I think he would do well in the world.'"

How strange it was to think of Lesage as having once been an ordinary man with a wife and sons—although it was said that even the Devil himself had once been an angel. "And what is his name? The younger one?"

Lesage said nothing for a long time, as if he had not heard her. "We named him Étienne," he said at last, as she prepared to repeat her question. "He was . . . there was something wrong with him. Not like the other boys. He was dim-witted somehow, you might say. We kept him inside a lot for fear the villagers would think ill of us. He did not speak for some years and then only in a strange tongue that could only be understood by those in the family. His mother could understand him. Me not so well, on account of being away on business so much. In fact, I met some of these people'—he gestured vaguely towards Madame Filastre—"in Paris because my friend Galet knew them. He thought Catherine Monvoisin might be able to help Étienne with a charm or a remedy of some sort. We had already tried the village priest. He performed an exorcism on Étienne, but it had no effect on the boy. So Catherine tried various spells, but nothing worked. My wife was against such things, but I felt I should do whatever possible to help my son, even if it was at risk to myself. I would have done anything for him. I *have* done all sorts of things. I was here in Paris a lot, in Italy, in Spain. But André would translate for us. And Étienne enjoyed the children's rhyme I sang for him. He insisted on my singing it to him at night when I was home. '*Les Cloches de Vendôme*'—you know the one?"

Shyly, he sang a few bars of the song, which Charlotte did indeed recognise, before his voice faltered.

"You would not wish to return to Normandy and see how he is faring?"

There was real irritation in his voice when he answered. "Yes, but it is not always possible to return home, Madame Picot. Not when a man has done certain . . . things; not when he has travelled a certain distance from that particular place. This is something that perhaps you are fortunate not to know. I have brought great shame upon my wife. Once innocence is lost, madame, it cannot be regained. One cannot"—he paused to glance again at Madame Filastre—"unlearn what one has learned. My fortunes are bound with yours, are they not? My freedom is still limited. Perhaps, if you were to release me from your service, I could indeed return, but you have made it plain that such a turn of events is impossible—regardless of the outcome."

Charlotte felt herself flushing to have this apparent cruelty of hers pointed out and she drew her shawl tight around her shoulders.

Madame Filastre chortled. "Is this woman your wife, Adam? For what you are describing sounds very much like a marriage."

"Very funny, Françoise. Now, to the matter at hand . . . " Lesage held up the wax ball containing her message. "I shall send this off immediately and soon we will know more."

"But how is it delivered?" Charlotte asked.

"Through fire. This will not take long."

Lesage produced from his satchel a short stick of hazel, then kneeled awkwardly in front of the coals glowing in the grate. He closed his eyes and touched the stick to his forehead with a brisk flourish, mumbling incomprehensibly to himself in some foreign language as he did so. A wand. His stick was a wand. His cheek twitched and his neck glistened with sweat. He seemed excited, prepared for his unholy communion.

A few more invocations, then he turned to Charlotte and

Madame Filastre with one arm raised to his face. "Cover your eyes, please."

He tossed the ball of wax containing Charlotte's message into the coals pulsing in the grate. Charlotte placed a hand over her eyes in time but she glimpsed, from behind interlaced fingers, a sputtering crackle and flash. She cried out in alarm and cowered on the sofa. When she removed her hand, bright shapes—orange, white, blue—danced in the air in front of her and the room was filled with a pungent odour, like that of gunpowder.

Lesage got to his feet and, with one of his characteristic, slightly comical bows, he turned to her. "Your message has been delivered, madame."

Madame Filastre was coughing and waving the smoke away from her face. "Ugh. What is that stench, Monsieur du Coeuret?"

"There are always side effects, as you well know, madame."

"What happens now?" Charlotte asked.

"Well. We wait."

"And we will receive an answer?"

"Ah, yes. Or maybe a sign of some sort. I shall be vigilant for it, and you should be, too. Perhaps it will be you who receives the sign. These matters are extremely hard to predict and the information sometimes comes from unlikely sources."

This didn't sound very persuasive. "But how long will it take?" she asked.

Lesage straightened his wig. "Who knows? Probably only one day, two days. Not long. The ways of such things are really quite mysterious, madame—even to me."

Charlotte felt sick to imagine a message written in her own hand being cast into the underworld. She peered into the coals in the grate, which had, by this time, returned to their slumber.

"Don't worry," Lesage said, as if reading her thoughts, "I'm certain we will find your son."

22

The following afternoon, Catherine ushered Lesage into the dim pavilion at the rear of her property in Rue Beauregard. The room was warm and its air was thick with her musky perfume, gamey as a vixen's den. Lesage was most impatient to know whether she had discovered anything about Nicolas's whereabouts, or ways to unhex him, but he knew better than to hurry her. Catherine Monvoisin was a woman of strict and meticulous formalities and it was fruitless and unwise to expect otherwise; things would happen in her own good time. Nothing would be revealed until she had fussed herself into a comfortable position.

The heavily curtained consulting room was unaltered since he last visited. A wooden statue of the suffering, crucified Christ stood on a side table, there were piles of books and papers on the carpeted floor and a water-stained map of the heavens pinned to one wall. Bundles of dried lavender, a variety of candles, a low table where she did her palm readings. A locked trunk contained her more dangerous substances—vials of vitriol and her forbidden black books. He averted his gaze from the compact stove in the corner.

Finally, when they were seated and she had settled herself, Lesage could bear it no longer. "So? Tell me, Catherine. Have you found a way to unwitch me?"

Catherine shook her head. "I searched all my books but have found nothing so far. I will be seeing La Trianon later this morning and I expect she will know something of these charms. Don't worry, Adam. I will free you. Stall Madame Picot for as long as you can and we'll think of a solution."

"Did you look in *all* the papers you have? The Enchiridion must have something. What about the other books? I cannot go back, Catherine."

She pressed her lips into a thin line. "Do you not trust me, Adam?"

"It's *Lesage*, remember," he hissed. "And yes, of course I trust you. I just . . . "

"What, then?"

He tried to smile, to compose himself. He wiped away his tears. How shameful it was to weep in such a manner in front of a woman. "I'm sorry, Catherine. I'm sorry. It's been a terrible time."

"I know. In any case, I'm not sure why you are so afraid of a woman like that. I paid a visit to Madame Picot."

"What? I told you not to. Really, Catherine, I—"

"Calm down, man. She didn't know who I was and it was all very friendly. She's a peasant. Old woman's magic, probably knows a cure or two for the ague. I'm surprised a man like you is so afraid of her. She didn't frighten me in the least."

"I told you, Catherine: I've *seen* what she can do. The wolf . . . "

"Bah! If her magic is as great as you say, then why could she not do something to find her beloved son? Make him come back?"

It was a good question, one Lesage had already asked himself over the past few days, and he responded with the only conclusion he'd been able to draw. "Magic cannot accomplish everything we want, as you well know. Some things are God's will and that's all there is to it. Life, death. There are forces that may never be harnessed."

Catherine leaned back in her chair. "I think we can find this boy and bring him back here."

"And then?"

"Then we tell her that we'll kill the boy if she doesn't release you immediately."

Lesage groaned. Why did women always complicate things? "But what if she doesn't?"

"Oh, I think she will."

"I would die before going back, Catherine. Honestly. I would drink poison myself."

Catherine leaned forward and patted his knee. "No need to be so dramatic. We'll find a way, I promise." She sat back with a terse smile on her face. "But you'll be pleased to know that I did hear something of a fellow who might be involved in the trade of children."

"Monsieur Horst?"

"I don't know if that's his name, but he and his assistant bring orphans to Paris and deposit them somewhere outside the city while they wait to sell them on. Perhaps they trade with one of those brutes like de Rais—who knows? Hopefully the woman's son has not yet been passed along the chain."

Lesage shuddered at consideration of the terrifying Gilles de Rais and the hundreds of children he had slaughtered in the years after serving alongside Jeanne of Orléans. Although already long dead when Lesage was a boy, his father would threaten to sell him and his brother to such a monster if they didn't do as they were told. *You go into his castle*, his father would taunt, *but you never come out. He kills you and then he fucks you in every hole he can find—and then he makes new holes with his halberd . . .*

Catherine went on. "The man who arranges to sell the orphans in Paris is called Willem. A Norman, one of your countrymen. He could know something of the boy's whereabouts—if he's alive. You can find him at La Pomme de Pin in Rue de la Cité. Go there tonight and buy him a cup or two of wine and I'm sure he'll tell you what he knows."

Lesage pondered this information. What a nightmare this was all proving to be. Freed only to be enslaved again. "Should I tell Madame Picot?" he asked. "After all, I'm only useful to her while her son is missing."

Catherine was silent for a moment, then shrugged. "Yes. Tell her. What's the harm? You haven't freed the boy yet, so you're still useful to her. Keep stalling her while we figure out exactly what to do. Get the boy, bring him to me."

It seemed as wise a course of action as any, and it was better than nothing. Lesage moved to get to his feet, but Catherine motioned for him to stay where he was. From the house she fetched a bottle of ale. She poured them each a glass and sat back, as if toasting a bargain concluded to their mutual satisfaction. "Did I tell you about Madame Aubervilles? My God . . . "

Distracted, Lesage shook his head. Catherine didn't quite seem to understand that he had been in prison and heard almost nothing of the happenings in Paris. She rattled off any number of scandals, revelling in her tales of infidelity and murder. Dukes and duchesses trying to kill one another, someone's lady-in-waiting who had three abortions in a single year, the baker near her on Rue Saint-Étienne who couldn't get it up. Lesage suspected that Catherine's love of gossip had, in fact, been the impetus for her career in magic and fortune telling. After all, what better way to encourage all manner of people to reveal their deepest secrets and desires? What Catherine Monvoisin and her rivals really traded in, of course, was trust—which led to the sharing of intimacies. How many times had he watched her farewell some lady of the court who was visibly distressed after revealing a terrible family secret, a secret that—often accompanied by gales of laughter—would promptly be shared with him?

He sipped his warm ale and smiled or nodded when it was required.

"You know," Catherine said, "sometimes I have terrible moments of doubt about my own powers and I rush to Bonne-Nouvelle and ask the Lord for guidance. I light a candle and I pray and eventually the feelings go away. None of us know what we are truly capable of. Our hearts are quite mysterious even to ourselves, aren't they?"

Lesage glanced down at his palm. Spitefully, he thought again of the treasure map tucked away in the purse next to his heart. Sometimes, like now, he detected its reassuring warmth, as if it were a promise merely waiting to be fulfilled.

"Don't fret," said Catherine, placing a hand on his knee. "I'm sure we can find a solution to your problem with this damned Picot woman and, soon enough, we will be more powerful than ever before. And richer. *Imagine it*, Adam. We are thriving here as never before. They cannot get enough of our services. Later today there will be so many people here seeking our assistance. People from court, men and women from all across Europe. Last week a woman came all the way from Florence to see me about a problem she was having with her lover. There are people of great quality waiting to get in. Sometimes there are so many clients waiting that we employ musicians to entertain them while they wait. It's like a festival here in summer. Everyone comes to us now. And when they hear you have returned to Paris, well . . . "

She went on with her grand plans for their future together. Astrological charts, charms for effecting marriages (always his forte, admittedly), the rates they could charge. Perhaps they could even move to larger premises? She got up from her chair and flung open the curtains. A knife-strike of daylight pierced the room. Motes of dust fussed about angrily in the air like tiny creatures roused from their slumber. Lesage's attention wandered. Sparrows twittered in the tree outside and a mule brayed on the street somewhere beyond the walls. So much had happened, so little had changed. It was as if he had never left.

Back in her tiny room, Lesage relayed this information concerning her son to Madame Picot.

"And this Willem person knows where Nicolas is?" she asked.

"He might. Yes."

She pondered this for a moment. "And the Devil told you this?"

He couldn't stifle a chuckle. "Well, you know what the Germans say—where the Devil cannot go, he sends an old woman."

She gathered up her shawl. "Then I will come with you to meet this fellow."

Alarmed, Lesage moved towards her. "No, madame. That won't be necessary. It's probably best if I meet with him alone. These sorts of men are often no better than villains themselves. Dangerous. Very dangerous. You will be much safer here, I think. Such taverns are the drinking houses of rogues. They are not fit for women."

"Nowhere, it seems, is fit for women, monsieur."

"But what if something were to happen to you?"

She waved away his protest. "I appreciate your concern, monsieur, but much has already happened to me in recent days."

Why would she not listen? Lesage opened his mouth to speak, but managed to quell the urge to tell her that his anxieties were not for her wellbeing but, rather, for what her continuing good health meant for his own; if he had a choice he would poison her without delay.

They walked along Rue Saint-Denis towards the river, past the cemetery, then cut through to Rue des Lavandières so as not to venture too near the Conciergerie—about which he was fearful and superstitious. Carts and hubbub, the hoarse cries of the fishwives and vinegar girls, battalions of pigeons parading about in the dirt. Madame Picot walked beside him, gazing around at the city's buildings and people. Lesage recalled his first trip to Paris all those years ago, and in the terror and amazement in her eyes he recognised his younger self.

He was young, perhaps seventeen years old, when he first came here with his father, who had been born and grown up in nearby Rue Saint-Martin. How provincial he had felt when his father pointed out the places he knew: the huge bridge with the muddle of houses across its length; La Place de l'Estrapade, where boys rented out lanterns to guide visitors through the labyrinth of the university quarter; the stinking tanning factories alongside the River Bièvre; the enormous gardens alongside the Quai des Tuileries where, it was said, a tiny red man cavorted at night when the French crown was under threat. Even at first glimpse, the city exerted a strange allure for Lesage, which was twinned with a sort of disgust—like lusting after a whore.

He and Madame Picot emerged onto the Quai de la Mégisserie to the hearty stink of fish offal and mud baking in the summer sun. A grey cat sat on a low stone wall serenely licking its paw. There, above the bustle of the Pont au Change and the other quays to the east, loomed the two towers of Notre-Dame Cathedral, gleaming in the setting sun as if placed there by God himself. It was one of his favourite views of the city and he felt an odd surge of pride at being able to show it off to Madame Picot.

"Is this not the greatest city in the world, madame?" he said to her as they picked their way around a pile of food scraps. "I have been to many others in my time, but Paris is by far the greatest. Rome is a terrible place, Marseille. No. Paris has it all. In that cathedral over there they have the crown of thorns, madame. Yes. Yes, they do. The one worn by Christ himself. A true relic."

Madame Picot shaded her eyes with one hand and gazed around her. She did not seem as enamoured of Paris as he, and he felt disappointment that she did not share his reverence.

"When I came here as a young man," he went on, "I, too, was fearful. The city seemed so large and impossible to understand. Streets like a maze, the noise and chaos. But I have come to love it." He felt an inexplicable desire to expound on this affection, as if such an explanation were a door he might hold open for her to share in his appreciation.

Madame Picot did not seem to be paying him much attention, however, but was instead staring down at the riverbank in front of them. He followed her gaze. Down among the fishing boats and baskets and laundry boats and sails and nets, men were shouting and a woman was pointing towards the river. A shirtless man was wading into the murky green water towards something floating further out. It was a dark and bobbing shape, a vessel or some bundles of goods that had perhaps come adrift. There arose more shouts and cries of alarm in all sorts of languages. "*Quickly, quickly. There she is!*" Some of the horses roped to boats shook their withers and stamped their hoofs in fright. Residents in the houses honeycombed atop the Pont au Change had flung open their shutters and leaned from their windows to watch the commotion and call out advice and encouragement.

People bustled past them to see the cause of the hubbub and Lesage and Madame Picot found themselves drawn towards the river, where a crowd was gathering. The shirtless fellow was staggering back to the bank, stopping now and again to steady his footing in the greasy shallows. In his arms he cradled a person. It was a woman with her head thrown back and her dark hair trailing in the water like wet cords connecting her to the river.

Finally, the man was able to make it clear of the water, where he squatted among the bales and baskets and lowered the woman to the muddy bank. The crowd had, by this time, obscured Lesage and Madame Picot's view of the scene but they managed to push their way through to the front. A woman was crying and praying, someone else called for a priest. The woman on the bank was clearly dead and probably had been for some time. The skin of her face was blue and her mouth was agape. Eyes dull as oysters, mud smeared on her cheek and a yellow birch leaf stuck to her neck. Truly a ghastly sight. Lesage had, of course, seen plenty of corpses in his time—who hadn't?—but they never failed to shock him. Death was not something he liked to think about.

Men and women in the crowd crossed themselves and murmured prayers for the poor woman, as did Madame Picot.

He looked down again at the body. Beside him, Madame Picot uttered a cry and Lesage reflexively grabbed her arm, as if to prevent himself from falling, for they had both at the same time recognised the dead woman on the riverbank.

It was the troubadour Madame Leroux. Drowned in a river, precisely as he had foretold.

23

L a Pomme de Pin was dim and low-roofed, and its air was grey and soupy with tobacco smoke. Lanterns and a few candles glimmered in the gloom like the lights of distant villages glimpsed through fog. In one corner a boy played a boisterous tune on his violin, and a crone slumped on a low chair by the wall. The customers were mainly men, an ill-assorted lot with filthy breeches, hunched shoulders and restless eyes. In the middle of the room, at the largest and best-lit table, five or six soldiers were arguing loudly over a game of cards.

As a rule, Charlotte did not frequent establishments built for men and their whores and wine. Such places intimidated her, and she was relieved to have Lesage as a companion on this occasion. Perhaps he had been right to scold her for disparaging the very qualities for which she had summoned him? After all, it was akin to having a soldier for a valet.

They paused in the doorway while Lesage peered through the smoke at the groups of drinking men. "Wait for me here," he said, and then he moved among them before she could object, asking if anyone knew of Willem the Norman. One group shook their heads in answer to his query, then another. Eventually, someone pointed to the corner, where a man sat alone at a table fondling his clay pipe. This fellow was thin and ancient, the skin of his face as darkly wrinkled as an old apple.

Lesage approached and conferred with the stranger, but Charlotte was unable to hear what they were saying over the noise of the tavern, its music and gruff din. Several of the soldiers were yelling at each other. Lesage motioned to the tavern keeper for a jug of wine, then he and this stranger talked for some time with their heads close together in a distinctly conspiratorial manner that made her uneasy. Despite his professed loyalty to her, Charlotte regarded Lesage with suspicion. Most men were untrustworthy at the best of times and this creature was really no man at all. She recalled what Madame Rolland had told her of the unpredictability of magic. Yes, he was a queer fish, indeed. Eventually, Lesage swivelled on his bench, pointed to Charlotte and, after further whispered consultation with the stranger, indicated for her to join them.

"This man has my son?" she asked as soon as she sat.

The stranger glanced at her, then at Lesage, who spoke to him in a foreign tongue before turning back to her. She heard her son's name, her own name.

"What did he say?" she said. "Is this the fellow we hoped to meet? Does he know something?"

"Yes," said Lesage. "It's him. But you have to speak quietly. Please. He says he has your boy and that he is in a house outside Paris."

Her relief was immediate and intense. She crossed herself. Under her breath she thanked the Virgin. "And he's alive?"

"Yes, of course. Of course, madame. He is talking the language of my country. You know, we are fortunate I can speak with him."

Charlotte was aware of the stranger's idle gaze, like that of a sceptical buyer inspecting a cut of meat. The Norman and Lesage conferred again in their own language. One or two words she recognised, but nothing else. The two men haggled further.

She grew impatient. "Can he get my son for me? Can we see him?"

Both men ignored her. Finally, Lesage leaned across to whisper in her ear. "Yes, but he wants money in exchange for him."

"My son is not his property to sell, monsieur. He was stolen from me. Does he even know that?"

"This is Paris, madame, not the provinces."

"Are you telling me the truth?"

Lesage looked aggrieved. "Of course I am, madame."

"But I have no money."

The stranger smiled a benign, wet-lipped smile, slid the stem of his pipe into his mouth and puffed repeatedly until smoke bobbed from its bowl. Then, taking the pipe from his mouth and jabbing it occasionally at Lesage for emphasis, he launched into a long and croaky monologue.

When he had finished, Lesage turned once more to Charlotte. "He says your son is well and seems a good boy. He is safe for now, but another person is interested in buying him—"

"But Nicolas is my own son! I do not need to buy his release."

"Quiet, woman. Keep your voice low. Someone is coming to buy him tomorrow afternoon."

"Who?"

Lesage asked the swindler. "Another witch, he says."

"For what reason?"

Lesage hesitated, frowning, but the stranger, perhaps sensing the juncture at which the translation had faltered, drew his pipe stem across his whiskered throat.

Charlotte's heart felt as if it had been drained of its blood. "But Nicolas is my son," she whispered weakly. "Did you tell him that? That he's my son?"

The vile Norman shrugged and muttered some more before looking away. She did not need to understand his language to know how inconsequential he thought her. She resisted an urge to strike him.

Lesage, perhaps sensing her anger, placed a hand on her arm. "Stay calm, woman. He says if the boy is truly your son then you will be glad to pay for his safe return. He says the other party has promised one hundred and fifty livres. If we want him, we need to offer at least the same amount."

Charlotte sat quietly. Her mouth was dry and her hands were shaking in her lap. Men, she thought, who are so full of wickedness and deceit. She took Lesage's cup, filled it with wine, and drank. The liquid burned her throat. Instinctively, she pressed one hand to the book in her dress pocket. Her son. Her poor son in the control of these hideous men. How had such darkness come to pass? How could the world be so evil? *Your blood, your blood, your blood.* The fire crackled and spat as several of its glowing logs collapsed in the grate, prompting the tavern keeper to waddle over and prod at it with his poker before returning to his corner stool. Sparks swirled into the chimney and were quickly spent. Lesage shifted on the bench beside her.

She had an idea. "You will get your money, monsieur," she hissed at Willem the Norman. "Tomorrow I will give you two hundred livres for my son." The man stared at her and in his blank gaze Charlotte detected a mute challenge. "And tell him," she added, "that if any harm comes to Nicolas, then I will send you to murder him."

The two men conferred a moment longer, then Willem belched and rose to his feet. "I will see you tomorrow morning, monsieur," he said to Lesage in Charlotte's language. "But don't bring this woman or the arrangement is off. I don't trust her." He listed, then blew Charlotte a kiss before weaving out the door into the street.

Lesage turned to her with an expression on his face that might have been vindication or incomprehension.

She spoke before he could object. "That treasure you mentioned? You said it was in Paris. Take me there. Now. Tonight."

He paused for a moment, thoughtful. Then a delighted

smile broke across his mouth. He got to his feet and leaned over her until his face was directly in front of hers. "Ah," he said with satisfaction. "Yes, indeed. Of course, of course. Come outside, madame, where we might talk without being overheard. This is a serious business."

Outside it was cold and Charlotte drew her shawl about her shoulders as Lesage, with a hand on her back, steered her deeper into the darkness away from the tavern. The voices of boatmen echoed from across the nearby river. "*Watch out! Careful of the rope . . .*" Laughter, singing, clank of chains, the hollow thump of oar against hull.

"Where is this money?" Charlotte asked.

"Oh, it is somewhere in Paris."

Furious, Charlotte grabbed the lapels of Lesage's tunic and pressed him against a wall. These disgusting men with their hearts bulging with treachery. "Where is it? I have had enough of your riddles. Do you know or not? Where is it? Tell me now."

"I will tell you," he said with a smug grin, his palms raised in surrender. "I will. I will. But do you not think I deserve some . . . reward if I complete such a task?"

"I was warned not to bargain with a creature like you. Shall I send you back immediately? Tonight? A few words from me is all it takes to cast you down again, monsieur."

"Wait, madame. Wait! Wait! Listen to me. You *could* send me back, but then you would not have time enough to locate such a sum of money. More than one hundred and fifty livres. Can you conjure such a sum?"

Charlotte didn't answer.

"Your son will be sold tomorrow and, well, I do not wish to think what might become of him. There is untold wickedness in Paris. Besides, you will never survive here without me. I know Paris, all its streets, almost every one of its people. You

. . . you need me. You are your son's only hope and I am *your* only hope."

The horrible man was right; she didn't have enough time to summon anyone else to help her. He was right, too, about her chances of surviving in this city alone; it was doubtful she could even find her way back to the widow Simon's lodging house in the dark. These realisations filled her with a cold despair. Had he planned it this way all along, conspired in his language with the horrible Willem? Was there no end to his trickery and mischief? She let go of his jacket. "What, then?"

"Listen, madame. It's a simple request, one I have already made. I will help you locate the treasure if you pledge to free me from your servitude."

"This is an ambitious request, monsieur."

"And I am an ambitious man. But you can surely see my predicament? If I help you find the boy, you will send me back. And if I don't find him, you will send me back. Please. I can't return. I have done all you asked. It is not so much, is it? You are condemning me to a terrible fate. Have mercy on me."

Charlotte hesitated. "Show me the map."

Lesage rummaged through his coat pockets, eventually brandishing a purse from which he drew a square of paper. He glanced around to ensure they were alone, then unfolded it.

The map was brown with age and deeply creased. In the dim light Charlotte could make out letters and symbols, the faint outlines of streets and buildings. Along one edge of the paper were scrawled rows of words and a drawing of a lascivious, prancing figure—a loathsome, goatish manikin, not unlike Lesage. She shivered at the sight of it. Lesage snatched the map out of sight, deftly refolded it and returned it back inside his coat.

"How do you know it is a true map?" Charlotte asked. "That this fellow who gave it to you was not a swindler?"

Lesage appeared dumbfounded by the question. "What,

madame? Well, I . . . The man who gave it to me, he had it on very good authority that the . . . *money in question* was buried by—"

"But was he not a criminal like yourself? What did you give him in exchange?"

"I promised to pray for his soul."

She laughed. "A man such as yourself? Praying like a good Christian?"

"A person in an unfortunate predicament will make all sorts of deals to save themselves—or, indeed, to save the ones they love."

"Why should I believe such a thing? Do you take me for a fool, monsieur?"

"No, no, no. Why would you mock me so cruelly? You have my word, madame."

"The word of a . . . what?"

Lesage squared his shoulders. "A man. That's all. Not the most upstanding, certainly—I admit that in front of you and in front of God Almighty himself—but not the worst, either. I make my confession. I have atoned for my sins. *I have been a slave*. Madame, please, I . . . A fellow in the galleys gave it to me: Bertrand. He was a master blacksmith from Avignon. I had done him a few favours while we were chained together. Assisted him. He loved me like a brother. He . . . he threw himself from the boat one very hot summer because he knew he would never be released and couldn't bear the agony of it any longer. He wanted me to share in the fortune that he was unable to possess. So it is a true map, madame, he swore it upon his loving mother's grave. I have carried it with me for three years. Hidden it from the authorities, and from the other men who would give anything to know where such a fortune is buried."

"Why have you not taken this treasure already?"

"Because not any person can say the words of the spell and

have them work. I told you this already. It needs to be someone . . . like you, Madame Picot. Someone with particular
skills, you see. Not just anyone can attempt it or they would be
destroyed immediately. You have the black book with such a
spell. And a witch's knife. The money is guarded by ferocious
spirits, who must first be cast aside."

"More ferocious than yourself?"

"What?" he stammered, apparently affronted at her insinu-
ation. "Yes! Of course. Much more ferocious than me."

"What if the money is not there? Someone might already
have taken it. Or it was never there at all."

Lesage cleared his throat. "Then all of us—you, me and
your son—are in serious trouble, madame."

She gazed up over the pitched roofs of houses. Low on the
grubby horizon there loomed a mountainous fortress, larger
than anything she had ever seen. The building, or group of
buildings, was utterly dark against the sky, except for a lantern
burning in one of its high windows like the glowing eye of a
silent, stooping giant. "Is that the home of our King?"

"What? That? No, that is not the palace, madame. That is
the Bastille. The prison."

Charlotte was so tired, and her palm was sore where
Madame Rolland had cut her. Her heart keened at the memory
of Saint-Gilles—its owls in the trees like solemn watchmen, its
smoky familiarity. How she wished she had never left. Might it
have been better to die of fever in her own country than travel
all this way to meet death in this shabby city full of strangers,
this city of crows?

Lesage, perhaps sensing her momentary vulnerability,
pressed his case. "I am assisting you, Madame Picot.
Remember that. Did I not escort you safely to Paris from the
provinces? Find you lodgings? Have I not located your son?
Who else might have been able to accomplish these things? I
ask you. Who else? You know nobody here. Do I not deserve

a tiny something? My freedom is not so much to give in return for your own son, is it? Hardly anything at all, when you think about it."

She looked at the wretched creature she had summoned. On their journey to Paris with the troubadours, Charlotte had observed Lesage as he slept with his arms flung above him as if warding off his own ravenous spirits. Sometimes his head was uncovered and she had seen the scars gleaming among the bristles of his shorn scalp, the twitch of his dreaming cheek, the ways he whimpered and thrashed. And, strangely enough, she had pitied him on those nights, as—even more strangely—she pitied him again upon consideration of his greasy cheeks and little yellow teeth. It's true, she thought. It's true my heart is so disordered. Besides, he was right; it was not so much to ask for her son's return. "Very well," she said at last. "When I have my son safely in my arms, I shall release you."

Lesage clapped his hands together. "And what of the money, madame? If there is as much treasure as I've been led to believe, then there will be a substantial amount left over—even after we have paid for your son's release."

"I only wish to have Nicolas back. Now, let's go. Quickly."

Lesage bobbed up and down with excitement, but made no move to leave. Instead, he thrust out his hand to formalise their compact. "Do I have your solemn word, madame?"

Charlotte hesitated; Madame Rolland had warned her against bargaining with such a scoundrel, but what else could she do? "Yes. You have my word."

Instead of releasing her after they had shaken, Lesage raised her hand to his lips and kissed it fervently, as if she were a womanly cardinal and he a grateful supplicant. "Thank you. Thank you, madame. Now. We should go immediately. The quicker we get there, the sooner you might be reunited with your beloved son. We have no time to waste. The treasure is buried in a cellar west of here. Do you have your black book with you?"

She retrieved her book from its pocket.

"Very well. Now. The map says that the spell requires a crow to offer these spirits in return. But it must be a stolen crow, not bought. Let me think. Yes! We can go past the bird market at the quay. Come. This way. Yes. This way, madame."

Charlotte followed him once more through the Paris streets. Around them, she heard the city's inhabitants. Men sighing at their nocturnal labours, women murmuring in their dreams, arguments, babies mewling. Some of the houses looming over them were so high it was impossible to see the night sky. Paris. A dark and terrible place, almost treeless, where one could barely tell whether it was night or day, let alone what season it might be.

Perhaps divining her apprehension, Lesage glanced at her and smiled. "Don't worry, Madame Picot. We will be able to free your son soon enough."

She didn't answer, but was grateful for his reassurances. He was certainly an intriguing combination of characteristics; at times malign, at others quite tender. She hitched her dress to step over a ditch.

Stealing a crow was no problem for Lesage, who had clearly done this kind of thing—among worse crimes, no doubt—many times before. Charlotte waited in the shadows near the river while he crept among the crooning birds and their sleeping handlers and emerged shortly afterwards with a tiny wooden cage doused in black cloth.

They pressed on through the city. More muddy streets and tilting houses. Eventually, Lesage stopped in front of a large stone building. Bidding her to be silent, he ushered her through a low, broken gate into an empty courtyard. There were no animals, no signs of human habitation, although the night air was thick with the smell of pigeon shit.

Lesage pulled out his map and squinted at it, turning it this way and that and mumbling to himself. Finally, he motioned for Charlotte to follow him across the courtyard, where he squatted by a trapdoor. He produced a tinderbox with which he managed to light a candle stub he took from his satchel. "Help me with this," he said.

They lifted the heavy, creaking trapdoor as quietly as they could. Stone stairs disappeared into the darkness beyond the candle's light, and Charlotte felt on her cheek an exhalation of stale subterranean air that carried on it smells of mildew, cold rock and sour wine. Lesage looked up at her and grinned. In the candlelight he resembled a gargoyle invested with life; his face shone with sweat and his cheek twitched.

He tapped the map triumphantly. "It's down here. Yes. You see? Exactly as the map indicates."

Lesage turned around and began clambering backwards down the stairs. He motioned for her to do the same. Charlotte followed him, but before closing the trapdoor she heard a series of high-pitched squeaks and glanced back in time to see a cat trotting jauntily across the courtyard with a baby rat wriggling in its jaws.

24

The stairs were extremely steep and Lesage's breast swelled with excitement with each step downwards. He could scarcely believe how well his plan was coming to fruition. Not only would he soon be free of this damnable witch, he would be wealthier than he had ever dreamed. Thousands of livres, buried by some foolish old duke many years before. Money. Freedom. Soon he would have plenty of both.

At the bottom of the stairs, Lesage held the candle aloft. Although its light was thin as gruel, he could see they were in a large and crumbling cellar with high, vaulted ceilings. It was the cellar of the townhouse for a former monastery, where the monks stored olives and wine to sell at market. It was damp. Hot candle wax dripped onto his knuckles. He consulted his map again. His hands were shaking and his breathing was shallow. He was so excited that he stared at the map for some time, uncomprehending, before realising he was holding it the wrong way around. "Ah. In the . . . south wall there should be a door leading to another part of the cellar. The money is behind a rock in a tunnel through there. Come. It's this way."

They crossed the cellar and began moving aside old sacks and barrels and pieces of rubble and timber as quickly as they could. It wasn't long before Lesage located the battered wooden door. It was waist high, with a brass handle in the shape of a child's hand. The hand's knuckles shone with wear. He could scarcely believe it. "It's here," he whispered. "It's here. As the map says."

With some effort, Lesage wrenched the door open and, holding the candle in front of him, peered through into another dark passageway. "Come," he said to Madame Picot.

Almost on hands and knees, he clambered through the doorway, followed by Madame Picot. Once inside, he held the candle high. It did not look promising. More piles of plaster and broken rock, like the leavings of a quarry. The tunnel in which they found themselves seemed to stretch far into the distance, much further than their paltry candlelight could illuminate. A musty breeze, like a man's dying breath, arrived from its furthest reaches.

"The treasure should be hidden behind a large stone with an eight-pointed star scratched into it," he said, and began scouring the walls, running his hands over the rough and crumbling bricks. He felt nothing aside from slicks of moss, rusted bolts and occasional lengths of old chain. Deeper and deeper into the tunnel he ventured, stumbling over debris and broken rocks.

What if the witch had been right—what if there was no treasure, or it had already been taken? It wasn't likely, for Bertrand had assured him that he possessed the only map in existence, but it was possible. Lesage pressed on, his enthusiasm somewhat diminished. A shadow fell across his heart at consideration of the fate of the poor blacksmith, not to mention his own destiny. His conviction that the treasure existed was the only thing that had given him determination enough to survive his years in the galleys; but what if this was proven to be false? What then? He paused and looked around. At his feet lay a coil of rusted chain and at his shoulder were rough stone blocks, their surfaces scored with the markings of the tools from which they had been hewn. Dear God. He muttered a solemn prayer under his breath—for poor Bertrand, for himself—and, strangely, the words upon his tongue were like a balm.

Then, there, to his astonishment, almost directly in front of him: a large block of stone with an eight-pointed star scratched into its surface, its dimensions roughly that of a man's splayed hand. Lesage stepped back. He was panting and, despite the cellar's cold air, his brow was slick with sweat. He could barely speak. During those long years in the dungeons and galleys among those common criminals he had thought himself cursed, but now the opposite appeared to be true. It was merely the shape of things was so difficult to discern; hidden away it was, like the bones beneath one's skin.

"There it is," he managed to say eventually, and in the confined, echoless space his voice sounded thin and weak.

Madame Picot peered over his shoulder. "What is that written underneath it?"

Lesage held the candle up and peered closer. The witch was right. Below the star, a word was scratched into the stone. He wiped away some of the loose dust. "It's Latin. *Cave.*"

"What does that mean?"

He did not like to say it aloud. "It means: Beware."

The candle flame flickered in a draught, bent low, then wriggled upright. Lesage was uneasy. He had been involved in many magical ceremonies over the years and they never failed to infuse him with fear, for one never really knew exactly what would happen. There were countless tales of men and women being molested by those they had sought to control. The Spaniard, for instance, who was driven mad and threw himself from a belltower; the furrier from Toulouse who was devoured—skin and hair and nails and all; the woman who was afterwards compelled by them to murder a baby. Catherine had always said of demons, *Treat them as you would a disobedient child.* Spirits were violent, temperamental and greedy by nature and it was evident that Madame Picot, despite her powers, was inexperienced in these matters.

Madame Picot touched a hand to her shoulder. "When I

was injured, I had a strange encounter. A meeting with Hellequin, the overseer of the Wild Horde."

Lesage scrutinised the witch for signs of mockery or pretence, but she appeared as candid as ever. She stared at the ground and, in that strange moment, imbued with such stillness, and with candlelight flickering on her cheek, she resembled a statue. Most unexpectedly, Lesage was reminded of how his mother had been in the weeks after his brother drowned, her expression that of a woman resigned to perpetual sorrow. It seemed an eel squirmed through his heart at consideration of his family; it had been so many years since he had thought of Pierre—or his mother, for that matter—and decades since the terrible day suddenly brought to mind. "Hellequin? You spoke with him? Truly?"

"You have not seen this creature?"

"Of course not."

Madame Picot appeared annoyed at this response. "He is a tall man. He rides a black horse. His breath smells of bones and old meat. You know, I have wondered more than once in the past few days if I have been transported to hell. This city is . . . "

Lesage shuddered at the thought. "Oh no, madame. I can assure you that there are a great many people in Paris who are very much alive."

She hesitated for a moment. "He told me that death is a great palace with many rooms and magnificent gardens. A place with no earthly concerns, free of disease and pain. It sounded . . . very peaceful."

"Perhaps it was a dream, madame? Or a vision?"

"I fear he was attempting to lure me to my own death."

"Or to console you for the deaths of those you have loved."

Although outwardly calm, it was clear Madame Picot was in the grip of a delirium. Grief was an unpredictable burden for a woman; it killed or deranged some, yet made warriors of others.

His own mother had not coped well after Pierre's death, and he feared that Madame Picot was also of the former variety.

"Tell me, monsieur, what do you recall of that place? The place from where I summoned you? Were you free of disease and pain, as Hellequin told me?"

Lesage grunted bitterly. Hardly. "I think the man you spoke with was a liar, madame. Perhaps for some particularly vile men it resembles a garden or palace, but for me it was nothing like that at all. Before we left Paris, they branded us so we might be more easily identified should we escape."

"Is that the Devil's mark then, on your forearm?"

Again he was disturbed by how much the woman knew; she couldn't have seen the brand, for he was most careful to hide it beneath his sleeve at all times. The Devil's mark, indeed. It was as good a name for it as any. "When we finally arrived in the dungeons we were beaten and shackled. We rowed all day long in the summer. There were battles with filthy Turks and the Genoese. The winters were spent locked in the port prison, but it was not much better there. Men volunteered to pull the bodies of fever victims from the streets to get out of the prison for an afternoon. I saw so many horrible things. Each day was an eternity."

Madame Picot looked at him with the confused expression of one who has been roused from a deep slumber. She squatted and began to scratch a circle on the ground with her knife. "They say that all things might be forgiven. Do you think that is true?"

Only those who have sinned terribly need to believe such a thing, he thought, although he said nothing. He felt an intense urge to piss. "Make sure there is no break in the circle," he reminded her. "And we must stay inside it. Whatever happens. Whatever they might say."

The woman was clearly afraid. Her eyes were dull and her mouth was tight, as if sealed against the very air. "I know this," she snapped. "But tell me: how many spirits are there? Does your secret map tell us that?"

"I'm not sure. One or two, I think. The demon named Baicher is the master of hidden treasure. He is the most . . . the most dangerous, I've heard."

"What does he look like? Is he terrible?"

Lesage tugged at his sleeves. "That I don't know for certain, but I think so, yes. They might take any human or animal shape."

The crow fretted and flapped in its cage. Perhaps the creature knew something. Yes. Probably. So close now. So close. At Madame Picot's invitation, he stepped into the circle she had scratched onto the ground.

"Should you not take the crow from its cage?" she asked.

"I'm sorry, madame. Wait one moment." He placed the cage on the ground. Unable to suppress the inconvenient bodily urge any longer, he scurried along the tunnel until he was out of her sight and pissed against the wall. Sweet relief. Then he returned, stepped into the circle and removed the thick cloth covering the cage. Then, using the cloth as a makeshift glove, he grasped the unwilling crow and angled it through the cage door.

"Are you prepared?" she asked.

"Yes, yes. Say the spell, woman. Let's be done with it and get away from here. I do not like this place one bit."

Madame Picot gave him a cold look before taking out her black book and holding it unopened in her hand. She seemed to be taking a long time. Then, instead of reading the book, she closed her eyes and gripped it tighter, as if absorbing the conjurations through her skin. What on earth was she doing?

Lesage waited for Madame Picot to begin, but before she said a word, her eyes snapped open and she swung about to stare along the tunnel, into the inky darkness beyond the candle's light. With her free hand she crossed herself.

"Dear God," she said. "I can hear them."

"What, madame? Hear what?"

"Demons."

Lesage stood absolutely still, but he couldn't hear anything. A distant plink of dripping water, then silence. The crow struggled under the cloth in his hands; he could feel its delicate bones, its tiny thrashing heart. Then it fell still. He looked around, sick with fear and anticipation. Again he listened. Still nothing. He was about to tell the witch to hurry when he heard them. Madame Picot was right. Voices, yes, certainly those of demons, even a chilling shriek of laughter that uncoiled from the darkest reaches of the cavern. This was followed by some vile and tuneless singing: "*Hands on her hips, the little Antichrist wheezes, and howls and swears by the death of Jesus. Oh, I'm a dirty old man and a whore suits me fine . . .*"

"Stand fast," he sputtered, although he himself had a powerful compulsion to flee. "And don't step out of the circle or we will both be devoured."

25

Lesage cowered as the voices drew closer. More hideous cackling. Presently, a man and woman stumbled from the tunnel's gloom, growing larger as they approached, their features becoming more distinct. They were a rough-looking pair indeed, wild-haired and grinning at some private joke as they lurched along arm in arm. Upon seeing Lesage and Madame Picot, however, they halted their carousing and drew apart, but shakily, as if only by holding each other had they stayed upright at all.

The fellow was fat and greasy-cheeked, wigless, but with a cloth cap on his head. In contrast, his companion was pinched, with the waxy complexion and demeanour—cringing, but defiant—of a woman much used, doubtless in assorted unpleasant ways. If Lesage did not know the two strangers, he was at least familiar with the type of dangerous and unpre-dictable people they had undoubtedly been when alive; the drunken boor and his boorish whore, each made bolder by the villainy of their crony.

The man scratched his face and looked unsmilingly back and forth between Lesage and Madame Picot. "Who are you?" he demanded. Then, when he received no answer: "What are you doing down here?"

"We might ask the same of you, monsieur," replied Lesage after a short silence in which it was clear Madame Picot was not prepared—or not able—to answer.

"No business of yours, my friend."

"As is ours here none of yours."

The unpleasant fellow nodded at this—as if Lesage's response accorded with the unfavourable impression he had already formed of him. Then he snorted energetically and turned aside to spit thickly against the wall. He wiped spittle from his mouth before again regarding Lesage and Madame Picot with a wary contempt. He peered over Lesage's shoulder. "Who else is with you two?"

"Nobody," said Lesage.

This was true, and yet, quite unnerved, Lesage glanced behind. There was nothing, of course. Only the darkness, their own shadows juddering along the wall in the candle's light, the door through which they had come.

He waited for Madame Picot to perform her banishing spell—to do or say anything—but it seemed she had been struck dumb in the presence of these two curious fiends. He elbowed her, but could elicit no response. The crow wedged under his arm, which had been silent until this moment, squirmed and squawked forlornly.

The strangers flinched and exchanged nervous glances. "What have you under that cloth, monsieur?" the woman asked. She affected a gruff tone of voice, but it was plain to see she was afraid.

"It's only a bird," Lesage said.

"A bird? A *bird*? What for? Who are you people?"

Still Madame Picot was silent; clearly it was up to Lesage to deal with these horrible creatures. Thinking to ingratiate himself somehow, he bowed. "I am the magician Lesage and this is Madame Picot, the Forest Queen."

The woman snickered and wiped her nose along her chalky wrist. "The Forest Queen, eh? I see. Which forest would this be? Up to mischief, I'll bet. Well, this is my patch down here, sweetheart, not the fucking forest. No trees in these tunnels that I can see. Anyway, I don't remember seeing you here before."

Silence followed. Lesage sensed a cool breeze emanating from the darkness behind the strangers. He glanced at Madame Picot, who was as immobile as a statue. Her lips were cracked and strands of hair had unravelled from beneath her scarf and hung loose around her temples. In one hand she clutched her black book. Why would she not do anything? Perhaps these demons had already performed some diabolical trick on her? Either that or Madame Picot was lying about her book containing a spell to evict them, even though she had boasted of it. She blinked, and something throbbed in her neck, but in all other ways she was inert.

With a nod of her bony chin, the woman indicated Madame Picot. "Why does this Forest Queen of yours not say anything? Tongue stuck in her pocket, eh? Eh?"

Perhaps emboldened by the whore's witticism and by Madame Picot's continued inaction, the fellow produced a pistol from his belt and, brandishing it in front of him, took several steps towards them. "I'll shoot you in the face and then cut out your tongue and stick it in *my* pocket if you don't say something, bitch."

Terrified, Lesage took a step backwards, almost stumbling in his haste. "Say it, madame," he hissed. "*Do something.*"

The fat fellow holding the pistol hesitated—puzzled, somewhat fearful. "Say what?" A pause. "What is it exactly you are doing down here?"

His whore grabbed his upper arm and pointed to the ground at Lesage and Madame Picot's feet. "Look! They're standing in a circle. Be careful, Louis. I think they are witches."

The fellow nodded assent, then wrestled with the flintlock of his pistol before aiming it at them. "No. I think they look more like devils. Are you devils?"

The man waved the gun around and, as he took another step towards him, Lesage felt his guts slacken. A groan escaped his lips. *Pater Noster*, he thought, don't let me come so close to my treasure only to have me killed at the final test.

"Are you devils?" the man repeated.

"No," Lesage stammered. "I am a . . . man."

The woman grinned. Her teeth glinted like tools when she spoke. "Prove it to us. Prove you are a man."

Lesage opened his mouth to speak, but could make no sound. He stared at the pistol's long and narrow barrel. What could he say? How to prove he was a man? How to itemise for them the myriad ways he felt pain, or love, or fear—if indeed these were signs of mortal life? He thought of his parents, of his wife Claudette. He recalled, inexplicably, a summer's afternoon when he was a boy and he tried to jump a low fence and failed, how his brother had laughed and laughed. The earthy flavour of bruised grass in his mouth, a yellow bug crawling along a fallen leaf, sun hot on his back. Life, his life.

The man pulled the trigger of his pistol. Lesage yelped and flinched, but the weapon failed to fire properly. Instead, it discharged no more than a disgruntled fizzle and flash. The man jumped back and swore as a loosed ember or shard of powder burned his wrist. The pistol clattered to the ground.

Then, finally, Madame Picot spoke, and her voice was loud and authoritative. "I conjure and exorcise Baicher to come to me by the three names of God, Eloy Afinay, Agla, Ely Lamazabatany, which were written in Hebrew, in Greek and in Latin, and by all the names which were written in this book, and by He who drove you from high in the heavens. I command you by the great living God and by the sainted Eucharist which delivers men from their sins that, without delay, you come and put me in possession of the treasure you own unjustly and leave without noise or smell or terror towards me."

The two fiends stared at them in alarm, their faces like milky puddles in the gloom.

"Take the crow and be gone," continued Madame Picot with a wave of one hand. "*Venite. Venite. Ainsi soit-il.*"

With shaking hands Lesage unhooded the crow and held the creature out, its claws gripping his skin like the talons of a shrunken witch. He shrank back; the crow, after all, was a clever and most sinister bird. But rather than flying off, as he would have expected, the bird merely hopped from his hand to the floor, where it shrugged its glossy black feathers back into place and looked around with displeasure, its black eyes glinting. Lesage half expected the creature to speak—pass sentence, perhaps, in a provost's grave and scrupulous tones.

All four of them stepped backwards and stared at the crow with trepidation. The bird stretched its wings experimentally before taking several steps towards the two strangers. Then it flattened its body and opened its beak to caw its terrible caw. The strangers winced. The woman gasped and gripped the man's arm. She pulled him away and they moved silently backwards, far beyond the candle's wan light, as if sinking beneath black waters. The crow then cocked its head as if in silent discourse with itself before launching into the darkness after them. The clatter of its wings—the sound like that of a woman shaking out her cloak—was followed by another shriek from the far reaches of the tunnel, some distant swearing. Then nothing more.

It was a terrifying ordeal. Lesage bent down to retrieve the pistol and turned to Madame Picot. They waited, for what exactly he couldn't be sure. Another sign, perhaps. The candle flame flickered. Lesage put his hand to his cheek, felt his own body's anxious tremble and jerk. His apprehension was replaced by fury. "Why the hell did you not act sooner, woman? He might have killed me. Killed us both, for that matter. What were you doing?"

Madame Picot didn't answer. Her gaze was fixed on her hand—the one with its wound—and on the book, as if she had been unaware of them until this moment. "I was too afraid to speak," she murmured. "I'm sorry."

Lesage closed his eyes and crossed himself. "*Ave Maria.*" Opening his eyes, he inspected the heavy pistol before jamming it into his belt.

Madame Picot closed her book. "That was most strange."

"Yes. A devilish pair. Did you notice how they travelled without lanterns, without any light at all? Horrible creatures. Do you think they have gone?"

"Yes. It seems so."

They waited a while longer but detected no further sign of the unwelcome pair. Finally, with trembling hands, Lesage set about shifting the stone block bearing the star and the inscription. He could scarcely believe what was happening. A dream? Dear God, who knew? But no. The rock was hard and rough beneath his hands; this was certainly a real thing, at least. Its corners crumbled as he wrestled with it, but eventually, by setting his shoulder to its rough bulk and pulling it back and forth a number of times, he dislodged it. The sound of it thumping on the ground echoed along the tunnel, prompting them both to peer anxiously into its darkness for any further signs of those they had recently dispatched.

Lesage took up the candle and peered into the space he had exposed. He thrust a hand through. Another prayer under his breath, to whomever might listen. Please. After everything I have endured, do I not deserve some wealth, some success? He touched something that felt like a leather-bound trunk. Yes, a trunk! His heart jumped.

Still with his arm deep in the hole, he swung around to Madame Picot. "Help me. Quickly. I've found it!"

Together they dragged the trunk from the gritty crawl space. It was secured with a padlock but the iron was old and corroded, and Lesage was able to break it off easily with a rock. He flipped open the lid with shaking hands. And there, anticipated but also so surprising—like a baby's birth—were coins and other items of treasure. Money. Treasure. Freedom. *At last.* Even Madame Picot was pleased and they embraced clumsily with the sudden joy and relief of it.

Dawn was breaking by the time Lesage and Madame Picot returned with the trunk to the room on Rue Françoise. The trunk contained treasure from all sorts of countries. Thalers, Roman and Spanish coins, doubloons, an assortment of bejewelled necklaces and rings. There were also hundreds of livres in the trunk, perhaps thousands—enough to free the woman's son, with plenty left over for him. As if he were a parched man and the coins water, he sifted them in his hands as a terrible pleasure coursed through him.

26

It was late morning when Lesage met his countryman Willem outside the tavern where they had encountered each other the previous evening. They travelled in a hired carriage as far as La Porte Saint-Antoine, then walked along a broad road into the nearby countryside. Farmhouses loomed here and there over fields and orchards in which the heads of field workers bobbed around in the heat haze as if on green and fragrant seas.

The day was growing hotter and they conversed little as they walked. This Willem was a scraggly, ill-built fellow—a scarecrow broken free from his post—and Lesage trusted him even less in the daylight than he had the previous night. He held a hand protectively across his satchel containing the money. What if this were an elaborate ruse to rob him? Away from the shadows and alleyways of the city, he felt alone and rather exposed. The sunlight, all these birds, strangers, the horizon. A carriage rumbled past, leaving in its wake a drift of woman's laughter, like petals strewn along the road; doubtless some nobles on the way to their country estate.

"Where is this place?" Lesage asked, stopping for a moment to wipe his face with his scarf. "Is it much further?"

"Perhaps another league or so. Do you see that hill over there?"

Lesage squinted into the distance. He saw stands of cypress trees, occasional huts and houses, windmills endlessly churning. A man on horseback moved through a field and Lesage was reminded of the tale he'd told the stupid tavern keeper Scarron—of monkeys riding on the backs of dolphins. Eventually he made out the low, wooded hill Willem was pointing to, a patch of green darker than its surrounds.

"And can you see the house to the side? It's there, monsieur."

"You're sure Nicolas will be at the house? It's most important to me that he is safe and well."

"If you have the money, they will have the boy. I have already sent them word. They are waiting for us. Across the field there. Not far now, monsieur. Don't worry—they will provide a carriage for our return."

Willem must have noted the puzzlement in Lesage's eyes, for he went on: "Sometimes the children resist being taken. They expect something terrible to happen to them. And we do not wish for anyone to notice boys coming and going, do we? Especially in the condition they are sometimes in."

They left the road and tramped through a wood of birch and maple trees, their trunks bristling with glossy ivy. It was cool and peaceful after the harsh sun. Bees lumbered in the dappled light and bracken crunched underfoot. Lesage wanted to lie down and rest in the shade, but felt the nagging urgency of his task. Soon, he thought. Soon he would be free at last. Free of Madame Picot and—thanks to the treasure—free of La Voisin, too. Then he could lie down in glades as much as he wished.

After telling Madame Picot about his sons at La Filastre's, he had started thinking; perhaps he could return to Normandy and be finished at last with La Voisin, Mariette and the rest of those scoundrels—those vile abortionists, poisoners, witches, priests and conjurers; that entire realm working away industriously beneath the world, like worms and beetles beneath the forest floor. Yes. Why not? The treasure had been as plentiful as he had hoped, and, with it, there would be no need for him to help La Voisin or Guibourg or any of them. He might escape their nasty domain. He had been fortunate to be sentenced to the galleys on the last occasion instead of being executed, but if he were caught engaging in such impieties again, not even God himself—let alone Madame Picot—would be able to summon him back to the world of the living.

There was, of course, the matter of Catherine, who was highly sensitive to even the merest hint that she was being spurned; he had seen her roused to inarticulate fury at the slightest suspicion a customer was thinking of visiting another sorceress in Paris. Those who facilitated betrayal in others were often the most sensitive to it. God alone knew how she would receive knowledge of his intended departure, but he could always attempt to mollify her. He would buy her a gift. Some wine, perhaps? No, he would need something more than that. A bonnet or some perfume from one of the luxury stores? New shoes? He shook off thoughts of her. He would consider that particular problem later.

They emerged from the forest into bright sunlight and crossed a muddy stream. The house was a short distance away, its tall windows shining in the sun. Lesage and Willem approached and mounted some stairs. At the top, in the shade of the large house, bright red geraniums tumbled over the sides of large pots with nymphs carved on their rims. From nearby drifted the reassuring noise of a fountain. A servant wearing blue livery and carrying a large silver platter under one arm nodded to Willem in greeting as he trotted around a corner. Willem opened a side door and ushered Lesage through a warren of humid kitchens and storerooms in which cooks and maids bustled about, none of whom paid them the slightest attention; obviously Willem was a familiar sight.

Willem tugged on a rope hanging by one wall and presently a footman appeared. The two of them conversed in low tones. When they had finished, the footman spun on his heel and walked away. Willem indicated for Lesage to follow and together they walked through more tunnels until they arrived at a cellar stocked with dried meat and barrels of wine. Braces of rabbits and pheasants hung from ceiling hooks. Lesage's anxiety was only barely allayed by the promise of finally securing the boy's release—and freeing himself from Madame Picot's power. He sensed the twitch at his cheek.

The footman turned to Lesage, acknowledging him for the first time. "He says you have money for one of the boys?"

"Yes. The one called Nicolas."

"Two hundred livres? Show it to me."

Lesage opened his satchel and pulled out the smaller sack into which he had placed the amount needed to buy Nicolas's freedom. He began to explain who the boy was in relation to him and why he, Lesage, was here, but the footman silenced him with a wave of his hand.

The footman sighed and began counting out the coins on a low table. This took a long time. When it was done, he slipped several coins to Willem and took up a three-pronged candelabrum. Without another word, he led them up a dim stone stairway until they emerged into a room with a parquetry floor that squeaked beneath their shoes. The footman handed the candelabrum to Willem while he drew aside the corner of an enormous coloured tapestry bearing the scene of a boar hunt. Men on horses, dogs with spiked collars, a tusked boar running for its life across a clearing. With a huge key on a ring taken from his pocket, the footman unlocked a door hidden behind the tapestry. Lesage recoiled. From the dark passageway that had been exposed there emanated a powerful and all-too-familiar dungeon smell.

Lesage's eye was drawn to a painting of King Louis high on the opposite wall. In the scene, the King was wearing buckled black shoes, white hose and a luxurious black wig that tumbled over his shoulders. A magnificent blue and white ermine-trimmed cloak cascaded like a foaming sea on the carpet around him. His right hand rested on a gold sceptre and a gold sword hung at his left hip. Red curtains embroidered with gold thread billowed behind, an intimation of a thick black column. Power and restraint, beauty and terror. France's king was known to be wise and witty, to have an enormous appetite for women and food. Those who had met him all agreed he was charming company, but from the painting he gazed down upon Lesage with an expression of benign disapproval. Lesage wondered what King Louis was doing at that moment. Entertaining courtiers, eating vast mouthfuls of suckling pig, lounging naked in bed with one of his lovely mistresses? He might have been put on the throne by God Himself, but did he have the slightest clue, this king, about what happened across his vast realm? Did he know about Catherine Monvoisin and her sorceries or of the lengths to which Athénaïs de Montespan had gone to swell his heart—not to mention his cock? Did he know how many men and women of his own court journeyed from the palace at Saint-Germain to a pavilion in Villeneuve where they paid the drunken wife of a failed jeweller to cast spells, fashion amulets or organise black masses to secure his continued patronage?

The footman bade them enter. Willem crouched low and indicated for Lesage to follow. Then he disappeared from sight. Lesage felt sick. He glanced away and muttered a prayer. The clacking of the footman's shoes on the wooden floor grew faint as he attended to duties in other parts of the huge house. Outside, glimpsed through the window's rippled glass, he saw a young woman on a gravel path playing with a brown terrier. He heard the dog's yelp and her soft laughter, saw lawns stretching green to the darkness of the distant forest.

27

Charlotte heard scuffling noises coming from the passage outside her room. It's Nicolas, she thought. My son. So soon, at last. She leaped up from her stool and opened the door.

But, instead, it was the troubadour girl, Marguerite, who began to cry as soon as she saw Charlotte. "My mother is dead," she sobbed, and fell into her arms.

Charlotte embraced her. The girl's entire body shook as she wept.

"She should have known," the girl was saying between breaths, "she should have known to stay away from the river. Lesage saw it in her cards. He warned her about water, but she still went to visit a friend who worked on the quay."

Charlotte recalled the scene by the river when she and Lesage had come across the poor drowned woman. Lesage seemed shocked—not only by the sight of the woman's corpse, apparently, but at the fact that he had forewarned her of such a fate.

Charlotte's shoulder grew damp with tears. How terrible it was to lose one's mother so young. She searched for the words with which others had comforted her in her own times of mourning, but they were meagre pickings: faith and prayer, life and the afterlife, where all former things have passed away. There was nothing to be said; death, after all, was the final word.

Eventually, the girl stopped crying and Charlotte led her to the lumpy mattress on the floor. "Has she been buried yet?" she asked.

Marguerite shook her head. "It will be later today. My father is most distraught and has hired mourners at some expense. He is already sick from grief himself. He was out all night. This morning some friends brought him back to the fair and he was dirty, and as drunk as a bellringer. The performance cannot go ahead today, of course. We'll have no money if we cannot work, and we'll be ruined."

Charlotte had always thought of grief as a nasty unwanted visitor who encouraged the bereaved to act in ways contrary to their true natures. Grief took them carousing or goaded them to fight in the street. Sometimes he lured them to their own deaths, or forbade them to speak at all. And—this worst of all—he whispered the names of the dead in your ear, over and again; the things you should have done; the words you should have said; his bony finger tap-tap-tapping against your heart.

When their daughters died, she and Michel retreated into their own private silences, where they remained for so long, careful with each other, barely touching, as if fearful their hearts were made of glass and might break. They didn't speak. When at home, Michel gnawed on his pipe while Charlotte went more often than necessary to her vegetable garden, where she made a show of tending her crop, for only there could she succumb to the urge to sag to her knees. *Why did you not seek help sooner?* Tap. *Why did you not see they were sick?* Tap. *Why did you not pray harder, woman?* Tap. Henceforth, the smell of fresh leeks always reminded her of that bitter summer. With Philippe it was different; he was barely formed, and Charlotte herself was only seventeen years old; it was as if she didn't have time enough to know how best to love him before he was taken from her.

"Sorrow makes people do strange things," she murmured. "Your father will return to you soon enough."

Marguerite gazed around the room with her head angled to compensate for her bad eye, a mannerism that gave her the bearing of one listening to voices in other rooms. "Did you find your own son, madame?" she asked.

Charlotte nodded. "Yes. Lesage has gone to fetch him and bring him here. They will be here any moment. When I heard you on the stairs I thought you were him."

The girl managed a crumpled smile. "Ah. That is good, at least. Something good."

"Yes. It is. He is alive and well. He should be back here soon and we will return to our country."

They listened to the noises from the street outside. A child singing a nonsensical rhyme, a butter vendor, pigeons on the roof. "*Beurre frais, beurre frais . . .*"

Marguerite wiped her nose. "Do you still remember your own children, madame? What they looked like, I mean?"

She took the girl's hand and stroked it. "Yes. Of course I do. How could I forget them? Béatrice was pale, with freckles. She hated to wear a bonnet, even in winter. A serious child. Sturdy, I would have thought, not fearful of anything. But Aliénor was—what?—she seemed older than her years. Always telling Béatrice what to do, tugging her along; you know how girls are sometimes. But cheerful, always finding something to laugh about. Clumsy as a foal, my husband used to say. I was holding her hand, like this, when she died, and looking her in the eye as if I might keep her in this world with me. We sat like that for a long time, but for one moment I glanced away at something Michel said, and when I looked back she was gone—as if she had merely slipped out the window."

"To heaven."

"To heaven," Charlotte said at last. "Yes." She paused until her breathing regained its balance. "You'll not forget your mother, Marguerite. Don't worry. You'll always carry her with you."

Perhaps seeking to lighten the atmosphere, Marguerite fumbled beneath her blouse and retrieved the amulet containing the pigeon's heart that Charlotte had assembled for her.

"I am wearing your charm around my neck, madame. As you told me."

Charlotte felt a fresh surge of affection for the girl and squeezed her hand, unsure whether to be envious of her as-yet-unlived future—or fearful. Life and all its endless variations. There was no order to it. "Good girl. Remember to bury it where your handsome man will pass by. You need a husband now more than ever, for he can help your family."

Marguerite nodded. Then she began to weep again.

Charlotte embraced her, felt her shoulder bones moving beneath her clothes, beneath her skin. "Your father will come back to you. I promise. I can tell he is a decent man. Grief will have its way with him for a while, but he will take care of you. Your mother's death is a terrible loss for him. And for you."

But the girl shook her head. There was something else. "I need your help again, madame. Monsieur Lesage told my mother to take special care with baby Jean. He said he could die of plague. The card he drew for him was terrible. I saw it. It was a skeleton. Can you make a charm for him, for his protection? Please. I know you can. *Please.* My brother is so weak. I'll pay you, of course."

"Where is your baby brother now?"

"He is with my uncle. He does not want him to be too far from his sight. He cries all the time."

It was unclear if she were referring to the baby or her uncle, Monsieur Boucher. Charlotte considered the poor girl before placing her left hand on her book and closing her eyes. *Paper blessed by a priest on which are written prayers to Saint Roque. Lavender flowers, dragon seeds, amulets bound with twine and sprinkled with the purest vinegar. Save us from such vile pestilence and fevers. Praetectio. Place the charm around the neck and wear it at all times.*

She opened her eyes. "I have none of the ingredients to make such a charm, Marguerite."

The girl wiped tears from her face and scrambled to her feet. "There is an apothecary near the fair at Saint-Germain, on the other side of the river—Monsieur Maigret on Rue des Canettes. He has everything. He is the best in Paris, they all say. He'll have what you need. Come, madame. We can go there now."

Marguerite's eagerness was heartbreaking, but Charlotte shook her head. "No. I cannot leave here. Not now. I have to wait for Nicolas. I can visit the apothecary later. Come back tonight. And bring your brother with you. I was intending to leave Paris as soon as Lesage returned with Nicolas, but I'll wait for you."

28

Even with only three of them travelling in it, the carriage was stuffy and felt extremely crowded. Its shades were drawn and Lesage was forced to sit sideways on his bench to avoid touching the boy's bloodied knees with his new breeches. The added disadvantage with this awkward sitting position was that it brought him into even closer contact with Willem's sweat-damp thighs and grubby elbows. His many years on the galleys—chained day and night to other convicts—had instilled in Lesage a horror of other men's bodies and a suspicion they were composed primarily of lice, wretched oaths, pus-filled sores and blisters. Truly a debased half of humanity.

He was unnerved, too, by the boy's miserable condition—not to mention the experience in taking him from the house. Rather than resist it, as Willem had warned he would, Nicolas had meekly acquiesced to being led from the cellar, even though—as he made clear—he was certain his fate was to be used in some vile manner by the criminal gangs of Paris. He'd already seen what happened, he'd said, and no amount of reassurance was enough to allay these fears. Willem's snickering and general sinister demeanour had certainly not helped.

Lesage had told Nicolas that he was taking him to see his mother, to which the boy had merely nodded and said, "Well, that is a curious thing, because my mother is dead."

"No, no, no," Lesage had replied. "She is not dead at all. No. This is the miraculous thing. The injury was not as bad as she first thought. She is not well, certainly, but she is not dead. I saw her already this morning, Nicolas. She is very eager to see you once more. Please. You must believe me—I intend you no harm. Quite the opposite, in fact."

But the boy clearly did not believe him at all. And, now, as they travelled in the carriage, Nicolas sat with his hands tied together in his lap, staring over Lesage's shoulder—like a cur avoiding the eye of the man he knows to be the instrument of his demise. If the boy had ever possessed any fight, then it had clearly been squeezed from him by his time entombed in that cellar. Hardly surprising, Lesage supposed, considering the horrible state of the place and the other boys held there— its reek of shit, blood on the floor, wet straw and weak murmurs.

Nicolas muttered something incomprehensible. The boy lisped slightly, probably on account of the cut on his upper lip. There was also a thread of blood between his two front teeth.

Lesage leaned forward slightly. "Pardon?"

"You seem a decent fellow, monsieur." A glance at Willem, as if to make clear this decency was only relative to his companion. "Perhaps you might untie me? My wrists are so sore."

Lesage knew the pain of captivity only too well, but he could not risk the boy escaping before he'd been delivered safely to Madame Picot; after all, his own freedom depended wholly on it. He shook his head. "I'll not be at ease, Nicolas, until you're safe in your mother's arms. We have come a long way to find you, and at great risk. I'll not take any chances now. Don't fret, there's not too far to go."

They had entered through the city's eastern gate and were travelling along Rue Saint-Antoine, past the Jesuit church and the Hôtel de Ville. The clamour of Paris filled the air outside the carriage—merchants and maids, voices and clatter. The carriage driver called out to someone beside the road and urged his horses on with a wild curse. There was the smell of burnt wood, a song sung by a girl, laughter fading away to nothing as they shuddered to a stop.

Then, quite suddenly, the sounds of the street gave way to a lone voice crying out, hoarse and urgent. Alarmed, Lesage drew aside the shabby curtain and recoiled momentarily from the blinding burst of daylight. When his eyesight had adjusted, he squinted through the window. He saw crowds of men and women of all descriptions, a boy with a sack of apples at his waist, a donkey, a cobbler with his box of tools slung over a shoulder. There were pilgrims setting forth on their journeys, merchants selling candles and crosses. And, above the heads of the assembled crowd, a thin, bearded man with arms outflung in appeal. It was the same monk he had seen preaching on Rue Saint-Denis several days earlier. Yes, the fellow was still at it.

His audience had grown. It spilled all over the road and had wedged their cart in, preventing it from moving forward. The carriage driver yelled at the crowd to part so they might pass, but he was no Moses, the crowd no Red Sea, and no one paid him the slightest attention.

The monk's voice, meanwhile, was swelling with passion as he paced back and forth and delivered his wild prophecies. "Fear the abyss!" he was saying. "This city—with its whores and thieves, its unbelievers" (a chortle from the crowd; of pride or indignation, it was hard to tell) "—you can feel it in the air here. You can smell it on the women, despite their *civet* and their *rosewater*. The men, with their . . . disgusting habits and clothes. Decadence, sodomy, all manner of sin. There are those who murder children and drink their blood. Yes. There are! You know this to be true as well as I do. All that you can imagine exists. Witchcraft, pacts with the Devil. I sense there are those among you here today who have indulged in all manner of despicable acts, who have allowed your darker selves to reign in the kingdom of your soul. Why? *Why?* Because we are all sinners. We are all wicked. We are all doomed. The end is coming. Oh, yes. I have heard the word of the Lord. I have listened to the Lord. Allow me to tell you what happened, friends. Out there in the fields where I lived near Rodez, He came to me, while others quailed in the face of fevers and plague. To me alone. Because I believed. He came as a great light, a great voice, all thunder and noise. The clouds were churning, the trees caught fire, birds fell like rocks from the sky. A terrible thing it was, and I fell to the ground and covered my head and trembled. Like a lamb I trembled! Soon now, He told me. Infidels are at the gates. Fear the scourge, oh yes. Fear the barbarians. Fear apocalypse and damnation. But it is not too late. No. Go forth and tell them. Save them. Save their souls."

Crowds in Paris usually had little patience for these sorts of itinerants; Lesage had seen them beaten away with rotten fruit and scraps of offal, with curses and mockery and din. But for some reason, this fellow had struck them dumb and—despite his frustration at their lack of progress—Lesage was also oddly compelled. The preacher possessed an unusual urgency of delivery. With his weathered face and straggly beard, he resembled any number of preachers who roamed the land, and yet heads in this crowd nodded like rain-burdened stalks of wheat, as if what they heard were utterly new to them. Others muttered prayers or raised their hands in apparent spasms of ecstasy. A woman was weeping. The monk had stopped pacing and he searched the crowd with his hard, black eyes, assessing them, it seemed, with hope and regret, alighting here and there before moving on.

"The Kingdom of the Lord has no borders," the monk continued, his gaze still appraising them as if he were a ship's captain and they a storm-racked ocean through which he wished to chart a course. His voice then became so quiet that Lesage had to strain to hear what he was saying.

"The Kingdom of the Lord is not at all like this world.

And He will welcome you into His mansion of numberless rooms. He will forgive you. He will salve your wounds and ease your heart. All of you. The fallen butcher's wife, the greedy gem merchant who beats his three children. The boy who lies to his father about where he's been, who pinches his sister's arm when no one is looking. The girl with lust and avarice in her heart. The Lord knows everything about these men and women and children. He sees directly into their hearts. He knows of the merchant from Normandy who has been led astray by an evil assembly right here in Paris, who has committed unspeakable acts in exchange for money and power . . . "

The monk's gaze had, by this time, alighted—could it be?—on or near Lesage. He shrank back slowly, reluctant even to pull the curtain for fear of drawing further attention to himself. There followed a silence so lengthy and strange that members of the crowd turned to see what had caught the monk's eye. General murmurs, baby's bleat, the distant cry of a girl.

" . . . how he lied and deceived and has had so many dealings with demons and witches. Do not gasp in such a manner, good people. Do not *pretend*. You know as well as I do there are people in this very city who engage in terrible crimes. In magic and impieties. The Lord knows you are in pain, but there is relief at hand. There will be a reckoning. But there will be mercy, too. Imagine it. Hunger and disease no more. No agony or trouble, no heartache. But you must repent. Otherwise it will be hell and eternal damnation for you all. Here is the truth: if you do not go towards the reckoning, then the reckoning will surely one day come to you. Yes. And you will have to choose."

Lesage let the thick curtain drop. He reeled back and shut his eyes. Dear God. Dear God Almighty. The heat. It was the heat in this horrible carriage and the sun and the terrible strain of his predicament. The words of the raving monk retreated like an ebbing tide. "*The divine*," the monk was saying, his voice fading as if he—or perhaps it was Lesage—were drifting on those waters. "*The divine and the magnificent and it is there for us, we only need to choose.*" The words of the monk. The words of the monk. "*Damnation. Salvation. A reckoning.*" Words and clamour and the shuffling of the throng.

Then there was a new commotion, the ringing of a single bell becoming ever louder. Again Lesage peered out. The crowd's attention wavered, then drifted to some new spectacle further along the road. He followed their gaze. Heads turned, someone urged the mob to make way. Women leaned out from their windows. A group of people jostled their way through. Cowled heads, weeping women, children wailing, a bier for a corpse. It was a ragtag funeral cortège, as if conjured by the preacher himself.

The funeral procession was unable to pass and the two groups began to bicker. Lesage thought he recognised some members of the funeral party. Yes, one of those carrying the bier was the troubadour fellow. It was Monsieur Leroux, and the procession was for his wife Madame Leroux, who had drowned in the river. The girl's monkey was perched on her shoulder. Monsieur Leroux was haggard, drunk, and he remonstrated with a woman in his path, gently at first, but then with increasing hostility. Spittle flecked his beard. His grip on the bier's handle slipped and the body, wrapped in its burial sheet, sagged at one end. The others supporting it hurriedly compensated for the tilt, but a portion of the woman's sheet came adrift. One of her arms flopped free. A clawed, yellowed hand with bruised fingernails. A few boys jeered. A member of the funeral party punched someone, a woman screamed. A furore, the crowd was roiling now as a pair of rat-faced dogs squirmed through their legs.

Many years ago, Lesage had been in the Low Countries doing business with a burgher of Amsterdam called Egbert van

Roos, a self-important and fastidious fellow (as they so often were in that part of the world) who, as part of their transaction, insisted on escorting Lesage all over Amsterdam—a city of which this van Roos was most proud. Lesage had hoped to sell this man a fair quantity of wool, and so he bore Monsieur van Roos's amiable bullying in good humour. He ate a wide variety of pickled seafood—some of it quite repulsive—and generally partook in all manner of social intercourse with other merchants in the city. Guilds and fur-lined coats on broad-shouldered men, the discreet aromas of northern wealth. It was winter. The canals were rimed with ice and the streets treacherous with sleet. Upon leaving a tavern, Lesage, who was slightly drunk, slipped and tore his breeches at the knee, so Monsieur van Roos escorted him to his house, where the maid could mend his trousers and provide a bandage to sop the bleeding. The canal house was narrow, but the man's upstairs study, in which a fire blazed, was warm and smelled reassuringly of pipe tobacco and furniture polish. The man's family fussed about, running here and there fetching blankets and cushions. At one stage, Lesage was left alone on the narrow sofa, his head throbbing, feeling altogether unwell and not a little embarrassed at what had occurred and the trouble it had occasioned.

Hanging above the fireplace was a large painting that, at first glance, appeared to be no more than a dull mess, perhaps not even properly finished. Could it be the work of Monsieur van Roos himself, or a relative of his? The man certainly struck Lesage as the type to display his own amateurish efforts in his house. When his eyes adjusted to the light and afforded closer examination, however, the painting resolved itself into one of immense detail and skill. It was a scene of extravagant debauch. Hundreds—no, thousands—of tiny figures swarmed over a blighted landscape committing all manner of atrocities. Men were garrotted and impaled on spears. Armies of grinning skeletons rampaged on the horizon and swarmed from dark caves. Corpses in piles. Farting nuns, strange-faced priests, a dog licking blood from a dead child's face. A merchant was fucking a pig, a woman was hoisting her skirts for a goat. Great fires burned orange and the sky was dark with smoke. Vile creatures—half bird, half deer—played cards. Frogs wielded cutlasses, a bear wore antlers.

Lesage was familiar with depictions of damnation, but that night on the burgher's sofa he quailed, for he had never seen it illustrated in such ghastly and exhaustive detail. He could almost hear the cries of the wretched and the glee of those who pursued them.

He never discovered who had painted the monstrosity in Amsterdam—nor did he care. As soon as his knee was bandaged he made some hasty apologies to Monsieur van Roos and his family before fleeing into the freezing night as if the house were collapsing into the icy canal. The transaction with Egbert van Roos was never completed. The painting had horrified Lesage so deeply that he never mentioned it to a soul and, in fact, had banished its memory altogether—until that hot afternoon on the corner of Rue Saint-Denis and Rue des Lombards, when it seemed to be coming to life before him.

He let go of the thick carriage curtain, reeled back against his bench and shut his eyes. He scrambled through his doublet in search of a kerchief with which to wipe his face. No luck, but in one of his pockets he found instead the ball of wax containing the message Madame Picot had written to be delivered to the Devil. He was cheered at the thought that his sleight of hand had deceived not only a peasant like Madame Picot—no great claim, perhaps—but also a much worldlier woman like La Filastre. The wax was dirty from having been in his pocket. He prised it open with his thumbs and took out the folded piece of paper. *please where is my son nicolas please.* Madame Picot's writing was like that of a child's and he was unexpectedly affected by it. Merely lines on a piece of paper—but how much yearning they contained! He held the message in his hand for a long while. It was all anyone wanted, wasn't it? Their loved ones near them, safe and prosperous.

When at last he returned to himself, Lesage was startled to realise they had left the riotous funeral procession and were again lumbering north along Rue Saint-Denis. If Willem and the boy noticed anything amiss in his demeanour, they gave no outward sign of it. He wiped his sweating face on his sleeve.

The three of them travelled in silence for some time before the boy leaned forward. "Please, monsieur," he said. Then, when Lesage didn't answer, he went on. "Please. It's not too late to save yourself, no matter what evils you might have committed."

"I'm saving *you*, boy. There are some in this city who would murder you for their own purposes."

"You do not appear to be such a terrible man."

"And what would you know of my life?"

"Oh, but your life is written on your face, monsieur. It's not too late to save yourself from hell."

His *face*? He was tempted to slap the boy, but managed to restrain himself. The driver called out to his horses and the carriage shuddered to a halt. Willem pulled aside his shade. A sudden burst of daylight illuminated the boy's eager and despairing features, the blood on his lip, the frayed seam of the leather seat on which he slumped. Lesage would be most pleased to see the back of him.

"I think it's too late for that," Willem said with a chuckle as he dropped the curtain and the carriage returned to its upholstered gloom, "for we have arrived."

Lesage helped Nicolas from the carriage and escorted him beneath the archway into the cool courtyard. The boy looked around fearfully. Chickens fussed and clucked among the sticks of straw, a goat stared at them. Water trickled from the hand pump's spout. "Don't worry, boy," he said, "your mother is waiting for you up here."

Behind them the carriage rattled away. Gripping the boy's upper arm, Lesage guided him—perhaps more roughly than he needed, for the boy had irritated him with his whining—through a narrow door, along a passageway, up the dingy stairs. Murmur of other tenants from behind flimsy walls, the wail of a baby, a man's laughter.

Lesage was excited, not only at the prospect of his own imminent release from Madame Picot's power, but also—and this almost despite himself—for the woman herself. Clearly she had suffered a great deal in her life. Husband dead, three of her four children dead. Not an unusual story, to be sure, but no less terrible for that. He was pleased to think he might play a minor role in securing some happiness for the poor woman. He felt exceedingly pleased with himself that he had decided against Catherine's suggested course of action of bringing the boy to her so that he might be ransomed. No, he thought with some satisfaction, the accounting for his soul was not yet done with.

Finally, the door. With his knife, he cut away the rope tying the boy's hands behind his back. Despite Lesage's endless reassurances, the boy still looked terrified. No matter; soon he would see for himself that Lesage had been telling the truth all along. Then Lesage flung open the door and propelled him into the room.

As he expected, Madame Picot was sitting on her low stool by the window. At their entrance she turned to them. Lesage sensed the grin on his own face and was bewildered not to see it mirrored on her own. She did not even rise from her stool. Instead, she looked between him and Nicolas with confusion. "Who's this boy, monsieur?" she asked.

"This is your son. Nicolas."

She shook her head. "But this is not my son."

29

L esage was first to break the lengthy silence that followed. "Pardon, madame?"
"That boy is not my son."
This seemed impossible. Lesage shook the boy roughly by the shoulder. "Is that true?"
"I told you my mother was dead."
Enraged, Lesage slapped the boy's face. "Did you lie to me? Your name is not Nicolas?"
The boy shrank back, crying. "Yes, monsieur. I am named that, but—"
"What? But what?"
"Did you see my son?" Madame Picot asked the boy, rising from her stool. "My son who is also called Nicolas? Nicolas Picot. He is around your age. With black hair . . . "
The boy paused, sniffling, then nodded. "Yes, madame. I think so."
Madame Picot glided over to him. "Where is he now?"
The boy glanced at Lesage, then shrugged as if the answer should have been clear. "But he is dead, madame. As I told this man . . . "
Lesage staggered back against the wall and slid down until he was sitting on the hard floor. Any slim hope of freedom had vanished. The witch would now surely send him back. He was truly cursed. Money, freedom—he should have known such things were forever unattainable. But how cruel it was to place them momentarily within his reach! He closed

his eyes and dropped his forehead onto his knees. The boy, tremblingly, between sobs, told Madame Picot what had become of her son, but Lesage didn't wish to hear any of it. He shut his eyes tight and clasped his hands over his ears so that the words were, if not completely obscured, at least partially muffled, as if heard underwater. "*Chains . . . blood . . . murder.*"

When at last he opened his eyes again and looked up, Madame Picot was perched on the edge of the bed. Wan light, absence of movement, a spider's web dangling from a corner of the window. But the boy was nowhere to be seen. "Where is he?" Lesage asked.

Madame Picot looked at him for a long time as if unsure of who he was or what he might have been talking about. Then she waved a hand. "That boy you found? He's gone. Back to his own village, I assume. Who knows?"

His scalp itched beneath his wig and he wedged a finger under the lining to scratch it.

"He has a scar under his jaw," Madame Picot muttered, running a finger along her own jawline. "Here, on the left side."

"What? The boy had a scar?"

She clucked her tongue in annoyance. "My son. *My* Nicolas. That is how you might have known. That's all. You might have seen it. He slipped from a fence when he was a few years old and cut his jaw open. A terrible sight it was."

"Ah. Yes. Young boys . . . "

"But he is now dead. Murdered by some men for their pleasure, it seems."

He longed to tell Madame Picot of La Voisin's idea of ransoming her son rather than reuniting them, of her plan to murder the boy if she did not release Lesage. And of how he had elected—from the kindness of his heart alone—to bring that boy here instead of offering him up to that terrible fate. But he couldn't speak. And, in any case, there was no point, for he had rescued the wrong boy.

"What should we do now?" he asked after a thick silence.

The sorceress regarded him bleakly, and although she was no further than a few paces away, her gaze seemed to alight upon him from deep within the cavern of her skull. Lesage knew better than to ask for further details of what had become of her boy. Madame Picot closed her eyes and muttered under her breath. A prayer, perhaps, or a curse. He noticed that she was stroking her black book in her lap.

"*Avaunt,*" she said suddenly. "*Avaunt, avaunt.*" Then she crossed herself with her free hand, shivered and looked directly at him. "You are now free to go. The charm yoking us together has been undone. Wreak whatever havoc you wish to in the world, monsieur."

Lesage could scarcely believe his ears. He clambered to his feet. "Pardon, madame? I am free? You will not send me back? Truly?" Confused, uncertain, he stood before her. "Thank you, madame. But . . . what of our arrangement, Madame Picot? The *money*? What about—"

"I dragged you out from hell, monsieur. Do you not think that is enough?"

He opened his mouth to protest, but thought it wiser to keep the peace. No need to antagonise the woman at this stage. He picked up the satchel containing the tools of his trade: the pot of ink, the tarot cards and shards of paper.

"What will you do now?" she asked.

It was a good question. The prospect of freedom overwhelmed him. He gazed around and shook his head. "I don't know, madame, I . . . Perhaps I shall return to Normandy? See my sons, my wife?"

Lesage thought of the trunk crammed with money and jewellery. He had twenty livres left over from the money Catherine had given him, but it would not last long. He gestured towards the trunk. "You will need to be careful of that treasure," he said, hoping a reminder might prompt in her some gesture of charity or recompense. "Wary of thieves, I mean."

But Madame Picot didn't acknowledge him and seemed barely aware he had spoken. It looked, in fact, like she might never speak again, so firmly did the tomb of her mouth appear to be sealed. No, he would not be able to change her mind. Nevertheless, he hesitated. He had been desperate to get away from the poor woman, but now the time had come, he was strangely reluctant. "Is there anything else you need, madame? Some wine, perhaps? A piece of bread? Should I hail a passing merchant for you?"

When she again declined to answer Lesage sidled towards the door, where he paused. He felt there was something more that needed to be said. "I'm sorry, madame. About your son. I'm sorry I wasn't able to help you. I will pray for his eternal soul."

And, despite everything, he truly did feel sorry for her. The woman had lost all that moored a person to the world and she seemed drastically altered, as if some vital element had been stripped from her. If it weren't for the lank hair framing her face, she might again have been mistaken for a statue of an anguished saint. She frightened him, for a grieving woman was a wounded thing, likely to strike out in any direction. "Goodbye, madame."

And he left the room and closed the door behind him, gently, so as not to disturb her further.

Somewhat dazed, Lesage walked south along Rue Saint-Denis towards the river, then veered east to avoid passing too close by the stinking cemetery. The street, the city, the earth. He stopped for a moment, unsure how to make sense of what had happened. People brushed past him. The smell of a brazier, a carriage rattling by. *What will you do now?* It was a good question indeed and the more Lesage considered it, the more he felt it was time to leave Paris—as much as he adored the place. Yes. It was a good idea. The time was right. Yes, why not return to Normandy, as he had said? The coast, the sea air, green fields. His eyes watered at the thought of a homecoming after all these years. His house, his *sons*. He imagined the villagers remarking on his fine hat and his lovely shoes. Claudette would throw something at him—probably many things, actually—but he was sure he could win her over again. Besides, she was still his wife. What else was she to do?

He considered visiting Le Berceau over on Pont Saint-Michel, assuming the old tavern was still there. Yes. Why not? He had a few coins. He should celebrate his release, but not ostentatiously, for he felt superstitious about abandoning himself to even the vaguest sense of elation; after all, the last time he was unexpectedly released it was to fall immediately under the spell of Madame Picot.

Merely a quiet drink of cider, he thought, some time to reflect on his change in fortune. Yes. A tavern with a fire and some hot food was precisely what a man needed on such an evening. Le Berceau used to have a decent soup or roast on offer and there might be one or two old acquaintances of his there—perhaps even a whore with whom he might flirt? Yes. This time he was *truly* free—freer than he'd been in many years! He was unable to supress a sob of triumph. Then someone called his name and he turned to see a boy trotting towards him.

"You are Lesage?" the runt squeaked, out of breath and doubled over in front of him with his hands on his knees. "La Voisin . . . wants to see you."

Her name punctured the pleasurable swell of anticipation in his chest. "What?"

"Madame Monvoisin, monsieur."

"Yes, yes, I heard you. But it's much too late now, boy. I'm busy." He continued walking. "Tell her I'll come to see her tomorrow."

But the boy shook his head. "No, monsieur," he said gravely. "She says you must go see her immediately. She was most serious about it. Says it's very important."

30

Charlotte sat for a long time, as if she had been struck by a blow. Outside, clouds covered the sun. She had neither the strength nor the inclination to light a candle, and the room around her—its walls, the bed—crumbled away until she was quite alone, drenched in sorrow as heavy as blood. Perhaps this was how it was to die, she thought, and half expected to see Hellequin on his awful black horse leering at her from the window. Certainly I could feel no worse than this. My husband, all my children. If I sit here then surely I, too, will vanish completely. At last. At last my heart has been picked clean. From outside came the cry of a water merchant, a gust of wind. Someone, somewhere, calmed a skittish horse and this evidence of the world continuing as if nothing untoward had happened seemed an affront fashioned for her alone.

She inspected her hands. The left palm still bore the wound Madame Rolland had carved into it. The gash was encrusted with black blood and still tender to the touch—a fact which surprised her, for the encounter with the old sorceress seemed so long ago. Her other hand had its own old scars; the time she nearly sliced the end off her thumb as a girl while helping her mother skin rabbits, the marks on the backs of her hands and wrists from her own encounter with fever. She supposed there was a whole life contained in a person's hands; all they had done, everything they were yet to do. It was no wonder some people could read a person's past and future there.

She cupped her hands over her mouth and nose and closed

her eyes as if in prayer; indeed, within the tiny space there loomed a claustral world of scent and memory. There was her own familiar smell, of course, almost undetectable; sweat; and that of Paris's musty air. Everything, it seemed, she had handled in her life. The pigeon's heart, the pages of her book. Her village, her father's sour breath and his arm around her shoulders as they strolled back to their cottage through the winter dusk. A bee's sting on her wrist. The day her brother Paul broke his arm when a cow crushed it against a fence, and his terrible cries of pain when it was set by the midwife. How hard he had squeezed her hand. Smoke gathering in the morning breeze, the flavour of lark. The darkness of a pine forest after rain, beech leaves she had shredded through her fingers on summer days, a snuffed candle wick. She recalled Michel's bristly cheek against her neck. The smell of autumn soil and summer clouds, sunlight seeping into the mist-shrouded valley at dawn. She heard her children singing in their plaintive voices and the nights when Béatrice, the youngest, still the youngest and somehow the most forlorn, had cried out in her sleep. *Mother. Mother. Mother.* When Charlotte had been pregnant with Philippe all those years ago, her hair had thickened and her breasts swelled. One warm afternoon she sat to rest on a tree stump and she felt her baby turn inside her—feet hard against her womb, his head pressed to her ribs. Some of the other women from the village passed by on their way from the fields, but they didn't mock Charlotte for her idleness, as they might usually have done, but merely smiled at her. She had remained on the stump with her hand cradling her drum-tight stomach, caressing the child who had given her the clearest sign yet that he was waiting to be born. She wondered what kind of boy Philippe would have been had he survived infancy.

She withdrew her hands from her face. Enough. How unbearable it was to be so alive to the world and its endless comings and goings. She lit the candle. In her lap was her black book, as warm as a rabbit or cat. Idly, she thumbed its torn corners and the tiny clasp securing the forbidden pages. Then, barely aware of what she was doing, Charlotte held her left hand over the candle flame until the skin of her palm blistered, whereupon she pulled it away. Foolish, but at least it was a pain that would eventually ease.

Then she opened the clasp that secured the secret pages in her book. Ghostly whispers and dark murmurs drifted up to her like the scent from a long-smouldering fire. *Help yourself, woman, and God will help you. Anything can be done, everything can be done. Unicorn horn, blood of a week-old lamb, hazel ash soaked in brine. Astaroth, Alazan, Ambriel. Anything you desire.* Many other things. *Some devils can take your toes without you even knowing.* Eerie sigils without name or sound, but whose dark meanings were unmistakeable. *Parchment of deerskin, a knife, a child less than a season old who has been willingly given like a gift. Demons can make storms appear. Thistle and goat fat. Thyme and blood. A woman's heart contains all things. She creates life, gives suck to her baby; her heart is tender and loving. But it has other elements as well. It contains fire and intrigue and mighty storms. Shipwrecks and all that has ever happened in the world. Murder, if need be, and dragons and quakes. All that is, is God. Agnus Dei. The lamb. Kyrie, eleison. Mercy on my soul. Have faith and he will surely rise again. I ask of thee. I ask of thee. I ask of thee. Your eyes will be jewels, your bones will be cast of silver and your veins will run with gold.*

It was dark inside and out when, finally, she closed her book, and by that time a new and thrilling strangeness had entered her. *Your blood, your blood, your blood.*

When she could bear herself no longer, Charlotte rose from her chair and, dreamily, as if operating under a power not her own, she took some of the coins from the treasure chest, put on her cloak, departed the house and walked in the direction of the river. The late-afternoon streets were busy with people hurrying to finish their errands or return home. When in sight of the river she hesitated, uncertain. Here, spread out before her, was the view Lesage had shown her—the bone-white towers of the church on the island, the washed-blue sky, thick ribbons of golden sunlight rippling on the water. To her it looked an unruly place, fit only for chaos and ruin.

She left the busier thoroughfares and wound her way south through the labyrinth of smaller, meaner streets until—after getting lost several times—she found herself at a bridge larger than any she thought possible. Along its great span were crowded all sorts of people offering any manner of service or entertainment, a sinister carnival of dancers, children, parrots, merchants and men all cackling and shrieking with pleasure. A group of laughing nobles were carried past in their sedan chairs and a pair of rough-looking men leered and gestured towards her. She wondered where Lesage had gone, what would become of him, and she realised she missed the ungainly reassurance he had provided. Perhaps she had been unwise to send him away?

She waded into the throng of jugglers and teeth-pullers, past the scribes and priests and braying aristocrats having their fortunes told. There was a family with a dancing bear. Grinning faces and feathered hats and the smoke from braziers. Several times she found herself unable to continue, so thick was the crowd, and on one of these occasions a man grabbed her arm and put his hot mouth to her ear. "Want to fuck me, whore?" She tried to pull away, but he was stronger and determined to detain her. A hand clutched at her breast. She gasped, and was horribly aware of her own pathetic, outraged gasp. A few people turned around, then glanced away. A woman's grin, the smell of cooking meat, flash of sweaty neck. "Because I want to fuck you . . . " Finally, she broke away and jostled through the crowd to the other bank, where it was much quieter, more to her liking.

She asked an old woman for directions and, eventually, found her way to Rue des Canettes. Over a shopfront hung a sign of tin beaten into the shape of a mortar and pestle. On it were painted the words *Monsieur Maigret, Predictions herbs and unguents.* Through the murky window burned a lamp. She cupped her hands against the glass and peered through, but could make out almost nothing in the aqueous gloom. Shadows, the glint of metal, a bubble captured in the window's thick, green glass.

A carriage startled Charlotte as it passed close behind her, leaving an acrid smell of horse sweat in its wake. *Gloria Patri, et Filio, et Spiritui Sancto.* She waited for a moment with her hand on the door handle before forcing it open and stepping inside. The shop was as dark and silent as a cave and smelled powerfully of things dried and salted. She blinked and waited for her eyes to adjust. When they did, she found she was standing amid all manner of objects. Flasks, vials, books, instruments on benches, barrels and boxes on the floor. Pelts hung from the ceiling, maps and charts adorned the walls.

A shape rose like a great leviathan from the darkness. It was a man. "Good afternoon, madame."

She started, then caught her breath. "Good afternoon. Are you Monsieur Maigret? The apothecary?"

A pause as his gaze travelled up and down her body, as if assembling her limb by limb with this eyes. "Yes, yes. What is it?"

"There are some things I need. I'm told you can help me."

The apothecary nodded. He was an immensely tall, ill-dressed man with dark eyes and a beard the colour of pewter that reached to his waist. On his head was a grubby coif, and around his neck was a leather strap with a medallion bearing an astrological design of some sort. He stood tilted slightly forward, with his arms behind his back like wings; indeed, there was something in his bearing reminiscent of a giant, peevish bird. "What do you need, madame?"

She hesitated. "Some unicorn horn. The blood of a week-old lamb. Hazel ash."

Monsieur Maigret arched his eyebrows with surprise, but made no other movement. Then he narrowed his gaze. "I have not met you before, have I?"

Charlotte hesitated, unsure if his question were designed to trick her. "No, monsieur. Do you not have these items?"

"Yes," he said, ducking his head. "I do. It's only that . . . Might I ask what it is you intend to do with them?"

"It is a charm for a baby, monsieur. To protect him from plague. The child's mother is recently dead and his older sister fears for his life. She begged me to help her."

"There is certainly fever about this summer. I can feel it in the air, a sort of thickening. It must be a powerful charm."

"Oh, it is."

"Ah, yes. You are not from Paris, are you?"

"No. I'm from a village south of here."

"Where is your husband?"

"Dead."

"Children?"

"All dead."

"Ah. And why did you come to Paris?"

"I was looking for someone."

"I see. And did you find this person?"

She hesitated. "Not yet."

"What do you think of our fair city?"

"I think it's a wicked place."

The old man laughed, displaying long yellow teeth. "Yes. That's certainly one word for it."

She held out her handful of coins. "I have the money, monsieur."

He looked at her coins and muttered, whether with appreciation or contempt, it was difficult to tell. "Very well. Wait here, madame."

Lighting a candle for her and taking the lantern for himself, he shuffled to the rear of the workshop where his shadow bobbed about among the countless racks of grimy flasks, mandrake roots, bird skulls and bones. Charlotte gazed around. Scattered across a nearby bench were sheets of paper covered with numerous numbers and diagrams and symbols. Circles, pentacles, the girdle of the earth. Calculations or spells in unknown languages, the splayed figure of a naked man. *Forty is the most powerful number there is, for it was the number of years Moses wandered in the desert.* Charlotte gazed at the illustrations and ran her fingers over them. They possessed a kind of majesty. Distance to the moon, various stars, the measure of all the things in heaven. Saturn and Mars, beams of light. All the means by which men tried to understand their world.

A bulbous mirror on one wall reflected the room back to her, everything it contained—her own face included—small and jostling in on itself as if in a globe of quicksilver. In the reflection, her features were inflated so out of proportion that she resembled a pinch-cheeked, bulge-eyed mantis. She was dismayed to see a smudge of dirt on her forehead and wiped it off with a finger wetted with spit. She peered again at herself quickly before glancing away. *I was not a witch, but they made me one.*

On a shelf above her was an array of animal skulls, a human one among them, the white of it almost luminous in the murk. She looked around to ensure that Monsieur Maigret was otherwise occupied, then reached out to touch it. The surface was cold and grainy. She drew back. Then she touched the bony globe again. Like a wooden rock, she thought. She tapped it several times with a fingernail.

"Ah," came Monsieur Maigret's voice close at her shoulder. "I see you have met my old friend Monsieur Joffroy."

Charlotte spun around in fright. "I'm sorry, monsieur."

"You couldn't resist."

"No, monsieur. I'm sorry, I shouldn't have touched it."

"Knocking will get you nowhere with him, I fear. The door is well and truly locked behind him."

But rather than displeased, Monsieur Maigret appeared gratified, as if by her gesture a long-held, private theory of his had been proven. He placed his lantern on a bench where it sputtered momentarily before falling quiet. In his other hand was a cloth sack. "It's the irresistible call of the dead. They require so much. But we also make our demands of them, don't we?"

Charlotte was unsure how to answer this. She stayed silent and watched a greasy tendril of smoke issuing from the lantern.

Monsieur Maigret picked up the skull, balanced it on his palm and raised it to his face as if preparing to kiss it, but instead he peered into its large, eyeless sockets. "I wonder what he sees now. The fires of damnation, no doubt. Devils."

Charlotte shuddered and stepped back, out of the man's reach. "Was he truly your friend?"

The apothecary chuckled and shook his head. "No. I think perhaps that Monsieur Joffroy was friend to no man. This gentleman met his death at the end of a rope. A thief and the murderer of several people. Not that you could tell any of this from looking at his skull. Looks the same as any man once the skin has fallen away, doesn't it? No eyes. No face. Larger at the back, perhaps. They say he was brave at the end, that he looked the hangman in the eye without flinching. I often wonder if he and his victims have met in the afterlife and what they might have said to each other. The executioner Monsieur Guillaume sometimes passes them along to me. A hanged man's skull is a most powerful thing, you know."

Charlotte felt her lips tighten with distaste. "What can it do?"

"It reminds us of our fate, that's what. Dust to dust . . . "

"I think perhaps the world provides us with plenty of such reminders, monsieur."

"Indeed." He considered the skull once more. "And it tells me secrets about people. The dark things people might hide—-even from themselves."

"Is that so?"

"Yes." And, with a glint in his eye, he lifted the skull to his ear, nodded and made a face as if hearing incredible things. "If I hold it here like this. You don't believe me?"

Charlotte laughed. "Why, yes. I do, monsieur."

The old man chuckled again, this time more heartily, and lowered the skull. Then he held out the little sack of green fabric. Its contents clinked together. "I have what you asked for, madame."

"Everything?"

"Of course."

She made no move to take it.

"You appear to be disappointed," he said. "Perhaps you hoped that I wouldn't have all that you requested?"

"No, monsieur. That would not make sense."

"Tell me, madame, what do you intend to use these ingredients for?"

"A charm of protection. I told you, monsieur. A baby . . . "

"Ah. Yes." The apothecary pursed his lips as he considered this. Then his eyes widened comically and again he raised the skull to his ear. "What's that, Monsieur Joffroy? Is that true? Yes. I see. I see." He turned to her. "He tells me you are preparing to do something terrible."

Charlotte caught her breath, but made no answer.

Monsieur Maigret placed the skull back on the shelf. "You know, they are hanging Justine Gallant and Monsieur Olivier at Place de Grève tonight. For murder. Witchcraft. They say they tried to summon the Devil himself." He shrugged and rubbed at his nose. "Some might interpret the event as a warning," he added.

They stood in silence. Eventually, Charlotte gestured towards one of the papers. "Tell me, monsieur, these diagrams—are they magic? What is the word that is written here?"

The apothecary made a small movement with his head, like a self-satisfied heron. "No, no, no, madame. Not magic. Of course not. No. This is science. *Science*. You don't know how to read Greek, I suppose?"

"No."

"Ah." He bent over the workbench to peer at the documents, tucking his beard aside as he did so. Muttering to himself, he smoothed the curling papers against the bench with his hand. "I doubt a woman could understand such complex astrological matters. The movement of the heavens and stars and so on." He arranged his fingers as if gripping invisible eggs, which he had circle each other in the air between them. "That word is *eclipse*. An eclipse is when the moon moves in front of the sun, which causes the earth to go dark."

"And this happens when night falls at the end of the day?"

The old man smiled. "No, no, no, no, no. An eclipse sometimes happens in daylight, and it is *as if* there is a brief night in the middle of the day—but it's only for a short time."

A brief night in the middle of the day. It sounded preposterous. Charlotte's scepticism must have shown clearly on her face, for the apothecary held up an admonitory finger. "Oh yes. And not so rare as you might think. No. There was an eclipse only a few days ago, which is why I have been consulting these particular documents. It's vital to know about these matters when it comes to making predictions for someone's future success, you see. Even minor miscalculations could mean the difference between life and death. Now, madame. If you look here at these particular illustrations . . . "

The apothecary rambled on nonsensically about the heavens and the movement of planets and stars, but Charlotte's mind drifted. Instead of paying attention to the papers on which the apothecary was pointing out various diagrams and formulae, she gazed at the old man's grey hairs wavering about in the buttery lantern light. So much had happened. She wondered about her village of Saint-Gilles and imagined its inhabitants going about their business—Louis beating his flock of sheep from pasture with a switch, old Fournier lounging in the doorway with his pipe clamped between his teeth, the clatter of children and animals underfoot, the earthy stench of the dungheap. Such a place now seemed utterly impossible to her, as distant and ethereal as a dream. Dread keened across her skin. What did the villagers imagine had become of her—if they considered her fate at all? Was this how it was to be dead, to wonder about the living and whether they went about their business without you?

"No," she murmured when she wearied of his lecture.

"Pardon, madame?"

Her heart swelled with a feeling of pleasurable discomfort, like a pulse of illicit desire.

"That was not an eclipse, Monsieur Maigret. No. I darkened the sun. It was me."

The apothecary could barely contain his mirth. "Pardon, madame? *You?*"

She took the sack of ingredients and gave him her handful of coins, then took her leave before the old man could say anything more.

Power, she realised as she stepped into the street. That feeling was power.

31

Most disgruntled, Lesage trudged to Catherine Monvoisin's villa in the city's north, where he found her strolling in her rear garden. It was clear she was quite drunk. She moved deliberately, as if in accordance with instructions audible to her alone; her blouse was askew; the red pigments she had applied to her mouth and cheeks were smudged and this granted her a ghoulish appearance. She greeted him with fond kisses before escorting him with some force into her consulting pavilion. She was excited as she closed the door behind them and gestured for him to sit. The room was stuffy, its air still.

"Come, my dear. Come. Let's sit. It's so wonderful to see you again. Now. It's as well you came, Adam."

He flinched at the use of his former name. "You asked me to come."

"Oh yes. Of course. Now, did you manage to see this fellow at La Pomme de Pin? What was his name?"

"Willem. Yes, and we found the boy, but things did not quite go as I might have wished."

"Oh? But why?"

Briefly—and leaving aside the crucial matter of the treasure—Lesage explained how he had retrieved a boy only to find he was not Madame Picot's son after all. "Unfortunately, it seems that her son was killed by these men."

"But he was not her son?"

"What? The other boy? No."

She belched. "Another boy altogether? With the exact same name?"

"Yes."

Catherine sank back in her chair, seemingly aghast at the thought of two boys with the same name, common as it was. A fly hovered near her left shoulder, alighting momentarily before lumbering away again. "I thought we agreed you would bring him here? To hold him ransom for your freedom?"

Lesage gestured and shook his head to indicate the matter was too complicated to explain and, in any case, was now of no importance.

Catherine grunted. "Strange. Well. I have some interesting information."

"As do I, Catherine—"

She waved for him to be silent and poured herself a generous amount of red wine—a good portion of which slopped onto the carpet—but offered him none.

"I have—or *we* have, I should say—been asked by someone important to help with something. Someone *very* important."

Catherine gulped from her glass then stared wide-eyed at Lesage and nodded intently, as if these actions alone might communicate to him who this person might be and the nature of the assistance required.

Realising that an offer of wine would not be forthcoming, Lesage stood and poured himself a cup. He sensed he would need it. "Well?" he asked, when he had resumed his seat. "What is it, then?"

Catherine leaned forward and dropped her voice to a whisper. "The King is away inspecting the borders. And yesterday, old . . . *Quanto* came to see me herself. Privately."

This wasn't completely surprising. The King's mistress was known to be a regular customer of the sorceresses of Paris and, in fact, Catherine—quite rightly—claimed a great deal of credit for ensuring her success in obtaining the title of *maîtresse-en-titre* in the first place. Although it was unusual for Madame de Montespan to come to Villeneuve herself—a maid usually picked things up for her—it was hardly unprecedented. Lesage sensed, however, that some further sinister revelation was forthcoming, and he sipped his wine to settle the queasiness in his innards. He glanced at the door.

Catherine sucked her teeth. "Madame is worried about a young woman, some whore at court. You know what I mean. Our King is most restless in his desires, as I think we all know. Madame is getting older, of course, and it's true she has . . . *filled out* somewhat. What does she expect, after several children? She's past thirty, after all. What does *the King* expect? I think she is still charming, very vivacious. The King, however, is tiring of her. The other woman is, of course, much younger, and extremely beautiful, but she is notoriously stupid. *Caput vacuum cerebro*, if you understand my meaning. I forget—do you understand Latin, Adam?"

"Yes, yes. Of course. Empty-headed. Yes."

"Completely stupid. And I fear she has met her match in Athénaïs de Montespan. After all, one does not maintain such a position by kindness and wit alone. She wants another ceremony. She's desperate to have her children recognised by the King. Now, I need you to go to Les Enfants Rouges to pick something up for us. Some slut had her baby last night and—"

"No, Catherine."

She looked at him, puzzled, as if these two words were a riddle. "What do you mean, *No, Catherine*? Madame has expressly wished for your participation in this and I have assured her you would be able to help. She has a great deal of respect for you, Adam. You should have heard her in those years you were away." Catherine fluttered a hand in front of her face in imitation of a fan and affected a noblewoman's accent. "*Oh, I wish Monsieur du Coeuret were here to assist us,*

she would say. And then you returned," she clicked her stubby,
beringed fingers in the air, "like magic."

Lesage exhaled and ran a finger around the rim of his wine
cup. Buried like broken glass in Catherine's chronicle was an
accusation, as if all his years in the galleys had been contrived
to inconvenience her.

"Besides," Catherine went on, "do you know what this is
worth to us? One thousand *écus*."

Lesage let out a low whistle of astonishment. It was certainly an enormous sum of money. He wondered about the
woman who had so riled Athénaïs but, fearing he was already
too implicated, he jumped to his feet, spilling wine over his
breeches in his haste. "No. I cannot be involved. You see,
Madame Picot has released me from her power."

He had not intended to disclose this in such an abrupt fashion—indeed, he had not expected to see Catherine so soon
and had not had the time to formulate a wiser approach to the
matter.

There followed a long, strange silence as Catherine digested
this. If nothing else, Lesage had at least succeeded in deflect-
ing the conversation away from the ghastly ceremony
Catherine was planning.

"She freed you?" she asked at last.

"Yes!"

Catherine clicked her fingers again. "Just like that? How
curious. But you didn't find her boy?"

He was annoyed, but hardly surprised, that she did not
appear as pleased by this announcement as he had hoped.
"No. I did my best to find her son and it was not my fault we
couldn't. The boy is dead and she finally understands this.
Why would you doubt it? She is a kind woman at heart, I
think."

"A kind woman, eh? The kind Forest Queen. You were not
so complimentary about her when you first returned to Paris."

She affected a whining voice. "*Oh help me, Catherine, I have been bewitched. Help me, help me. I can't go back . . .*" Catherine downed the rest of her wine and wiped the back of her hand across her mouth. "Well. What now for your friendly sorceress? Is your Madame Picot leaving Paris at last?"

"I don't know. She told me nothing of her plans. It is enough for me to be finally free of her."

Catherine laughed and refilled her glass. "Gone mute, has she?"

Lesage bristled. "The woman has lost all her children, Catherine. And her husband. I think perhaps even *you* would be somewhat melancholy after such an experience."

"Would that I were so lucky. My children are miserable fucking whelps . . . "

"Catherine!"

"*Catherine*," she mocked. "Scandalous, I know. I think you became soft in the galleys. Soft in your cock it seems, too, eh? Where is the man I knew all those years ago? Gelded by that witch, I think. Or perhaps you acquired a taste for sodomites in there, eh?" And she wriggled obscenely on her chair as if attending to an intimate itch.

"Anyway," she went on. "That's enough about that fucking sow. Good. Congratulations. Here's to your health and freedom. It's about time you got out from beneath her. Hardly manly, is it?" She raised her glass to her mouth and gulped from it. Her gullet bobbed up and down furiously as she drank. God help any woman who'd allow Catherine to poke about inside her this evening, for she would surely damage them even more than usual.

"I can't help," Lesage said. "The risk is far too great. Madame Picot has released me from her power, and I would be a fool not to take the opportunity to get away from . . . all of this. What of the arrests of Madame Gallant and her lover? They are hanging them both tonight. What if they put her to the question and she talks? Things are changing in Paris. And they will certainly burn us alive if we are caught."

"You are afraid?"

He paused. "Yes. Besides, it's my chance to return to Normandy and see how my sons and my wife are faring. It's been so many years since I have visited—"

"I beg your pardon?"

He drew breath. "I thought I would return to Normandy."

"Oh. I see. Well. Even after all I have done for you."

"Catherine . . . "

She poured herself another glass of wine. "You were nothing when you first came to Paris. A wool merchant."

"Not quite nothing, Catherine. I did have a most successful business if you recall."

"Nothing!"

He sighed again. There was no point in arguing with her. "I know, and I am most grateful."

"I raised you up, introduced you to fine people. Nobles, influential men. Made you a lot of money. Do you think a man such as yourself might have been able to visit the court without the assistance I have given you? Do you think you would have met any of those people while dealing in fucking *wool*?"

"No. Nor would I have spent several years in the galleys."

She scoffed and straightened her hair viciously, as if this were the source of her anger.

Lesage sagged. This was not going well. They sat in a prickly silence. He sensed her formulating some new line of attack.

"Did you hear what I told you about Madame de Montespan requesting your involvement?" she asked. "She believes—and God alone knows why—that you are crucial to the success of the whole thing. *Crucial*. You're talented, Adam. And now I will look an utter fool, thanks to you. All you need to do is—"

"No, Catherine. I will return to Normandy as soon as I can."

"Don't be ridiculous, Adam. How will you survive? With what money?"

"I shall make my way. There is no reason why I could not return to my former profession. I am not so old, Catherine."

She inspected him from head to foot very slowly, very suspiciously, taking in his hat, his coat, his satchel and, finally, his boots, as if tracing the progress of a falling feather visible to her alone. It made him wary. La Voisin was adept at reading people, of locating and exploiting the chink in any man's armour. It was, after all, a large part of her success as a clairvoyant.

"Phht," she said at last. "I know you too well. You can't live anywhere but Paris. *The centre of the world*, you always used to say. And never has it been truer. There is everything here. You think you'll return to the family life in Caen and live a merchant's life on a merchant's salary with your pathetic wife and your imbecile son—assuming she'll even take you in after all that has happened? In the *countryside*? No. I've shown you too much. Do you think you might simply go home as if nothing had happened? After all these years? After all we've done together? You think you have not been implicated, but you have blood on your hands as much as I do. You imagine you are above it all, but you're not. One cannot return home after the nest has been fouled. You have a new home—here, in Paris. Now. Enough foolishness. Sit down, man."

He sensed his resolve faltering, but shook his head. "Goodbye, Catherine." He stood and bent to kiss her cheek, but she recoiled, bumping a side table and sending quills and a ledger clattering onto the floor.

She swore, then composed herself. "Very well, Adam, go back to Normandy—but do this one last favour for me. Madame won't go ahead if you are not involved. One final thing. It's all I ask. Please. With the money we will make from this, you'll never have to work again. I'll give you two hundred *écus* of it. Two hundred. That's six hundred livres. Think about it. Don't abandon me, Adam."

Lesage straightened his wig in preparation to depart.

"Leave here now and I'll curse you, Adam. I swear to God I will."

He hesitated with his hand on the door handle.

"That got your attention, eh? Yes. It doesn't take much to kill a man, as you well know. I, too, have become more powerful over the years. I certainly don't wish for it to be like this, but you have given me no option. A few words is all it takes . . ." She got unsteadily to her feet and rummaged through her pockets, heedless of her wineglass, which toppled to the ground. "You of all people should know what I am capable of. Now, let's have no more of this foolishness."

"You would do that, Catherine? Truly?"

She chuckled as she threaded her arm through his. What a question; of course she would. She held out a purse clinking with coins. "Now," she went on brightly, "here are two hundred livres. Go immediately to the orphanage. They are expecting you. Ask for Monsieur Vicente. He is in charge of the young mothers there now. He will have something for you. Bring it back quickly. We'll leave for Montlhéry this evening with Guibourg. Madame de Montespan will meet us there tonight with her maid. She'll travel in her own carriage, of course." She flung open the pavilion door, paused to inhale the evening air, then belched and giggled. "Phew. I'm a bit drunk. *You* have made me drunk, you sly old devil."

Catherine escorted Lesage through the house to the high wooden door that led to the street outside. He succumbed, like an unmoored boat drifting on an ebbing tide. Without another word, she unlatched the heavy door, pulled it open, kissed Lesage on the cheek and propelled him gently into the street.

32

Charlotte hurried to the Place de Grève as the bells for vespers began to ring. A large crowd had gathered to witness the execution of Madame Gallant and Monsieur Olivier. Although it was not yet dark, lanterns burned in the windows of those who had assembled in the houses lining the square to observe the spectacle. Several guards lounged in front of the scaffold, but in general the mood was convivial, as if the crowd had gathered for a fete. A man and his wife were roasting chestnuts. There was much chatter and recounting of the crimes the pair had committed. "How foolhardy they were to think they might summon the Devil and not be harmed by it"; "The poison was supplied by an Italian, of course"; "I always heard she was a sorceress." Fervent prayers, also, from the nuns and monks moving among them with their rosaries and crosses pressed to their lips.

Charlotte stood on the outskirts of the assembly. Some time passed without any sign of the condemned, and the crowd grew restless. There were mutterings that La Gallant had died after being subjected to the water cure, or that she had been mysteriously pardoned. Some became annoyed and wandered home. Eventually, reports were passed along that the condemned pair had left Notre-Dame, where they had completed their penance, and would arrive shortly in their separate carts.

Charlotte saw them soon enough, moving above the heads of the crowd. They were dressed in ill-fitting white linen shifts and wore on their heads coarse hoods fastened beneath the chin. They each held a large flaming candle in one fist. Their confessors stood near to them with Bibles open, hoping for a final confession, an expurgation of every last sin.

As they drew closer, Charlotte could make out their features more clearly. The woman, La Gallant, was tight-faced, while Monsieur Olivier was sobbing, and when he glanced up and saw the gallows he faltered at the knees and had to be supported by his priest. The crowd grew solemn, for although their crimes had been wicked and they were eager to see the criminals punished, it was terrible to die in such a public and shameful manner. Those nearest to the carts drew close in the hope of hearing something or of offering some consolation, while those who had been praying grew more fervent.

The carts stopped beside the scaffold and the poor sinners were escorted down and taken to the platform. A clerk spoke to them and the prisoners shook their heads. Various other officials conferred among themselves and papers were signed before a guard ushered the pair to the platform and handed them over to the care of the executioner, Monsieur Guillaume. A quiver of anticipation, relief, pity and disgust coursed through the crowd. The prisoners then mounted the steps and stood in full view of everyone. "They look like anyone," a girl said. A drunk lamented they would only be hanged, for he wished to see something more theatrical. An official read out the sentence.

Monsieur Olivier had stopped weeping but Madame Gallant's face now contorted with barely contained terror and she glanced repeatedly up at the gallows overhead. Although she had been in prison for several months and the sentence passed some time before, she seemed unable to believe that the moment—her final moment on this earth—had actually arrived. Her mouth overflowed with prayers. The executioner and his assistant now moved swiftly, for it was growing late and the crowd, having waited for so long in the evening heat, would not be accommodating to delays.

The prisoners' hands were tied behind their backs. They looked confusedly out over the crowd. Their confessors stayed at their sides, praying for their eternal souls. Then, suddenly, it was time. The executioner took Monsieur Olivier while his young assistant handled Madame Gallant. They hauled their charges to the top of their ladders and fitted nooses around their necks. La Gallant moved her head around in an almost comical attempt to avoid the noose and delay her fate, but it was soon done. The crowd fell quiet. At a signal known to them alone, Monsieur Guillaume and his assistant shoved the prisoners from the ladders. They cried out, or someone cried out. Weeping, dull cheers, gasps and a ripple and hum through the crowd as many, including Charlotte, crossed themselves and offered up prayers for the poor sinners. "*In nomine Patris, et Filii, et Spiritus Sancti. Amen.*"

Monsieur Olivier died quickly, and it was not long before his face was empurpled and a dark stain was visible at the front of his shift. Some in the crowd sniggered. Madame Gallant survived longer. With her hands secured behind her back, she bucked frantically on the rope, much to the amusement of some, who jeered her vain attempts to dislodge herself from her noose. "*Look. As if she might escape her fate now!*" Her eyes bulged and her mouth twisted. She blinked and blinked. From her lips came a choking sound and it seemed, at times, that she was attempting to say something, whereupon some in the crowd pleaded for her to be shown mercy and be permitted to speak. But the executioner Guillaume paid no attention, merely stood by with his assistant, who sat on the back of a cart behind the scaffold staring at the ground.

Eventually, the executioner inspected the prisoners and pronounced his work complete. The crowd dispersed and the guards drifted away. Charlotte waited. She watched the executioner stuff his pipe, light it from one of the torches and sit on the edge of the gallows platform to smoke. His assistant busied himself packing things away on their cart. The bodies swung stiffly behind them.

She approached, but stood a respectful distance away. Guillaume didn't see her, or chose to ignore her. Eventually, the executioner looked at her and it was clear he had been aware of her presence all along. She nodded a greeting and he nodded his own in return. He puffed several times on his pipe and his face glowed orange in its light. He was bearded, dark-eyed and broad of forehead. She glanced around. The square had emptied and even those watching from the windows had closed their shutters. The city had tired quickly of the display.

"Can I assist you, madame? Did you know one of these sinners?"

Charlotte shook her head. The executioner got to his feet and spat into the dirt at the base of the platform. He bent to pick something up.

Charlotte drew closer. "I need the woman's heart, monsieur," she whispered.

Guillaume stopped what he was doing. "Pardon, madame?"

"Her heart."

Guillaume glanced up at Madame Gallant, or at the body she had occupied until a short time earlier. Her cropped scalp was exposed after her hood became dislodged in the course of her struggle. The hem of the shift was frayed and the slipper on one of her feet had fallen off to reveal a foot with its sooty sole. Her tongue bulged obscenely in her mouth, but otherwise her face was impassive, slate blue, empty of life.

The executioner retied the red scarf at his throat and flicked dust from his shoulders. "People come to me for all manner of things, madame. Fingers, hair, nail clippings, bones. Blood, of course. But I have never before cut the heart from a hanged woman. That is quite a job."

"I will pay you, of course."

"That is just as well, for I would not do it for free." He looked down at her from the platform. "Why would you need such a thing, madame?"

"A woman's heart contains all things, monsieur."

Guillaume considered this deeply. "I suppose that is true. Very well, but I cannot do it here. Come up to my house shortly. The price will be fifty livres."

Monsieur Guillaume's house was in the north of the city. A thin woman opened the door and ushered Charlotte into the kitchen where the executioner sat at his table with an empty bowl and a cup of wine. The house was orderly and clean, and in such surroundings he seemed an ordinary tradesman, no different to a furrier or boatman.

He bade her sit. "I thought you might not come, madame."

"Did you think I was afraid?"

"You would have reason to be, for what you have asked for is against the law."

"As it is for you, I expect."

Guillaume acknowledged this with a wry smile. "The hangman gets away with a lot, for no one else wants his job. He is not so easily replaced."

The woman placed a cup of wine on the table in front of her. Charlotte sensed Guillaume watching her. There were some who felt the mere presence of men who traded professionally in death, let alone the food they ate, was severely tainted. She lifted the cup to her mouth and drank. The wine was syrupy and tart. She sensed it dissolve through her body.

Guillaume waved for the woman to leave them. When she had left the room, he fetched a bloodstained linen sack from a box and put it on the table. Charlotte averted her eyes. He watched her from beneath his heavy eyebrows. He was elegant, in his way, not as brutish—nor as handsome—as she'd feared.

There was a certain kind of woman, Charlotte knew, who desired such men for the dark power invested in them, but she had no wish to be mistaken for such a woman. She produced a small bag of her own that clinked when she set it on the table. "Here is your payment, monsieur."

He nodded and a drop of wine gleamed in his beard, like a miniature bauble caught in a bush. "You do not appear to be like the others who come to see me for things. The other sorceresses, I mean." She made no answer and Guillaume, with an air of satisfaction, added, "But a woman's heart contains all things, or so I have heard."

"And you do not look like a man who . . . kills people for a living, monsieur."

"How do you think such a man should look? More like a savage?"

"I have not given it much thought, monsieur."

"But not like me."

Charlotte felt herself flush. "I did not mean to offend you, monsieur."

He waved away her concern. "Everyone wants to see a felon punished, but no one wishes to do it themselves."

She sipped her wine. "Tell me. How does it feel?"

"What?"

She was sure her meaning was clear enough but the hangman, for his own reasons, wished her to say it aloud. "How does it feel to kill a person, Monsieur Guillaume?"

Guillaume shrugged and poured himself another cup of wine. He gave her question some consideration before answering. "It is not the profession I would have chosen for myself, but it is an honour. It cannot be done lightly. A great burden and a great responsibility. I try to ensure they are dispatched the proper way. I pray for their eternal souls. Women are not called upon to do it, luckily for them."

"They say everything can be forgiven."

"Do you think the two I executed tonight will be forgiven, madame?"

"Yes. If they were duly confessed. God forgives everything."

"And me?"

"You are doing God's work, are you not? Is it not for the greater good?"

The executioner looked down at his hands as if the answer might be found there. His fingernails were blunt and Charlotte wondered how he had freed the woman's heart from her body. "I will find out in the end, I suppose," he said.

"As will we all, monsieur."

Gingerly, she placed the heart, still wrapped in its cloth, in her pocket. Then she straightened the scarf on her head and returned to her room in Madame Simon's house. The terrible day was drawing to an end, but she was no longer afraid.

33

L esage walked in the direction of Les Enfants Rouges, brooding on his conversation with Catherine. Her words echoed about in his skull as if it were a cavern. You have blood on your hands. One cannot return home after the nest has been fouled. The damned woman was so adept at turning anything to her own advantage. For good reason was she feared throughout the city. Over the years Lesage had seen her bend all sorts of people to her will—and not only illiterate merchants and greedy soldiers and their ilk. No. There had been duchesses and dukes, and now it seemed that Madame de Montespan herself was the King's official mistress thanks to their diabolical intercession. Catherine had spies in virtually every quarter of the city, people over whom she held great influence, mostly thanks to some shard of compromising gossip she wouldn't hesitate to leverage for her own purposes. After all, someone was always fucking someone they shouldn't be or generally up to mischief. She probably wouldn't rest until she had been installed in her own apartments at Saint-Germain.

The streets were busy with all sorts of merchants and carriages and idlers and animals. Horses, a flock of geese, a herd of pigs. He paused at an oyster stall and quaffed several with a sprinkling of lemon and salt. Unpleasant things they were—like warm dollops of coagulated sea water—and yet he invariably felt compelled to eat them if the opportunity arose.

Nearby a blind beggar woman crouched in the shadows

with her hand out, murmuring prayers and imprecations. The woman was ancient and her scalp and cheeks were dotted with blisters. In an Italian church many years ago Lesage had seen a saint who had been dead for several centuries, but who looked more likely to rise up and walk than this old woman. Consideration of the beggar—and of the saint—prompted in him thoughts of Madame Picot and he experienced an unfamiliar spasm of guilt. Should he have done something for the poor woman, offered some further sort of—what?—*assistance*? She had no husband, no children. She was not old, certainly, and quite pretty—but she wasn't young enough to attract a husband of great quality. And she was so provincial, not suited to the city. Paris swarmed with unscrupulous and calculating rogues. This he knew better than most; after all, he was one of them. The fate he had hastily predicted for her when they encountered the family of troubadours in the forest might yet prove to be accurate. Perhaps he truly *was* possessed of clairvoyant abilities? How else to explain Madame Leroux's drowning, not to mention the money he'd seen in Madame Picot's tarot cards? Unaccountably moved by the beggar's sordid fate, Lesage took a few *sous* from his pocket and dropped them into her outstretched claw.

He turned into Rue Pavée, its fancy paving stones underfoot like turtle shells, and skirted around a stinking pile of fresh ordure. A rat darted past and vanished into the shadows. Soon he became aware that the cacophony of children playing and babies squalling was louder than the general noise of the street. He had arrived at the orphanage of Les Enfants Rouges. He adjusted his hat and straightened his wig.

When he rang the bell, the peephole set into the door slid across, revealing a pair of eyes as dark and as oily as olives. "Yes?"

"I am here to see Monsieur Vicente," Lesage told the concierge.

"For what purpose, monsieur?"

"He has something for me."

"What is your name, please?"

"My name is Lesage."

The eyes bobbed out of sight, then returned. "We have no record of an appointment for anyone by that name, monsieur."

"Catherine Monvoisin sent me."

"Ah. I see." A puzzled pause. "You are Monsieur du Coeuret?"

Lesage sighed. "Yes. That's me."

The peephole closed, then the bolt was retracted and the door swung open, releasing the institutional whiff of the orphanage. He hesitated, but the concierge gestured impatiently for him to come inside, so he muttered a prayer and crossed himself before covering his nose with one hand and stepping into the courtyard full of children.

The concierge—waddling with arms akimbo like a duck drying its wings—led Lesage across a courtyard and through the swarm of orphans, most of whom were dressed in red in accordance with the name of the orphanage. Children of all ages, and in varying states of health and disrepair, eddied about. A group of girls perched on a nearby bench darning, while some younger boys at their feet played a game with pebbles. Others were engaged in lessons.

They passed through a dim colonnade into a passage and then down a flight of stairs until they entered a high-ceilinged ward. Several lanterns and candles cast a greenish light over the dozen or so beds arranged haphazardly on the floor. It was cooler and calmer down here. Young women sat on benches nursing babies, while others glided as serenely as mermaids through the shadows. Female murmurs and the squawk of a newborn, glimpse of a pale young breast. The world of women. So lovely.

"Through here, Monsieur du Coeuret," said the concierge, and he ushered Lesage into an office on the far side of the ward.

Monsieur Vicente was a portly man who wore a pale wig and a grey apron spattered with blood. He shook Lesage's hand and whispered some instructions to a midwife, who glanced at Lesage before bustling from the room. Although it was many years since Lesage had been engaged in such a transaction, the procedures were depressingly familiar. It was a secret, this kind of arrangement, but really no secret at all. Everyone knew what occurred, even if they didn't acknowledge that they knew. Besides, the babies were bastards, unwanted and delivered of whores—what did anyone expect? At least this way they would be of use to someone.

"Please, Monsieur du Coeuret. Sit down. You must be hot. Would you like a drink? Some chicory water, perhaps?" Monsieur Vicente poured a cup of the water from a clay jug and handed it to him.

"It's Lesage."

"Pardon, monsieur?"

"My name is now Lesage." He raised the cup to his lips and drank. It was refreshing, but at that moment he wished for something stronger.

Monsieur Vicente ran his tongue over his lips as he considered this, but declined to respond. "And how is Catherine?" he asked.

"Pardon?"

"Madame Monvoisin?"

"Oh. She seems well. The same as ever, I suppose. Little truly changes . . . "

A chuckle, a steepling of the fingers beneath his chin. "Indeed. A formidable woman. Now. I trust you have the money for this baby?"

Lesage pulled the purse from his satchel and placed it on the table. The midwife returned with a bundle in her arms. Lesage stood and the woman moved to give the baby to him but, evidently reconsidering this course of action and, momentarily confused, she opted instead to place it in a cradle by the door before leaving the room. Monsieur Vicente stood and opened his mouth to call after her, but faltered.

"Ah," he murmured, manoeuvring somewhat awkwardly around his desk. "She's gone already." He opened the door and summoned a boy walking past carrying a bucket. "You there. Boy. Come here a moment."

The dark-haired boy flinched when he was addressed, as if he apprehended Monsieur Vicente's words as blows, but he shuffled into the room and listened as Monsieur Vicente instructed him to escort Lesage to the side entrance of the orphanage.

The boy looked at Lesage and, at that moment, in the light entering through the barred window set high into the wall, Lesage saw the boy had a thick scar along the side of his jaw. He started in disbelief. Could it be true? He rose from his chair and pushed past Monsieur Vicente to inspect the boy, who cowered further under his scrutiny. Lesage tilted the boy's head to one side. Yes, there could be no doubt. Along the left side of his jaw was a thick scar, exactly as Madame Picot had told him.

"How did you get this scar here?"

"I fell off a fence when I was a child, monsieur."

"You are Charlotte Picot's son, are you not? Nicolas Picot?"

The boy shrank away and stared at him. "How did you know that, monsieur?"

34

Charlotte sat on the low stool in her room with the black book in her lap. It was hot and her brow was damp with sweat. To one god she prayed that Marguerite would come with her baby brother Jean, but to another god she prayed she would not. All her life she had been taught to read the signs for all manner of things: comets foretold death, of course; a dream of a woman standing by a man's left hand meant she would become his wife; a child who does not cry when baptised will not live long; the wounds of a murdered person will bleed afresh if the corpse is touched by its killer. She listened with her ears, with her fingers and her skin. But for this, there was nothing.

She prepared the ingredients according to the instructions from her book. Eventually, she heard voices echoing around the courtyard, followed by a knock on her door. She flinched. Another knock, louder this time.

The girl called her name. "Madame Picot. Open your door. It's Marguerite."

Charlotte unlocked the door to find the troubadour girl standing in the dim passage with her baby brother heavily swaddled in her arms. She stepped aside to allow the girl to enter.

"I am here, Madame Picot. As you said."

Marguerite pulled the blanket free of her brother's face as if to prove her word. Charlotte looked at the baby, but unwillingly. Thatch of dark hair, his lips like a twist of blood in cream. A child freely given. She glanced away. "Put him down. There, on the bed."

The girl did as she was asked. "Do you have the ingredients to make the charm?"

"Yes."

"But why are you trembling, madame? Are you sick?"

"No. No reason. I am tired, that's all."

Marguerite looked around. "But where is your own son, madame?"

"He will be here soon."

Baby Jean made a sucking sound, whimpered, then fell quiet. For a moment they both looked at him.

"When was he born?" Charlotte asked.

"In the spring."

Less than a season old. Charlotte nodded. "You should say goodbye to him. Quickly, before he frets."

"I cannot stay with him while you make the charm?"

"It's better if you're not here. Come back later when I have finished."

"But he will need to be fed by then, madame . . . "

"There is a woman in the street who will do it. If need be, I will organise it. Don't worry. Quickly now."

The girl seemed puzzled and disappointed, but she acquiesced and kneeled beside her brother. She murmured quiet words and nuzzled him, as all sisters do with their younger siblings. It was unbearable.

35

Monsieur Vicente ushered Nicolas Picot from his office and returned to his desk. He rummaged through his papers until he located a ledger, opened it and ran his finger through the many names scrawled in its pages, muttering to himself as he did so.

"So many orphans in these times. So much degradation, so much disease. Ah," he exclaimed at last. "Here he is. Picot. I can hardly read the entry. Says here that . . . His mother and father are both dead. Of course. The boy told us his mother was attacked when he was taken by some men. Terrible business. The father died of fever. Also . . . both his brother and two sisters are dead. Tragic. No relatives, perhaps an uncle somewhere, he says. Some days ago he was found wandering the streets near the river in the east of the city in a most agitated state. Claimed he had escaped from some men who had kidnapped him."

"Yes," said Lesage. "It's true that his mother was injured but she did not die. No. She is alive and I have been helping her to find the boy for the past few days."

"His mother is alive? But he says not."

"Yes. I was with her today at a lodging house in Rue Françoise. This is the truth. That's how we came to be in Paris. We heard of a man called Horst who stole children and brought them here. There is a trade, monsieur." He paused. "As I'm sure you know."

Monsieur Vicente perused his ledger for a moment longer

before looking up at Lesage with his hands clasped together on the desk. It was clear he did not believe what Lesage had been telling him. "If that is all, Monsieur du Coeuret, I have work to attend to. And please, take that child away before it starts crying."

Lesage sat silently. He gazed up at the high ceiling. A grille set in a corner afforded a view of the street, of people's boots as they strolled past. A thread of sunlight, a strand of spider's web. "I don't want the baby, monsieur."

Monsieur Vicente looked up. "What?"

"I wish to take the boy instead."

"I doubt Catherine Monvoisin would be pleased. In any case, I cannot simply *release* the boy to a man like you. That would be most unethical. The regulations of the institution state quite clearly that—"

"And what kind of man would I be?"

Monsieur Vicente spread his palms, as if his objections were obvious to anyone who cared to look.

Lesage removed his hat and straightened the wig upon his head. "I think you have misunderstood me, Monsieur Vicente. I do not want the boy for . . . for sorcery or anything else of that nature. Nothing like that. The boy needs his mother and Madame Picot is desolate without him. He is her last living child. Think of it. Her husband is dead, her three other children . . ."

Monsieur Vicente clucked his tongue and set about fiddling with his clay pipe. He gestured to the baby sleeping in the cot. "And this baby you are purchasing for La Voisin? You wish to give it a good home, I assume? Raise her to be a good Christian? No? I didn't think so."

"The boy is a different matter. He can be reunited with his mother and they might return to their village."

"Your reputation precedes you, Monsieur du Coeuret. You have been away for several years, but you are still spoken of in the darker corners of our city. A new name cannot disguise a man's character any more than some fashionable new clothes can."

Lesage was indignant. "Can a man not change himself? Can he not perform a decent act in his life?"

"You wish to perform—what?—a noble deed?"

It sounded like an accusation and, indeed, Lesage felt as if he were engaged in an unnatural act. "How much would it cost to free the boy?" he asked.

Monsieur Vicente smiled as if Lesage had at last solved a problem he had set. "Ah. You wish to hire him out to do some work for you? *That* can certainly be arranged. Many of our wards are useful in the community as labourers and mourners and servants. Cooks, cleaners . . . "

"Yes. What would that cost, then? To hire him?"

Monsieur Vicente puffed on his pipe, then withdrew it from his mouth. With its stem he jabbed at Lesage. "How much money do you have with you?"

Lesage sat in silence for a moment, unable to speak. "I have the two hundred for the baby and an additional twenty livres of my own," he said at last.

"But you don't want the newborn?"

"No."

"But what about Madame Monvoisin? She will not be happy."

Lesage shrugged. He did not wish to think how Catherine might react.

Monsieur Vicente sat back, impressed. "Well, noble deeds do not come cheap, monsieur. The boy will cost two hundred and twenty livres."

Lesage sank back in his chair. Dear God, he thought. That raving monk was right. Here it is, then. My reckoning.

36

W hen Marguerite had gone Charlotte sat on the low stool. She avoided looking at the child and listened instead to the pigeons purring in the eaves. The setting sun had broken through the low clouds and the city was saturated in its sumptuous twilight. The city roofs, the distant spires. All things—everything great and terrible—seemed equally possible. To make and unmake, to rise and fall, murder and beget. On a shard of paper she wrote a word. Her single fervent wish. She stared at it for a long time and her skin hummed with terror and anticipation.

She picked up the boy. It had been several years since she had cradled a child so small. She recalled the kinds of babies her own children had been, how their characters had been stamped so early and so visibly upon them. Aliénor with her ferocious gripping fingers, Béatrice's smile, Philippe with his ruddy cheeks and Nicolas, oh, Nicolas, his seriousness, his bony chest, the afternoons he spent practising tying knots. The sheer wonder of her children, how they had inflamed in her breast a subdued sense of her own glory. Had she carried them in her belly for all that time for nothing? Entire seasons? Kept them warm, bundled them securely, reassured them when they fretted? Be brave, my son. Have courage, my daughter. Your mother will protect you. Was she not entitled to have a single child survive? *We must have done something terrible to be visited by such things.* Did you pray to God for his help and guidance? Yes. Did you live as well as you could? Yes. And what did God do? Did He save them? Did He ease your suffering? No.

From where she had hidden it, she took out Madame Gallant's heart, still wrapped in the executioner's cloth. She unwrapped it and held the strange and bloody fruit in one hand. Veins, tubes of yellow gristle, dried blood. It weighed about the same as the book Madame Rolland had given her. It was hard to believe that something which balanced so easily on one's palm was the source of everything.

The baby on her lap was light, as much blanket as flesh. He pursed his lips and gave a squeak. Instinctively Charlotte leaned over to inhale his rejuvenating scent. Each child who survives its birth is a miracle, her mother used to say. The curé said similar things: hope in a troubled world; the child to save us all. One is all it takes. Our saviour. Yes. How true. She opened her black book and listened to its pungent voices. *Nigromancy, according to the wisdom of Agrippa, taken from the Book of Soyga, The Book of Buried Pearls and the Clavicle of Solomon. A babe at the breast is required. Say the words at the moment of cutting. Ask of the Angel Uriel for his assistance. Innocence and possibility. Tabula rasa. Balance is restored. Say the words thrice. Agnus Dei. The lamb.*

She took up her knife. The baby knew nothing. "I'm sorry, little boy," Charlotte said as she closed her eyes. She muttered secret words under her breath and pressed the point of the knife to the baby's doughy chest. *Κύριε, ελέησον. Κύριε, ελέησον. Κύριε, ελέησον.* Mercy on my soul. *Your blood, your blood, your blood.*

It was done. In one hand Charlotte still gripped the portion of paper on which she had written Nicolas's name. It emanated a soft heat, like that of a stone warmed by the sun. She wiped her hands as best she could, then wrapped the baby in his blood-thickened blanket and placed him back on the bed.

Exhausted and afraid, she sat on the stool and waited. The drying blood was tight and heavy on her skin. It had splattered on her hands and neck, all over her forearms. It had soaked thickly into her dress. Some of it resembled clumsily applied lacquer. Other portions were still wet and sticky. Puddles of blood, too, on the floor, seeping into the cracks.

She thought of the moments directly after her own children were born. The throbbing agony of delivery, the midwife's muttered prayers, bloodied sheets, terror and exultation. "*Pater Noster, qui es in caelis . . .* " We are but parcels of organs and bone. The smell of meat. Would the child be still living, have the correct parts, seem sturdy enough to survive? Does he breathe as he should? How is his colour? Please, show him to me, put my baby to my breast.

Charlotte barely breathed, hardly altered her position on the stool, as if to do so might jeopardise her terrible request. It grew gloomy as the day slipped away but she lit no candle, accepting that darkness was more suited to her desires.

Eventually, there was a knock at the door. Charlotte started, but did not respond immediately. A dreadful silence. Another knock. She tried to speak, but her voice failed. No matter. The door opened with a low creak and there, in the dim passage, stood Nicolas. Her son. He was dirtier than when she had last seen him, certainly, but it was him. Her heart caught, a sleeve on a twig. Her beloved son had returned at last. Behind him on the landing a face dissolved into the darkness—the face, presumably, of the hateful creature who had delivered Nicolas to her.

Cautiously, Nicolas stepped into the room. He was filthy, barefoot, and his clothes were red and torn. He was trembling. "Mother," he whispered. "Is that truly you?"

With a hand over her mouth she stifled a sob.

"But are you injured? What is all the blood?"

"No, Nicolas. I am quite well."

"But they told me you had been killed. I saw the arrow . . . "

Charlotte opened her arms. "Come to me, my son. Here."

Nicolas approached slowly, as if he suspected her of being a phantom. Charlotte stood until hesitantly, wordlessly, he allowed himself to be enfolded in her bloody embrace. Her son. Yes. It was him. He was warm, he breathed in the way of the living.

She grasped his hand. "Here. Put your hand here. Do you feel it? My own heart? How it beats? Yes. And you? Are you . . . are you truly alive, my son?"

She placed her own palm to Nicolas's chest. Yes. There. His own heartbeat, like that of a bird. She ran her hands feverishly along his thin arms and sensed the blood thrumming beneath his skin. "Did they hurt you?"

The boy looked stunned. He shook his head.

"Don't be afraid, my son. I have brought you back. And now I will protect you."

Only then did she permit herself to weep.

Lesage watched from the shadows as Madame Picot embraced her son. He had seen terrible acts performed by terrible people. Black masses, executions and murders, brutal fights in the galleys. And he had been present, of course, when Catherine and Abbé Guibourg had sacrificed babies and chanted dreadful incantations over the bodies so that Madame de Montespan might win the favour of the King.

But this seemed so much worse because Madame Picot had hitherto seemed so innocent. The blood on her hands and clothes, the blood-soaked bundle on the bed. What had the woman done? People were capable of all sorts of inexplicable things, weren't they? Horrified, he fumbled his way down the dark stairs, across the courtyard and into the street, where he ran into the troubadour girl, Marguerite, coming the other way.

"Good evening, monsieur," she said. "Have you been to see Madame Picot? Did her son return?"

Lesage nodded. Then, without a word, he fled.

Over Nicolas's shoulder, Marguerite materialised on the dim landing, pale as an apparition. She looked at Charlotte and Nicolas with great puzzlement as she stepped into the room. "My brother, madame? Is he with you? But what has happened? There is so much blood."

The girl moved to the bed and bent over her brother, cooing endearments as she did so. She picked him up and drew aside his wrapping. Charlotte watched as if she were trapped within a dream's thick amber, unable to act as the girl gasped, then recoiled in shock. "Dear God. What happened to my brother? He is dead?"

Coming to her senses, Charlotte detached herself from Nicolas and moved to prevent Marguerite's escape, but the girl was nimbler than a cat and managed to push past Charlotte and slip from the room. There was the clomp of her feet on the stairs and yelling, followed by voices in the courtyard as she screamed and screamed.

"Help! Help! She has killed my baby. The witch killed my baby. Help!"

Charlotte hesitated momentarily before grabbing Nicolas by his tattered red tunic and dragging him onto the landing. To judge by the commotion echoing around the courtyard downstairs, it would be impossible for them to make it through the house and onto the street without being caught. They would surely kill them for what she had done—kill them both and burn their bones. She glanced around. A narrow flight of stairs led to an upper room. Nicolas was weeping and muttering. She shoved him in front of her and they clambered up into a tiny attic, where the ceiling beams were so low she was unable to stand upright. She closed the door and bolted it. Then, with Nicolas's help, she pushed the only piece of furniture—a low bed—in front of it as a makeshift barricade.

"But what are you doing, Mother? What has happened?"

She looked around. A shutterless window offered a glimpse of the evening where pink clouds and smudges of brown smoke hung in the pale blue sky. Voices drifted up from the street below and there came the clatter of boots on the wooden stairs. Doors slammed, cries and lamentations. "*Catch them. Call someone. The baby. Dear God, where did they go?*"

Charlotte pushed open the dormer window and leaned out. It gave onto a flat portion of the tiled roof that abutted the neighbouring building. She held out a hand to Nicolas. "Come."

"But we'll fall into the street, Mother. There is nowhere to go."

"There is. Trust me. Quickly now."

Voices closer now on the stairs behind the closed door. Nicolas relented and they slipped through the narrow window onto the roof. Charlotte had never in her life been so high above the ground and, once on the roof, she stood still for a moment to orient herself to the unnerving sensation. Several men burst into the room behind. Crouching low for balance, almost on all fours, Charlotte and Nicolas scrambled along the lichen-spotted tiles as quickly as they dared, but the flat section of the roof was short and ended in a long drop to the street below. The old slate cracked like pie crust beneath their feet. A wet-lipped woman in a window opposite screamed at them. "There! The sorceress. There!" The entire quarter, it seemed, was yelling and crying out.

Charlotte hesitated, putting a hand to the pitched roof for

balance. There was no way they might escape over the rooftops and they would almost certainly not be quick enough to out-run the men who, at that moment, were clambering through the window with daggers and shovels in their hands. Nicolas was sobbing and shaking his head.

The men would be upon them in no time at all. "Come down," they were saying. "Come down now, woman. There is no escaping us. Think of the boy . . . "

Think of the boy. As if she had thought of anything else. Charlotte hauled Nicolas up the steepest part of the roof. It was difficult. Her shoes slipped on the slate. Nicolas, barefoot, made swifter progress and reached down to assist her. They ascended the roof's peak and clung to a crumbling chimney. The grimy streets and rooftops of Paris spread out in all directions. A crowd had formed in the street below. People cried out in fury. Merchants, a trio of monks, a swineherd with his pigs. Boys were throwing stones and women were jeering. *"There on the roof! Child-killer. Kill her. Break all her bones. Push the bitch off!"*

But Charlotte had stopped listening. These ordinary people, with their meagre words. She smelled smoke from the evening's fires. She saw a flock of geese and the pale crescent moon. Closer at hand, church bells tolled for evening prayers. Three crows flew in low and landed on the chimney of the neighbouring roof, where they watched her with interest. What did they see, these crows? A woman and her son. What could they know? One of the birds shrugged and turned to its companions, as if to confer on the matter. It was almost dark, but not quite; the time between the dog and the wolf. *When all great and wondrous things happen.*

With extreme care, Charlotte stood with one foot on either side of the pitched roof. The crowd in the street fell silent and the men below paused in their sinister entreaties. After taking a moment to steady herself, she retrieved the black book from her pocket and held it aloft. She grasped Nicolas's hand. My beautiful son, at last; his fingers so warm and alive in my own.

Above the racket of Paris, through her skin, Charlotte absorbed the black book's whisperings. Then she closed her eyes and spoke aloud its incantations. An awful majesty swelled in her breast; her heart was a cathedral, her chest a city, her body the world and all it contained. Delight and murder and eruption and quakes. Babies and fire. Dogs. Mountains. Cities. Language and rivers and trees. Its people, its knowledge, its many winds and vast oceans. *Command the elements and they can be yours*, Madame Rolland had told her. And this was what Charlotte did.

There was a swirl of wind. She was buffeted, but then became light, as if swelling with air. She felt the slate roof shift beneath her. Nicolas cried out and gripped her hand more tightly. Those in the street gasped in terror and amazement. A woman's wail of alarm, a prayer. Charlotte opened her eyes and saw the buildings fall away beneath her feet, saw the street thronged with terrified people. Their upturned faces, their furious eyes, their tiny round mouths opening and closing soundlessly like those of baby birds awaiting food. And she laughed with unexpected delight.

On the cool evening breeze she and Nicolas were borne away as if weightless. Over squares and spires and over the river running golden in the last of the day's sunlight. Over the city's black, jagged rooftops, its rickety carts and muddy streets. There a man hoisting his basket of apples, there a boy chasing a grey cat. The city made miniature—all its walls and churches, its great prisons and bustling gates, the roads laid out like lengths of pale rope. Travellers the size of ants. She saw lanterns flickering in windows, smelled rabbits cooking in pots. A pair of nuns giggled at a lewd joke, a distant woman sang to her child. She detected the melancholy scent of autumn as it rolled over the land. Spring, summer, autumn, next year's summer. She heard the distant, bitter laughter of the Wild Horde. She smelled the fragrances of foreign bazaars, of rank battlefields, of oceans and bundles of rags in meadows; of remote cities, those terrible places where they spoke in languages that resembled so many mouthfuls of broken glass.

Other visions she didn't understand. Vast skies, icy wastes, the severed heads of kings, blasts obliterating entire cities. Multitudes. Everything, nothing. Chaos and beauty, the future and the past, the manifest and the obscure, the sacred and the profane, terror and pleasure, the living and the dead. Yes, she thought. Yes. My eyes are jewels, my bones are of silver and my veins now run with gold.

Your blood, your blood, your blood.

The magician Adam du Coeuret—also known as Lesage—remained in Paris for several years, working with Catherine Monvoisin—or La Voisin—among Paris's network of abortionists, poisoners, sorcerers and fortune tellers. On 22 March 1679, he was arrested in connection with the scandal known thereafter as the Affair of the Poisons, in which Parisian police unearthed what they feared was a plot to poison King Louis XIV. As a recidivist on charges of sacrilege, Lesage faced execution if guilty, but when the Chambre Ardente established to investigate the affair was dissolved in 1682, Lesage was imprisoned without trial for the rest of his life in the Chateau de Besançon. The date of his death is unknown.

The fortune teller and abortionist Catherine Monvoisin was arrested on 12 March 1679 on suspicion of involvement in a plot to poison King Louis XIV and for her role in black masses designed to secure for Athénaïs de Montespan the affections of King Louis XIV. She confessed to witchcraft and was burned alive on 22 February 1680.

In March 1680, the daughter of Catherine Monvoisin, Marie-Marguerite Monvoisin, was interrogated and described all she knew of her mother's involvement in an alleged plot to poison Louis XIV. Although only in her early twenties and not charged with any offences, she was imprisoned without trial for the rest of her life on the island prison of Belle-Île-en-Mer. As with other female prisoners jailed in the affair, she was guarded by women to ensure she could not use her feminine wiles to escape. The date of her death is unknown.

Athénaïs de Montespan, King Louis XIV's official mistress, or *maîtresse-en-titre*, had several children with Louis XIV over the course of their thirteen-year relationship. These children were recognised officially by Louis in December 1673, several months after the black mass conducted for that purpose by Lesage, Abbé Guibourg and Catherine Monvoisin. Although numerous people arrested in the Affair of the Poisons mentioned Madame de Montespan in connection with the sorcerers of Paris, there was never any proof of her involvement in witchcraft. In 1691, Madame de Montespan retired to a convent, where she died in 1707 at the age of sixty-six.

Françoise Filastre was arrested in December 1679 and burned alive in October 1680 for practising witchcraft.

Nothing further was heard of Charlotte Picot, although mention of a prophetess living in a forest near Lyon by the seventeenth-century English essayist Joseph Addison could be a reference to her.

ACKNOWLEDGEMENTS

All books are, in some way, engaged in conversation with other books, so it is fitting that *City of Crows*—which has a book at its centre—began taking shape several years ago when Arwen at Brunswick Street Bookstore suggested I might be interested in *Grimoires: A History of Magic Books* by Owen Davies. She was right, and the book sent me further down the rabbit hole to others such as *The Affair of the Poisons: Murder, Infanticide & Satanism at the Court of Louis XIV* by Anne Somerset, *Strange Revelations: Magic, Poison, and Sacrilege in Louis XIV's France* by Lynn Wood Mollenauer, *Europe's Inner Demons: The Demonization of Christians in Medieval Christendom* by Norman Cohn and *The Discovery of France* by Graham Robb. Although fiction, *City of Crows* is based on historical incident and real people, and anyone interested in witchcraft or the general period of French history in which it is set (and how could you not be?!) would be advised to read the above books.

I was incredibly fortunate to be able to spend time in France researching *City of Crows*, thanks to a grant from The Australia Council for the Arts—for which I am truly grateful. While in Paris, I spent time with some wonderful people, each of whom assisted me in all sorts of ways and made my stay there particularly fruitful and memorable. My appreciation firstly to Marie Furthner for her invaluable assistance in unlocking the occult mysteries of the Bibliothèque nationale de France. Thanks also to fellow flâneur Alex Landragin for his companionship, and Francis Geffard for his unflagging friendship and support. Thanks to Chloe Baker, Melissa Cox and Chris Kenna for the dinners, drinks and music. Thanks to Aude Sowerwine for the apartment in Paris and to Rob Annema and Els Zoon for the room in Pampelonne where Charlotte Picot truly came into focus.

My gratitude also to my wonderful agent Jay Mandel for his encouragement and sound advice over the years of writing *City of Crows*. My thanks also to everyone at Pan Macmillan Australia for making me feel so welcome, particularly my excellent publisher Geordie Williamson and editor Mathilda Imlah—both of whom worked long and hard to make this book as good as possible.

And, of course, special thanks goes to Roslyn and Reuben for their love and support. Love you both.

ABOUT THE AUTHOR

Chris Womersley's novels have been awarded the Ned Kelly Award for Best First Fiction, the Indie Award for Best Fiction, and the ABIA Award for Literary Fiction, and have been shortlisted for the Miles Franklin Award, *The Age* Book of the Year, and the ALS Gold Medal for Literature. His short fiction has appeared in *Granta*, *The Best Australian Stories*, *Meanjin*, and *Griffith Review*. He lives in Melbourne, Australia.